ELEVATOR
Pitch

L.B. DUNBAR

www.lbdunbar.com

L.B. DUNBAR

L.B. Dunbar
ROMANCE. FOR SEXY SILVER FOX LOVERS.

Copyright © 2024 Laura Dunbar
L.B. Dunbar Writes, Ltd.
https://www.lbdunbar.com/

All rights reserved.

No part of this book may be reproduced or transmitted in any form or by any means, electronic or mechanical, including photocopying, recording, or by any information storage and retrieval system, without written permission from the author.

Without in any way limiting the author's exclusive rights under copyright, any use of this publication to 'train' generative artificial intelligence (AI) technologies to generate text is expressly prohibited. The author reserves all rights to license uses of this work for generative AI training and development of machine learning language models.

This is a work of fiction, created without the use of AI technology. Any names, characters, places, and incidents are the products of the author's imagination and used in a fictitious manner. Any resemblance to any actual people, living or dead, events, or locales is entirely coincidental.

The author acknowledges the trademarked status and trademark owners of various products referenced in this work of fiction, which have been used without permission. The publication/use of these trademarks is not authorized, associated with, or sponsored by the trademark owner.

Cover Design: Mae Harden
Editor: Nicole McCurdy/Emerald Edits
Editor: Gemma Brocato

Other Books by L.B. Dunbar

Sterling Falls
Sterling Heat
Sterling Brick
Sterling Streak
Sterling Clay
Sterling Fight

Chicago Anchors
Elevator Pitch
Catch the Kiss

Parentmoon

Holiday Hotties (Christmas novellas)
Scrooge-ish
Naughty-ish
Grouch-ish

Road Trips & Romance
Hauling Ashe
Merging Wright
Rhode Trip

Lakeside Cottage
Living at 40
Loving at 40
Learning at 40
Letting Go at 40

Silver Foxes of Blue Ridge
Silver Brewer
Silver Player
Silver Mayor
Silver Biker

Sexy Silver Fox Collection
After Care
Midlife Crisis

L.B. DUNBAR

Restored Dreams
Second Chance
Wine&Dine

Collision novellas
Collide
Caught

The Sex Education of M.E.

The Heart Collection
Speak from the Heart
Read with your Heart
Look with your Heart
Fight from the Heart
View with your Heart

A Heart Collection Spin-off
The Heart Remembers

BOOKS IN OTHER AUTHOR WORLDS
Smartypants Romance (an imprint of Penny Reid)
Love in Due Time
Love in Deed
Love in a Pickle

The World of True North (an imprint of Sarina Bowen)
Cowboy
Studfinder

THE EARLY YEARS
The Legendary Rock Star Series

Paradise Stories

The Island Duet

Modern Descendants – writing as elda lore

ELEVATOR PITCH

DEDICATION

Because I love baseball and the Chicago Cubs,
and the memories both have built for my family.
Go Cubbies. Play ball.

This one is all for me.

L.B. DUNBAR

Chapter 1

November
Offseason

[Vee]

"Hold the elevator."

My heels clack against the tile floor of the Autumn Hotel's lobby as I race for the elevator. I can't wait to take off these shoes and the constricting panties beneath my dress.

A masculine hand grips the closing door, triggering it to re-open, and I skip into the lift. Collapsing against the back wall, I tip up my head and let out a sharp, singular laugh.

I made it.

With my heart racing from the sprint, I'm breathless when I say, "Eleven, please."

The doors close and I lower my head, giving a cursory glance at my elevator mate and dismissing him. Then I do a double take.

Holy cow! I mean, Holy. Speckled. Cow. Baseball legend Ross Davis is standing in the elevator with me, staring at his phone. Baseball cap slung low over his eyes. Three-quarter zip shirt. Dress slacks. Not going to lie. I totally objectify his backside in those pants that curve around his firm ass and outline muscular thighs.

With my back to the interior wall, I plaster myself even tighter to the panel. The gold-colored rail lining the space jabs into my lower spine. My gaze drifts to the shiny chrome bank of floor numbers, finding eleven is the only button glowing.

That isn't as consequential as the fact I'm standing—*alone*—with not only a present icon in baseball but someone I have the biggest sport-celebrity crush on.

Some people have book boyfriends. I have a baseball boyfriend.

Ross Davis was the pitcher for the Chicago Anchors when they won the World Championship eight years ago. As a die-hard fan of the royal blue and red, he stood out in the league because of his age. He was thirty-nine back then, making him forty-seven now.

However, I'd recognize him anywhere. Hidden beneath the ball cap on his head is the buzz-cut of salt-and-pepper hair but the beard on his jaw is what distinguishes him. Silver, gray, and white in an artful blend on a man with a fuller face. He's very tall up close with mile-wide shoulders and a solid stance.

Ross Davis as a fantasy in my head is nothing compared to Ross Davis in the flesh. My hands grow clammy, my mouth sticky like caramel corn. My heart rate is slightly more erratic than usual.

When he left the Anchors, he took a year off before becoming manager of the Philadelphia Flash. Neither of us are near our home states as we stand in this elevator in downtown Houston on the final night of the current championship series. The last game of the season for his team.

I'm here for a writers' conference.

And again, I'm the only person in the elevator with him.

I should say something. Then again, I shouldn't say anything. The game was rough. He's clearly focused on his phone. He probably doesn't want to be interrupted. Definitely does not want to be fangirled over. Although, since I'm forty-five, I guess I might be called a fan*woman*. However, I'm not a ball chaser. The women who toss themselves at baseball players for their fame and status. Not to mention, any overzealous attention from me might make me look like a stalker.

But I'm absolutely crushing on him.

Suddenly, the elevator jolts. The lights flicker. A grinding sound *kathunks*, and the lift abruptly stops.

With my fingers clutching the railing behind me, I glance at Ross, who lifts his head, and squints at the electronic square that blinked through the once-ascending numbers.

"What the fuck?" he mutters under his breath. He presses the number eleven, but we are obviously not moving. Next, he jabs at the emergency call button. Nothing happens. We wait in silence. He triple-jabs the offensive button. *Poke-poke-poke*. Still, nothing.

"Maybe you should use your phone."

ELEVATOR PITCH

His shoulders stiffen, head lifting higher, before twisting only his upper body to face me. With the device in his hand, he stares at me like he'd forgotten someone else was present.

His eyes narrow before he gazes down at his phone and rapidly types out a message.

With his head bowed, he shakes it side to side. "No service."

The elevator jolts. My knees buckle and I clutch the railing harder. We seem to rise a few feet and then abruptly halt, rocking the lift.

Dear God, I'm going to die. In an elevator. With Ross Davis.

There could be worse ways to go but plummeting to my death still wasn't on my bingo card. As we rapidly descend to the end of our lives, I'm going to scream like I'm watching a horror flick, pee myself, and then die in a pool of urine at the feet of Ross Davis.

Graphic. I get it. My overactive imagination is what makes me a great writer.

And the thought of peeing sparks the urge.

No. Just no, no, *no.* My weak bladder is not allowed to kick in right now.

I. Do. Not. Need. To. Pee.

The mental command only stirs more urgency. My palms sweat on the railing. I can smell the tainted mixture of metal and perspiration. Or maybe that's me, as my pits are beginning to moisten as if I hadn't already been a little damp from my race to the elevator.

My pajamas, a lush bed, and a good romance novel were calling my name.

Trapped in an elevator would make a great meet-cute, but this was not romantic.

Peeing myself in front of Ross Davis is not the fluff of fantasies.

Lifting a hand, I fan my face, which has no effect but I'm internally telling myself it helps.

"Are you alright?" Ross asks, finally acknowledging my presence.

"Is it hot in here?" *Mother of baseball, this can't be happening.* On top of the sudden need to pee, panic is setting in, triggering a hot flash. Not that the scorching-curse can be called forth. The devilish hormones inside me have a mind of their own and they've chosen this moment to strike, adding to my discomfort. Starting at my shins, heat rises up my body like the vines of the ivy wall in the iconic Chicago Anchor stadium. My skin goes up in flames. Steam is probably wafting off my flesh.

Ross stares at me as I frantically wave one hand in front of my face while clinging to the railing with my other hand. The restrictive, uncomfortable, possibly size-too-small spandex I'm wearing is making everything worse. My stomach is tight, pressing down on my bladder. Once I shed these control-top panties, I plan to never wear them again. I bend a little at the knees, clenching my thighs together. Any second now, the full-on *I've-got-to-potty* dance will commence. Momentarily, the hot flash is distracting me. I'm certain the additional heat turns my face Anchor red.

"You're not claustrophobic, are you?"

Now that he's mentioned it . . . "Maybe a little bit." *Are the walls getting closer in here? Is the oxygen lessening?*

"Fuck." He tips back his head and glares at the ceiling for a second before tugging off his baseball cap and rubbing his thick hand over his head. I have never in my life had a thing for tattooed or nearly bald men until this man. And with that silvery beard and the winning smile I've seen him give a crowd of cameras, he's panty-melting.

Only I don't need my panties to melt. I need them to stay intact.

"It will probably only be a few minutes."

"Yep." I dig my teeth into my lower lip as I continue the hand-fanning, knee-bending, thigh-clenching dance.

"Rough game tonight," I add, then mentally curse myself. Now isn't the time for small talk. In fact, it might be best if he goes back to ignoring my existence and I peacefully die a slow death unacknowledged by him.

"You a baseball fan?" He resettles the cap on his head.

"Go Anchors," I muster.

"Shit," he mutters, lowering his head again. He played for our team for six seasons before that record breaking one. We were sad to see him go when he'd announced his retirement after a personal tragedy. He was a worthy coach, though. Players adored him. Front offices respected him.

ELEVATOR PITCH

He lifts his head again, tipping it back to stare at the ceiling. "I miss Chicago."

"Oh, yeah?" I grasp for something more intelligent to say. "What do you miss?"

His shoulders lift as he inhales deeply. He removes his cap again, scrubs over his head, and replaces the covering once more. "I miss the fans."

"For baseball," I interject, dropping my gaze to the Philadelphia logo on his shirt. Of course, he means baseball. Isn't that the topic?

He tilts his head, confusion scored in his expression. "Yeah."

"What else do you miss?" Maybe small talk won't be so bad. Keep him chatting. Then maybe he'll ignore the perspiration dampening my neck and the excessive wetness at my pits as I fight through the hot flash, the need to pee, and the onset of my height-phobia which involves additional sweating on my palms and feet.

"Walks along the lakefront in the summer. Hell, even the frigid temps of winter. Although my bones appreciate springtime in Florida." The Flash's spring training takes place in the sunshine state.

"Summer in the city is the best." Still not the most conversational statement but the truth. Chicago has this strange dichotomy of beachfront town and major metropolis divided by a famous highway, still affectionately called Lake Shore Drive.

"Ever done the polar plunge, though?" Ross shivers.

The idea of throwing myself into the frigid winter lake isn't helping with my need-to-pee emergency.

I cross my legs and bounce once. Ross notices. His brows cinch tight. He rubs his forefinger and thumb around his mouth, circling his lush-looking lips before drawing them together along the thick edge of his chin. His eyes are blue which I've only ever seen on a screen. Up close, they are the same royal shade as my beloved baseball team.

"Hello?" A scratchy voice projects through the emergency call speaker.

"Yes. Hello." Ross quickly turns toward the box and bellows louder than necessary for such a small space. "We're stuck." He glances at the floor numbers, none of which are lit to tell us where we've stalled.

"Sir, it should only be another minute."

"Someone in here is on the verge of a panic attack. If she goes into cardiac arrest, it will be on your conscience."

Oh my. "Was that necessary?" I demand, surprised by the sharpness of his tone and the terse insult to someone only trying to help us remain calm. Not to mention, he's calling out *my* verge-of-hysteria. The only heart attack I'll have is if my bladder gives out.

The elevator thuds, rumbling the lift before a loud clacking occurs, and we move again. I drop my fanning hand to my lower belly and squeeze my thighs tighter together. Knowing I'm *this close* to exiting this thing and reaching the safety of my room has the urge to pee ratcheting sky-high.

The sweat lingering on my skin is no longer related to the hot flash but to the potential mortification of *not* making it off this elevator and into my room in time.

Suddenly, the doors whoosh open.

Without a word to my *former* celebrity crush because he'd just lost all his points by reprimanding the elevator attendant, I rush toward my room. I have a vague sense of him turning in the same direction as me but I'm hyper-focused as I fumble with my room key. My hands tremble as the plastic card swipes over the electronic lock.

Red.

Red.

I flip the card over.

Red.

What the hell?

My hips rock. My knees knock. My thighs are pressed together tighter than a ballpark hotdog in a bun.

"That's my room." The masculine voice, embodied by the man standing beside me, watching me struggle to enter a hotel room, only irritates me further.

ELEVATOR PITCH

Glancing at the marker beside the door, I read the number. 1113.

Shit. I step to my left, forcing Ross Davis out of my way, and swipe my card over the keypad for my room. 1111.

Green. *Click.*

Without a glance backward, I step inside, allow the door to slam behind me and enter the bathroom. The potty dance continues as I struggle to roll down my nude-colored shaper briefs and settle on the toilet. Relief hits instantly and I bow my head, resting my forehead in my hand with my elbow on my thigh.

Holy cow, that was close.

Taking a deep breath, I linger on the porcelain throne as sweat cools on my skin. Pushing the body-contouring torture garment over my knees, I let it fall to my ankles. After kicking off my heels, I jiggle my feet for the final stage of removing the underwear.

With another deep exhale, freedom comes for my once constricted belly while I wiggle my toes, now released from my pinching shoes.

Placing both hands on my thighs, I lean forward, shaking my head back and forth.

No one else. To no one else would such a moment happen. I nearly peed myself in an elevator in front of Ross Davis.

Who really wasn't a conversationalist, nor was he particularly polite. Not to mention he sort of threw me under the bus without compassion, like I was one hand wave away from smacking myself or dropping to the floor in a frothing panic.

I hate when you learn your crush isn't really *all that* in the end.

Sitting upright, I reach over my shoulder and attempt to lower the zipper on the back of my dress.

Single-Woman Issue 171: Zipper lowering. Equally as difficult as zipper lifting.

My arms don't bend behind my back quite like they once did to operate zippers on a dress. I only have the closure lowered a few inches before I take care of personal hygiene and stand from the toilet. With my shaper on the floor, I push the garment aside with my foot and wash my hands, taking a second to stare at myself in the mirror.

My blonde hair shows evidence of finger combing throughout the long day of attending seminars. My eyes are bloodshot from straining to read in low-light ballrooms, plus, I've had two glasses of wine. Reaching for a washcloth, I wet it and scrub my face with the warm terrycloth, removing any remaining makeup.

As I wring out the washcloth, a knock comes on my hotel room door. Being that I was kind of in a hurry to enter the bathroom, I hadn't bothered closing the privacy slider. Plus, I'm the only one staying in my room. Either way, I haven't ordered room service, and someone evidently has the wrong room. I pause, waiting out the sound.

But another knock occurs, a little harder, a little more insistent.

Setting aside the washcloth, I pick up a hair band and tuck my hair into a messy bun at my nape while I cross the room for the door.

Peeking through the peephole, a sight I never in a million years imagined seeing stands in the hallway.

Even with an overactive imagination, I couldn't make this situation up.

And for a full minute or more, I stare at the peephole, as if I have imagined him. My stomach ripples like stands full of fans attempting The Wave. Unhindered, I observe him. Even though he was rude in the elevator, the tilt of his head gives a vibe of bone-deep weariness. A vulnerability that has me stepping back.

I tug at the loose twist of my hair then smooth my hand over my belly, hoping to calm the fluttering within me. I'm highly conscious that my dress is partially unzipped. *And*, I'm not wearing underwear.

With a flourish, I open the door and stare into the hall.

Ross Davis's gaze drops to a cut-crystal bottle of amber-colored liquid he cups in his hand. "I was saving this for tonight." He lifts the container. "For the big win."

I nod, suddenly sympathetic. Nothing excuses his tone or behavior earlier, but I instantly recall he's had a tough night. Maybe rougher than getting stuck in an elevator with a woman fanning herself, but not quite as desperate as my near-urination emergency. I will not concede the direness of *that* situation.

ELEVATOR PITCH

"I'm sorry about the loss."

Yep. Ross Davis and the Philadelphia Flash lost the biggest night in baseball in a gut-wrenching sixth game match up with Houston. The game came down to the ninth inning with bases loaded and a double play when the centerfielder caught a fly ball and then threw to the second baseman, who tagged the runner for the game ending out. In a mediocre game, the play was a major blow.

Ross nods once. His demeanor melancholy as he lowers his gaze again to where his thick fingers circle the neck of the crystal container, which he cradles like a prized possession. Albeit a poor substitute for a championship trophy.

For some reason, I envision what it would look like to have those thick fingers wrapped around me in some way. My thighs. My wrist. My throat.

"And I'm sorry for my behavior in the elevator. I called the front desk to apologize to the kid." He lifts the bottle in his hands and shrugs, the subtle movement almost bashful. "Anyway, I wondered if you'd like to share a drink with me. Even though, I can't promise to be the best company."

Holding onto the door, I shift to one leg and rub my bare foot over my ankle. Ross watches the motion. He's no longer wearing his team's three-quarter zip shirt or those ass-complementing dress slacks, but a plain black sweatshirt made of waterproof material and athletic pants.

We might be total strangers to one another but the aura of defeat around him has me stepping back and silently waving him inside. A hint of freshly-showered man mixes with a splash of spicy, masculine cologne as he passes me.

Was I really sitting on the toilet long enough for him to shower? Then again, I remember the days when Cameron could shower in under five minutes and be prepared to go in a total of eight. It's a man-thing.

However, the man-thing I'm most curious about right now is why Ross Davis wants to share a drink with me and how we're doing it in my hotel room.

Chapter 2

[Vee]

"I just need a minute," I state, pointing to the bathroom while Ross helps himself to the coaster covered glasses on the dresser. With my back to him, I rustle through my suitcase, conscious that I'm standing in a hotel room with Ross Davis *sans* underwear.

"Need help with your dress?"

I freeze with a clean pair of comfy underwear and folded jeans at my chest.

"Uh . . ." I turn to face him.

Ross stands with both hands raised in the air, emphasizing his innocence. "I just noticed the zipper is only partially undone and thought . . ."

He isn't wrong. I do need help. "I was trying to do the contortionist thing." I lift one arm, showing him how I bend it over my shoulder, attempting to unzip my dress.

What the heck am I doing?

Lowering my arm, I clutch the clothing to my chest again. "Anyway, I'm not as flexible as I used to be."

Somehow that sounds as dirty as him asking if he can help with my dress. I clear my throat, and he inches closer. Unconsciously, I step back, and he lifts both his hands again.

"Just offering my services." There isn't a drop of seduction or innuendo in his rugged voice. He looks beat down, and he doesn't need the ridiculousness of me imagining he's making an advance.

Why would he do that? He's Ross *Freakin'* Davis. Hot manager of a major league baseball team who can get any woman he wants, and he has. According to the snippets I've seen online, his latest conquest is Chandler Bressler, a reality TV diva, roughly fifteen years younger than him.

We lock eyes a second before I slowly turn and give him my back.

"Thank you," I whisper over my shoulder as his fingers come to the zipper and he smoothly lowers it. I ignore the chill rippling down my spine and the tingle between my thighs. Don't even think about the pulse thrumming at my bare core.

Holding the front of my dress pressed to my chest along with my change of clothes, I head to the bathroom with the back of my bra exposed. I don't give Ross another glance. I couldn't stand to witness him turning away from me while I walk away from him.

Which is as bizarre a thought as this entire evening so far.

Once inside the bathroom again, I decide against slipping into my jeans.

He's casually dressed. I'll dress comfortably.

I put on my plaid flannel pajama shorts and a graphic T-shirt which I'd left hanging on the back of the bathroom door.

Stepping back into the main room, Ross has taken a seat on the edge of the king-sized bed. A glass of amber liquid awaits me on the nightstand between the bed and an over-stuffed chair with a matching ottoman. Picking up the container, I take a seat on the ottoman and face him.

"What should we drink to?"

"Not losing," he huffs, before lifting his glass without clinking against mine and draining it.

I sniff the alcohol in my glass and risk a sip. Instantly, I sputter on the sharpness and struggle with the burn scorching down my throat. Holy hellfire, it's been a long time since I've drank the strong stuff.

Glancing up, I catch Ross watching me.

Can there be anyone less *impressive than me?* I nearly peed myself, had a hot flash, panicked about plummeting, and now I'm gagging on alcohol while dressed like a college co-ed, age advanced by twenty-five years.

"I'm Ross Davis, by the way." He tilts his head. "But somehow I think you know that."

"I do," I admit but remind myself of a few things that tamp down the stalker-effect. *He* came to my door. He asked to enter said room.

"And you are?"

"Verona Huxley. My friends call me Vee." I smile, like *we* are old acquaintances when we are not.

Ross observes me as he takes another sip of his drink, eyes watching me over the rim of his glass. He starts at my bare toes, which I dig into the lush carpeting, and he travels up my exposed legs, lingering on my knees a second. Then his gaze leaps to my hair, before dropping to my chin, mouth, nose and eyes. His slow perusal is so intense. Not sexual, just focused. His gaze is almost tangible, sending goosebumps over my skin.

"Why do you look familiar?"

The question startles me, and I realize he isn't checking me out so much as trying to figure out who I am. *If* he knows me, how does he know me. But there is no way I am familiar to him.

"Maybe because we just shared ten minutes together in an elevator."

His thick strained chuckle sounds like sandpaper on wood. "Why does that sound dirty?"

I sit up straighter. Not a suggestive hint filled my voice. I wouldn't know *how* to seduce a man like him. While I've been on a slew of dates over the years, sexually enticing were two words I would not pair together to describe myself. Then again, neither were the men I'd swiped on.

"Let me have a look at your social media." Ross doesn't appear to have a phone and the command implies he wants mine.

"What?" I scoff. "Why?"

"I swear I know you."

"I'm certain you do not."

Ross Davis and I are not likely to round the same social circles nor have our paths crossed in any manner other than I'm a baseball fan and he was once a well-known player.

My phone is plugged into the base of the lamp on the opposite nightstand. Earlier, I'd left the dead device behind to charge when I met friends in the lobby bar. Ross sets down his drink and shifts on the bed, suddenly lunging across the wide berth of the mattress and extending his long arm for my phone.

"No," I canter, scampering after him, reaching for the back of his sweatshirt and missing. Instead, I catch the back of his leg using it for leverage to climb up on the bed and partially over his broad body as if I can get to my phone before him. His arms are longer. Once he has the device in his hands, he shifts, forcing me to fall to his side while he flops to his back and holds up my phone.

"Use your own phone," I argue, irritated by his intrusiveness.

"Nope. Coaching makes me a strategist. I always look for the straightest path forward. And right now, that's to open your apps, not search mine." He rolls his head to look at me. "Passcode?"

Is he serious? "So invasive," I mumble.

Our eyes meet. Blue to blue, we're a matching set, yet we couldn't be more opposite. Think book nerd and popular jock in high school.

"Fine." I grumble out the six-digit code, knowing he'll never remember it nor hold my phone in his hands again.

Once the device is unlocked, he easily finds my Instagram, scrolls through the images, and pinches his brow.

"You really like books." Curiosity fills his voice.

I reach for my phone, but he rolls to his left side, body-blocking me and forcing me to drape over him a second while he holds the device out of my grasp.

I hitch my shoulder. "I like books." The truth is more complicated than that, but he doesn't need to know my life's work.

Ross pauses to glance at me again, reading my tee.

Cool Girls Read Hot Books.

Without a comment, he turns back to my phone and continues to scroll. My heart hammers the longer he searches. Then he taps over to the reels and my stomach drops. There aren't many saved videos, but there's one I'd rather he didn't see. His roaming thumb stills, and he presses on the screen.

"Put Me in Coach" screeches into the room and gives away exactly what he's watching.

A thirty-second blip on the jumbotron at Anchor Field of a woman dancing. Arms raised. Hips swaying. Exaggerated movements which express enthusiasm and suggest one too many margaritas. There's no way Ross watched the screen during that game or recalls a video from years ago.

However, the video hit social media and went viral.

Ross quickly turns his head; eyes searching my face once again. "I knew you looked familiar."

"How would you remember thirty-seconds from eight years ago?"

Yep, that embarrassing moment captured on film and shared across the internet was me.

Wiggling. Jiggling. Shaking my then-thirty-something groove thing.

Slightly ashamed by the antics on the video, I tug the phone from his grasp and collapse on my back, holding the device so the screen faces me.

The video replays, splashing the image of me dancing in the bleachers of Anchor Field, rhythmically waving my arms and over-enthusiastically rocking my hips, when the girl beside me holds up a posterboard with a giant arrow pointed at me that read:

Hey-hey Ross Davis. Date our mom.

The video captures me turning toward my then teenage daughter and jumping up and down as she holds the poster beyond my reach. She's six inches taller than me.

"She was grounded for a month after that stunt," I mutter, knowing not only was the poster humiliating, but the timing was insensitive.

"How many children do you have?" His voice lowers.

My attention returns to him. "Two girls." Although I'm aware of his marital status and family dynamics I still ask, "You?"

He scoffs and hikes himself upright, scooting to the edge of the bed. "Two boys. But I bet you knew that, too."

I sit up as well, but don't move from the middle of the mattress. With his back to me, I hold my breath, assuming he's about to leave. To my shock, he pours himself another drink.

For some reason, the need to defend myself and my daughter arises although that video was innocent enough. "My girls love baseball, and they'd been pushing me to date, but I wasn't ready." I swallow around the lump in my throat, around a word still difficult to say after all this time, but one Ross might relate to as well.

"I'm a widow."

Ross shifts, lifting a bent knee to rest on the mattress while his other leg hangs off the side, foot braced on the floor. He eyes me suspiciously, but I'm quick to remind myself he asked to enter my room, not the other way around.

"Me too. Widower. But you probably know that about me, too."

"I only know what the media shared." Shame fills my tone. The confession feels intrusive and wrong. "Your boys are adorable." *Your wife was, too.*

"Show me your social media," I add, still a bit defensive. "It's going to tell me exactly what I'm spitting back at you."

Maybe I follow him, but that doesn't single me out as a stalker. The point of a public profile is to put yourself out there. Making your status or stature or sensitivities accessible.

"I also know you date Chandler Bressler." Where the heck is she tonight?

"*Dated.* We broke up." He lifts his glass and swallows the entire pour once again.

I'm not interested in watching him get drunk, nor do I intend to be a rebound for him. Safe in believing I wouldn't be, I'm still not willing to be part of his pity party.

Nevertheless, I say, "I'm sorry." They each have high profile lifestyles, albeit she's fifteen years younger than him. He's another forty-something man chasing after a much younger woman, and I wonder what the issue is. Sure, she's beautiful, and has youth on her side, but is he trying to reclaim a part of himself by being with her? The question leaves me a little disappointed.

"Don't you have other people waiting on you?" What is he doing here with me? "Other coaches? Players, maybe, whom you can drown your sorrows with?"

"Am I drowning?" He glances up, eyes flaring the brightest blue I've ever seen.

"You look like a man who can hardly tread water."

Silence falls between us before he huffs and reaches for the bottle.

I scoot forward and catch his forearm. "If you want to drink your night away, I can't stop you, but I don't think alcohol is the answer."

He glances at my slim, short fingers on his forearm. "Want to know a secret?"

I release his arm, and he watches my hand retreat.

"I needed that win."

"What do you mean?"

He sighs and sets down the empty glass, shifting to prop himself against the headboard. His head tips back. His eyes momentarily close. "They're going to fire me."

"The Flash?"

He doesn't look at me. "Failure to perform."

"How did you fail?"

His head pops forward, eyes flashing like lightning. "I just lost the fucking Series."

"Your *team* lost the Series, on a double play that couldn't have been predicted. Most plays can't. A bat hits a ball and there's a bit of hope and a large prayer it goes where you intend. But the object of the game is for the opponent to try and catch that ball. And tonight, someone did."

"He sure fucking did." Ross's sandpaper voice rises.

I don't flinch but my skin pebbles. He isn't frightening. He's sadly angry or angrily sad but, most of all, from the set of his shoulders and the cinch of his brows, he looks defeated. Plus, his eyes are stormy, his mouth tight.

"I'm sorry," he mutters, placing his hand on my forearm and absentmindedly rubbing up and down the hairs standing erect on my skin.

ELEVATOR PITCH

Twisting, he grabs the bottle on the stand, and one-handedly pours himself another sliver.

"Want to know a secret about me?" Leveling the playing field might ease some of the tension around him.

He finishes his pour but doesn't drink. He simply holds the glass in his hand. His eyes brighten a smidge. Intrigued. Possibly eager to know something about me.

"I'm an author." He doesn't need to know I'm currently struggling with writer's block. Or that I'm on a deadline that looms closer every day. Or that I haven't published in over six months.

He stares blankly at me which is exactly the reaction I expected. People don't know how to respond to such a declaration.

"What do you write?" he asks.

While again a typical response, Ross tips up his chin, his voice full of intrigue, and I'm thrown off by the genuine curiosity in his tone. His eyes are focused again on me, not glazing over as some people's do.

"I write romance." Here I brace myself for a detached *huh* and wait on the inevitable question of whether I write something similar to *Fifty Shades of Grey*, as if that book is the only example of romance on the market. *God bless the author.*

"Anything I've heard of?"

"Do you read romance?" I tilt my head. *Color me purple if he does.*

"No."

I laugh. "Then no. It would be nothing you've heard of."

He sets down his newest glass of alcohol, without taking a sip, and gazes at me. "Tell me more about what you write." With his legs stretched outward, he crosses his ankles and clasps his hands in his lap like he's settling in to listen.

I only told him this piece of me because he told me his secret. I anticipated that being the end of our truth sharing session, but Ross continues to surprise me. I can't get a read on this unpredictable man. And I'm not certain what details to share about my career.

"Come on. Tell me. Give me the ten-second explanation."

"Like an elevator pitch?"

He nods toward the hallway and a soft chuckle leaves his lips. "Is that what they call it? Feels appropriate."

I swallow before I begin. "Currently, I'm toying with writing about a woman who enjoys two men. At once."

Ross reaches for his glass again and gulps down the contents, then sets the empty container on the nightstand with a heavy *thunk*. "Is that what you want?"

"*My character* wants two men."

"At the same time?"

"Something like that."

"And you want two men to share you."

I clear my throat. "*My character* wants two men to love her."

"Love?" He scoffs. "You're not talking about love."

"Okay, maybe not," I defend. "Maybe she just wants pleasure. Maybe she wants to feel desired . . . by two men at the same time. Maybe she wants to feel so irresistible that she can't make a choice and doesn't have to. They both want her, and they are willing to share her."

"And that's what you write . . . because that's what you want." An accusation rests in his rugged tone, one almost patronizing and pitying.

I don't need his judgement. I didn't follow him to his room. I didn't invite him over to mine.

Plus, I only said I was *toying* with the idea, not actually certain I would write such a thing. Not that I'm against a polyamorous story, I'm just not convinced I *could* write it.

Regardless, Ross Davis might be pretty on the outside but maybe he's just as shallow, bitter, and judgmental as any other man voicing an opinion about what woman should or should not want. If I wanted two men at once, who is he to say different? And how dare he judge me when he doesn't know me. We aren't talking about me. We're talking about a fictional character. Maybe some women want two men at once, but in reality, I could hardly handle one when I had him.

"And what do you want in life, Ross?"

"I want to manage Chicago."

His honesty stumps me. His answer doesn't compare to the judgment he was placing on me.

"Not that the Flash guys aren't great men and my coaching staff exceptional, but I want to go home."

Rawness exists in his wish. A yearning for something more.

"Then go home, Ross." My voice softens but it's also a command. He needs to leave my room. He needs to get on a plane, petition Chicago for a coaching position, or however that works, and do what makes him happy.

Frustrated and concerned, I exhale. "What are you even doing in my room?"

His eyes widen, meeting mine with a dullness I unfortunately recognize. A withering look of exhaustion. A hollow haze of loneliness. "I just want to talk."

My shoulders fall and I reach out for his hand, wrapping my fingers around the edge of his.

"Then talk."

Chapter 3

[Ross]

I didn't know exactly what to say to her. I didn't have an honest answer for why I wanted to share a drink with her or crack open this bottle I'd been saving since the season started, when I didn't have a cause to celebrate.

My team lost the world championship.

The woman I'd been dating broke things off with me three weeks ago in the middle of the playoff mayhem.

My sons don't like me very much.

After the season is my motto, and the season is now over.

I'm in this weird in-between state where it hasn't sunk in. Only a few hours have passed. In another couple months, I'll be itching to coach again, but I won't have a team. I don't know where I'll be. Maybe these are the things we should talk about, but I don't want to discuss the stuff weighing me down. I just want to have a drink and share some company without a crowd.

Plus, Vee is . . . intriguing.

A woman shared by two men? *Fuck me.*

And that dance in the elevator. The panic in her face. Her rush to escape and her struggle to enter . . . my room. Her frustration made her cute. Pretty in a way I hadn't noticed at first. Shoulder-length hair that's dirty blonde. Medium height with toned legs and curvy hips. Her blue eyes hold wisdom. Her face tells the truth. She's shown me her feisty side.

I won't mention how I checked out her tempting back as I lowered her zipper.

I want to know more about this two-men thing. *Was she into that?* I could never share a woman with another man. Plus, she gives off a good girl vibe, sweet and soft, feminine, yet her wit and tongue are sharp like steel cleats. She isn't afraid to say what she means or what she feels. She's a welcome contradiction.

With her hand still clutching the side of mine, I flip my palm and grasp her fingers. They're tiny compared to mine. Delicate. She said she's an author. She must type a lot.

"Tell me more about you. Another secret." With my focus on her hand, I spread her palm over mine, before dragging my thumb and forefinger down the length of her index finger, massaging the extremity as I go.

"I think you should coach Chicago."

My head snaps up. "That's not a secret of yours." I chuckle bitterly. "And what do you know about baseball?"

"My dad loved the sport. I go to the games for the atmosphere." Her smile says she's joking, which loosens the tension in my shoulders.

The fact that I remember her is mind-boggling. That damn video made a social media sweep, and I was tagged over and over again in it. People begged me to find her. Fans suggested I ask out a stranger.

At the time, I wasn't in a good headspace. A relationship was the last thing I wanted after Patty's sudden passing. Dating was nowhere on my bingo card then.

I had sex, though. Something physical to distract me from my grief, without any fear of becoming attached to anyone on a deeper level. I lost myself to the flashing lights and superficiality of a revolving door of celebrity women, because they never wanted anything from me other than orgasm and a picture splashed on some high-profile website or gossip magazine.

But when Chandler came along, I realized something was missing in my life. Something is *still* missing, and I feel unsettled, adrift almost. Our break-up had not caused any heartbreak.

"What do you love about the atmosphere?" From a coaching perspective, the vibe in a huge stadium is indescribable. The sense of grandeur. A place of pride. A feeling of belonging. The thrill of competition.

"The community. Everyone dressed in team colors. The enthusiasm over a game. The love of a team. When the Anchors win, the fans feel like winners." She raises her fist in solidarity. "Plus, Anchor Field serves a mean margarita."

I smile at the simplicity she's made of my career but understand what she's saying. In my psychology of sport class back in college, I learned about winning-team fan-pride. The BIRG Effect, where fans bask in the reflected glory of their chosen team's success.

It's abundantly clear how they feel about a loss, too.

The taunts. The insults. The cry to fire the coach.

Verona has just emphatically described every fandom that exists.

"You're kind of adorable." A chuckle that feels unfamiliar and rough from disuse follows my compliment.

"Ugh." She groans, glancing down at her hand which I'm still massaging finger by finger. A sharp contrast exists between her creamy fingers, nails polished in a dark purple, and my rough ones.

"Puppies are adorable. And if you compare me to a dog, I'm kicking you out."

The last thing I want to do is go back to my empty room and sit there alone. I could have met up with the other coaches. Hung out with the players. But they have their own rituals after a loss. I didn't want to share in the misery. I also didn't want to be by myself.

Being here, in her room, is just what I needed. A distraction from everything. Then again, isn't that how I ended up in Philadelphia nearly seven years ago? I'd needed to escape reality.

"Let's not talk about baseball."

"Okay," she whispers, dropping her voice to something huskier, alluring even.

"Let's get back to that two-men thing."

"It's called polyamorous. And I know . . ." she projects louder, pursing her lips as she lifts her head. "Let's chat about why older men like younger women. I mean, age-gap is popular in romance right now but what's really the appeal?"

My brows hitch, suggesting she must know the answer. *Sex.* Call me shallow, but there had been a mutual benefit between me and former partners.

Without waiting for a definitive answer, Vee continues, "I mean, I might not be twenty years younger, but I'm twenty years wiser. I know what I want. I know my worth, and I know a thing or two about the bedroom. Is that it? Is it that an *older* woman has an opinion, specific desires, a set standard, and we aren't willing to settle for mediocre once we cross a certain age threshold? Is it that we're more selective? We want a unicorn, instead of a work horse, hammering away at us." She jostles her hips just the slightest to emphasize her meaning.

"A unicorn?" I chuckle, wondering if this is another genre among the romance book industry, but Vee is on a roll, and I like her enthusiasm and her defense.

"Is it more effort to be with an older woman? We don't want trinkets and the tropics. Okay, maybe I wouldn't turn down a man willing to take me to Hawaii, but really? What's wrong with confidence and companionship? What's wrong with being feisty and wanting friendship, plus some damn good foreplay."

My brows hitch. I'm certain she isn't propositioning me. She's simply stating a case which has me considering something.

Being with Chandler had never been about her age. Chandler wanted a nice dinner, some publicity, and sex. However, I'd finally concluded that fancy restaurants, a flash photograph, and consensual sexy times did not garner strong sentiment. And I wanted to feel something again.

"Don't you want someone who appreciates you?"

Her question strikes a chord.

"Someone who can commiserate with your need for reading glasses and the ache in your joints."

"Commiserate?" I chortle.

"Yeah, I mean, getting older sucks, but wouldn't it be better to be with someone who can laugh with you about it versus someone who calls you *old man*. Unless you're into that daddy stuff, which is a whole other shelf in the romance section." She waves dismissively and releases a long exhale. The fight has gone out of her. "Besides, getting older is a privilege."

The final gavel drops on her argument, and I ignore the sudden thud in my chest. She's absolutely correct on her last point.

With a deep rumble in my throat, I say, "Romance certainly sounds like an interesting industry."

"We even have sports romance for those of us who love both, but we won't talk about baseball." She hitches one shoulder, teasingly dismissing the topic.

My focus shifts to her other hand, reaching for it and rubbing down each of her fingers, marveling at the delicacy of them. Vee's spirit and spunk don't match her tender frame.

She hums.

Eyeing her hand, stroking over her fingers, the moment feels strangely intimate. Why am I touching her? More importantly, why am I afraid to let go? Most surprising is the question that escapes. "What kind of story would you write about us?"

"Oh, are we a story?" She ticks up a brow, her eyes flashing a playful blue.

My gaze flicks up to meet hers. "Aren't we?" *Could we be?* The thought is ridiculous. Life is not fiction. It's hard facts like losing spouses and important games, not equivalent in any manner, but life is full of deprivation. If Vee did write us a story, I wonder if she would make us a success. What do they call it for romance? A happily ever after.

Do I want that?

"We'd be a stalled elevator meet-cute turned only one bed."

I glance around us, taking in the king-sized bed.

"But we aren't talking about beds or sex . . . or baseball," Vee confirms, a twitch in her smile.

Slowly, I return her smile. "Isn't baseball somehow related to romance? I remember something about first base and second base."

Her head tilts. "Is there something romantic about reaching second base?" Implying getting felt up might not be special.

My gaze drifts from her lips to her chest which is ample beneath her tight-fitting tee.

Cool Girls Read Hot Books. Cute.

Then, I shake my head, ridding myself of all thoughts of happily ever after and fictional tales. I'm here to chat, not check her out.

I don't want a rebound.

I'm not looking for sex.

I just want company. *Her company.*

Something unfamiliar and rare aches inside me. She isn't completely wrong about me wanting a woman who better understands me. Not the baseball fame or the spotlight fanfare, but me, Ross Davis, an aging man.

Patty would have been that person.

And I'm not old. *Fuck that.* I don't have the cricks she's talking about, but the day I bought reader glasses had been a difficult one. And she's right. I didn't like it when Chandler called me old man. I never let her call me daddy, although she asked if she could. I'm a father, for fuck's sake. That's just— I shudder.

"What about first base in a hotel room?" The question comes from left field.

Vee's fingers stiffen within my grasp.

"For story-telling purposes," I clarify as my eyes flick upward to meet hers.

"Strangers kissing in a hotel room? It has potential." Teasingly contemplative, she pouts. Her head tilts like she's honestly giving the idea thought. Her gaze is focused on me, processing, thinking. Then, she looks puzzled.

Even I'm confused. Do I want to kiss her? Am I innocently flirting? Or am I making an ass of myself? And why would I care if I am?

I just lost the granddaddy of championships. Weightier things should fill my head. I might lose my job. I might not be marketable to a new team. I might have to retire. Again.

I'm failing at everything lately.

I clear my throat and drop my gaze back to her hand, concentrating on rubbing her thumb. "Why did you decide to become a writer?"

"It's something I always wanted to do. I have an active imagination. And at one point, I decided it was time to do something for me."

There's more to her story she isn't saying, but I don't ask. Instead, I kid her, "Like two men sharing you."

"Okay, that's enough of that." She yanks her hand free from mine, but I chase, catching her fingers before she can fully retreat.

"I'll drop it." I pause as I rub my thumb into her palm and her arm quivers. "Ticklish?"

"Maybe." She giggles.

"I just have one more thing to say about two men—"

She groans and tries to tug her hand away again, but I hold firm.

"I'd never share."

Her arm stiffens, forcing me to look up at her. "It's fiction."

"In reality . . ." I press down on the center of her palm, stroking the lifeline bisecting the middle of her hand. Her arm twitches again. She *is* ticklish. "I'd never share *you*."

"That's"—She swallows, watching my thumb work over her inner hand—"oddly sweet of you to say."

She's sweet.

Then I yawn, wide and large and out of nowhere. Suddenly, my head is heavy, my body weary. I blink as exhaustion hits me like I've just run into the ivy wall at Anchor Field. I should excuse myself and head to my room, but I don't want to leave.

Her room.

Or her.

Not yet.

Unable to stop myself, I scoot down on the bed and extend my arm along the extra pillows beside me. Wiggling my hand, I signify I want her to lay down next to me.

"What are you doing?" She watches me, curious, cautious, but also with a mischievous smile which lights up her face. Her blue eyes dance. She has a playful side, a silly one at that. She's passionate and talks with her hands a lot. That old video seems to embody her personality. Watching her reaction to the moment, her face turned a pretty shade of pink, hinting at both her embarrassment and the potential of a crush on me back then.

I pat the bed. "Lie down."

Her brows pinch once, the crease deep with concern. A second passes, and I brace for her to kick me to the curb. I'm actually holding my breath.

Then, she shifts, hesitantly folding down to her side, nestling her neck against my arm until I tug her closer to me, hooking her into my side so her head rests on my shoulder.

She places a hand on my belly and smooths over the material of my sweatshirt. "This isn't very comfortable."

The athletic shirt is waterproof and wind resistant, and the fabric is slippery. I sit upward, taking Vee with me, and reach for the back of my collar. In the reflection of the blank television screen, I see Vee dig her teeth into her lower lip while she watches me. Her gaze is appraising, appreciative even, of the muscle mass I still maintain. I tug the outerwear over my head and toss the sportswear toward the ottoman. Then, I kick off my shoes. They fall off the edge of the bed with a thud.

"Anchors," she whispers when I settle onto my back again and she reads the logo on the tee I have on. The one beneath the outerwear.

Vee remains propped up, her gaze running the length of my extended arm, taking in the tattoos that decorate my former pitching powerhouse. Quickly, she snags her eyes away and runs her hand over my chest, across the logo of my former team on my tee. Wearing the apparel of an opposing team could get me canned. Hell, I probably will be sacked. However, this shirt is also my lucky tee, and in baseball we have serious superstitions. I wore this worn thing the night the Chicago Anchors won the championship when I was their all-star pitcher. When my life imploded once before, and baseball had been my savior.

"Don't tell anyone," I hush.

"Another secret between us."

I've told her more tonight than I've told anyone in weeks. Not many know Chandler and I aren't together anymore. No one knows I want a coaching position with Chicago. Not a soul would believe how much I miss that city.

"Another secret," I whisper in confirmation, tugging her to me and innocently kissing her hair. She smells fresh and floral, which is expected. She's a hearts and flower kind of woman, and I'd never be the kind of man she deserves.

"Did you really want to go out with me?" Somehow, I don't think Vee would have been interested in me simply for a swanky dinner and some publicity. Maybe not even for great sex. Maybe she'd been chasing the same sentiment I had. She just wanted to feel something again.

She giggles nervously and pokes me in the chest. "Okay, no more secrets for you, mister."

We remain silent a minute. The fan of the air conditioner kicks on. The chatter of people passing the room in the hallway filters to us.

But I really want to know if my theory is correct.

"Why did she do it?" I shift so I can better see Vee's face. "Why did your daughter bring that poster to the game?"

Vee draws a finger along the anchor on my shirt. "She knew I was sad, and she thought you might be too." She shakes her head. "She was just a girl looking out for her mom, but it was incredibly insensitive, and I apologize on her behalf."

Insensitive? Because I'd been a new widower then?

Pressing my nose to her hair, I inhale her scent again. Am I *still* sad? Truth is, I don't feel much of anything. I'm numb lately. In comparison to the woman against my chest, who appears full of passion and drive. Playfulness and decisiveness.

"She sounds . . . fun."

"She is." Vee sighs wistfully, pride in the sleepy sound. "More fun than me. Her social calendar is so full. Kids these days . . ." She quietly chuckles, then her voice turns a touch more somber. "She was just a boy-crazed teen back then. Now, she's an adult."

I chuckle, bitter sympathy in the sound as I understand her meaning about aging children and packed calendars. I've missed out on a lot of my boys' activities from March to October. Missed their games and spring plays. Almost missed Harley's high school graduation this year. The time has passed so much quicker than I thought it would.

Without Patty present, I've been failing at fatherhood. *After the season.* But the seasons have rushed along.

Tightening my hold on Vee, she responds by draping her arm over my stomach and slinging her ankle over my shin.

My dick twitches at the contact. He's been ignored since long before Chandler and I separated, but sex isn't why I'm here tonight. Romance and baseball might go hand in hand, but tonight I'm alright with never leaving the batter's box. Crazy as it sounds, I don't want to strike out with Vee.

Another heavy yawn pulls up my throat.

"What are we doing, Ross Davis?" Vee's voice softens, hushed and sleepy.

"I think we're sleeping together."

She chuckles. "I miss sleeping with someone."

It's like she read my thoughts. There were days the ache for Patty runs deep. And then there were empty nights with Chandler. She wanted to capture the allusion of cuddling, snapping endless photos for social media before we rolled to separate sides of a bed. We lacked a true connection.

I should ask if Vee has a man in her life now. Make certain she's not breaking any vows, although she isn't wearing a wedding ring. If there is someone in her life, Vee seems strong enough to have told me to hit the road instead of allowing me to enter her room.

Why would she do that with a man she doesn't know?

"You're not sleeping with just anyone, Vee. Tonight, you're sleeping with me. Only me."

Fuck the idea of another man. Or two men!

Vee hums. "Only you." Her sleepy voice drifts. "I'm sleeping with Ross Davis." Her relaxed chuckle rumbles over my chest.

Will she exploit this night to be a viral sensation again? Will she use this time against me? There isn't a bone in my body that believes she'd do that, even if I don't know her. Verona Huxley gives me strange comfort. A good kind of weird energy is coming off her. A sensation of good fortune and future luck.

"What kind of happenstance is that?" she mutters drowsily, continuing her thought.

"Happy chance?" I repeat.

"Happenstance. A coincidence. You and me in the elevator. And now you and me in my bed."

Definitely a happy chance. "I like my phrase better."

She quietly chuckles. "I think it's kind of the same thing."

As the sweet sound of her quiet laughter flutters through the room, I drift off to sleep imagining this is my life. I lose a game and come home to a woman who empathizes and supports my mood, because she understands *me*. She *appreciates* me, not just the fame of a game, and what it could mean for her status. Her image. Her brand. Her portfolio.

I snuggle selfishly into Vee, holding her tighter to me.

Silently, I thank an elevator for getting stuck and giving me an awkward ten minutes that have turned into a night of much-needed distraction.

No fooling around. No complicated sex.

Just some pillow talk.

It's refreshing. Like Vee.

A happy chance.

Chapter 4

[Vee]

At some point during the night, I pressed off Ross's chest and rolled to my side, giving my back to him. Like iron fragments chasing a magnet, Ross rolled with me, lining his body up tight against mine. His heavy arm draped over my waist. I fell into a restless doze.

The gentle hum of him snoring could have been the reason for feeling unsettled.

Or the fact I'm literally sleeping with Ross Davis, my imaginary baseball boyfriend.

My overactive thoughts wander through a variety of scenarios, if only I were a little more reckless and a lot more seductive. Like how I would have kissed my crush at some point. That strong hand of his would have cupped my neck, wanting more from me. Our tongues would have met, and I'd have had a connection like none other, taking us down the first base line to making out.

How long has it been since I've been kissed?

My wayward thoughts round toward second base. I didn't miss how his eyes raked over my T-shirt. His hands are the size of a baseball mitt and, in my fantasy, he'd cover my breast, squeezing, kneading, before plucking at the tight nub of my nipple.

With that mental image, I squirm a little and feel the glory of something solid and firm pressing against my backside. Baseball euphemisms abound. *He has quite the bat in his pants, and I'd like him to take a swing.* I dig my teeth into my lower lip to suppress a giggle. I'm so exhausted I'm not thinking straight, and I'm in this weird dream state with Ross Davis behind me and the firmness of his morning wood against my ass.

If I'd been braver last night, I would have run my hand lower than the Anchors logo on the tee covering his firm chest. *Down, down, down* to the wedge that wasn't hidden by loose fitting sweatpants. Slipping below his beltline, my hand would have stolen to third base. He would have placed his hand on my backside and tugged me over his firm body, coaxing me to straddle that big *bat* of his.

After that, we would have headed for a home run. Or at least I would have scored because there's no doubt what he's packing in those sweatpants would have brought me to an instant fireworks-over-the-stadium celebration.

I nearly burst out laughing at my own ridiculousness.

But when his hand flattens and he coasts it over my belly, I stiffen. Torn between the desire for his touch, and knowing I'd want so much more than a roll in these sheets with Ross Davis, I stay still. He nuzzles his nose into my nape while tightening his arm around my midsection and tugging me closer to him. His hips gently roll forward and then he stalls.

I sense his confusion. That awareness he's pressed up against a woman. A woman he doesn't know or recognize. I can almost hear his mind sprinting, wondering what he's doing in this strange ballpark, AKA my hotel room.

The arm hooked over my waist tenses. His breath catches. His solid length holds firmly against my lower cheeks.

"Mornin'," he grumbles, groggy and low.

"Good morning," I choke.

He abruptly rolls away and falls to his back. As I twist to face him, he swipes both hands down his face before blinking up at the dim ceiling.

"I'm still here," he whispers.

"You're still here," I echo. Why *did* he stay? Instead, I ask, "How did you sleep?"

He turns his head on the pillow and looks directly at me, taking in my eyes before lowering to my lips. His brows pinch, as if questioning himself before he answers. "Well. *Really* well."

His puzzled tone has me wondering if he normally doesn't sleep well, but I suspect someone of his caliber wrestles with stress, causing him sleepless nights and exhausting days. The responsibility for a major league team must be huge.

"How did you sleep?" he asks eventually.

I shrug. "Eh." But I can't fight the slow curl of my lips. *I slept with Ross Davis.*

As if reading my thoughts, he says. "We probably shouldn't tell anyone about this." An anxious edge rounds out his words. The underlying command is clear. No one can know and I'm instantly offended he thinks I'd share our moment with anyone else. I'm also hurt that our time together is suddenly being reduced like some kind of dirty one night stand he wants to keep hidden in the shadows.

Still, I shove aside the sting in my chest. "Your secrets are safe with me." With one hand over the top of the other, I wave them in a manner that crisscrosses them, weakly attempting the umpire signal for *safe*.

Silence follows before I clear my throat.

"I was thinking about what you said last night," I pause as he watches me. "You mentioned baseball players being superstitious. I've heard of unwashed socks, unruly facial hair, and lucky T-shirts." My gaze falls to his Anchors tee. "Maybe *this* is a conflict of interest."

I chew my lip, worried I'm opening a can of worms by hinting at last night's game and offering my opinion.

Ross tips his head in a way he glances at his shirt. He smooths his big hand over the soft cotton and I almost whimper considering I'd been daydreaming about that paw cupping my breast.

"Maybe, your heart lies somewhere else," I whisper, tiptoeing the line I've already crossed.

He gazes back at me. "Are you suggesting my heart is in Chicago?"

I dig my teeth into my lower lip.

With our eyes locked on each other, time stills.

I'll never forget this night, Ross Davis.

While my brain has bandwidth for endless fantasies, my heart doesn't have the capacity for our reality. He's a famous baseball coach. I'm just a fan. The two shall not meet again.

Clearing my throat again, and breaking the intensity of our connection, I say, "It's just a thought."

"You might be onto something." His heavy brows press together a second before he looks up at the ceiling, blinking several times again like it will bring him clarity. "Maybe I do need a scene change . . . or a new ritual."

"Maybe," I tease, quietly laughing before I offer another suggestion. "Like randomly sleeping with a stranger in a hotel room. Emphasis on *sleeping*."

"Yeah." A divot momentarily forms again between his brows, questioning, confused. "Something like that."

Ross shakes his head, then swipes his hand down his face once more, and abruptly sits upright, swinging his legs off the bed and giving me his back. Glancing at me over his shoulder, he says, "I should probably get going."

I roll my lips inward, fighting the desire to ask him to stay, maybe join me for breakfast. However, that isn't an option. This was only one night.

Suddenly, a loud bass mingled with the words "hit it" erupts from somewhere, and the sound of Rob Base and DJ E-Z Rock fills my room.

"What is that?" I laugh, slowly pressing myself upright as Ross turns for the nightstand where his phone and the prized bottle of alcohol remain.

"My alarm."

"Wasn't that . . . ." I chuckle softly. "Your walk-up song?"

He huffs out a laugh. "Yeah."

"Dude," I groan. "The 80s called and want their music back."

His blue eyes light up as he twists to face me better. "Do not disrespect a classic." He points a long thick finger at me in jest. I grip it with my smaller hand, tugging on it, while laughing harder at his serious tone.

This man is a mystery, full of secrets, and some serious superstitions. Or maybe it's just that he's holding onto history, afraid to let go.

"So, it's time for you to *hit it*." I follow my poor attempt at mimicking the rappers by throwing out my arms before crossing them in front of my chest which has him chuckling. Then, he slides off the edge of the bed and stands.

ELEVATOR PITCH

Instantly, this strange bond with him breaks. Like he's left the sacred island of the rumpled sheets and too many pillows, and I'm going to be stranded here alone.

Tossing my own legs over the opposite side of the bed, I stand as well, and we face off across the deserted land between us.

Ross anxiously scratches underneath his chin.

Deciding I need to be the one to break the sudden awkwardness of the morning after, I step toward the short hallway that leads to the door.

"It was a pleasure sleeping with you, Ross Davis."

He chuckles deeper, before slipping his phone into his pocket, and reaching for his shoes and sweatshirt. He picks up the bottle of precious booze, then rounds the bed, walking right up to me. Opening his arms, he tugs me to his solid frame. Held firmly against him, he squeezes tight like he doesn't want to let me go.

Or maybe that's just me wishful thinking.

The word *fan* comes from fantasy. Or fanatic.

I'll always be one for Ross Davis in his role as a player and a coach. But as a man, Ross has shown he's only human, flawed and complicated, real and fascinating.

"Thanks for last night," he mutters near my ear before slowly releasing me. He swallows hard and meets my eyes. "Maybe we'll meet again."

"Maybe."

Stranger things have happened.

Like getting stuck in an elevator with my baseball boyfriend.

Or spending the night with him. Only sleeping. Sharing pillow talk and private thoughts.

Silently, I hope we do meet another time.

Happenstance, perhaps.

Chapter 5

March
Spring Training

[Vee]

"There he is, Vee-Vee," my best friend teases as she sits beside me in the stadium seats.

Shortly after my night with Ross Davis, sports media announced that he had been released from the Flash and picked up by the Chicago Anchors to manage the team. When I heard the news, pride swelled within me. Ross had accomplished what he wanted. He returned to Chicago to manage a team with deep history and passionate followers. He wore red and royal blue once more.

Presently, I'm attending a spring training game in Arizona where the Anchors practice pre-season. The field is full size, but the stadium is closer to the size of an exhibition team setting, with limited rows of seats from left field to right. A grassy berm, appropriately named lawn seats, lines the edge of the outfield. Fans out there bring their own blankets and sit where they can find space. The overall atmosphere in this springtime setting is less chaotic than the grandeur of the home field. This place is more old-school, almost small-town, and all-around full of excitement for another year of baseball.

Maybe this will be our year.

My two daughters, Laurel and Hannah, are on their spring breaks, and we've traveled here with my bestie, Cassandra Culpére. Cassandra is the sister I never had, and my girls lovingly call her Aunt Sassy, which she requested when they were younger. At twenty-three and twenty respectively, my daughters maintain the tradition, while I call Cassandra Cee-Cee complementing her nickname for me, Vee-Vee. Besides, Cassandra does not like her name. She says it sounds too aristocratic and uppity. I've argued it's beautiful and classic, like a historical romance heroine.

"Okay, Cee-Cee, chill." I pat her forearm patronizingly as she sits with her feet up on the back of the seat in front of her while her body slouches down in her own chair. Months ago, I'd made the mistake of telling Cassandra about my night with Ross. Not all the details but the basics.

The elevator stop. The drink in my room. The fact he slept in my bed.

Just slept.

"But he's right there." She waves exaggeratedly toward the dugout and the back of Ross Davis, who fills out baseball pants like no man I've ever seen. The tight curve of his backside and the outline of his thick thighs makes my lower belly flutter. With seats only eight rows from the dugout and no one else immediately present, we have an unobstructed view of the man who has starred in my dreams a little too often over the past few months.

One would think with all the fantasies I've had, the spark to write would ignite, but I'm in a slump again. The current dry spell has been practically desert-like.

"Stop," I groan, cupping my hand around Cassandra's wrist and pressing it back to her lap.

Thankfully, Laurel and Hannah went to purchase snacks and the first round of drinks.

My best friend only chuckles, enjoying how she pokes at the bear—*me*. The grumpy cub, she calls me. I'm not grumpy. I'm stressed. I need a story. A flicker of inspiration. Just something to get the creative juices flowing again. I'm hopeful the change of scenery in Arizona will spark the flame I need.

"Hmm," Cassandra groans. "He sure is fine at forty-nine."

"He's forty-*seven*," I correct, knowing a few too many numbers about him. Six-four. Two-ten. Forty-seven until June. Formerly number thirty-three for the Anchors and the number I wear on my Anchor jersey with his name.

Cassandra hums again. "A slice of heaven at forty-seven."

The salacious wiggle of her brows causes me to giggle. When we met in college, I didn't know then how much of a ride-or-die sister from another mister Cassandra would be in my life. Watching me embrace motherhood when she didn't have kids. Holding my hand when Cameron died. Supporting my venture to write romance.

Cassandra is my biggest fan, next to my girls, who know what I do, but not exactly what I write. If they've ever read my books I don't want to know. Some things a mother never needs to learn about her daughters.

"You should go talk to him," Cassandra encourages.

"I wouldn't even know what to say." While I've thought about Ross for months, I never considered reaching out to him. We didn't leave things like that. We didn't exchange phone numbers or email addresses. Besides, he'd have people who had people who wouldn't pass on a message from some random woman with a name they wouldn't recognize.

Plus, Ross didn't want anyone to know he'd slept in my room that night. I'd only told Cassandra because I tell her everything, and three margaritas make for loose lips.

"Davis," Cassandra calls out, cupping her hands around her mouth to carry her voice.

"Cee-Cee," I groan, leaning forward and covering her mouth as best I can with her hands in the way. I feel like a teenage girl fighting her friend who is trying to cause a scene so the boy I'm crushing on will notice me. Cee-Cee is that embarrassing friend, although technically, she simply embraces life. She'd be more likely to approach Ross Davis on a whim than me.

That elevator brought us together. Nothing more.

Falling back into my seat, I'm grateful that Ross doesn't turn to the catcalling of a boisterous female in the stands. He's probably heard lots of chants over the years. Had phone numbers slipped into his hand. Had hotel keycards tucked into his pants.

Some nights, I'm still puzzled that he knocked on my hotel room door and asked to come inside.

"Looking good, Gee," Cassandra calls out next, cupping her hands around her lips once more.

My friend is in full-on courage-mode, innocently, but flirtatiously, heckling the younger set on the Anchors. She can't decide who she crushes on more: our newest recruit, Gee Scott; the team captain, Ford Sylver; or our prized hitter, Caleb Williams.

The Chicago Anchors should be good this year. They have youthful players with high talent, but they've just had a week-long losing streak. The start for the new manager and his team has been rocky.

Not to mention there was an altercation between team members roughly a week ago.

While my friend drools over the Anchors having some of the best-looking players in the league, I'm more intrigued by the coaching staff and glance back at Ross. With his legs spread wide and his ass tight, his arms are crossed over his chest, one forearm lifted so his forefinger can circle his lips. I don't need to fully see his face to know his signature move. His forefinger and thumb tracing over his moustache and around his lips is a contemplative tick while he assesses his team. The unseen action reminds me of his fingers stroking over mine the night he stayed in my room.

Finally, Chicago and their opponents from Cleveland head to their respective dugouts. Cee-Cee lifts her arms above her head to clap, then whistles her excitement with two fingers between her lips, a skill I've never mastered. The sharp trill in such close proximity is almost deafening, and the noise makes Ross's head lift as he follows after his team toward the dugout. As he glances into the stands, his feet falter.

The eighth row is low and with several empty seats around us, we're clearly visible from the field.

With her elbow leaning on the armrest between us, Cassandra wiggles her fingers in the air, waving at Ross.

Without looking at her, I grip her wrist and try to press her arm down, as if that will hide us somehow. As if Ross Davis hasn't already looked in our direction and keeps his gaze on us as he narrows his eyes and closes the distance to the dugout.

Then he disappears beneath the roof of the structure, and I exhale.

Whether it's a sigh of relief or a breath of regret is yet to be determined.

Does he not remember our night? Surely, he couldn't forget getting stuck in an elevator with a face-fanning, potty-dancing woman, or the fact he invited himself into her room to share a drink and talk romance and baseball. Then again, maybe he *has* forgotten.

His breakup with Chandler Bressler appeared to be an on-again off-again thing after last season's end. Last I'd read, they were on-again. And I know all-too-well how someone can forgive and forget often in a relationship.

It was only one night.

Something clearly forgettable for Ross Davis.

A month ago, I mentally scolded myself for continuing to follow Ross Davis on social media, and I unfollowed him everywhere for my own sanity. My editor would tell me I shouldn't be on social platforms anyway. I have words to write.

After the singing of the "National Anthem", my girls return to our seats. Laurel flanks Cassandra while Hannah sits beside me. My blonde-haired, blue-eyed girl is an all American beach beauty with a strong mind, sharp wit, and tough personality. She's my baseball girl, knowing more statistics than I'll ever remember about past and present teams and players. My dad loved the sport and took the girls often to the stadium back home. When he died, I'd inherited his season tickets, and I didn't have the heart to let the tradition pass as well.

Laurel helps me sell the tickets we can't use, earning back the exorbitant fee for eighty-something home games. With brown hair and brown eyes, she's the spitting image of her father with a lean build and average height. She's more of a social fan, attending games to see and be seen, talking through most of the innings and taking a gazillion pictures of herself and her friends in the stands. She adores Cee-Cee like a big sister and tries to emulate her in many ways, including commenting on the *cuteness* of the players.

"That Caleb Williams is a looker," Cassandra muses, chewing at her lower lip.

"He's a hooker?" Hannah questions over me.

"No one says looker, Aunt Sassy," Laurel chides.

No one says hooker anymore either, I want to chime in.

"He's still fine like a straight line," Cassandra continues.

"Are straight lines fine?" Hannah deadpans.

"Only if that straightness is his—" Laurel abruptly stops, catching her gaze on mine.

Cassandra turns her head, volleying glances from Laurel to me before bursting into laughter.

"Laurel Huxley, have you been reading your mother's books?"

My twenty-three-year-old turns bright red and shakes her head. "Absolutely not."

"Are you sure?" Cassandra scoffs playfully. "Because that comment sounded awfully close to a d—"

"Alright," I cut off Cassandra, squeezing my brows together in warning. I'm *not* discussing dicks around my daughters.

Cassandra only chuckles harder while Laurel appears to shrink in her seat. My girl props her feet up on the back of the seat in front of her like Cassandra and dips her hand into the popcorn container, filling her mouth to prevent further comment.

"You're such an instigator," I mutter, chastising my bestie.

"And you're a spoilsport," she counters teasingly. Cassandra accepts that while I have an open relationship with my girls, hoping they come to me for anything and everything, that doesn't mean we're going to share cock comments with one another.

"Play ball." The words ring through the stadium, drawing my attention back to the field.

Are there any better words to give me goosebumps?

In the first few innings, our pitcher is on fire and in perfect rhythm with the catcher. However, one of our long-standing stars is our centerfielder, Ford Sylver, who has made one error after another. A pop-up fly hit toward the scoreboard was missed despite his height and an impressive jump. Another time the ball dropped between him and Romero Valdez, our reckless short stop, who made a mad dash to the outfield to assist. The play looked like something from a T-ball game with both men staring at one another. Their body language suggested they were faulting the other.

I glance at Cassandra, whose brows are pinched with concern and curiosity as she stares at the field where the two players are still facing off. With her phone in her hand, she quickly looks up our center fielder.

"Did you know Romero Valdez is dating Ford Sylver's ex-wife?"

Our shortstop, his teammate, is dating his former wife?

"Also, rumor has it, Ford is dating the country music icon, Cadence."

Would not surprise me.

However, my attention snaps back toward the outfield, my eyes narrowing in sympathy. At thirty-eight, Ford Sylver has had a great career, along with a beautiful wife and three of the cutest little girls. And I'm sorry if their marriage ended because of adultery. My sympathy stands with him as I scan the stands as if I'd be able to pick out his ex or his girls in the crowd, which I wouldn't be able to do. Still, I wonder if they are here. Family men on baseball teams often bring their spouses and children with them during spring training season.

Then I consider Ross. Who is here to support him? Do his boys attend games? Does he have additional family? Is Chandler Bressler present?

If my calculations are correct, his boys should be in high school or college themselves.

Glancing over the crowd again, I search for Chandler next. Her dark hair and curvy body would make her easy to recognize. As I don't see her, my focus returns to the game. I interject my opinion on bad calls. Wave my hands in the air in frustration over an error. Jump to my feet when Gee Scott hits a homerun with a man on second for a two-run score.

The eventual win is the first W for the Anchors since spring training started, and I enthusiastically join the fans who sing our winning anthem.

The song ends, and I'm inspecting the space around us for trash, bending to pick up the short stack of beer cups collected in my cup holder, when I hear my name.

"Verona Huxley?"

Abruptly straightening, I peer around Cassandra, down our row, to a man dressed in baseball gear without a stitch of dirt on him standing in the aisle. He isn't someone I recognize and based on the wrinkles at the corner of his eyes and the silver scruff along his jaw, I'd say he isn't a player, but someone affiliated with the team.

"I'm Kip Garcia." He pats his chest as a form of introduction because of our distance.

I haven't identified myself, but he steps into the row in front of our seats, now empty of attendees, and nears me.

"Ross Davis asked me to give you this." The messenger holds out a piece of paper which Cassandra is quick to reach for, but Kip is faster to retract from her. "Said only Vee should take this."

My brows lift, shocked that Ross remembers the nickname. Surprised that he remembers me at all. Then I'm slightly embarrassed he recognized me in the stands. My face heats as I reach out for the slip of paper.

"Thank you," I mutter, taking the haphazardly folded strip that looks like it was hastily ripped out of a small notebook and bent in half.

Kip nods once then steps away.

"Good game," I call after him, talking to his back.

He casually lifts his hand, waves once over his head, and continues on his way.

"Hmm," Cassandra hums beside me. "Who is he?" Her salacious tone doesn't imply she wants his name, but him. His position, rank, and status with the team.

Ignoring Cassandra's blatant ogling, I flip open the paper between my fingers.

Happy chance?

Lifting my head, I glance toward the dugout, now empty of the team. Then, I gaze in the direction where Kip walked away.

The note includes no other words but the simplicity of two in combination makes me smile.

Ross Davis remembers me.

Chapter 6

[Ross]

What are the odds?

I hadn't forgotten Verona Huxley, or that night we spent together. For months, memories of her plagued me, haunting my thoughts and filling my dreams with things that seemed too ridiculous to imagine.

And there she was, sitting in the stands in our spring training stadium, some two-thousand miles from home.

Then again, the odds are one in fifteen thousand which is the number of people this stadium can hold, and it isn't uncommon for fans to vacation in our springtime destination to escape the lingering cold in Chicago and in anticipation for another season of baseball.

Vee is clearly an avid fan of the team.

Wonder how many margaritas she enjoyed today?

The thought makes me chuckle.

"What the hell was that?" Kip Garcia asks. My pitching coach stares at me, a puzzled expression on his face.

Over the years, Kip and I met many times on the field. As rival pitchers, he was my nemesis before he became a friend. He left the ball field for the sidelines long before I did, and he's become a mentor of sorts. He's one reason I have my new position as manager of the Chicago Anchors. He put the bug in the front office's ear to hire me and I'm forever grateful to him.

And because of him and the opportunity the Anchors have given me, I don't want to disappoint him. Our three-game losing streak against Colorado, followed by a losing streak against Cleveland until today, has been embarrassing. I typically don't get rattled by these things. Losses suck but this *is* spring training. We have an entire season before us. The team in March will not be the same team in October. Still, I need to iron out some kinks now, especially issues between Sylver and Valdez.

"What the hell was what?" I scoff.

"That noise." Kip wrinkles his nose while he watches me.

"What noise?"

"That little puff of air. Was that . . ." He pauses for dramatic effect and scrunches his nose again. ". . . a laugh?" He chuckles himself.

"I laugh," I counter.

"Not often." His brows lift while he observes me.

"There isn't time for laughter in baseball."

"The saying is about crying, and I've seen plenty of tears from you on the mound over the years," he jests.

"You're full of shit." I am not a crying man.

"Better than being full of myself."

The knock takes me down a peg. I never want to come across as arrogant or cocky. Baseball is a team sport, and my position here is a fresh start. I'm home on a ball field. But I'll be missing my boys.

Harley is a freshman at DePaul. Landon is a junior at Purdue.

"We won," I remind Kip, but we have a long way to go with only one win under our belt.

Kip gives me a knowing gaze before tipping up his chin. "What was that with me playing messenger? You know we have people for that shit." His eyes narrow, assuming I passed my phone number to a woman in the stands.

Only I didn't. I should have but that isn't who Vee and me are. We didn't exchange numbers. We didn't mention where we lived. We only briefly brushed on what we did.

She is a romance author, but I didn't find any books with her name on them on bookstore shelves. Heck, I don't typically enter bookstores, but I'd been drawn to one in my new neighborhood once I was hired by the Anchors. When I asked the clerk about Verona Huxley, she couldn't find the name in their database, and I accepted Verona might have been a fake name given to me by the stranger whose room I'd entered and then crashed in her bed.

"What did she say?" I try to school my voice, attempting not to sound too eager to know if Vee remembers our night together.

"She said, and I quote. . ." He pauses while I wait with bated breath. "Thank you."

"That's it."

"She also said good game." His monotone voice has me arching a brow, teetering with anticipation for more.

"She also mentioned how I shouldn't ever have to deliver a message like a schoolboy passing notes again. And she thought I was hot."

I snort. "Okay. Now you're just being a dick."

Kip chuckles. "Seriously, who is she?"

I shake my head. How could I explain Vee?

"Are you fucking blushing?"

"What? No." However, I slap my hands to my cheeks, feeling a twinge of heat.

"What you *are* is gullible." Kip laughs harder, picking up his iPad and tapping his finger against it. "And we have tape to watch."

He's right. I need to get my head in the game. We finally have a win and I have work to do.

+ + +

We're about to lose the final game of a three-game series with Arizona.

"What the hell is going on out there?" Kip mutters, staring out at the nine players on the field. Each talented. Each experienced. Somehow out of sync with one another, though.

Ford Sylver is captain of these guys and he's been off since I met him last fall. A certain pressure comes with years in the league, especially for married guys. Couple that with being a single dad with little kids, and the toll is showing on Ford, especially since his ex is dating a fellow team member.

I'm not at liberty to share my true opinion of our shortstop.

I don't know each of the guys on the team well yet, but one of the things I pride myself on is being a mentor for my men. The father they didn't have or the substitute many of them need. A person to remind them to keep their dicks covered and their heads clear.

The three Ds: Devotion. Drive. Determination.

However, I seem to lack those things myself today. We are about to lose another series, and I'm stumped.

And not for the first time this game, I tip my head out of the dugout in hopes to find a certain someone sitting in the eighth row. Or anywhere else in this stadium.

"Who are you looking for?" Kip mutters out the side of his mouth.

Snapping my attention back to the game, I stare out at the field. The pitcher for Arizona is a beast, and if Gee Scott doesn't fix his swing, he's going to strike out. Game over.

When that moment happens, the team hangs their heads while Gee returns to the dugout, swearing under his breath. Only the clatter of cleats fills the dugout as the guys disappear into the locker room.

I take a step up to the field, taking one more survey around the stadium. Unfortunately, I'm not sly or stealthy like I think, and Kip catches me.

"We need to talk."

Fuck.

+ + +

"And you think she's the answer?" Kip stares at me. His questioning eyes caught between *you're fucking kidding* and *you're kidding, right?* A joke or an inquisition.

I swipe my ball cap off my head and scratch my scalp. Replacing the hat, I stare back at Kip standing on the other side of the desk in my office.

"I don't know." I've just explained how I met Verona Huxley. And my thoughts about the connectedness between us. "But think about it. I get the call from Chicago, the same day I get let go from the Flash, and both things happened the day *after* I slept with her."

"Coincidence," Kip groans.

Happy chance, perhaps?

"Then she shows up earlier this week and we win our first game." My voice rises, cracking on the absurdity, but the possibility cannot be denied. "She's my lucky charm."

"You don't know anything about her." Kip watches me.

He's right. I only know her name, or what I assume is her name, and what she does for a living, if writing books is even true. Either way, I can't ignore that her presence changes things for me.

The job. The win.

"You're taking baseball superstitions to a whole new level," Kip chides, crossing his arms. "You don't know how to find her. *If* she's even still in Arizona. *If* she's actually from Chicago." His voice rises in frustration with every *if*.

He's right again, but I refuse to believe Verona lied to me. Maybe the name is a pseudonym. Maybe her presence in Arizona is a fluke. Maybe I'm just nuts.

"It's worth a shot." I shrug. "If you don't swing . . ."

Kip is already shaking his head while completing the statement. "You'll miss one hundred percent of the time." He continues watching me, assessing me. "What are you thinking?" His voice lowers, leery with uncertainty.

"I have an idea."

Chapter 7

[Vee]

After an amazing week with my girls, they each depart Arizona with a hint of sunshine on their skin and melancholy in their eyes. The week has been filled with late night movies, loads of alcohol, a little retail therapy, plus copious time together. Saying goodbye is always difficult.

Cassandra flies back to Chicago with them.

Hannah will return to college where she is studying physical therapy. Laurel goes back to her classroom. She's a fifth-grade teacher. Their spring break week lining up on the calendar was a small miracle. We haven't had this kind of time together for years, and I treasured every moment.

As for me, I plan to stay behind in Arizona for another few weeks. Nearly a full month without interruption in hopes of inspiration to write a damn book.

However, on day one, I found myself staring longingly out the window at the sunshine and decided I'd write outside, where I promptly took a nap in the shade on an outdoor two-seater. Suburban Scottsdale is blissfully quiet compared to Chicago.

The next day, I told myself I couldn't leave the house without writing one chapter. Instead, I cleaned out my email inbox and organized the photos on my computer.

Day three, I intended to escape the house and visit a local coffee shop, like I often do back home, but I stepped into a breakfast café and enjoyed a meal heavy enough to warp my focus.

By mid-week, I'd given up and decided to attend a baseball game, hoping something completely unrelated to writing might trigger creativity.

I've never attended a baseball game solo, but I am comfortable doing things alone. Plus, I'm a people watcher. Sitting among strangers, I often mentally sketch out their lives. Their hangups and heartbreaks.

Their loves and laughter. And sometimes, my fictional creations prompt an idea, that turns into an obsession, that becomes a story.

Yes, an overcast sky and a midday baseball game might do the trick.

Surprisingly, my seat is roughly in the same spot as the game I'd previously attended. The Anchors are on a tough losing streak.

With a cold drink in a souvenir cup and a small bucket of popcorn, I settle into the atmosphere, mindlessly staring out at the field.

Who is Gee Scott? What is Caleb Williams' story? Why is Ford Sylver so angry?

Ideas . . . concepts . . . scenarios . . . and a slow build.

Pulling my phone from the pocket of my Anchor hoodie as bags are not allowed in the stadium, I quickly type my random fictional thoughts about each of the young players in the Notes app.

Small town hero.

Hawaiian vacation mishap.

Heartbroken family.

When a person nearby groans and abruptly stands, I finally lift my head.

How have I missed most of the innings of this game? The Anchors are tied in the ninth. Ford Sylver is up to bat.

"He fucking sucks this year," someone behind me grumbles.

"He's an unsung hero," someone else replies. "His stats are impressive."

"I'd be more impressed if he did something here."

As the first man finishes his complaint, Ford's bat cracks against the ball which soars for the outfield and lands in the lawn seats.

Homerun!

The crowd goes wild as the players on second and third base hit home with Ford on their heels.

With the Anchors at a sudden seven-to-four advantage, their opponent is quickly struck out with only three at bats. The Anchors have their first W since the previous game I attended.

I stand proudly among the mass of fans around me and join in singing our winning anthem. Ross Davis and his team have done it. They might be slow out of the gate, but the season isn't lost. That's what spring training is all about. Arranging and re-arranging players and positions, and finding that fit, that rhythm, that *schtick* makes a team tick.

When the song finishes, I gather my empty drink cup and the tub of popcorn I'd devoured and prepare to exit my row.

Once again, a man, dressed in an Anchors uniform, stands in the aisle.

"Kip Garcia." I slowly smile as I now recognize him. With graying hair on both his head and his jaw, plus his sun-kissed skin, he is a good-looking man I'd place in his early fifties. I didn't know who Kip Garcia was a week ago, but Hannah had all the facts.

Former Boston player. Pitching coach for Chicago. Has been with the team for ten years, which means he'd been a coach when Ross had been a pitcher for the Anchors.

Kip returns my smile with the briefest hint of white teeth and a spark to his infield-green eyes.

"You wouldn't, by chance, be willing to follow me." He arches one brow, slowly shaking his head like he can't believe he is requesting such a thing.

I am equally surprised.

"There's someone who'd like to meet you. Rather, see you. Again." With those friendly eyes staring back at me, I know exactly who he means. The confusion comes with *why* he wants to see me.

"That certainly sounds mysterious," I tease, curiosity getting the best of me. "But I'd be willing to follow you, for an autograph. My friend Cassandra would never forgive me if I didn't get one from you."

Kip chuckles. "Not many people want the pitching coaches' signature."

Cassandra wants more than a penned scribble from Kip, but asking if he is available and if I can have his phone number for a friend feels a little forward, not to mention awkward.

"My best friend is a huge fan."

"Anything for a fan, then." His smile widens before he tips his head to the side. "The question is, will you do anything for your team?"

As my brows crease at his cryptic question, he nods and adds, "This way, then."

Kip steps back, allowing me to exit the row, and leads me up the aisle to the concourse behind the stadium seats. Once there, he walks in front of me and I follow him through the maze of excited fans, grateful for a win. The smaller stadium doesn't house much of a dugout or locker rooms, and I am guided across a lawn space doubling as a parking lot to another building adjacent to the main field.

"Ask for Ross. Tell the security guard your name."

The direction sounds rather cloak and dagger, and just as suspicious as his earlier question. *Would* I do anything for my favorite team?

As players head in the direction Kip points, I make the assumption that the team's locker room is in the other facility, and the management offices must be in the same location.

Offering Kip a smile, I catch the skeptical shake of his head once more, like he knows a secret he can't believe he's keeping.

Like he knows something about me, and he doesn't understand it.

Why would Ross Davis want to see me again?

+ + +

Standing across from Ross feels a bit surreal.

His office door was open, still I rapped on it before entering. He'd been pacing the small confines and stopped abruptly at the sharp knock. His eyes race a cursory scan down my body taking in the replica Anchors jersey I'm wearing. The one with his name and number on the back. His gaze catches on the team's logo across my chest and then he glances away. He swallows hard. Quickly, his gaze returns to me, and we stare at one another for no more than five seconds. The time shorter than it takes a batter to reach first base after hitting the ball, and yet, time seemed to stand still.

Finally, Ross speaks, rubbing his hands against his thick thighs. "Vee."

"Hiya, Ross Davis." The cheer in my voice doesn't match the shaking in my knees or the fluttering in my belly. How could I forget how strikingly good-looking Ross is up close and personal? That stubble on his jaw. The strength in his arms. The thickness of his thighs. I'd spent a night in a bed with this man and the memories do not compare to the reality.

Those piercing blue eyes. That brilliant silvery scruff. The rosy lushness of his mouth.

"Good game," I add.

Ross chuckles gruffly. "Yeah, about that." He swipes at his hat, tugging it off his head by the bill and rubbing his palm over his buzzed hair. With the cap still in his hand, he lowers it before him.

"How have you been?"

"Good." I drag out the word and tilt my head, eyeing him suspiciously. There's no way Ross Davis asked me to his office to question how I've been for five months.

"Still writing?" He lifts his head and meets my eyes a second, narrowing them like he's trying to get a read on me, before he glances away.

"Yes," I lie as I haven't written anything of substance in three months. Today was different, though. Today was a good idea plucking day. "And I see you're still coaching."

My corresponding smile hints at our secret. He wanted to be exactly where he is, managing the Anchors.

"Yeah, about that, too."

I lean against the open door, crossing my arms and willing my legs to stop shaking. "And what exactly *about that*?"

Stepping closer to me, Ross cups my elbow and gently tugs me forward, moving me further into his office before closing the door behind me.

"Want to take a seat?"

"Am I in trouble, Coach?" Suddenly, I feel like a player called into the office to discuss my lack of talent.

Ross chuckles, tosses his hat on his desk, and takes a seat behind it, folding his hands on the surface. With the furniture as a barrier between us, I become even more anxious as to why I'm in this office. The distance between us is like a gap in mountain ranges considering we shared a bed and a night together, offering secrets to one another.

Ross flattens his hands against the smooth top of his desk and then stands. Rounding the desk, he stands in front of the steel-gray piece before leaning against the edge, folding his arms over his broad chest and crossing his ankles. Then he shifts again and lowers his arms, curling his hands around the frame of the desk to brace himself.

"Are you alright?"

Ross lowers his gaze and I glance down at his big feet as well, wondering if, as the saying goes, his shoe size equals the length of another body part. Then I wonder if staring at his shoes will give me a hint as to why I'm in his office and why the heck he seems so nervous.

"Did you lie to me?"

"What?" My head snaps up like a player watching a pop fly to centerfield.

"About the writing? About being an author?" He stares at me. "I never found your books."

"I write under a pen name," I state, not offering the name. That's a secret he hasn't earned yet, but an additional flutter flits through my low belly.

Ross Davis sought out my books.

He nods once, slowly, as if understanding the anonymity.

"Why would I lie to you?" If I'm here for an inquisition, then I don't need to be here. I don't owe Ross Davis an explanation about my life or my secrets. He's the one who asked me to come to his office.

"I don't know." Ross swipes over his hair again with a thick hand, nervously glancing at me before looking away again.

I stand. "I don't know why you called me into your office. Just like I still don't understand why you came to my hotel room, but if I'm here to be interrogated or something, then . . . I don't need to be here."

Nothing I said made sense, but Ross had me tongue-tied and weak-kneed, and he stands too close to me, although I'm the one who stood up.

"I have a proposition for you."

The word has me blinking and my heart hammering. The strangest thought occurs. *Would Ross propose he and Kip share me?* It was improbable. It was also absurd. It was so out in left field I don't know where the thought came from.

With a shaky hand, I rub my forehead, as if my fingertips can erase the thought.

Is it hot in this office? I'm suddenly too warm and I'm having an out-of-body experience.

Ross Davis is too close. His manly, spicy scent invades my olfactory senses. Like being stuck in that elevator with him, my body wants to squirm. Thankfully, I'm not experiencing a bathroom emergency.

With trepidation, I question him. "What is the proposition?"

"As you know, baseball players are highly superstitious."

Why is he using that tone with me? One that sounds instructional and distant.

"And once we have something set in our head, a routine . . . a ritual, we don't like to break the pattern."

I nod, mouth opening with no ready response to what feels like schooling in baseball lore.

"And I've noticed a pattern." He pauses, lifting his head and meeting my eyes. "With you."

"With me?" I squeak out, like I'm about to be reprimanded. Like he knows I've been skipping out on writing to do anything but write.

"Yes. You." He folds his arms over his chest again. "And I'd like to propose an experiment."

"With you?" I ask, tipping my head forward and wide-eye staring at him, like opening my eyes wider will help me confirm I'm hearing him correctly.

"Yes. With me."

"And what exactly is this experiment?"

"I'd like you to sleep with me." He exhales. "Again."

I stare blankly at him, certain I misheard him. His voice has been so off-putting and detached, and yet, I think he just asked me to sleep with him again.

"You want me." I point to myself. "To sleep with you." I point at him. "Again."

"Yes."

"Just sleep."

"Yes."

"In the same bed?"

"That's how it happened the first time."

"And this time?"

"In the same bed again."

"Why?"

Ross sighs, lowers his head and squeezes the back of his neck, like he can't believe what he is about to say. "Because you might be my lucky charm." He slowly lifts his gaze. "My happy chance."

"Your happy chance?" I sound like a freaking parrot with all the repetitiveness. Because I'm confused.

Ross waves toward me. "That happenstance thing."

"That—" I cut myself off from echoing him again. *This* is ridiculous, but because I'm mid-forties and fully in my F-it era, I ask, "And how exactly would that work? Me. In your bed."

He rubs his knuckles beneath his chin, the gesture bordering on anxious. The sound of his skin against that coarse hair causes a quiver in *my* belly. His mouth is tightly smug, like I've said yes when I'm still trying to process what he's suggesting.

"I guess, you'd come to my place."

My mouth gapes.

"Or I could come to yours," he states, noting what I'm certain is a horrified expression on my face.

Finally, I smack my lips closed and blink once. "You know, typically, a man asks if he can buy me a drink or dinner before suggesting his place or mine."

From his casual position, still perched against his desk, his eyes narrow. "And how often do men propose his place or yours to you?"

More mouth gaping. More lip smacking. *Never.* "I don't see how that would be any of your business."

My dating history is not the discussion at hand. This preposterous proposition is.

Those blue eyes of his become flames before he rolls his gaze down my body, the look causing a feather-like rush right down my center. A ripple of lust skitters over my skin, and I shiver.

Then I shake my head. "I'm sorry. I'd like to help but I just can't—"

"This was your idea."

"Mine?" I choke, back to one-syllable questions.

"The morning after."

My lips part once more, prepped to repeat what he's stated. Instead, I stare at him, my brows knitting tightly together in confusion.

"You said I needed a change in routine. Like sleeping with a stranger in a hotel room."

"I never said that." More blinking. More staring. "But if I had"— because I'm slowly recalling I might have said something similar— "How do you remember that?"

"Because I remember everything." His eyes laser in on mine. The look intense, electrifying even.

About that night? About me?

"And I'm thinking it can't be just anyone in my bed. It needs to be you."

Me? A virtual stranger?

Truthfully, we aren't complete strangers anymore. Did ten minutes trapped in an elevator make us besties? Absolutely not. But we shared roughly nine hours together in one bed in a hotel room in Houston. We learned a thing or two about one another. However, that didn't make us friends or bed fellows.

His final request stalls all higher functions. My brain stops trying to make sense of his thought process. My breath hitches. My heart, however, continues to hammer because deep down in my gut, I want to be significant to him, which is a puzzling concept.

"The facts are, I wanted this job, managing the Anchors," he continues. "And the only person I'd told about my fear of being fired from the Flash, and my hope of being hired here, was you. Then it happened."

Coincidence, I want to argue.

"Then we hadn't won a game in the first week of this training season, until you showed up a week ago. Then we win."

"Not exactly scientific evidence of—"

"And then . . ." he continues as if I wasn't speaking. "Today. You're here and we finally win for the second time."

I stare at him. He can't be serious with this nonsense, and yet, staring at him, the hopeful gleam in his eyes tells me he's convinced this is how things evolved. My presence, not the talent of his team, brought about a win.

"So give me training season tickets, and I'll attend a few more games." I can't believe I'm playing into his theory. This preposterous idea that I'm lucky for him. But as I'm not writing like I should be, maybe attendance at a couple more training games will be good for me, too.

Silence falls between us like a ball-drop in the outfield. I turn my head, glancing at a whiteboard with a baseball diamond embossed on it. Players on a team working in sync are vital to success, not a silly talisman. And certainly not some random set of happenstances.

Facing Ross again, I prepare to present my argument.

"Look." He holds his hand up, stopping me before I speak. "I know it sounds outrageous. Strange. Ridiculous even. But I'm not beyond begging you to take a chance on me. On this little experiment. Just give me one night. Maybe two. I'm staying at the hotel here on the campus."

I glance behind me as if I can see the four-star chain hotel on the opposite side of the stadium grounds.

"I need you," he states, his raspy voice softening from sandpaper against wood to soft grains of sand falling. His eyes lighten, vulnerable, hopeful.

And herein laid the problem.

I didn't want to be some hairbrained experiment for Ross Davis.

Chapter 8

[Vee]

"I'll think about it," I eventually tell Ross, which in mom-speak, typically means a silent *hell no*.

There are a number of reasons why I don't like his idea, top of which is being a woman who sneaks into, and then out of, his hotel room, like we're having a clandestine affair. I am assuming he wouldn't want anyone to know about our arrangement since he thought it was best we did not share what happened that night in Houston with anyone else.

There's also that pesky thing called *his girlfriend* to consider.

Everything in me screams to call Cassandra and immediately tell her about this bizarre proposal, but something holds me back.

That something being the sudden inspiration to write. Within ten minutes of returning to my rented condo, I've shed the flummoxed emotions of Ross's suggestion, and found a hint of creativity.

Just the beginnings of a story. Roughly twelve-hundred words to set a scene. Nothing profound or earth-shattering, but the sentences start to flow. The page was no longer blank. By the time I'd finished my thoughts, I'd filled one and a half sheets in a word document.

Word by word. One sentence at a time until a paragraph forms. Then a page. Then a chapter. Basic writing steps in their most rudimentary form.

The spark to create felt good. I needed a flame, but a flicker was still something. A flash of hope.

Maybe I need Ross Davis as much as he claims to need me. Or at the very least, I need that spring training stadium as plot ideas sparked during the game.

As the scene I'm concentrating on nears the end, and my characters are no longer telling me where they want to go next, other thoughts creep into my head, like Ross's ridiculous proposition and my own curiosity.

With my phone in my hand, I pull up Ross's number. *His direct number* as he clarified earlier. My finger hovers over the new contact before I switch to the texting app and I press the writing icon.

Was I really considering his proposal? Should I do this? Could I *sleep* with Ross Davis again? He isn't propositioning me for sex. *That would be preposterous, right?* I huff aloud to the empty room as if the vacant space can hear my thoughts.

At the very least, though, I had logistical questions and I type out a text, then press send.

How would this work?

His response is instantaneous, as if he'd been waiting for my reply.

Is this a yes?

Me: **This is me asking for details.**

Ross: **Maybe we should have that drink after all?**

Aren't we past the formality? He'd already proposed I sleep with him.

No question about sex. There won't be any.

No emotion implied. There wasn't a place for them.

This was just your average request from a man to a relative female stranger to spend the night with him in a bed. Sleeping. *Mentally insert all the sarcasm.*

But as an avid Anchors fan, shouldn't I do what I can to help my favorite baseball team be successful?

News articles are written about all kinds of people—*superfans*—and their strange game day traditions. Like the guy who washes his dog every Tuesday during a home game for the win. Or the woman who eats tacos for breakfast on Saturdays for the win. Or the elderly fan who dunks his donut three times into his coffee during the fourth inning for the win.

Lucky shirts. Lucky socks. Lucky hats.

Processes. Beliefs. Faith.

If I, an ordinary person not playing on the team, do this or that then my beloved team will win.

Maybe *if* I have a drink with Ross Davis, he'll change his mind about all this nonsense.

Then again, curiosity has me by the throat. The same place I want those thick hands of Ross Davis to cup me when that isn't on the table.

Or should I say bed?

Me: **When and where?**

+ + +

Professional baseball's spring training season is roughly a month long, and with the Anchors two weeks into their schedule, they didn't have much longer to be in Arizona. That meant their calendar was packed with three-game series either at their spring stadium or at the stadiums of their fellow Arizona-based opponents.

Since Ross had a series of late-afternoon away games the next three days, he opted for a coffee date to discuss the particulars the day after his proposition.

Anxiously, I sit on the patio of the farm-to-table breakfast place I'd suggested near my rental. The food here is exceptional, although I don't have an appetite. Since our meeting yesterday in Ross's office, my stomach has been in knots, but my mind has unraveled.

Ideas for my next book were flowing, like the lazy trickle of a stream, a little bumpy over river rocks, but still a puddle of clarity moving forward.

I couldn't wait to get back to my place and type.

For now, I fidget on the wrought iron chair that is slightly unbalanced on the cement patio, causing me to teeter back and forth if I shift too far to the left on the seat.

Back and forth. Back and forth. Like my decision about Ross's suggestion. Should I, or shouldn't I?

"Hey, sorry I'm late." His deep voice behind me startles me, then his hand casually strokes over my shoulder, and I twist to look up at him.

Ross Davis is just too good looking. Dressed in lightweight athletic pants and a T-shirt that stretches over the expanse of his chest, he looks like he walked off the pages of a sports magazine. His full sleeve of tattoos on display. His head is not covered by a baseball cap, a bit of an anomaly compared to most photographs of him, and my personal fantasies, which include him wearing the signature hat. Mirrored sunglasses cover his eyes and when he removes them to lean in and place a quick, surprising kiss on my cheek, his eyes match the vibrant-blue Arizona morning sky when he pulls back and looks at me.

That look alone has a resounding *yes* on the tip of my tongue. I'll do whatever he asks.

Then, I shake the thought and reach for my tea, lifting the mug for my lips and taking a too-fast, too-large sip, scalding the inside of my mouth on the still hot liquid. Instantly, I reach for my water glass, desperate to down the entire eight ounces to cool my tongue. So, I'm guzzling the cold liquid, ice hitting my teeth which causes water to dribble outside the glass and probably spill on me. I'm a mess.

Ross's thick brows crease as he watches me drown myself. His gaze flicks to my shirt, then he quickly glances away, his Adam's apple rolling hard before he points toward the inside of the café. "I'm going to get a coffee."

While continuing to drink, I nod and hum my approval. When Ross steps away, I set down the half-empty container and slam my elbow on the table, placing my forehead in my hand. Glancing at my shirt, I find I'm speckled with water drops.

Of course. Amid the 'food-catchers' as Cassandra likes to teasingly call our ample breasts that nab stray crumbs and splashes of liquid, I have an array of dots, but the most embarrassing one is right over my nipple, which is now peaked and prominently on display beneath my white tee. *What was I thinking wearing a white shirt?*

I do the boob swish next, which involves using my forearms like windshield wipers to rub out the hard nipples in an attempt to smooth them.

This is just my luck. Hard nipples. Wet T-shirt. Not even going to think about how much liquid intake I just consumed and how quickly that will process through my body. I'll need to pee before Ross takes his first sip of coffee. Let's just hope the stress doesn't trigger a hot flash.

Maybe Ross will change his mind and decide I'm no charm for him after all.

Lucky is certainly not a term I'd use to describe myself. The real blessing in my life is my two girls. I've been fortunate to have a short career as a librarian and then a second one as an author. But I wouldn't say *luck* has necessarily been on my side.

Ross returns rather quickly—mid breast swish—and I lower my arms, attempting to disguise what I'd been publicly doing. As for the water stains, there is no hope.

"Drinking hazard." I laugh at myself. "Definitely not an amulet of good fortune."

He snorts as he takes the chair opposite me at the round café table. "I told you before, you're kind of adorable."

I roll my eyes, marveling that he remembers he said such a thing, and wishing he'd come up with another adjective.

Setting his forearms on the too-small-for-his-limbs table, he cups his to-go coffee mug and smiles at me.

"So," he begins.

"So." Suddenly, I can't look at him. His blue gaze is too intense, too hopeful. His sunglasses are tucked into the collar of his shirt, dangling near his collarbone and I focus there instead.

"I've been thinking . . ." he begins.

That doesn't sound like a good idea as this is how his proposal began.

"And I thought maybe I should come to your place. Less risk of being seen. Plus, that's what happened the first time. I came to your room."

Less risk of being seen? Because he certainly wouldn't want anyone to know about this ludicrous plan. Or is it that he doesn't want to be caught with someone like me? The T-shirt stained, nipple-swishing woman. The former hot flash, potty dancing, elevator queen.

"What would Chandler think of all this?" I blurt, wondering where his girlfriend is, or what her opinion would be on this situation.

His thick brows divot. "I told you we broke up."

"And I've seen your social media which showed you together again." Deceit and disloyalty are two things I cannot abide. And what was I supposed to think when Ross is asking me to share his bed while his social media showed him and his stunning former flame together again back in January? I hate that I'm admitting I've stalked him. That I've checked out his Instagram a time or two, or twenty, driving myself crazy when I saw him dressed in a tux for some gala with his curvaceous, young girlfriend in a slinky white dress clinging to his arm. That's the moment I stopped following him.

His gaze drops to the table, his fingers sliding up and down the side of his to-go cup. "Back in October, she called things off. Not that we were on. We only went on a few dates together, but she'd wanted me to call her my girlfriend, and I wouldn't do that. But we had prior commitments to fulfill, and we weren't each other's date in the traditional sense."

"I didn't realize there was a non-traditional sense." I tilt my head.

"Well, *we'd* certainly be in a non-traditional position." His gaze flits between us before he glances over his shoulder, checking the nearness of other customers before he leans closer to me. "I mean, how often does a man ask a woman to sleep with him, only for sleep." He pauses, his forehead furrowing. "Out of necessity."

I snort. A deep, obnoxious honk. Covering my nose with my hand, I fake a cough.

His eyes widen, a smile tugging at his mouth. "Was that a snort?"

"It was a snortle."

He chuckles. "What the hell is a snortle?"

"More like a snort slash laugh, but not a true snort. A distant cousin of sorts."

His mouth slowly ticks higher, spreading wider before he lifts his mug to cover the fact he wants to laugh. At me.

"And what is that sound all about?" He tips up one brow while bringing his cup to his lips, sipping at his fresh coffee.

"There is no way sleeping with me is a necessity." My voice is too loud, the absurdity echoing around us.

Ross chokes on his drink before glancing over his shoulder once more. Then he turns back to me, expression firm and serious while vulnerable and raw at the same time. He lowers his voice. "This is important. To me."

We're silent a second while he stares at his coffee cup again.

"However," he clears his throat. "I haven't asked if you have someone in your life. Maybe this would be a conflict of interest *for him*."

What if it's a conflict of interest for *me*? My real concern is the close proximity of our bodies in a bed. That first night, something special occurred. Something magical and spontaneous, and trying to recreate that moment is like setting words to paper when you can't summon a coherent thought. Or sending a steal signal to a player when he doesn't have enough time to reach the next base. You can't force something that might have been a one-time occurrence. *A happy chance.*

I'd like to think Ross knows this is an awkward, even stressful, predicament he's requesting of me.

Lowering my head, I slowly shake it. "There isn't anyone else." He knows I'm a widow, if he remembers everything as he claims he does.

Silence lingers between us another second. My thoughts scramble between Ross not wanting to call Chandler his official girlfriend and his proposal for me.

"What would I get out of this arrangement?" I'm not trying to sound greedy or even selfish. I hadn't considered that I should get something out of this bargain until this moment.

"Do you want to be paid?" His brows lift, wrinkling his forehead.

My mouth falls open. "I'm not for hire." Collapsing back in my chair and crossing my arms over my midsection which only accentuates the wet stains and hard nipples, like headlights announcing an approaching disaster, I glare at him across the table.

Ross clears his throat. "I didn't mean to insult you. Of course, I want this to be mutually beneficial, but I don't know what I can offer you in return." His eyes sheepishly meet mine, and then lower for the cup between his large hands.

I'm not suggesting tit-for-tat. I'm simply bamboozled by his idea that this kind of arrangement might help him. Help the Anchors.

"I am just trying to understand your thinking. Your reasoning."

Ross extends his arms while not releasing the to-go mug centered on the table between his hands. "I need this. I need to make an impression. I need wins."

"You're the manager, Ross. You'd been a player a long time before you took to coaching. You're a *good* coach. You know what to do." I emphasize. "You've done this before with the Flash."

His gaze lands on mine. "And look how that turned out for me."

He might have been let go from the Flash, but he also wanted to return to Chicago, or at least, that's what he told me months ago.

"Look, Coach," I chide. "It's the beginning of the season. All teams look rough. You move players around like chess pieces if you need to, but they'll get there. *You'll* get there." Wherever the proverbial *there* is.

"Is this supposed to be a pep talk?" His mouth crooks upward again. His eyes blaze with heat, but the flame is soft.

"Whatever it takes," I tell him.

"What it *might* take is another night together." His entire demeanor shifts, and although I'm a writer, I can't find the words to describe his expression, other than a puppy-dog plea despite the white scruff along his jaw suggesting he's more like man's lifelong best friend than a scrappy pup.

Now who is the adorable one?

I sigh as thoughts collide in my head. What would it really hurt? We've already spent a night together. It's only a bed and a few hours. We don't need to touch. We don't even need to talk. One night might prove his superstition is simply unwarranted. *I* am not lucky for him.

"Okay," I mutter, lowering my gaze for the tea I've left untouched since burning my mouth.

I'm not a superstitious person, so I'm hopeful that scalding move wasn't a foreshadow that Ross Davis could burn me in this process. However, as I appear to have lost my head, I can't be trusted to interpret symbolism.

"Yeah?" His voice lifts, hopeful while hesitant.

"Yeah."

And the next question I ask is almost as ludicrous as this entire idea. "What time is your bedtime?"

Chapter 9

[Ross]

I can't believe she agreed to my plan. However, I could have leapt over the table, and kissed her for accepting it.

I know how it sounds. Kip told me I was being ridiculous. Hell, even she's said as much, but the fact she believes me, or believes in helping me, means the world to me.

Maybe it is preposterous to think spending another night next to her would change anything. She's right. I'm the coach. The beginning of the season always has bumps, especially as I'm new to the Anchors, and the team has undergone some major shifts in players.

The last-minute addition of Bolan Adler as a catcher.

The tension between Ford Sylver and Romero Valdez.

Not to mention the young, scrappy new guys, like Gee Scott and Caleb Williams.

There's a lot of raw talent to mold and seasoned talent to support us.

Still, the need for Vee has become almost an obsession. I just want to try. One more night.

Which says more about me and my desperation than her. She's just as cute as ever, wet stains on her shirt, pert nipples and all. Nice to see she reacts to me just a little as I'm the one who woke up next to her with raging morning wood last November.

Thankfully, she hadn't addressed the elephant in the room, and I'm not saying I'm large like an anaconda, but she couldn't have *not* noticed what she'd done to me with the way I was pressed up against her, taking a moment to grind against her firm ass tucked tight to my front. Vee had featured in my dreams that night.

Not to mention, that momentary action was the most my dick had seen in almost a year.

I hate that Vee saw images of me with Chandler. Hate that she assumed we were still together when I'd told her the truth. We separated during the playoffs last season. I would have broken things off anyway, *after the season.* She wanted me to call her my girlfriend. Something I wasn't willing to do.

The pictures Vee might have seen were a gimmick, as we both attended a fundraiser for a children's hospital separate from one another. An event scheduled long before we broke up, otherwise Chandler wouldn't have been in Chicago. I don't pay attention to social media, but I can imagine what the reports might have speculated. A reunion between us, which was never going to happen.

Chandler is not invested in anything other than her career, which is her prerogative. But her drive to advance came some faulty characterizations about her. Like images that appear as if she's compassionately speaking to a sick child in a hospital room when she's really grumbling to the photographer to hurry up and take the picture, and then muttering about a foul smell as she exits the child's room.

Or the fact she openly flirted with the younger members of my team when I brought her to a team function, but she'd staged photos of us to look like we were a devoted couple.

Vee, on the other hand, is a little more . . . real. Genuine. Curious. Quirky even, and I liked every trait. She's like complementary contradictions on a coin. Confident while not full of herself. Funny while thoughtful. She's sweet and sincere but I suspect beneath the wholesome vibe is a sensual, untamed wildcat. A good woman with a big heart and a dirty imagination. She's a winning combination.

Was I being selfish like Chandler, though? Possibly. I would definitely owe Vee.

She'd asked what was in this proposition for her, and I didn't have an answer. I'd been wracking my brain for a trade, but I couldn't think of anything she'd need as compensation from me—a grumpy, growing-older guy, with two college aged kids, and a professional baseball team in need of some spirit lifting. Not to mention, pressure to succeed from a front office giving me a second chance to prove myself and a fanbase with legendary love for the Anchors.

Nope, not much to offer her.

She mentioned spring training season tickets. Attendance at the games sounded more like a consolation prize and wasn't enough of an exchange. I needed something grander, but what?

There is no denying something powerful happened the night we spent together. Like tectonic plates shifting. It sounds absurd, but that night changed the trajectory of my life. Again.

I got the call from the Anchors within minutes of the Flash letting me go. Like, who would have even known I'd been released in the four-minute span? The news hadn't broken in the sports media. There hadn't been the typical chatter prior to the team firing me that would generate interest from another team possibly interested in hiring me.

Everything happened by chance. *Happenstance.*

And dammit, I haven't been this happy in a long time.

I firmly believed Vee was the catalyst for all that occurred. Maybe talking to her simply put my desires into the universe. That I wanted—*no, needed*—this second chance. This golden opportunity.

However, I didn't believe in that sort of thing, which was strange considering how much faith I had in superstitions, like thinking a woman sleeping beside me brought me good fortune.

+++

As I wanted to start this trial immediately, we agreed I'd come to her place around ten o'clock. She balked at the time, and I sensed it was later than she typically climbed into bed, but I had a game on the other side of Phoenix, plus tape to review, and dinner with the coaching staff before I could settle in for the night.

When Vee opens the door to her rental, she dramatically waves her arm, inviting me inside.

"*Mi casa es tu casa.* Or should I say, *mi cama es tu cama*? My bed is your bed." She laughs at herself, as she shuts the door behind me. "That was just weird wasn't it." She blows out a deep breath. "I'm nervous."

ELEVATOR PITCH

I take in her baggy pajama pants and oversized sweatshirt. Her hair is swept off her neck like it had been that first night. Her cheeks are sweetly flushed. Her eyes dance. When we met for coffee, only this morning, I remember thinking she's so pretty, and I have the same thought as we stand across from one another. I am greatly relieved and extremely grateful to be standing across from her.

I'm also anxious. Strangely, I hadn't felt this much nervous energy the night she rushed to her hotel room, slipping away from me after our elevator interlude, and I made the sudden decision to take my prized bottle of scotch to her room and ask her to share a drink with me.

This night shouldn't feel dissimilar, and yet, it feels monumentally different.

"Would you like a drink?" she offers.

"Are you having one?"

She slowly shakes her head. "Not this late. Hot flashes will haunt me."

Hot flashes? "You can't be more than forty."

A smirk graces her soft mouth. "You're sweet, and I'm forty-five."

My gaze roams her from tip to toes, taking in her blonde hair, the color of wheat in sunshine, and the curves of her body which are subtle like the hills near home. She only comes to my shoulder like a petite package, but she has spunk and spirit, and I *like* her. She reminds me a little bit of Patty.

"Honestly," she interjects before my thoughts race to my late wife. "It's past my bedtime." She softly chuckles. "And as lame as that sounds, it can't be any weirder than this arrangement." She waves between us.

I toe off my athletic shoes and nod. "Want to show me to your room?" I'm not sure I've ever asked the question in such a strangled tone or said it in a way that sounded so disconnected.

Vee offers a lopsided smile and tips her head, leading me to the left of the living room and kitchen combination. I should ask for a tour or take her up on that drink she offered, but I'm not here for more than a good night's rest. And hopefully some success at tomorrow's game because tonight's was a fiasco.

We lost when Bolan Adler's hit toward first base was an easy out and our final one of the night. Things were reaching an embarrassing level but as the leader of our team I had faith in our future.

Which is why I am here.

I follow Vee into the large primary bedroom with a raised king-sized bed that has a puffy headboard, matching nightstands on either side of the mattress, and a long, low dresser against the opposite wall. An ensuite bathroom is off to the left of the room. A sliding glass door that leads outside is to the right.

"Nice room." Slipping my hands into my black joggers, I sound like an awkward teen being taken to a girl's bedroom for the first time.

Vee walks to the left side of the bed and picks up a few of the numerous throw pillows. "I made the bed today, but I hadn't accounted for all these extra pillows." Slowly, she tosses them to the right side of the bed then pauses. Quickly, she glances up at me. "Actually, you'll be sleeping on that side, if you don't mind."

"You're doing me the favor." Could I sound anymore stilted? Maybe I'm more nervous than I'm letting on.

She rushes to the right side of the bed, picking up as many pillows as she can, which isn't more than two because of their size and shape, and stalks toward me.

"I'll just put these in the other bedroom." Her voice lowers as does her gaze.

Holding out my hands, I take the pillows from her. "I'll take them. You get ready for bed."

Her eyes leap upward to meet mine. "I am ready."

My gaze wanders down her once more, taking in the large sweatshirt and flannel pants she's wearing. Speaking of hot flashes . . . "Won't you be warm in that?" I nod at her attire.

I hadn't really considered what she'd wear. Not going to admit I momentarily fantasized about her wearing that *Cool Girls Read Hot Books* tee and another pair of loose-fit shorts. I also imagined her wearing the Anchors jersey she was wearing during the games she attended.

My replica Anchors jersey. With my name. My number.

She glances down at herself. "I didn't know what to wear." She scoffs. "What does one wear to a non-traditional sleepover date?" Looking up at me again, her eyes narrow. "Not that this *is* a date, it's just . . ."

"I'm nervous, too," I tell her as if this will reassure her. Maybe settle my own unease.

Our awkwardness is ridiculous. We've done this sleeping thing before. It shouldn't feel so different and on the tip of my tongue is a retraction, where I tell her I've made a mistake. But being here doesn't feel like an error.

Standing here, as tension filled as the moment is, feels strangely right. And now that I'm here, I'd have trouble pulling myself away.

"Why don't you get more comfortable?" I nod at her outfit. "Unless you are comfortable. Because the last thing I want to do is make you feel uncomfortable." And now I'm the one being weird.

She laughs, the sound stressed but quiet and sweet. Placing her hand lightly on my forearm, she says, "I'll change. You get in bed."

I glance at the large mattress. One difference between then and now is the number of damn throw pillows on the bed. The other difference is we didn't climb beneath the sheets that night but remained on top of them. I hadn't thought about the logistics of our sleeping arrangement other than being next to her, but somehow crawling underneath the covers feels more intimate.

Still, I carry the pillows to the other bedroom and then return to pull back the duvet. Glancing toward the ensuite where Vee is changing, I still. Perhaps she doesn't realize she didn't close the door between the bedroom and the bathroom. With a second glance at the doorframe, I notice there isn't a closure. The shower and double vanity sinks are open to the main bathroom while the toilet is inside a closet.

With her naked back to me, I take in this enticing spot on her. A straight line cascades between her shoulder blades, like a beautiful riverbed, flowing to the swell of her ripe backside. I recall admiring her back when I helped her unzip her dress that first night. Her skin looks smooth. Her legs are toned.

Quickly, I glance away. Admiring her back has no place in our arrangement.

I'm not typically a man who sleeps in sweats or a tee but out of respect for Vee I'll be wearing both tonight. I might experience my own hot flash at some point, but this overnight will be worth the heat.

I can already feel the positive energy buzzing around me.

Slipping beneath the sheet and light blanket, I turn my head when Vee pulls down the coverings on her side of the bed. She's wearing a graphic tee and loose shorts after all. Only a lamp on the nightstand lights the room, and she stretches to turn it off before settling to her back, her head against the long bed pillow. I do the same.

Silence ensues as darkness takes over the room and we both stare at the ceiling.

"Can I ask you a personal question?" Her voice is low, almost a whisper.

Rolling only my head, her profile comes into view. A sliver of light slips through the vertical blinds covering the sliding glass door and I can make out the jut of her chin, the straightness of her nose. What I want to see are her eyes.

"Of course." I might be opening a can of worms, but any conversation is better than this muted tension.

"When you spend the night with a woman, do you feel like you are cheating on your wife?"

I deeply exhale, feeling like a soft punch hit my gut. "Jumping into the deep end, are we?"

Her head shifts on her pillow, her face angled toward me. "Is that question too much?"

Again, I wish I could see her expressive eyes. Instead, I focus on her face in general. "No, it's not too much. And yeah, I guess I did feel a little like I was cheating on Patty. At first."

In the twelve years of my marriage, I hadn't been with anyone else *but* my wife. Up until the bitter end, she had been my heart.

"I didn't date for a long time," I explain. "Probably more than two years." However, I'd had sex in the interim. Random, one-night stands. Quicky hookups. Like a devil inside me had been unleashed. The anger and rage consuming me at the loss of my wife.

However, returning to casual sex in my late thirties did not offer the same thrill as the recklessness I'd indulged in during my early twenties. Instead, I fell in lust with several starlets and models of varying ages, resulting in short-term stints and several months-long situationships like Chandler.

"But at some point, I accepted that Patty wasn't ever coming back, and I had not cheated on her while we were married. I'd been faithful and loyal." I'd loved her. *Until death parted us.*

Silence falls between us for another painfully long minute. I wonder if Vee has fallen asleep on me. Then her head rolls, profile outlined once more. "My husband cheated on me during our marriage."

Fuck!

"And yet I'm the one who struggled to accept I was not cheating on him once he was gone."

"I'm so sorry that happened to you, Vee." Some men are such dicks. Women, too, as I've witnessed by Ford Sylver's ex-wife flaunting her affair with his fellow teammate. "But you got through those emotions, right?"

Is she feeling adulterous right now? I roll to my side facing her, wanting to reach out to her, wanting to reassure her that we aren't doing anything remotely similar to infidelity. But I'm afraid to touch her. Afraid she won't want my touch.

"Vee," I whisper. "When you spend the night with a man, you don't still feel like you're cheating, do you?"

With her face still aimed toward the ceiling, she brushes at her cheek. *Shit.* Is she crying? Did I press too hard? Did I push this arrangement too fast without thinking it through? Thinking enough of her?

"Vee." My voice cracks. I'm fucking this up and taking her down with me.

Slowly, I press up on my elbow, desperately wanting a better glance at her face. The light filtering in from the outside offers only enough illumination to see her cheeks are dry, her eyes not glistening, but she refuses to look directly at me, even knowing I'm staring at her.

She rolls her head back and forth on the pillow once. "I'm okay."

"But when you spend the night—"

"I don't spend the night," she cuts me off. Despite the dim lighting, I see her eyes flash momentarily to me, and then away, as if she's embarrassed or ashamed. "I've never spent a night with a man other than you."

The shocking reality is like the crack of a bat on a powerful hit.

"And no, I don't feel guilty. I was just curious."

Her eyes are still pointed away from my face. Her head even shifts, drawing away from my concerned gaze, but I remain pressed up on my arm, staring down at her. Taking in the line of her cheek, the shape of her nose again, and the roll of her lips.

"Good night, Ross," she whispers, putting an end to this confession.

I collapse back to my side, still watching her, mentally making out her profile. Her mouth when she smiles. Her eyes when they sparkle. Wishing for that snortle sound she makes to dissolve the tension between us.

I roll to my back, hyperaware of Vee's closeness and yet sensitive about the distance between us. Her arms remain on her chest, holding the blanket near her collarbone. I cup my forehead for a second, stunned by what she'd just admitted. Her husband's adultery and the fact she hasn't slept through the night with any man other than me. I'm honored in the strangest way.

Do I tell her her admission is important to me? Do I explain how I feel special? I don't speak. Instead, I lower my arm and slowly stretch for her with my fingers.

"Vee," I whisper, knowing she isn't sleeping yet. "Give me your hand."

There's something about her fingers that brings me comfort, and when she lays her palm against mine, I rub my thumb the length of her pinky. Then, I shift so I'm stroking down each digit, until I sense Vee relaxing beside me.

And while my body settles into the bed, my thoughts continue to race, wanting to know everything there is to know about Vee.

Chapter 10

[Vee]

In the morning, a rousing call to *hit it* fills the bedroom, and I jolt awake. Ross is softly snoring behind me. At one point during the night, his arm was draped over me, but it is now removed from my hip. Instead, he lays flat on his back, wedged against me in a manner that doesn't allow me to turn over.

"Ross," I whisper, although what's the point of whispering to a sleeping man you wish to wake?

As I attempt to roll, my elbow nudges his chest. And his phone drones on with Rob Base and DJ E-Z Rock rapping about how it takes two people to make something right.

When Ross doesn't budge with my elbow at his belly, I flip as best I can so I can reach over his chest for the phone. Only his phone is somewhere near the opposite edge of his pillow. He's sleeping on mine.

I have no sense of what time it is, but I'm awake now, stretching over Ross, practically lying on him, to find his phone and turn off the sound that is apparently *not* waking the person intended to be awakened.

With my body draped over his midsection, I skim my hand beneath the pillow, reaching and seeking until my fingertips hit the edge of the device. My fingers are too short to grip the corner of his phone, so I'm up on my knees, preparing to climb over Ross when his hand connects with my side, just above my hip.

"What are you doing?" His voice is groggy, rough and sandpapery once more. His palm is warm against my skin exposed by my stretch for his phone.

I crane only my neck, glancing over my shoulder, and looking him right in the face where I'm met with bright blue eyes, fresh as a new day. Slowly, I blink, mesmerized by the color. Ross is also giving me a delicious, cheeky grin while watching me from his prone position.

Pulling back over his body, the movement causes my breasts to casually, accidentally, drag over his firm chest, sending a ripple of excitement throughout me and causing my nipples to pebble. Without a bra, my reaction to Ross is evident. "I was trying to reach your phone."

Ross turns his head so sharply it's a wonder I don't hear his neck crack. His expression suggests he's startled, like he doesn't hear the thumping beat of the 80s rap. Slowly, he twists his body opposite the direction of mine, and I sit back on my knees.

"Still have something against my song?" he chuckles, deep and rich.

"Nothing against your song. I'm just more of a Marvin Gaye "It Takes Two" type of person."

Ross rolls to his back again, phone in hand and taps off the alarm. "What?"

"Never mind." We stare at one another for a long, quiet minute. His morning eyes are sleepy while alert. His mouth slowly curls.

"So, now what? Do you feel like it's a winning kind of day?"

Ross blinks, stares up at the ceiling, like he's considering the question, and then lets out a slow exhale. "I'll say this. I don't think I've slept so well since . . ." He moves his head just the slightest, eyes meeting mine. "Since the night we met."

My cheeks heat. "That's sweet."

Startling me, he abruptly sits upright, his face coming close to mine. For a half a second, I think he's coming in for a morning kiss, but as my knees are close to the edge of the bed because he'd encroached on my side, I slip off the mattress. Ross catches my wrist at the same time my feet find the floor.

"Sea legs in the morning?" he teases as I wobble.

"More like someone hogged the ship." I nod toward the vast mattress and Ross glances around, realizing one half of the bed hasn't been slept in.

"Do you typically sleep on the left?" I question, wondering if he felt like he slept on the wrong side of the bed, thus encroaching on mine. Since Cameron's death, I bought a new bed. For me, sleeping comfortably isn't a matter of the right or left side of the bed, but a need to be closest to the door or exit. My Feng Shui is off otherwise.

Ross shakes his head, not commenting on his position while scowling at the empty space a second. Then, he says, "I should probably get going."

He scrubs both his hands down his face before flipping back the covers and scooting out of the bed toward me.

I step back but suddenly, I'm panicked. "We did it wrong."

Ross stills, standing upright in front of me. "We did what wrong?"

"Getting out of the bed. I went one direction. You went the other. We're messing up the shui or the vibe or the jujubeans."

"The jujubeans?"

"Whatever," I snap, waving around him toward the bed. "What if this messes up your win?" If this sleepover didn't work, Ross won't be back. He won't want to be friends if I don't bring him luck. This could be the last time we sleep next to one another. And none of this should matter, but strangely, I feel my chest constricting. My breathing ragged with fear.

Ross chuckles softly, setting his large, warm hands on my upper arms and rubbing up and down my suddenly goose bumped skin. "I think we'll be okay."

While he slept well, I feel like I've hardly slept and I'm out of sorts. So, I don't understand how he's so calm. Then again, this arrangement is *his* plan.

He bends at the knees, lowering his bulky body a bit to look me more directly in the eyes. "Let's just see what happens. If we did it wrong, we'll fix it."

My head lifts higher, body stiffening. "Are you saying you want to sleep with me again?"

He laughs a little deeper, louder, while shaking his head. "I don't want to be presumptuous—"

"I think we're beyond that."

"But if this works, I'll definitely want a repeat."

We stare at one another, the seconds ticking by slowly. The warmth of his touch seeps into my skin. A spicy cologne scent lingers on him. His nearness makes my legs wobble once more, before his brows pinch, and he removes his hands, instantly breaking a new kind of tension between us.

Suddenly, a pensive look fills his rested eyes. "Do you think I'm taking advantage of you?"

"No." I swallow. "Why would you ask that?"

"Because you said we're beyond presumptuous, and I don't want there to be any assumptions. I don't want to come across like I'm monopolizing you or this situation. I don't want to hurt you somehow. I want you to feel comfortable. Safe."

Just mentioning his concerns settles my anxiety. He's considerate of my comfort and worried about my emotions, and that right there says more about Ross Davis than Cameron. I don't like to think ill of the dead, but a decade later, I still have some serious mental scars from what he put me through.

And the truth is, I do feel safe with Ross Davis. Safer than I probably should.

I nod to calm his concerns, forgoing my own. I don't want him hurt either. I don't want him upset or disappointed when he discovers this little experiment of his does not help his team.

Instead, I say, "You should probably get going."

He nods once, but we both remain still, watching one another, eyes trying to read the other. Finally, he clears his throat. "I'll call you later."

The comment feels like a dismissal of sorts and as much as my chest pricks, I muster encouragement for him instead.

When he turns, I slap his ass, like they do in sports. The crack is hard and loud, resonating through the room. My palm stings from the firmness of his fine backside.

Ross spins, staring at me in shock. I'm a little startled myself.

Then he lets out a deep laugh, one that comes from his belly and fills the room, while he shakes his head. His laughter brings on my own, forcing a snortle out.

"There's my sound," he states, his voice quieting while still full of chuckles.

"Go get 'em, Coach," I say cheerfully, while struggling to quell my own anxious giggles. "Bring home a win."

+ + +

I hold my breath until the soft click of my front door echoes back to me in the bedroom, then I dissolve into hysterical laughter.
Oh. My. God. I just slapped Ross Davis's ass.

I fall face first into the bed, getting a whiff of his distinct cologne mingled with the laundry detergent scent of the sheets.

With Ross gone, the urge to write should overwhelm me but that doesn't happen. Within an hour, I'm stymied again, staring at the blank page, wondering where my characters should go next. Which collides with my thoughts retracing every step of last night with Ross.

I was relieved when he broke the tension by taking my hand. I don't know what it is about him massaging my fingers, but the delicate touch from his thick fingers sends shivers through me. *Good shivers.* Shivers I probably shouldn't be thinking about.

An hour passes as I mindlessly scroll social media, stalling instead of daydreaming, before I decide I need physical activity.

With a heavy sigh, I accept defeat for inspiration and head outside into the fresh, brisk morning air. Whoever says Scottsdale is constantly hot hasn't been here mid-March where the weather fluctuates from forty to eighty in a day. The desert air is dry making the temperature feel cooler at times than the humidity-filled air of the Midwest under similar temperatures.

I take a walk at a local riparian preserve, which is quite opposite Chicagoland's Forest Preserves. On the sandy paths between large man-made water tables filled with ducks and other waterfowl, my mind wandering as I circle the ponds and cut through the middle of the preserve on the various trails.

Cameron and Ross both cross my mind along with the variety of differences between them. I'd known Cameron since high school and Ross for less than five months with no more than four encounters, yet I felt more attracted to him as a stranger than the man I'd once called my husband. I don't like to think about Cameron's adultery. I often *don't* think about that time in our lives, but sneaky reminders creep up on me, like last night, laying silently staring up at the ceiling, feeling awkward and tense in my own bed, distant from the man beside me.

I wasn't sexually experienced or wise on dating, and when I asked Ross about cheating, the question came about because I figured he'd have a better perspective on how to separate my mind from my body. Not that Ross and I were doing anything physical. We were *sleeping* beside one another. But I couldn't dismiss the sensation fluttering inside me. That rumbling pull to know more about him. The attraction was real. For years, I have crushed on Ross. Like I'd once longingly stared with heart-filled eyes at Cameron when we were teenagers, before he noticed me.

I worry that despite being older and wiser, I am setting myself up for the same kind of failure. Perhaps not giving twenty years to a man, fifteen of them in marriage, but still, failure all the same. Because my feelings were evident, even if only lusty desire, and I'll need to work on keeping my emotions under control. I couldn't risk the physical attraction turning into a mental connection, like Ross Davis held some secret key to unlock my heart.

One thing that didn't worry me was taking advantage of Ross. I would never throw myself at him, despite the playful smack on his backside this morning.

I also didn't want Ross thinking about his late wife while he was with me. Silly, considering he'd been in a long-term relationship with Chandler Bressler, and several short-term ones with supermodels and beauty queens. If he'd been through all those women, a sense of guilt was no longer on his mind.

I didn't know what I should feel guilty about, but the familiar twinge was present all the same. Like maybe I was using Ross for some ulterior, unknown motive. I couldn't imagine what that mysterious reason would be. It couldn't be that a warm body in my bed made me feel safe and secure. Or that the presence of his arm over me was a comfort. Or that his side wedged against my back, keeping us connected even when he rolled away, made me feel important to him in some way.

Those feelings would be as ridiculous as this arrangement.

On that note, I head back to my place and watch the Anchors' afternoon game on a sports channel.

And, the Anchors win.

Chapter 11

[Vee]

When the knock comes to my front door around nine, I shouldn't be surprised, yet I am. I open the door with a flourish and stare at the man waiting on the stoop.

Ross is dressed in pants made of a light-weight material and a plain T-shirt, exposing the colorful inked arm I have yet to inspect. In his hand, he holds a bottle of wine. The moment reminds me of the night he stood outside my hotel room door, cradling a crystal bottle of scotch.

"I got your message," he says, watching me from where he remains on the stoop, and I stand inside the condo entryway.

Earlier in the day, I sent him a congratulatory message to which he replied with a simple, "Thank." Not a thank you; not even a thanks, the *S* glaringly missing on the end of the word.

"I got yours," I tease, leaning against the open doorway. "Not a very verbose man, are you?"

He chuckles. "My kids complain about that all the time." He glances down at the bottle in his hand and lifts it higher. "But the first person I wanted to share the good news with was you."

"Because the experiment worked?" I tip my head against the door, my heart hammering because I'm excited for him, while wishing he was here for more reason than winning a baseball game under the duress of a superstition. Like he wanted to share the winning moment *because* of me.

His mouth purses. A smug smirk forming. "Because it worked."

Without an additional invitation, I press off the door and step back, allowing him space to enter my place. *Presumptuous?* Because I'm assuming he's here for a repeat of our sleeping arrangement.

"I thought we could celebrate together," he says, walking through the living room to the bar-like counter that separates the living space from the kitchen area. "Have an actual drink."

"Versus a fake one?" I tease, moving around him and the counter to enter the kitchen and find wine glasses.

"Versus coffee." His voice drops low, gritty even, like wine implies something more intimate than a caffeinated drink.

Stretching up on my toes for the wine glasses on a high shelf, I wiggle my fingers for the first stemless glass when I sense Ross's warm, bigger body behind me, his spicy cologne invading my senses. He brushes against me. One hand lands on my hip to steady me, while his tattooed arm reaches over mine, stretching for the glass.

"I got 'em," he says near my ear, his voice that sandy sound, his proximity close, as he squeezes my hip.

"Thanks." I lower my arm and glance over my shoulder, meeting a heated gaze from him. Time seems to stand still a moment, then two.

Ross clears his throat, blinking once before retreating, and I'm left feeling a bit breathless and light-headed from both his nearness and his touch.

I search through a drawer for a wine bottle opener, noticing my hands are shaky. Ross rounds the counter with the glasses in hand. Once I find the corkscrew, Ross holds out his palm, doing the honors to open and then pour each of us a glass of rich red.

"You don't seem like a wine man," I admit.

He lifts his glass and sniffs the contents before swirling the dark liquid around inside the glass. "I've been known to enjoy the finer things in life." His gaze meets mine again, smoldering a second, before he chuckles and then taps his glass to mine even though it isn't in my hands. "To winning."

He sips his wine, closing his eyes and humming at the taste. I lift my glass and take a hearty gulp, knowing I'll pay later for this late-night drink. The peppery flavor tickles my throat and instantly relaxes me.

"What else do I seem like?" he asks, lowering his glass to the countertop. He helps himself to one of the two stools beneath the counter on the living room side. I remain standing in the kitchen.

"A man who'd hang out with movie stars and models, speaking of the finer things in life."

His gaze drops to his glass, one hand holding the bulbous goblet and slowly shifting the glass side-to-side so the contents slosh lazily around the glass. His lowered lids have me questioning if I've somehow hurt his feelings. Maybe he's missing Chandler. *She* should be his lucky charm.

Ross clears his throat. "You mentioned last night that your husband cheated on you."

The statement is like a stab to my heart. Perhaps I deserve it after what I've said about him.

"And I'm wondering . . . what happened?" He lifts his gaze. "How could he do such a thing to you?"

Genuine concern filters beneath the question. Almost as if he can't believe someone would do that to me. That someone being my husband.

"It was a long time ago," I state, preparing to brush off this soul-baring conversation. "And I guess none of it matters now." The affair ended. Cameron apologized. He is gone. My attitude wasn't so simplistic, but there wasn't any use dwelling on the past infraction even if it caused me to have major trust issues and trouble committing to someone else. Definitely a reason why most dates never made it past the first one.

And yet, here Ross Davis sits across from me for the fourth or fifth time.

He nods once, lowering his gaze again, then lifting his glass for another sip. Setting his wine back on the counter, he says, "So tell me what you did today? Did you write?"

"Tell me about the win," I deflect because his day was much more productive than mine.

"Did you watch the game?" His voice is hopeful as he peers back at my face. His eyes brighten. He chews his lower lip, like he's anxious about my answer.

Slowly, I smile. "I did watch. Very exciting, Coach. Ford Sylver's catch and then the double play to second . . ." I whistle low, expressing how impressed I am by the Anchors' star center fielder.

Ross shakes his head, his expression sobering. "Yeah, but I'm worried about him."

"Because of his ex?"

Ross's brows hitch. "Because of his arm."

"Oh." I lift my glass, taking another pull of the flavorful wine.

"What do you know about his ex-wife?" Ross tilts his head.

"Only what social media tells me."

Ross's hand stills, where he'd been twirling his glass again. He looks up at me, eyes earnest. "Please don't believe everything you see or read in those spaces."

Our eyes lock on one another for a moment before the intensity becomes too much and I pull away. "Okay." I know better than to believe in sensationalism. Real people are behind most tabloid rumors.

Ross clears his throat again and sits straighter on the stool, sliding his hands across the countertop to extend his arms. With the length of them, his hands come to either side of mine, where one holds my wineglass, the other is clenched loosely on the countertop. His thumb runs down the knuckles of my fist, and I flatten my hand on the cool surface.

Ross takes my hand and begins massaging my fingers. Starting with my pinky, he kneads and tugs at the length, like he did the night we met, like he did last night. The sensation is like he's pulling the tension out of me, one finger at a time. With my eyes fixated on his hand, I concentrate on how good his touch feels.

He says, "So now . . . Tell me about your day. Did you write?"

"Oh, we don't need to talk about that." I chuckle, the sound a bit bitter, maybe defensive. More likely deflection.

"Why not?" Ross stills, forcing me to look up at him.

I shrug. Cameron wasn't ever interested in my writing, and the subject became one to avoid. Not difficult to do when the topic hardly came up. However, Cameron was not upset to see that first deposit in our bank account after my initial publication.

The other reason not to discuss my writing is because I'm currently stumped. *Again.*

"You don't like to talk about it?" Ross questions, his tone almost hurt. Like he really wants to know more, but he'll respect if I don't share.

"I'm just not used to discussing it."

Staring at me like he's trying to read me, I don't give him any hints to better understand me. I don't want to discuss Cameron right now. That isn't who Ross and I are, and in order to protect my heart, we probably shouldn't discuss the difficult stuff.

Like old loves, big hurts, and larger disappointments.

"How did the woman who wanted to be shared by two men turn out?"

My laughter is more of a choking sound. "You remember that?" I still can't believe I told him the plot I was considering.

"I told you I remember everything. And why do you think I was looking for your book in a bookstore?" He smiles. "I was riveted and invested in knowing how things worked out for her."

His confession only makes me laugh harder.

"But seriously, why didn't I find Verona Huxley in a bookstore?"

The question sobers me up a bit. "It's complicated, but I'm independently published, which means I'm the CEO of my own publishing company and the author. Kind of like the publishing house, production team, marketing department, *and* the creative." I pause, wondering if I'd already lost him, searching for signs of glazed-over eyes, a look Cameron would get whenever I spoke to him about the process and procedure of self-publishing.

Finding no visual evidence that Ross has checked out on the conversation, I continue. "So, not all my books are on the shelf, as the industry calls it. Your typical large scale, or even small business bookshop, isn't going to carry my work."

"Why the fuck not?" His sharp intonation along with the hint of outrage warms my heart.

"It's just how it works, I guess. Plus, even though romance is eighty-something percent of the fiction market, it takes up only a few shelves in most bookstores."

"That's ridiculous."

"I know." My own voice rises with indignation. "But the truth is, there just isn't space for everyone. So, I live off digital copies, audiobooks, and paperback sales directly from my website."

"You have a website?" His surprise isn't condescending. He's impressed I have my own space on the internet in my name.

"Yep." Pride fills my voice as he moves from stroking one hand to the other. I use my now relaxed hand to lift my wineglass. *Cheers to me for working hard.* Sometimes it's exhausting, though, being a lone ship in a sea of successful storytellers.

"So, if I looked up Verona Huxley, I'd find you on the internet."

"Actually, I write under V. C. Hux."

"Ah, a pseudonym. Very clever, and mysterious." He shifts his voice to sound both impressed again while a bit deceived, almost scandalized. When he wiggles his brows, I'm not certain I've ever seen him so relaxed or playful.

"And *she's* who will tell me what happened with the woman who wanted two men at once?"

I snort, covering my nose with my hand.

"A snortle. The story must be a good one." Ross winks, and I might melt into a puddle right here on the tile floor.

"Just tell me what happens. Does she choose one of them over the other?"

I shake my head, zipping my lips, like they are a vault, before teasing him. "You'll just have to read the book." Although I didn't write that story, and I know he won't read a book of mine anyway.

"Okay, Coach. I'm assuming you're here for a second night's sleep beside me."

Ross lowers his eyes sheepishly, glancing at his near empty wine glass. "Well, if there's space . . ."

"Says the man who hogged my side of the bed last night," I tease.

"I'll try harder to not cross the line tonight." He turns his hand sideways and draws an imaginary line on the counter.

I shrug. "You're fine."

His brows lift and our eyes meet again. "As in, you don't mind that I cuddle up against you?"

My face heats, giving away an answer.

I don't mind him cuddling up against me.

Chapter 12

[Ross]

Vee was the first person I thought of when we won. The first person I wanted to celebrate with. The first person I wanted to call. Only, when her text came in, I'd been tackled in a hug by Kip, who knew my secret, and couldn't believe it worked.

My pitching coach was suddenly on board the sleep-beside-Vee ship. And I didn't want to do anything to rock the boat.

Showing up at her place unannounced *was* a bit presumptuous. I didn't want to assume she'd give me a second night while I was hopeful she would. Either way, I simply wanted to share a glass of wine and cheers the Anchors' success.

Instead, we talked about her, which was like pulling a bone away from a lion. She was holding fiercely to her writing success secrets and I didn't understand why. She wasn't bashful about speaking once I prompted her to open up, but she definitely held back on the finer details, especially concerning that one book she'd mentioned writing back in November.

She never answered my question about if she'd been writing today. Instead, she told me about her walk at the local riparian preserve and I considered asking her if she'd take a walk with me one day. Then decided that might be crossing the imaginary line.

The one I can't seem to help crossing because the pull to sleep close to her, to be closer to her, not just physically, but in a get-to-know her better way, was strong. The force of my eagerness hits me like a pitched ball giving in to the curve of a throw.

I didn't only want to be strangers sharing a bed. I wanted to know Vee. To be *friends*.

Somehow, I didn't like the descriptor. It didn't feel complete, and there was something strangely fulfilling about spending time with Vee. The numbness I'd been feeling for a while wasn't so crippling when I was around her, but I didn't want to confuse our experiment with new emotions. As in, I didn't want to develop feelings if this was only a fleeting arrangement between us.

My focus needed to stay firmly on the ball. And today, my head had been nowhere else during our meet up against Boston. When thoughts of Vee wandered into the dugout, I shut them out. I had clarity.

Devotion. Drive. Determination.

The motivation worked.

So had sleeping beside Vee.

I couldn't dismiss the thought our experiment had been in my favor, but now I was out to prove it wasn't a one-off moment. A second night with her had been necessary.

"So," I clear my throat. "Another night?"

She sighs. Her lips pinch before she twists them side to side like a classic vaudeville comedian. And I only know what a vaudeville comedian is because of my son, Harley.

After a brief contemplation, she says, "One more night."

She finishes her glass of wine while I re-cork the bottle and push it to the side of the countertop. The set up of her rental is cozy compared to my hotel room. Every year I tell myself I'm going to splurge on a short-term stay location and every year I end up in another hotel room for a month.

When Landon or Harley would visit during their spring breaks, they'd tuck into the room with me, sharing the space for the week. This year, Landon will be spending his spring break at school, opting to work instead of visiting his old man. Harley wanted a week in Philadelphia, to see friends from high school, missing them since they all went in different directions for college.

I'd gotten a text from each of my sons after today's win. Surprising, since Harley doesn't pay as much attention to baseball as Landon. Then again, Harley's congratulatory message came after Landon's which probably prompted him to respond.

I needed to check in with both of them soon.

However, tonight, my focus is another night of rest in Vee's bed.

She rounds the counter and stops beside me where I've spun on the stool to face her. I want her to take my hand and lead me to the room, but the thought doesn't feel fair. She isn't trying to seduce me. She doesn't *need* to seduce me. I'm going to follow her regardless. Still, I wish she'd take my hand, like we're in this together, not just me selfishly asking her to give me time and space in her bed.

Instead, she smiles, bashfully lowering her lids. "I'm going to get ready for bed."

As far as I can tell, she's already ready, dressed in silk pajama shorts and another bookish T-shirt. This one reads: *Will spread my pages for books*. Earlier when I read it, I tried not to react, but reading the phrase had me imagining her legs spread wide, her delicate folds on display, allowing me to read her.

The image is too much, and I swipe a hand down my face in an attempt to cool down before heading toward that bedroom.

Giving her a few minutes to do what she needs to do, I finish off my wine. When I eventually enter the room, she's already in bed, sheets tucked over her lap, her back propped against the headboard as if waiting for me, and not just in limbo for our new nightly ritual to begin. But like she might be anticipating me joining her in bed, for something more.

Again, I shake the thought. *That* isn't what I've propositioned her for.

"I put a spare toothbrush on the counter. In case you'd like to use it."

Her thoughtfulness has my face heating, and I slide my hands into the pockets of my pants while I tuck my head. I wore casual linen slacks in an attempt to dress a little nicer, not look like a baseball coach on a mission. More like a man intent on spending time with a woman.

"Are we jumping ahead to where I have a toothbrush at your place?" A joke is the only way to diffuse this sudden swirling in my chest. A feeling that's been dormant until now, stretching and yawning, and seeming to wake up.

Vee chuckles, the sound sweet. "Maybe." Again, not a seductive tease but a playful giggle.

The sound puts me at ease.

I nod and enter the open bathroom space, taking time to brush my teeth and slip into the toilet closet a moment. Stepping back out, I wash my hands. I'd really like to strip off my pants and remove my tee, but I don't want to appear like I'm expecting more from Vee.

She's already given me more than I deserved, more than I should have asked for.

Vee watches as I circle the bed to my *official* side. One I need to try to stay on, but I also know I'll inevitably cross during the night.

"Those pants are going to be mighty wrinkled by morning." She eyes the linen material, already creased from sitting.

"I typically sleep in only my boxer briefs and nothing more." My mouth crooks upward, taunting her. Or maybe torturing myself, because I want to be wearing less and asking her for more when it isn't right.

She sighs, glancing at her lap and spreading her hands across the sheets folded over her legs. "If it makes you more comfortable, you can take them off." Her voice shakes, eyes continuing to avoid me.

"Would you be uncomfortable if I did?" Because I won't do anything to make her think this arrangement needs to become something else. I've had no clear sign Vee is attracted to me, even if she once had a crush on me.

She shakes her head and twists for the lamp, turning off the light to douse us in momentary darkness. I take the cue as permission to remove my pants, keeping on my tee, as if that offers some protection.

My dick still twitches, and I adjust myself. It might turn out to be a long night.

I slip under the sheets and mirror Vee's position again, both of us staring up at the ceiling where a sliver of light dances through the vertical blinds.

"I want to apologize. I didn't mean to insult you earlier when I implied you only like supermodels and movie stars, especially considering who Chandler is to you."

"Vee," I immediately rotate to my side. "I cared about Chandler but we're over. It wasn't love. It was . . ." *Companionship?*

"Sex," she adds for me.

"Well," I clear my throat. "There was that, but I'd like to think we had a little more than just sexual chemistry." Upon mentioning it, I'm not certain Chandler and I fully had that either. I mean, we had sex, but was it a chemical attraction, something higher level, or just simple biology?

"But we don't need to share our sexual histories," I tell her.

"Because we aren't having sex," she states, a little too forceful, almost adamant, like a reminder of that invisible line between us.

Feeling strangely shot down when I didn't have any reason to be up, I don't reply. I shouldn't be hopeful of something else with Vee. Something more than just sleeping here beside her.

"Good night, Ross," she whispers, before turning to give me her back. A position I loathe but try to respect that she doesn't want me near her.

Try as I might, though, I don't last more than five minutes before I'm scooting closer to her, molding my chest to her back, and slinging my arm over her waist.

Thankfully, she signals she's okay with this position when the slightest tickle of her fingertips runs up and down my forearm a second before her hand rests on the bed, just out of reach from holding onto mine.

Chapter 13

[Vee]

In the morning, I wake before the alarming *hit it* disturbs us. Ross has his arm tucked across my chest, hand cupping my shoulder while my arm is wrapped over his, holding his wrist. At some point during the night, I must have pulled him closer, held onto him tighter.

Slowly releasing him, I gently push his arm off me and set it on him, then attempt to slip from the bed. The sudden rustling of the sheets and shift in my position has Ross's arm locking around me again, keeping me in place.

"Where you going?" he groggily mumbles.

"Bathroom." I chuckle softly, having been caught trying to escape our little nest. If only that nest was more of a love one than a just-friends one.

I'd heard what he *didn't* say last night. How his relationship with Chandler was sex, and probably good sex at that. I miss sex. How pathetic was I that I might even accept bad sex at this point? Then I remind myself I'm not interested in settling for less than I deserve. I'd done that when I took Cameron back after his affair. I'd settled.

Ross gives me a second squeeze, then loosens his arm so I can slip from the bed. Entering the toilet closet, which is a weird concept to me, I do my business, exit the small space and find Ross beside the double vanity brushing his teeth, wearing only his boxer briefs. The outline of his morning wood is prominent, and Ross doesn't seem the least bit shy about his condition. He isn't exactly flaunting it, but he isn't protecting that thick wedge either.

With my cheeks heated, I quickly glance away from him and wash my hands, then reach for my own toothbrush. Our eyes make contact in the reflection of the mirror.

"Would you like coffee this morning?" I don't want him to feel like he needs to rush out of my place. I also don't want him to feel like he needs to linger. I don't know what I want him to feel, and maybe that's more a reflection on me because I'm a bit of an emotional mess this morning.

The idea he had sex with Chandler shouldn't make me envious. She was his girlfriend. He'd been married. He'd had sex with other women in between, but maybe the mind scramble was that he wasn't having sex with me.

Or maybe it was simply that Chandler is beautiful, and I don't compare.

Glancing at myself, I take a long look at my face in the mirror. There are signs being mid-forties is having an effect. Some wrinkles here and there. Frown lines around my lips. A deep crease across my neck. I once read you can tell the age of a woman by looking at her neck, not her face. Mindlessly, I cup mine and smooth down the skin, watching it retract back into place.

"You're beautiful," Ross says, gaze meeting mine through the mirror again.

My face flames, the pink evident in the reflection. An argument is on the tip of my tongue, but Ross continues.

"Every freckle. Every wrinkle. Every scar is a testament to the life you've lived. Getting older is a privilege, remember?" He winks at me, our connection still through the reflective glass. "And I think who you are is pretty spectacular."

Dropping the connection of our gazes in the mirror, I fight a smile.

Quietly, he says, "I should probably get going."

"Of course." I exit the ensuite bathroom and make the bed while Ross finishes up in the bathroom, stepping out a few minutes later dressed in his clothes from yesterday evening.

Maybe he should bring a bag with him? A change of clothes? Should I give him a dresser drawer in this temporary place?

Dismissing all those thoughts, I'm hit with the overwhelming realization that I have less than two weeks remaining in Arizona and no manuscript.

"Walk me out?" Ross asks, surprising me.

I nod before following him to my front door. While I stand near the wall to the left of the entrance, leaning my back against it, Ross puts on his shoes. I hadn't noticed last night that he wore men's flip flops, his toes on display. For some reason, I giggle.

"What's so funny?" He's standing to his full height and steps closer to me, caging me in a bit against this narrow wall space.

"Your feet. I didn't expect you to wear flip flops."

"Are you opposed to feet, or do you have a foot fetish? Like that two-men thing?"

"Oh. My God." I groan. "How do you compare a two-men thing to bare toes. And will you let the polyamorous thing go?"

He chuckles, knowing he's riled me up.

Suddenly, his arm extends, his hand on the wall beside my head. "Just don't like the idea of men sharing you."

"No one's sharing me." My voice lowers, dropping to a lusty cadence. *Would he share himself with me?* Instantly, I shake the thought and clear my throat. "Anyway, feeling lucky again today?"

His eyes dance with mischief, maybe forming his own interpretation of my question.

"No smacking my ass this morning?" He guffaws.

A strangled laugh catches in my throat. "Yeah, I don't know where that came from."

He tips up his chin, a smirk on his lips. "Next time you spank me, you might need to brace for a spanking in return."

Sweet baby Jesus. The skin on my cheeks goes from mild to flaming hot.

He brushes his knuckles against my neck, pushing my hair over my shoulder. Then he leans closer to me. His forehead almost connects with mine. I can smell the fresh mint of toothpaste on his breath.

I shiver beneath his touch and dig my teeth into my lower lip. *Will he kiss me?*

"It's gonna be a winning day." His voice drops. The sandpaper on wood rasp sound makes me shiver.

Slowly, I smile, while my heart hammers in my chest. At least he has the right attitude.

"I'll call you later." The statement is a canned response. He didn't call me yesterday. He hardly responded to my text.

And I need to save myself from getting too involved in his superstition act and sexual innuendos.

I clear my throat. "Actually, I have plans later."

He presses off the wall and stands to his full height, arms slowly folding over his broad chest and crossing as he stares at me.

"Plans, huh?"

I don't elaborate. It'd be easy to tell him the truth, but for some reason, I don't. Maybe because the sex thing is still bothering me. Maybe it's more that he could have sex with someone else before coming to spend the night in my bed. And suddenly, I'm thinking of Cameron and how he did such a thing. He'd fucked another woman before he slept with me in our bed.

Ross's brows pinch, watching my expression, which I try to school at the sudden flash from my past. I remind myself Ross isn't Cam. He doesn't owe me his fidelity, just like I don't owe him.

Taking a risk, I grip his warm forearm and give him a squeeze. "Knock it out of the park today, Coach."

Ross doesn't look as carefree as he did a few seconds ago, teasing me about toes and two men. Or reciprocal spankings. Instead, he tips up his chin again and mutters, "Have a good one."

Then he reaches for the door and lets himself out.

And I exhale a breath I hadn't known I was holding.

+ + +

That afternoon, the Anchors won. Operation Superstition was a two-game success.

However, we skipped last night's sleeping ritual due to my plans.

Today, the Anchors return to their stadium with a home game against St. Louis, and I have a ticket for the afternoon matchup. After another morning of minimal word count, I am excited to return to the ballpark, in hopes of some inspiration.

The day is cloudy, with the threat of rain, which the desert climate desperately needs. I've been here long enough to learn rain showers can be fleeting. Still, I brought a pullover sweatshirt with me just in case, along with my freshly charged tablet, prepared to make all the notes on a larger screen than my phone.

With a cold refreshment and a hot pretzel, I settle into my seat and the muse sings. Ideas hit, and I frantically type each thought.

Small town baseball success falls for his snarky agent.

Hawaiian vacation turns to secret baby.

League bad boy needs a marriage of convenience to fix his reputation.

Each idea could be their own storyline. For now, I let the fictions flow.

With my head bent downward during most of the game, I don't notice the heavier rain clouds swiftly roll in, although I feel the temperature shift. A cold front blasts over the stadium, and I use my pullover as a blanket over my legs. Every once in a while, I rub at my bare arms, grappling with myself as to whether the sweatshirt would keep me warmer over my upper half versus my lower body.

A drizzle begins to pepper the stadium, and I tip up my tablet, so it doesn't get wet. Within minutes, the sky opens up, and rain pours in the direction where I sit. I shove my tablet beneath the pullover and wrestle the material, attempting to stretch it over my bent knees, knowing it can only expand so far, protect me so much.

Some people quickly gather their belongings and head to the covered concourse. Others slip into plastic ponchos. And still, a few of us just sit out the brief shower.

The saying in Chicago is, *if you don't like the weather, stick around for a few minutes.* Inevitably, it will change. Sometimes we can experience all four seasons in a day. It's ridiculous, and I often wonder why I remain in such a temperamental climate. But I'm born and raised in the Midwest, and while I love Arizona, I don't see moving here in my immediate future. I still have a college tuition to pay, and maybe a wedding or two one day, which means mama needs a new book.

Despite the sudden downpour, the game goes on as the rain isn't strong enough to impair or delay play.

As I'm sitting with my feet on the seat in front of me, knees tucked up as tight as I can bring them to my chest, with my pullover stretched around my legs and my arms wrapped beneath my knees like a human pretzel, the man beside me hands me a jacket. He's an older gentleman, his wife beside him.

I glance down at the kind offering then up at him. "Oh, thank you, but no thank you. I'll be okay." My teeth chatter as the cooler temperature settles into my skin, but I fight through the rattle.

"I was asked to pass it down to you." With the jacket still in his grasp, held out to me, he points toward a young man standing in the aisle at the end of our row. Once again, I have seats near the Anchor dugout, a few rows back, with an easy view of the players as they trot out onto the field and then rush back for cover once their turn at bat is over.

The young man standing in the aisle wears black pants and an Anchors polo, plus a ballcap. He looks like an older batboy or a very young security guard. Either way, he nods for me to take the jacket held by the man beside me.

My brows pinch while I shift, holding up my hand as a sign of gratitude before taking the jacket.

"Thank you," I mutter to the man next to me, as I hold up the jacket, spreading it wide to read the front.

"Looks like the official coaching staff's attire," the man beside me states.

Lowering the offering, I glance toward the dugout. From my position, I can't see inside the covered space. Ross is down there somewhere, tucked in a corner, concentrating on the game. The Anchors are up to bat, so I envision Ross observing Gee Scott standing over home plate. Ross's fingers might even nervously round his silver scruff, circling his lips before tugging at his chin.

ELEVATOR PITCH

I bring the jacket to my face, inhaling the spicy masculine cologne scent on the collar, then I flip the outerwear around my shoulders and slip my arms into material that is dry and warm, like it has just been removed from someone else, their body heat lingering inside.

Tugging the two sides tighter around me, like a warm hug, I tuck my face once more into the collar and fight a smile.

That Ross Davis is a damn gentleman, and *dammit*, I don't want my crush to turn into lust-like or like-lust, or whatever the stage is after a crush, when your attraction grows deeper, your emotions grow fonder, your desire burns hotter, but you haven't crossed the line to another L-word.

One I don't dare to consider falling into with Ross.

Chapter 14

[Ross]

She left the game early.

"For a moment there, I thought we lost you," Kip teases, clapping me on the shoulder once we are inside the management offices.

"What do you mean?"

"You almost sprained your neck looking into the stands."

"I did not," I groan. But Kip didn't miss how I took off my jacket and sent it with a security guard into the stands. What was she thinking, wearing shorts and a tee to a game when rain was predicted? Not to mention, how had I not known she'd be here?

"Looks like your experiment is working," he chides next, shaking his head in disbelief.

Yeah, the experiment appears to be working as we won our game yesterday, finishing out the series with Boston. Then today, the game ended in a win as well, despite her leaving early. And suddenly, I'm not certain it's spending the night with her that's bringing me luck, or just her presence in the stands. Which doesn't make sense as she hadn't attended those two away games with Boston.

I force myself not to look at the bigger picture. Like maybe just having her in my life is the lucky bit.

However, I am not the only one in her life and I've been unsettled since the moment she told me she had plans last night. Which was a definitive rejection and warning not to spontaneously, or otherwise, visit her place.

I didn't like it. Didn't like the thought of another man taking her out or sharing her bed or even touching her, which was just plain ridiculous.

We weren't in an arrangement that demanded monogamy or loyalty. Still, she'd mentioned what her husband did to her, and I didn't like that he'd cheated on her. I might have had a string of situationships in my past, but I was loyal in each and every one of them. I couldn't fathom cheating on a woman, especially someone as sweet, kind, and funny as Vee.

"Yeah," I finally muster a response for Kip, who has been staring at me, waiting on a reply to his statement.

"You don't sound very excited about it." He narrows his eyes, placing his hands on his hips and tilting his head, trying to read me.

"I'm excited about the wins," I state, trying to lift my enthusiasm.

"But not the woman?" His eyes widen, as if puzzled by his suggestion.

I lower to my desk chair and tug off my ball cap, tossing it to my desk before rubbing the heels of my palms against my eyes. I sigh.

"I think that's the trouble." I glance up at Kip. "I like her."

Kip chuckles. "You like her? Like *like*-like her? Like you're a couple of teenagers and not middle-aged adults? Come on, man." Kip whines. "Find a better descriptor for your feelings."

My brows hitch while I tip back in my desk chair. "Oh, are we doing that now? Sharing our feelings with one another?"

Kip scoffs. "Don't be a dick, Davis. You haven't liked a woman since Patty."

I tip forward in my chair and brace my forearms on the desktop. "Tread carefully, Garcia," I warn him in return.

"Look, fucking the supermodels might be fun for a while." He grunts. "But that shit gets old, because we're getting old. And even though Chandler was hot, she was cold."

"Speak for yourself about age, old man," I tease.

"Act your age. An adult."

Kip isn't wrong. Chandler only cared about herself, and her temperament ran to the extremes. She could *appear* playful and spontaneous and yet *act* distant and reserved. Somewhere in between was the sex.

And dammit, I hated that I'd admitted to Vee the other night that sex had been a focus of my relationship with Chandler. I didn't want Vee thinking I used women.

Chandler for sex. Vee for superstitious sleeping arrangements.

Still, I wasn't giving much of an impression that I'd want anything more with a woman. Right now, I don't have time for more. I'm still too new to the team and need my eyes on the ball, not off in la-la land, daydreaming about a spunky author writing kinky plotlines.

Although she never did confirm that she wrote that particular book.

Anyway, I understand what Kip is trying to impart. *Be a grown up.*

"I honestly can't think of any other way to describe my feelings. *She's* the writer." I simply like her. Not poetic or romantic or frilly verbiage. I just *like* her.

I chuckle to myself, recalling how she called me out on not being verbose the other night. When I hadn't typed more than one word in a responding text to her. Patty would sometimes complain I wasn't in touch with my emotions. I was goal-driven instead. *Win.*

My boys certainly felt the absence of my feelings, as I struggled after Patty's death to deal with my grief and balance theirs at nine and eleven years old. I made a lot of mistakes.

"So, she's a writer," Kip singsongs, wiggling his brows. "Anything I've read."

I remember her questioning me when I'd asked her the same thing. "Do you read romance?"

He gasps like I've shot him through the heart. The shocked expression on his face looks more like an admission of guilt than a pained accusation.

"Do you?" I question again, leaning forward once more, reminding myself I need to look up her books.

Kip glances nervously to his left. "I've been known to indulge in one or two." His voice remains steady while his confidence waffles. His cheeks tinge pink. "Women like that."

"Like what?" I ask, like I'm not well-versed in women.

"When you take an interest in them. Do what they do or read what they read. Hell, they especially like it when you read what they read to them."

A minute passes while I process what he's explained. Then I scoff while leaning against the arm of my chair. "Who knew you were such a romantic?"

"Maybe you should try it. You're finally with a woman your own age. A woman you *like*," he drones. "Might be more fun than you expect."

With that, Kip turns on his heels and exits my office, leaving me feeling a little chastised and a tad hurt.

And I'm not certain which emotion lines up with what. The growing older jab, or the lack of interest poke, or the fact that I'm out of practice at being romantic.

+ + +

As romantic gestures go, presenting a woman with season tickets to the Chicago Anchors might not rank up there for some.

"That's a sweet gesture," Vee says half-heartedly once she lets me into her place and I present her the tickets.

For her service to the team, I'd said.

I'd sent a text before arriving unannounced and asked if I could stop by with something for her. I didn't want to intrude on any *plans* she might have this evening.

"But I don't need them," she continues, glancing up at me as we stand in the entry area. She hasn't invited me further into her place when I'd really like to finish that bottle of wine we started the other night, and talk.

Maybe she emptied the bottle with *her plans* last night.

"My dad was an avid fan. I can't remember if I told you that before."

I couldn't either as I was too focused on her eyes. The blue soft yet sparkling, like the flicker of holiday lightbulbs. Her mouth is coated in a pink gloss. Freckles sprinkle her cheeks as if she has recently been in the sun when today had been gloomy and cloudy.

She's pretty. Adorably pretty. *Enticingly* pretty.

"Anyway, he often took me to the games." She shrugs. "It was a special time for us. Like a date with Dad moment." She wistfully sighs in recall, while the memories cinch her forehead a second, like an ache exists in remembering such sacred times. "He took my girls to games as well, giving them precious memories, too. So, when he passed away, I couldn't let the tradition go. I took over his lottery spot, claiming the tickets in his memory. So, I have season tickets."

I'm caught between stunned that she has an entire season worth of tickets and relieved that this means I'll continue to see her. Not that we'd gotten to that particular discussion point in the experiment. The *what's next* moment. But still, she'll be around the stadium once we return to Chicago.

I also feel a little stupid, thinking I was offering her something special, when she already has season tickets and loads of memories mingled with them.

I slip the certificate I had printed which explained how she could claim her tickets back into my pocket, and we stare at one another a minute.

"So, you'll be at all the home games, then?"

"Well, not all of them. If I have plans, or my girls can't use the tickets, we sell them. Try to recoup a little bit of the cost." She grimaces, expressing her dislike of the rising ticket prices.

"Plans, huh?" I grunt.

When she doesn't respond or ask me to stick around, I invite myself to stay. "Want to finish that bottle of wine from the other night?" I arch one brow and slowly smile at my memory of us. Then my voice hardens. "Unless you finished it with your *date* last night."

"I didn't say I had a date last night." Her voice rises in surprise, eyes widening as her hands come to her hips.

"You said you had *plans*." But I can read between the lines, even if the lines seem to be blurring a little bit.

"I did have plans. I went to dinner with an author friend who lives in the area." She tilts her head. "Why would you think I had a date?"

I lower my head, pursing my lips then twisting them, debating if I should answer honestly or not.

"I just thought plans meant you had a date, but you didn't want to tell me." *And I didn't like the idea of you having a date.*

"Why wouldn't I tell you?" Her tone suggests this is a legit question. "Furthermore, why would it matter?"

I feel her gaze on me, but I can't look up at her. I'm being unfair, selfish even, but then I lift my head and answer honestly, "Because I don't want to share you."

Her sweet mouth pops open before she clamps her lips back together a second. Then she speaks, "You aren't sharing me. We're only sleeping together."

The statement sounds so absurd, the argument exact, that we both laugh, scattering the tension between us and loosening the pressure on my shoulders. I hadn't realized how tense I was over the idea of her having a date.

"How about that wine?" I nod toward her kitchen, and she leads the way, taking her spot inside the kitchen while I help myself to a stool on the living room side of the counter. She pours us each a glass and slides one closer to me.

"I just want to clarify, that if I had a date, I'd say date. And me saying I have plans, in order not to attend a home game, would also be exactly what I mean. Pre-scheduled or last-minute plans. If I had a *date*, I might bring him to a game." She lifts her glass, drinking a hearty sip of wine, while glaring at me over the rim of the stemless glassware.

I growl, upset at the thought when I have no right to be worked up.

"You're very grumpy tonight for a man who won today."

"Sent my jacket to a woman in the stands and she ducked out early from the game."

"Oh. And that woman was so appreciative of the jacket. Now *that* was a sweet gesture." She smiles, her voice shifting, softening. She wasn't offended by the gift of season tickets, but she looked a little put off by them. Maybe she was hurt by the presentation. Or maybe my gift should have been more personal.

She wasn't specifically helping the team, but more so helping me. By *sleeping* with me.

Maybe Kip was right. Am I out of touch with what women want? All I really care about is what *Vee* might want. What she needs. And my presentation should have been more thoughtful. Something that expressed more of my gratitude for her and what she's doing for me by playing along with my superstition.

"Speaking of your jacket, let me get it for you." She rounds the counter for the living room.

Shifting on the stool, I catch her wrist as she nears me. "Is there a rush?" She seems eager to get me out of here tonight.

Her head lowers, eyes aimed where my hand cuffs her wrist, my thumb gently rubbing the inner skin over her pulse point. "You don't need to spend the night tonight. You didn't spend the night last night and you won today." Her head lifts and our eyes meet. "I think that proves the experiment isn't necessary."

Panic hits like a hundred-mile-an-hour hit to the elbow, pain radiating over my limbs. I sense Vee is pulling away, about to end our arrangement. And if that happened, I might never see her again.

Shaking my head, I argue. "You were *at* the game today, though. And we won."

She sighs. "So what you're saying is now I need to start attending all the games, both here and back home?" She chuckles but the sound is strained.

Would it be selfish to say cancel any pre-scheduled plans that conflict with those home games? Probably. How about no fucking dates allowed? Yeah, that wouldn't be right either.

"We haven't talked about the regular season yet," I remind her.

"I don't think we need to go there *yet*," she counters.

But we both know, time is ticking, and the calendar dates are getting crossed off on our stay in Arizona, both hers and the Anchors.

"Let's just take it night by night then?" I lower my voice, noticing a quiver in it. A vulnerability I don't want her hearing. I'm not ready to say goodbye to her.

"You weren't paying much attention at the game," I state next, wanting to shift topics, but also curious what held her interest as she clearly wasn't attentively observing the team. Why go to a game if she isn't interested? Then again, I recall her telling me about the atmosphere and margaritas.

She shrugs again, lowering her head, and I realize I'm still holding her wrist. With my foot, I drag the other stool forward, away from the overhanging counter, then pat the seat with my free hand.

Vee slides onto the seat, facing me, and I bracket my legs on either side of her knees. Again with my foot, I draw the stool closer to me, wedging her between my spread thighs.

"I was writing." Vee reaches for her wineglass and sips.

"Really?" I arch one brow, both surprised and pleased that she found inspiration during the game. Then my expression folds and I bitterly chuckle. "Not two men again, I hope."

"A whole team of players," she chides, then she bursts out laughing and points at me. "You should see your face."

I grab her finger and squeeze. "Not fucking funny," I mutter. Then I lower her hand, massaging her finger like I've done before, tugging at the short length, and kneading along the fine bones.

Vee's gaze drops. "That feels so nice."

"You type all day, right?"

"Well, not all day." She chokes on a strangled laugh. "In fact, not most days, until recently."

"What do you mean?"

"I've been struggling to write. *For months*," she emphasizes. "Publishing is a hard industry. Everyone is looking for the next great *thing* to write. What plot sells? What do readers want? What fits best with my brand?"

Her eyes don't leave where I'm massaging her hand. "The first game I attended alone, inspiration struck. Might not be a best seller. Might be a plot already told. Might not even be what readers want." She scoffs.

"But it's a story. A romantic one, at that." Her voice lulls, offering another wistful sigh mingling with secret wonder. Like she's both pleased and surprised at the romantic nature of her own storytelling.

"What's it about?"

Her head lifts, eyes staring directly at me for a split second before darting away. "I don't think I'm ready to share yet. I'm in the early stages still."

"Well, I'm glad inspiration struck. And I look forward to reading it. Once you're ready to share." I dip my head, forcing her eyes to meet mine again.

She clears her throat. "Cameron was never interested in my books."

My fingers still from working her hand, and I stare at her face, where her eyes are avoiding mine once more.

"And Cameron is . . ."

"My late husband." She lifts her shoulders dismissively. "He wasn't interested in story lines, or reading my books, or even talking about the business side of publishing. He didn't care."

I hurt for her like I've taken a fast ball to the chest. "He probably cared, he just didn't know how to show his interest or what questions to ask."

She weakly smiles, her voice sad. "No. He really didn't care about my writing."

I don't want to believe it. What kind of man isn't interested in his wife's career? About the thing that brings her joy because writing certainly gives Vee pleasure. She lights up when she talks about her work. At least, the bits and pieces she's shared.

"I became used to *not* talking about my career, so I'm sorry if I sound standoffish about it. It's just hard to believe you'd really be interested in hearing about the book world, as we call it."

"Vee," I groan, tipping up her chin. "I'm interested." *In the book world, in her world, in her.*

"Talk all you want. Share plot ideas or storylines. Tell me about the industry. Because you know about mine. You know about baseball and superstitions. And you know that I'm right where I wanted to be, managing the Anchors. It makes me happy." I chuckle. "I'm stressed, but content. And I can tell writing books makes you happy, so share that shit with me."

She laughs soggily while blinking rapidly a few times, clearing her eyes of tears she doesn't want me to notice.

"Share the stresses, too."

She laughs a little harder, swiping at the corner of her eye to dissolve a tear before it falls. "Thank you."

The desire to pull her close, hug her, *heck,* even kiss her, is so strong, I find myself leaning forward, then stop the trajectory. Still, I want to reassure her I'm here for her. I even consider teasing her about her polyamorous plotline to dissolve her sadness, but reconsider that jest as well. Instead, I ask something I'm more curious about.

"So, is this a baseball romance? Did I get the terminology correct?"

She snorts softly. Not a full snortle, but a pleasing sound all the same, tells me I'm correct. "You're the one who mentioned baseball and romance go together."

I smile that she remembers something about our first night.

I also wonder how she'd feel about experiencing first base with me.

Chapter 15

[Vee]

To my surprise, Ross spends the night.

As he arrived closer to eight-thirty, we finished the bottle of wine, and then decided to watch a movie. Nothing romantic. Nothing graphic. Nothing baseball. The happy medium was a movie with a touch of intrigue and mystery but not a suspense thriller. I didn't need horrific dreams.

What I dreamt about instead were the developing characters for my book and Ross as the main man in my real-life storyline.

He listened attentively as I talked more about the publishing industry. He even asked thoughtful questions and offered compassion. We discussed agents, and how I don't have one. It would be nice to follow the traditional path, with an agent for support and services, like securing foreign translations and movie deals, but I could do those things on my own. Or at least, I had been for the past ten years. I was comfortable where I was in my career, although there was always hope for more. More sales. More ideas. More years.

For now, I am relieved the writing well is not dry.

In the morning, I give Ross privacy to dress and follow his wake-up routine while I make him coffee. I don't drink the stuff, so I'm grateful for a machine with a pod you pop into the top and add water which automatically brews the liquid gold, as coffee lovers call their caffeine jolt.

As Ross enters the living room, I present the coffee in a travel mug. "For the road." Although he doesn't have far to travel.

He accepts the cup but lowers his head, thumb running around the ridge of the cap. "I've been thinking."

This sounds like another dangerous idea. "Okay."

"And I promise this will be the last time I ask."

Oh, God. *What now?*

"But about that two men sharing one woman thing—"

"Jesus," I hiss, digging my fingers into my hair and holding the length against the back of my neck a second. "Look, I don't expect you to understand." My tone is defensive while I wave up and down before his body. "Because you're you."

His thick brows lift. His thumb stops rotating on the coffee lid. "What does that mean?"

"You're a beautiful man." Exasperation wrestles with my defensiveness.

His cheeks tinge pink while shock registers in his eyes, and then his brows crease. "And you don't think you're a beautiful woman?"

"I'm not saying I'm not." But my expression surely says I don't think I am. "It's about *feeling* beautiful. Feeling desirable." I'm pretty certain we covered this concept the first time I told him about my possible plot line, but maybe he needs the refresher.

"By two men at once?"

"By anyone!" My voice crackles with frustrated tears I don't wish to shed in front of him.

Maybe a beautiful man doesn't get it because he is desirable. He's had sex with beautiful women.

"You're a beautiful woman, Vee. And anyone who doesn't see it, doesn't deserve you."

I sigh. Now, he's placating me. Giving me compliments like I was fishing for one. I don't need this, and I step left, intending to open my front door and practically kick him out.

Only he catches my wrist and tugs me toward him. Stumbling over my own feet, I collide with his chest, then his hand is cupping my jaw, and he leans toward me.

When his mouth makes contact with mine, I'm so surprised I immediately pull back. Our eyes lock on each other's before his gaze drops to my lips again.

Then, he kisses me.

Full on, lips on lips. His hand moves to cup the back of my head. My fingers fist in his shirt.

I'm kissing Ross Davis. And it is heavenly. Divine. Spiritual and inspirational and . . .

He pulls back. "I probably shouldn't have—"

"I don't know that this—"

His mouth cuts me off again, swallowing my agreement, dismissing the fact that this probably isn't a good idea.

What is good, though, is this kiss. The connection of our mouths. His lips full but tender. The scruff around them tickling. His fingers fist tighter in my hair. He sips at me like I'm that liquid-gold jolt he needs to brighten his day. Then his tongue dives inward and I'm up on my toes, tugging him closer to me.

However, when his other arm comes around my back, and a travel mug hits me in the lower spine are we reminded of who we are, where we are, or perhaps, what we shouldn't be doing.

We break apart again.

With shock in each of our eyes, we stare at one another a beat. My heart races, as does his beneath his shirt, which I'm still clutching with tight fingers. Like I want to tear the covering off him or curl underneath it or just draw him closer to me again.

Finally, he speaks. "I should probably go."

"Yep." I release his shirt like I'm dropping a hot pan of cookies. The burn hurts. The cookies ruined. I step back and swallow hard, still tasting his minty tongue against mine. Still feeling his lips as if imprinted with mine.

"Good luck today, Coach."

He glances at me only briefly before darting his eyes toward the door, no doubt eager to flee from the awkward exchange of words and the desperation in that kiss.

Or should I say devastation?

Because that moment turned out to be the kiss of death.

The Anchors lost their game later that day.

+ + +

"I don't know what I was thinking, Cee-Cee," I explain to my best friend on the phone four days after the kiss.

"About which part?" She chuckles good-naturedly as I've just told her everything.

"The experiment. The kiss. Coming to Arizona. Take your pick."

"Why would going to Arizona be an issue?"

I sigh, tipping back my head as I sit on the couch, another blank page on my laptop resting on the ottoman. "Because I'm not getting any words in like I'd hoped."

"But inspiration did strike while you were at the ballpark, right?"

I nod although she can't see me.

"Maybe you need to go to another game."

"And look like I'm chasing after Ross Davis? No way, Cee-Cee." While my best friend has that kind of confidence, I do not.

In the dating game, there is a three-day code.

Day one, a call looks too eager.

Day two, too calculated.

Day three, make contact.

But I'm on the morning of day four with only minimal texts.

Team meeting tonight.

Coaches' dinner, I forgot about.

Late call with the front office.

Those dating rules are a suggested holding pattern after a first date. What are the rules after a first kiss? What does day four signify? The obvious. He isn't going to call. He isn't coming over. No more kissing and no more sleeping arrangement.

I don't know whether to feel grateful or depressed.

Instead, I'm pissed. Ross kissed me first, much like he came to my hotel room, and he came to me with his hairbrained scheme. Of which, the Anchors have flowed in a pattern of loss-win-win.

I feel used and tossed aside, like people who leave their half-eaten snacks behind at a stadium game. *Am I simply an unfinished hot pretzel?* Screw that. And screw Ross. No one leaves a hot pretzel unfinished, and Ross needs to man up and finish us. I deserve a phone call, or at least a full sentence text with an explanation, not this emptiness after a kiss that changed my life.

How am I supposed to kiss someone else after that kind of kiss? I might never eat a hot pretzel again at this point, and the idea of *that* is just disappointing.

"Look, you went there to write," Cassandra interjects, her tone sharpening in a way I recognize. She's about to get real with me. Picture a woman in riding boots, tugging them hastily on in preparation to get dirty and take charge of a situation.

"I know, but—"

"Aunt Sassy is imparting wisdom, so you need to listen."

"You are not my—"

"Shush."

My mouth falls open. She did not just shush me, and I'm ready to argue again with her when she begins her wisdom-incantation.

"You are strong. You are beautiful. You are kind."

I snort. "You cannot steal someone else's words as your own advice, Cassandra."

"Oh, fine. But it's the truth. You have resilience like no one I know. Cameron. Writing. You make decisions, and you go for it. You have goals and don't let some *guy* get in the way."

"If you go into the montage from *Say Anything* about men versus guys . . ." I warn.

"Oh my gosh, such a good movie," Cassandra croons. "But I digress."

"Yes, tell me how I'm all woman, hear my roar."

"You are all woman," she growls, giving me her best *rawr* for effect. "And you're a beautiful soul with an active imagination. It's a gift, Vee-Vee. And no guy, or *man*, or hot baseball manager with a tempting ass in baseball pants should make you question that worth."

"He didn't exactly—"

"And you're a good person, Vee. You're sweet and nice. God, so nice. And look what you did for him." Her voice rises. A shift in the tide is coming, a rolling whitecap curling into itself, where she does break into a montage of her own about women's worth and men being dicks, or thinking only with them, or acting like one, which never makes sense to me because dicks have limited purpose or action and . . .

"You will not hide, Verona. You will not be ignored."

"Are we moving over to the *Fatal Attraction* portion of this pep talk?" I chuckle but Cassandra takes in a deep breath, like she's about to jump into that rising tide and swim for her life.

"And you can go where you want to go, which is a damn baseball game for inspiration so you can write your next bestseller and take all the trips to Anywhereland."

"Anywhereland?" I scoff.

"You know what I mean?"

"Actually, I'm not certain I do."

"You don't need him. He needed you."

Basically, what she isn't saying is he used me, and I exhale at the thought again.

Then I retrace my steps a bit. Hadn't I let myself be used? Hadn't I opened myself up for this downfall? This stupid experiment. What was I even doing with Ross Davis?

We shouldn't have kissed. But it was just a kiss. A toe-curling, soul-awakening, clit-pulsing kiss, but still only a kiss. Like *only* sleeping together. Maybe I'm making the moment bigger than it is, or was, because the moment is clearly past tense. Ross isn't coming back.

Which means the kiss was a big deal to him.

One that has him reneging on his experiment.

"You're right," I sigh, although I'm not entirely sure what I'm agreeing with in her speech.

I am resilient. I weathered Cameron's affair and took him back because of the girls. Because I thought we would have a chance to rebuild our marriage and our family. Then, he was taken from me, and in the midst of our marital rebuild, the house collapsed, so to speak.

My subsequent grief conflicted with my already unstable emotions. I'd been broken by my husband's poor decisions. With his absence, I dove deeper into my writing, turning it from my little hobby, as Cameron mockingly called it, to a profitable career. One that has afforded me a sensible apartment, a few vacations, and college tuition for the girls.

And dammit, I need to write. The creative itch is a real rash, one that festers and grows until you either ignore it with some other interest or give into the scratch.

Not exactly the best analogy if I'm trying to wax poetic and romantic, but a good one, nonetheless. Writing was a part of who I am, and I needed to write.

I needed inspiration, and I needed that ballpark.

Chapter 16

[Vee]

I can't bring myself to wear the opposing team's colors as Cassandra suggests in order to disguise myself in the crowd.

"What kind of blasphemy would that be?" The thought of doing such a thing appalls me, especially as the opponent for the afternoon game is Chicago's crosstown rival, the Agitators, whose colors are black, white, and dark green to match the Tyrannosaurus Rex of their mascot.

After hanging up with Cassandra, I don my favorite team's signature colors of royal blue and bright red, buy a baseball cap at the stadium store, and wear sunglasses as the day is vibrantly sunny. Not that I really need the getup or the mystique of a disguise.

I'm confident Ross Davis isn't looking for me.

I sit in the outfield, officially the lawn seats, and force myself not to look directly at the dugout. Like glancing in that direction might burn my retinas despite the UV-protection over my eyes.

Instead, I focus on Ford Sylver's backside as he stands in centerfield in his sinfully snug baseball pants and mentally objectify him. I also concentrate on the other men acting as my muses, especially Bolan Adler, a new-to-the-team catcher, although his age suggests he's been around baseball for a while.

Without Hannah present, my resident in-the-know about baseball players, I don't have more of a story on him, so I make up my own, adding to the bits and pieces I'd already collected about several of his fellow teammates.

For their privacy and protection, all names will be changed and any situations that might look similar to real life circumstances will be amended or flipped. So far, I don't think I'd done anyone damage turning them into fictitious characters. In fact, my characters are becoming far removed from their real player muses.

As the Anchors are headed for a win during the eighth inning, I decide I've had enough sunshine and the one margarita I splurged on is giving me a headache, so I pack up my things and head back to the rental prepared to write for the remainder of the day.

Fresh air brought fresh thoughts, and back at the condo after the game, I am settling into a good writing rhythm when a knock comes to my door.

I ordered takeout from a local barbeque place that had some of the best brisket I'd ever tasted. Although Chicago isn't a mecca for barbeque lovers, in my opinion, some of the best BBQ can be found in my fair city. After talking with Cassandra earlier in the day, I'd also been missing home. I only have a week left in Arizona, but I am ready to return to my apartment, with all its familiar comforts and proximity to my girls.

As I cross the room for the front door, my mouth waters. Opening the door on a rush, I stare wide-eyed at the man who is evidently *not* the delivery person.

"Ross?"

He brushes past me like a man on the run and I spin, hand still on the doorknob, staring after him.

"I can't take it," he snaps, tugging his ballcap from his head. He looks like he came here straight from the game. "We lost again."

"What?" I snap, almost as horrified as him. "But you were winning when I left and—"

The sharp way his head whips upward has me holding my tongue.

Ross takes two steps closer to me. "You were at the game?" His eyes narrow, like he's trying to bring me into focus. "I didn't see you."

Was he looking? Probably not.

Guiltily, I lower my head. "I sat on the lawn today." Why was I hiding? Like Cee-Cee said, I didn't deserve to be ignored and that's what Ross had done. He'd been a coward. Instead of facing me, or speaking to me, he simply ghosted me.

With my hand clutching the edge of the open door, I lift my head higher and glare back at him. "I guess our arrangement is null and void. I'm so sorry for your loss."

Loss of the game. But more succinctly, his loss of *me*.

"Now, I'm expecting dinner any second, so . . ." I wave my hand like I'm sweeping out the dust onto the front stoop of this place.

"Vee," he pleas as another man says, "Verona Huxley?"

I turn in the direction of the delivery person and take the bag he offers me. "Thank you."

The aroma of barbequed brisket hits me despite the food being encased in the plastic bag and takeaway container. I just want to eat my dinner in solitude while I wallow in self-pity and try to make fictional men romantic. A daunting task when nothing in my life speaks of romance.

Ross pauses, watching me, glancing at the bag in my hand and the open door. Then he steps closer to me and places his hand beneath mine, like he'll pull the door shut behind him as he leaves.

I step back giving him space.

Only, the door closes with a sharp snick and Ross remains inside my rental.

"What are you doing?"

"We need to talk." He spins to face me.

"Oh? Now you want to talk? I'm sorry I heard you loud and clear. *With your silence*," I bark. "For nearly four fucking days."

I don't know why I'm angry. Because he ignored me? Because he avoided me? Because he kissed me, and it rocked my world when it didn't even ruffle his?

Stalking away from him, I carry my dinner to the kitchen and hastily open and close cabinet doors, slamming them after I've found plates. The cutlery rattles as I tug open the drawer and I fiddle through the forks and knives, removing what I need before slamming it closed as well.

Next, I grab the bottle of wine I'd purchased the other day. The same kind Ross had brought to my place, which was darn expensive and probably explains why it tastes so good. The flavor surely couldn't have been enriched by the company *who skipped out on me because of a kiss*.

And all the while, I'm having this self-induced tantrum. Because who am I really mad at, me or Ross? Okay, Ross mainly, who stands opposite the counter that divides the living room and kitchen while I work myself into a lather.

I struggle with the corkscrew until Ross reaches over and takes both the bottle and the opener from me.

"Let me." His voice lowers, sand sifting through an hourglass. His gaze drops as well as he efficiently works the opener into the bottle and pops the cork before sliding the bottle back toward me and sets down the wine opener.

Because I'm wound up, I pick up the wine and take a hearty sip right out of the bottle.

Ross watches me, eyes bright and wide. His arms are stretched outward, hands braced on the countertop that works as a wall between us.

"Damn, you're fucking pretty when you're on fire."

I snort with the bottle too close to my lips and I choke on the contents inside my mouth. Setting the bottle down with force, I bend forward, trying to catch my breath as I swallow hard and fight a cough that wins. As I gasp for air because I'm gagging on wine and anger, Ross rounds the countertop to the kitchen and wraps his arms around my middle from behind me.

With his head lowered, face tucked into my neck, he mutters. "I'm sorry. I'm an ass." I feel him swallow against my shoulder. "And I missed you."

Dammit.

I could argue that he isn't an ass, or that he has a fine one, but neither feels appropriate. He can own his error.

Common courtesy counts.

And the fact he admitted he missed me, well . . . I'd be a butt if I didn't admit that made me tingle everywhere.

As the choking subsides, a tickle remains in my throat, and I don't respond to his apology or confession. Instead, a few moments pass with him holding me, squeezing me tighter to him with his chin on my shoulder until he kisses the side of my neck and stands to his full height behind me.

"I'll go," he mutters, defeated.

Sighing, I close my eyes a second before opening them. With my back to him, I quietly say, "Or you could stay and tell me about the game."

Ross spins me so fast to face him I stumble over my own feet. He looks me directly in the eyes, a world of relief in his own, while still surprised by my suggestion.

"How do you feel about brisket?"

+ + +

[Ross]

I fucking love smoked, salty meats, and I think I love her for not kicking me out.

Of course, I don't say that second part.

The past three nights without her have been hell.

The torture started with that kiss. While I shouldn't have done it, I don't regret it.

That kiss knocked me on my ass. I'd thought I might see a few stars if I ever got to kiss Vee. Maybe a little fireworks-over-a-stadium kind of effect from her mouth meeting mine. Instead, I saw the sacred Northern Lights. Kissing her was magical and confounding.

I never expected one kiss from Vee to impact me so hard. Never expected how surprisingly right her mouth felt. How instantly turned on I was. How much I wanted her.

This wasn't supposed to happen. We had an imaginary line that we never officially discussed, and it had not only been crossed, it has been obliterated.

Now all I can think about is kissing her again, and how much I've been missing her, especially our nights together. This isn't only about the experiment. With every lost game, I found myself wanting to call Vee and talk to her. Just hear her voice, telling me something random or encouraging. Her little pep talks aren't inconsequential to me. *She* believes in me, and I feel that faith in my gut. She played along with our arrangement, but she also has these tiny tidbits of advice. Or reminders. I'm the manager. I've been in this position before. I've been a player on a team. Baseball is in my blood like writing is in hers. I got this. I just need more time to weather the kinks.

And thinking of kinks also reminds me of how I told her I might spank her if she ever smacks my ass again.

I want to touch her, and not just the smarting pain of a crack on her bare ass. I want to feel her skin, explore her breasts, experience her clit, and be inside her.

The rush of desire comes visceral and fast, but not out of nowhere, because I've been falling for her from the moment I met her in that damn elevator. Okay, maybe it was more likely when she was trying to get into my room, but still . . . I wanted to be close to her and I was slowly discovering all the reasons why I felt this pull.

The way she opens the door with a flourish, like she can't wait to let me in.

Or that damn snortle that tells me she's covering up what makes her want to giggle at forty-five years old.

Or the wistful sigh she has for memories of her dad or a romantic story she's plotting.

There is so much more to Vee than sharing her bed. I want her to share herself with me.

And I fucked up.

After that kiss, I hadn't panicked so much as pulled back before I did something rash like take her down to the tile floor in the entry way and dry hump her. My dick had been so hard, and my thoughts were so out of control the other morning, I had to escape.

Why did I stay away for nearly four days? Because I'd hoped the craving would pass. That the desire to be near her would subside with separation.

What's that saying about absence makes the heart grow fonder? It sure fucking had, because I couldn't take another minute of being without Vee.

I don't need to spend the night. If she wants me to leave after dinner, I will. I just want a little more time with her. I want a little more of her.

"What did you get?" I whisper because I'm too choked up that she's willing to let me linger.

"Sliced brisket. Coleslaw, French fries, and cornbread." She sighs, a sad smile on her face while shaking her head. "I definitely over-ordered for one person but I'm an anxiety eater."

Running my knuckles along her neck, I brush her hair over her shoulder. "I'm sorry if I am the cause of that, Vee." Because I know I'm the reason she's upset.

We should talk about that kiss, but when I glance down at the countertop and notice Vee has already set out two plates and two sets of forks and knives, I realize she intended for me to stay even while she was getting worked up.

"You sit. Let me serve you." Pressing on her shoulders, I force her around the counter to one of the two stools. Pulling it out for her, I gently settle her onto the seat and reach over the counter to distribute the food.

She's right. There is too much for one person and I quickly divvy up the brisket and side dishes. Then, I find glasses for the wine and pour a glass but stop before filling hers.

"Would you rather drink right out of the bottle?" In jest, I hold up the container.

"Don't tempt me." She smirks.

If only I *didn't* want to tempt her into giving me more.

Kip warned me emotions would get in the way of this experiment, and I'd argued no such thing could happen.

But watching Vee sheepishly smile back at me, twirling her finger in the air giving me permission to continue pouring her a glass of wine versus handing over the bottle, I can't help but accept my argument was a failure.

And I don't want to fail Vee.

Chapter 17

[Vee]

We don't talk about the kiss and steer clear of both baseball and romance. Instead, we discuss our kids.

I tell him about Laurel being a teacher and loving the quirkiness of fifth graders. Hannah is studying physical therapy but isn't certain what she wants to do with the degree. Possibly sports medicine.

"I might be able to hook her up." Ross winks as we sit side by side, decimated plates of food before us, with wads of meager paper napkins ruined from sticky brisket and warm cornbread.

Ross tells me about his son Landon who wants to be an engineer. And Harley who is studying musical theatre in Chicago.

When I'm surprised his sons aren't into sports, he explains their animosity.

"Landon played through high school, but I think they resent baseball more than admire it," he says, going into detail about his schedule—the trainings, practices, meetings, and conferences, and all of that on top of the games.

"It was hard on them that I didn't have a nine-to-five job. But Patty was great."

He hasn't discussed his late wife much, so I cautiously ask, "How did she pass?"

"Aneurysm." He lowers his eyes and picks at the remains of his meal with his fork. "She'd been experiencing a lot of headaches, but we didn't look deeper into the cause." When he finally looks up at me, his eyes are sad.

Setting down his fork, he sits up straighter and I place my hand on his forearm. "I'm so sorry."

"She was a good woman, who gave me lots of leeway to be the man I am. I missed out on a lot with my kids. When Landon was in sports, or Harley had plays, I wasn't present for them, and it's my greatest regret.

I didn't do enough for them." Remorse etches his round face, sharpens his cheeks and jaw. "I was a mess the year she died."

The year the Anchors won the championship.

"I was desperate to keep playing. To keep my head in the game and not on reality." He lowers his gaze, where his hand cups his stemless wineglass. "My kids suffered because I was suffering. I took a year off after that win, but I still needed baseball." He glances up at me, guilt deep in his eyes. "When the Flash was looking for an assistant coach, I jumped at the chance. Plus, I'm from Philly and my sister is there, so she offered to help."

"You have a sister?" I ask eagerly, trying to distract him from his sad history.

"Regina. We call her Rena. And a brother named Rocco."

"The three Rs."

Ross chuckles but the sound still holds his sorrow.

With my hand on his forearm, I say, "I'm sure your boys realize now you did the best you could then. Loss is so difficult, whether you anticipate it, or it's sprung on you. Grief is really an individual process. We all deal with it the best we can, which is even harder when you feel responsible for little ones and *their* grief."

Ross lowers his head once more, his thumb rubbing up the side of his wine glass in distraction. "I mentioned that Patty let me be me, but sometimes I wonder if I did enough for her. Did I even know who she wanted to be outside of a wife or a mother?"

His grief weighs heavily within him.

"Is that how it was with you?" He swallows and lifts his eyes for mine. "How did Cameron die?"

"He was a police officer. Shot in the line of duty."

"Jesus." Ross shifts, his knees brushing my stool until his thighs are spread and he spins my seat, so my knees are between his legs, similar to our position the last time we sat on these stools.

With his hand on my thigh, he says, "I'm so sorry that happened to him. To you."

I nod, a weak smile on my face. The one I'd perfected when people wanted to make Cameron into a saint at his passing when he was anything but, especially after falling for another woman.

"I actually felt fully aware of who Cameron was when he passed. He was a cop and while not all cops are crooked, Cameron wasn't exactly straight, which is how he got involved with someone else."

I push away the reminders of the woman Cameron hoped to save.

"The doubt I had in his ability to change made me angry when he died. I'll never know if he could have been a better husband, father, police officer. But when he died, I didn't grieve the man he *was*."

With Ross's hand on my thigh, his thumb rubs my skin in the same way he pressed at the wine glass. With methodical strokes back and forth.

"Do I sound cold-hearted?" It's a question I've asked myself over and over again. Then I remind myself I was willing to take Cameron back after he confessed his adultery. I told him we'd get counseling. We could work on us. He agreed but I'll never know if he truly meant it. If he'd be dedicated or stray again. If he loved me at the end or thought of *her* instead.

The grieving woman in the back of the funeral home.

"No," Ross interjects. "You sound like you're being honest with yourself."

"Well," I chuckle bitterly. "I've had ten years to figure myself out."

"And that's when the writing began?"

"That's how the writing started." More than just scribbling in notebooks or typing notes on my phone. "It was time to do something for me and not make my life all about Cameron. Something inside me felt the separation from him. Maybe I was preparing for when I'd be without him."

I don't want to give Cameron credit for my creative mind, though. My writing desires came from me.

We sit in silence for a few minutes before Ross squeezes my leg.

"Okay, no more sad storytelling," he suggests.

ELEVATOR PITCH

    The other night he said we didn't need to share our sexual histories. Somehow our marital ones feel just as fragile. A decade, or nearly a decade, has passed for each of us.
    "Want to watch another movie?" I question.
    "Sure. You pick." He stands and picks up our plates, carrying them over to the sink. I follow, dumping trash into the bin. When I turn around, Ross is close, and he tugs me to him for a surprising hug. One I'm not reciprocating at first, until he holds on a little longer than I expect.
    And when I'm finally giving in, I hadn't realized how much I needed that hug. *His* hug. One that's bear tight, and just as warm. As I melt against his chest, he kisses the top of my head, lingering in this position. We hold each other for a minute, letting our thoughts be random.
    Maybe his remain on the sad loss of his wife.
    As for me, I'm just grateful he's sharing pieces of himself with me.

Chapter 18

[Ross]

I'm grateful when Vee allows me to stay the night.

Then, I wake in a risky position. My large body is practically over hers where she lays almost on her belly. Her legs are spread apart because my thigh is wedged between them, pressed against a spot that is warm and inviting. My arm rests across her chest, hand on her shoulder while her hand wraps around my forearm as if she doesn't want me to let go of her.

I sense her waking as well. The way her foot runs over my shin. The way her backside brushes me just off center from my morning wood. I slip my hand to her throat and feel her swallow. She arches into me, as if seeking what I want to slip inside her.

Skimming my hand to her chest, I imagine what would happen if I slid lower. My mitt-sized hand would cover her breast, teasing her nipple, before lowering to her belly.

I press my face into her hair, inhale her fresh floral scent and rock my hips forward, just once. One tap. Then I drop my hand to her stomach, meeting her skin where her shirt has risen.

Vee moves her legs, tightening them around my thigh, holding me in place between them.

God, I want her. I want to feel where she's warm and kiss where she drips. I want her wrapped around my hips, and my body jolts with excitement.

But my head gets in the way. Or maybe it's my heart stomping on the brakes.

"Vee," I groan, nuzzling my face deeper into her nape, pulling her closer while knowing I need to push her away. "I'm trying to be a decent man."

"You are a decent man," she moans as she arches her back, her fine ass jutting toward me, narrowly missing my rock-hard dick. I shift my leg, the thickness of my thigh firmly pressing against her center. She's clutching my wrist, pressing at my arm, begging me to travel lower on her body. To take what I want from her. Or maybe give her what she needs.

Instead, I push off her and roll to my back, inhaling short, sharp ragged breaths and swiping both hands down my face.

"*Fuck*. I'm sorry, Vee." It isn't that I don't want her. It's that I don't know how to keep her. I've just started a new job, and things are rocky at best, near avalanche at worst. I *value* Vee in my life, and I don't want sex to mar what we have. For once, I want to do things the right way, not make it about sex.

Still, I ache for her.

"No. Don't say it," she mutters, burying her face into her pillow. Disappointment rings throughout the bedroom. Both hers and mine.

"I don't want to hurt you. But I need to keep my eyes on the ball."

Devotion. Drive. Determination.

"It's okay," she mumbles, her face still aimed into her pillow. "I only have a few days left in Arizona anyway."

She doesn't understand. I'm not rejecting *her*. Not in a traditional sense. I want her, I just . . . I'm messing up. I'm sending her mixed signals.

Hold or steal the base? Can I risk more right now? Should I only lead off a little or rush toward the next base and hope the slide doesn't burn?

Fuck, I'm so confused, and I'm not ready to let Vee go which makes me selfish. Hell, I've been greedy from the start. Hadn't I known, deep down, we might come to this point? This moment where I'd want her physically. Emotions were not supposed to get in the way of things. But I treasure her friendship.

Quickly, I roll toward her, perch up on my elbow, and press on her shoulder, forcing her to look at me. Which she won't. Tears fill her eyes, and she closes them.

"I hadn't thought about us leaving." I need more time. I'm not ready to let her go. "The Anchors don't fly out until Monday night."

"I leave early Saturday morning."

"I don't want to think about saying goodbye yet." I swallow hard. Will we have to say goodbye? "Sweetheart, I have this Tuesday off. Go out with me." Spend more time with me. More than this bed. More than late night wine and movies on the couch.

Vee finally opens her eyes and briefly meets mine.

"What about practices? A meeting or press conference? Spring training is so short. I'm surprised you have any time off at all."

I brush back her hair, my fingertips skating over her collarbone. It isn't fair that I keep touching her, and yet I don't want to stop. "The days off are rare. Spend it with me. We can do anything you want."

Then I'm tracing her face with my finger. Starting between her brows, I round her eye, down her cheek, and draw to the tip of her chin. Then I circle over her opposite cheek, around her other eye, and return between her brows.

Her face is a perfect heart. *Fuck.* You'd think I'm a connoisseur of romance novels.

With her gaze landing on my face, suddenly I can't look her in the eyes.

"Have you heard of the Hole in The Rock? I've been wanting to go there," she says.

"I have heard of it, but I haven't been."

"I'm not athletic like you, but I've read it has low peaks which are easy to climb."

"Hey," I quietly state, forcing us to look at one another. "Don't sell yourself short. You don't need to be athletic. And a hike sounds great. We can go at our own pace. Maybe grab lunch afterwards."

"Sounds like a date, Coach."

"Definitely a date," I say, meeting her eyes, wanting to kiss her but stopping myself.

This date won't be one in a swanky restaurant or one with hopes of publicity shots. This time will be just an average day, doing something outdoors, and enjoying the company of a woman I don't want to let go of yet.

Because I'm not ready to consider what happens next.

+ + +

I hated leaving Vee. Especially as I'd disappointed her. I'd disappointed myself as well, but I didn't want to use Vee to relieve the ache in my cock, even if my desire for her was the cause of that tension.

After she agreed to our date, I was almost giddy. I'd wanted to linger in bed, maybe grab breakfast together. I could hardly wait until Tuesday.

But like I told her, I needed my eye on the ball, and we had another game today.

"Well, you look rested," Kip teases as I enter my office after a quick stop to my hotel room for a shower and change of clothes.

I sip from my to-go cup of coffee. "I am," I casually state, glancing down at my desk, randomly flipping through papers without reading a word on them.

"Sleep with your lady friend again?"

My head lifts and I narrow my gaze at Kip. "Don't make it sound so scandalous."

"But isn't it? Clandestine meetings at her place."

"What the . . . Are you reading romance novels again?"

"I'm going to regret letting you know that secret, aren't I?"

Not as much as I regret that I'm *not* having a clandestine affair with Vee, although this morning came close. Her heat against my thigh. Our legs entwined. Her hand on my wrist, signaling she wanted more.

"Are you feeling lucky?"

"What?" My head snaps upward, my tone a little sharper than necessary.

"For the game. Did your good luck charm bring you the magic you need?"

I shrug. "I don't know." However, I certainly do feel good. Better, especially after Vee didn't kick me out last night, invited me to stay for dinner, and then we hung out. Things got a little sad for a minute, but the sharing of our marriages was inevitable, almost refreshing.

I never mentioned Patty with former situationships. She was a subject I glossed over, and one most females didn't like to address. Some didn't even like my single dad status which made them short-lived in my life.

But like Kip had said weeks ago, fucking the younger set had it's time and place, and now I wanted my time to be filled with one pretty forty-five-year-old.

As for places, I couldn't believe both of us were so close to going back home. Chicago awaits.

The thought made me anxious. Like a summer fling about to end. I didn't like the comparison.

Would I see Vee in Chicago? Could we keep this arrangement going? Should we?

Was I being fair? Was I only dragging out the inevitable by asking Vee out on a date? My heart slowly sinks to my stomach. Still, I want that time with her. The Hole in the Rock will be a fun escape and excellent way to experience Arizona together. Plus, it gets us outside her rental which is the only place we've been together, like an actual clandestine affair as Kip teased me. Only I don't want Vee to feel like a secret. She isn't something scandalous. We're consenting adults, building a friendship, and I want to see where we'll go. Before we say goodbye, *if* we say goodbye.

"So you saw her?" Kip questions, still reading my mood.

"I saw her." A slow smile ticks up the corners of my mouth with reminders of this morning and our future plans. Like a runner moving around first base and hightailing toward second, I'm racing toward a grin I can't contain. Glancing at Kip, he catches me smiling.

"It's a nice look on you."

"What is?" I school my expression.

"Happiness."

Fuck off rests on the tip of my tongue, but I fight the response.

I am happy. Happy I'm getting this chance with Vee. If only for a little while longer.

ELEVATOR PITCH

+ + +

On Tuesday, after batting practice in the morning, I pick Vee up and drive the half hour distance to Hole in the Rock, which is essentially a giant hole in a ginormous rock formation, and a small sightseeing venture compared to all the trails, hikes, and mountain ranges in the area. If only I had time, I'd take Vee to Sedona or up to the Grand Canyon. *Maybe next year?* It was an excuse I'd used too often with my boys when they were younger. And I didn't know if there would be a next year for Vee and me. I needed to embrace the moment.

While we drive, Vee chatters away about activities she's done while in Arizona and things she'd wanted to do. She was running out of time to fit it all in.

Once we arrive at the park, we take the rocky trail which curves around the back of the rock to natural indentations leading to the hole that provides a scenic view of Phoenix.

Vee takes picture after picture after having taken tons of photographs from the base of the rock.

"Here. Let me take a picture of you." I hold up my phone when she turns and smirks. *Click.* "What was that look?"

"I hate having my photo taken."

"Why?"

"I just never look like I feel in the images."

"You're fucking beautiful, Vee. You should *feel* like that in every photo taken."

Her mouth falls open at my compliment and I take another photo of her. Then I step next to her and stretch out my arm holding the phone. Wrapping my other arm around her, I say, "We'll take one together."

"Okay." She leans toward my shoulder and just as I'm about to snap the button for the photo, I turn my head and press a kiss to the side of hers. *Click.*

She pulls back and stares at me, and with my arm still outstretched, I click a few more pictures of us. I'm not only embracing the moment; I'm capturing it.

We hang out on the rock for a while before noticing trails leading to other rock formations. We descend one geological phenomena and hike toward another. The second formation is slanted like something from a pre-historic time, and Vee stands still in awe again.

"'What are men to rocks and mountains?'" Vee whispers.

"What?" I turn to face her.

"It's a Jane Austen quote . She was questioning the purpose of men in relationships to the peace of rocks and mountains." Vee turns her head toward me. "Or maybe she was wondering what's the value in a man when rocks and mountains are more stable?"

She laughs, and I realize she's teasing me. *Or is she?*

I haven't been very consistent in how I've handled our situation.

"She also said 'It is not what we think or feel that makes us who we are. It is what we do.'"

I chuckle. "Now that's something you should have printed on a T-shirt."

She tilts her head. "I do. And why would you say that?"

"Because you have all those book tees."

She stares at me in question.

"You know, *Cool Girls Read Hot Books*."

Her mouth falls open, like she's surprised I remember the T-shirt.

"I told you, I remember everything." I tap at my temple. And I'm going to remember this moment, right here, where I really want to pull her into my arms and kiss her again. Not just a surprise cheek kiss, but an earnest, *I want this moment to last forever* kind of kiss.

Instead, I swallow down the desire and squint off into the distance where a range of mountains stands tall behind a glimmering city, wondering if I'm *doing* enough to let Vee know I value her and the time she's given me.

+ + +

After our hike, we decide to head back toward Vee's rental for lunch, and later find a local taco restaurant that serves margaritas and beer. We talk about nothing important and everything random, and I laugh like I haven't laughed in a long time. Vee talks with her hands a lot, getting animated when telling a story, especially ones about her girls or her friend Cassandra, who she explains was seated next to her during the first spring training game Vee attended and the one catcalling my name.

I don't remember her friend, but I recall looking up in the stands and seeing Vee when I typically gloss over the crowd. Looking at no one in particular and everyone all at once.

Vee stood out in that sea of baseball fans. And it wasn't only that she was wearing that replica Anchors jersey with my number on it. Her bright eyes. Her light hair. Her stunned face then.

However, her smile is what captivates me now. I'm hoping I was able to capture that smile in the pictures I took earlier.

Will I find Vee in the sea of fans at Anchor Field once we return to Chicago? She'll never be someone nameless or faceless in a crowd to me. Will she look for me as well? Or will we end when she leaves Arizona in a few days?

My stomach knots because I don't want to think about goodbyes.

When we finally return to Vee's place, she looks a little buzzed from two margaritas, and I'm drowsy from the physical exertion of the morning hike and the rays of sunshine, plus my two beers.

"Want to sit outside?" Vee asks, pointing toward the brilliant late afternoon sun shining on her balcony.

"Actually, lets nap." I'm not typically a napper but I'm warm and comfortable as I toss myself on her couch. Plus, I want to be close to her again.

Vee stares at me until I turn on the television, set the volume to low and stretch out on my side. Then I hold out my arm and wiggle my fingers.

"Come here, beautiful."

Vee chuckles softly, like a dismissive snortle. Like she doesn't trust this position and I shouldn't be teasing her. I shouldn't be tempting either of us, but I just want to hold her for a little while and soak up the remainder of this day.

"Will this count as sleeping together?" she asks, still standing too far away from me, with her hands on her hips and her lip caught between her teeth.

"Sure." I lug myself back off the couch. "Now get that fine ass over here." Only, I don't wait for her to approach me. I catch her around the waist and carry her backwards to the couch, tumbling us both awkwardly onto the cushions.

"That went better in my head." I chuckle about my vision of a smooth transition to the couch versus her landing on my lap and then her head colliding with my chin before I wrestle us to our sides.

"I'm not certain we fit on this thing together," she laughs quietly again.

With her settled, her back to my front, and my arm wrapped over her middle, I squeeze her.

"We fit together, Vee."

And I mean it in more ways than one.

Chapter 19

[Vee]

We sleep for two hours.

The hum of the television. The margaritas in my system. The warmth of Ross at my back. I'm cocooned in comfort.

When I wake, I need to use the bathroom. Plus, I feel the telltale signs of Ross's arousal and I can't go through that kind of disappointment again. I shift beneath his arm, and he clutches me tighter.

"Where you goin'?" he mutters groggily.

The moment reminds me of the other day in bed. Same squeeze around my middle. Same question in his sandpaper tone.

"Bathroom." Not exactly a flowery answer but everyone uses it.

When I return to the living room, I sit on the ottoman across from Ross who is lying on his back, face aimed toward the ceiling.

The day has been fantastic. Sunshine, warm hike, and excellent company. A real date. One that was different from your typical dinner and a movie.

Ross continually surprises me. Like that kiss to my head when he took a picture of us, or the times he took my hand and held on a little longer than just assisting me up a rock.

Even moments some might consider insignificant, like placing his hand on my lower back while we scanned the menu in the taco restaurant or how he pulled out my chair before I sat, were precious.

Ross is a gentleman, and I don't think his attention was an act. He wasn't trying to impress me. And we certainly didn't have paparazzi following us with cameras where he'd need to put on a show.

But he also confuses me.

Why treat me like we are a couple when he wasn't interested in more with me? Heck, why even ask me out on a date if he wasn't attracted to me?

"What are we doing?" I finally ask, my voice lowered, my gaze aimed at my knees. Too often throughout the day, I had heart-eyes for

Ross, turning moments romantic, when he might intend us only to be friends.

I don't want to hurt you. I don't think he understood that it hurt more to be rejected by him the other morning. Then again, I wouldn't want him to do anything he didn't want to do with me. I'd feel worse.

"I was thinking we could order dinner or—"

"No." I flick my wrist, pointing a wobbly finger between us. "I mean us. We never addressed that kiss. And your rejection the other morning said a lot."

"My rejection?" Ross's head rolls on the throw pillow, eyes wide as he stares at me. "I want you, Vee. Make no mistake about it. I just don't think we should cross that line."

"Why?" My voice cracks. Disappointment mingles with the ache in my chest. "I just want to understand what's wrong with me."

"Nothing, Vee. Absolutely nothing." Ross swings upward and shifts so he's facing me, knees spread and either side of mine. "It's not you. It's me."

I swallow against the sudden lump in my throat and will away the burn of tears.

"That didn't sound right." He clears his throat and takes my hands, digging his thumb into the backs of each of them. "Vee, I haven't been on a real date in years. One where I just had fun with someone. Doing something easy like enjoying the day, not putting on a show."

I nod, knowing I'd had the same sentiment.

"And I don't want to ruin what we have."

My head snaps upward. "A sleeping arrangement?"

"A friendship."

The term was almost worse.

"I'm not in the best place to start a new relationship, what with starting this job." He squeezes my hands. "But I'm not ready for us to end."

End. That was the word I was looking for. An ending to this affair. Like a summer love, that fades when September arrives. Only in this case, our situation ends when his season begins.

I could curse that Ross used me. That he's tossing me aside in a new way, but I've put myself in this position and I don't exactly regret it.

He made me no promises in the beginning. He never offered sex. I'm the one with a libido out of control lately. Because of the way he curls into me. Because of the way he cupped my throat. Because of the way he moved his thigh between my legs.

I want him. But in many ways, I understand what he isn't explaining. He isn't looking for sex. He can have that with anyone. He wants something deeper, and we have it.

As friends. The friend-zone is where we need to stay.

Slowly, I pull my hands from his.

"I understand."

Ross shakes his head. "I don't think you do, and I'm not explaining myself very well. You're the first woman I've been with where you don't *want* something from me. And I don't want to have sex for the sake of having sex. *We* aren't like that, Vee. You're important to me. More important than turning this into something that is only going to hurt in the end."

I want to believe he's trying to let me down gently. I'm the one who had a crush on him, not the other way around. Even if he says he wants me, he doesn't want sex to blur the line. The one that points like an arrow to his superstition fix. We only sleep together.

"I think this afternoon should count as us sleeping together."

"Vee." Ross takes my hands again, flipping them to face palm up this time, and digging his thumbs across the lifeline on each.

We only get one life. And in that life, we might only get one month with a man and that month was quickly coming to an end for me.

To save myself, I politely said, "I have my work as well. And I need to write tonight." Although I doubt I'll have any creative thoughts in my mind this evening. My brain will circle over and over about all Ross and I did, and all I thought we might be.

Ross watches me for a long minute before lifting my hands and pressing a lingering kiss into each of them. When he stands, his full height towers over where I remain on the ottoman. He brushes my hair with the back of his knuckles and cups the nape of my neck a second, squeezing once.

"I had fun today, sweetheart."

I nod, silently agreeing with him.

"The most fun I've had in nearly ten years."

The prickle in my eyes turns to a burning sensation. The threat of tears is very real and very near.

"Me, too, Ross Davis."

"I'll see you later, Vee."

I have no idea if he means tomorrow, the next night, or in place of goodbye. Saturday is only a few days away.

Suddenly, it doesn't feel like enough time to finish saving an entire baseball team.

Or myself from falling further in love with Ross.

Chapter 20

[Ross]

The moment I left her, I wanted to turn back. I should have turned back, but I wanted to respect her wishes, and the distance she was trying to put between us.

The day had been so great. I don't understand what happened. However, I only made things worse by admitting I want her but didn't want more from her.

I was sending her mixed signals again and frustrating myself even further.

When she left the couch for the bathroom, I'd been having the most amazing dream. One that involved both of us naked on those cushions. A dream I couldn't act upon but wanted to.

Disappointed in myself, I enter my empty hotel room. The vacant space with the prospect of a night of solitude does not settle well with me, and I'm instantly turning around.

Once I'm in the hallway, heading for the elevators, I see Felicity Sylver leaving Romero Valdez's room. The guys know better than to have a woman in their room, wife, girlfriend, or whatnot. She catches my eye while coming up to the elevator bank and I have to reroute for Romero's room.

He answers on the first knock.

"Coming back for more, ba—" He sputters to a halt when he sees me, and I take in his bare chest and bath towel at his waist.

"No women in your room."

"Ah, Coach, a man can't be all work and no play."

"Yes, he can," I argue, but realize I've been more work than play most of my life, even if some would say I *play* a game as work.

"Romeo has needs," he jokes, patting his chest, using the nickname he no doubt dubbed himself about his behavior with women. Casanova might be a better term for him. He seduces and uses and leaves women in his wake. However, the rumor is Felicity and him were an item before Ford and Felicity were a thing. Reunited lovers.

Wonder what Vee would say about that plot?

Just thinking of her has me regretting again that I left her place and having to deal with Romero further agitates me.

So an hour later, I'm not surprised to find my rented pickup truck parked in the lot of her condo, before I'm stalking back up the walk to Vee's door.

When the door opens on a flourish, like she was anticipating my return, my heart leaps to my throat.

I'm a man on a mission, though.

"We had a date, Vee. And as such, there's a piece I forgot." I step toward her, cup her face, and kiss her hard and fast.

Pulling back, I stare at her. "Every date ends with a kiss." I lower for her mouth again, going slower this time. Moving my lips in a way that lead hers, and sighing with relief when she doesn't push me away. Instead, she grabs onto my shirt, tugging me closer to her, and we stand in the open doorway kissing in a way that doesn't feel typical for a first official date.

We kiss like long-lost lovers. Reunited ones. Future ones.

I just don't know how to make that work.

When I finally pull back, we are both breathless. I still don't think we should move further down the baseline, keeping us perpetually on the bag at first, but I can't deny my desire to kiss her.

"So you came back for a kiss?"

"I came back for you." I kiss her again and lean over for the front door, shoving it hard to shut it. When it slams, I pull back again. "My room was too empty without you."

"That's . . . sweet."

I'm tired of being sweet but I don't mention that to Vee. Instead, I kiss her again, then lower my forehead to hers.

"I know you said you need to write, and I won't press if you tell me to leave again but—"

ELEVATOR PITCH

"Writing?" Vee glances up at her me, her blue eyes round and dilated, sparking with her attraction. She *tsks*. "What are words to kisses?"

I chuckle, recalling her comment about men and rocks.

"Give me four more nights, Vee. Please." *Don't say goodbye to me yet.* I know I originally asked for only one night. Then pushed for two. How do we suddenly only have four remaining nights?

"Sleeping with some kissing tossed in?" Her eyes are bright as she digs her teeth into her swollen lips.

"Sleeping with some kissing."

Then, I kiss her again.

Chapter 21

[Vee]

The Anchors record over the next three nights is up and down. Win. Loss. Loss. Despite Ross being at my place each night for sleep and kisses. The last time I made out with a man so often I was in high school. And Ross is insatiable with his mouth and tongue. Our bodies press together when our lips meet—as we stand in my entryway, as we lean over the kitchen counter, as we enter my bedroom—but his hands never wander. And we never kiss while horizontal, like on the couch, or in my bed.

By Friday, I'm a mess of struggling hormones and conflicting emotions.

But my writing is off the charts. My female character pulled up her proverbial big girl panties and has been leading me in all kinds of directions for her whirlwind romance.

Being my last day in Arizona, I attend a final spring training game. It's a beautiful desert afternoon, and with a margarita in hand, I settle into my seat. I'm wearing his classic Anchors jersey with the number 33 on it and his name on the back. My phone is also ready for any last-minute note-taking needs as it's the final time to soak up some inspiration from this stadium.

Ross tips up his chin in distant greeting from his position on the field. The man standing beside him, turns his head and stares in my direction. Eventually, he lifts a hand and waves over his shoulder.

Kip Garcia is almost as good looking as Ross. Maybe too good looking with green eyes and tattooed hands. I wave in response, chuckling as I do. Ross must say something that has Kip turning his head to stare at his fellow coach's profile. Then Kip laughs and turns back in my direction. Even from this distance, I see his wink.

Knowing they are discussing me, I should feel uncomfortable, but I don't. Ross admitted Kip knows about our arrangement. I broke down

ELEVATOR PITCH

and told Ross I'd mentioned the situation to Cassandra, who is sworn to secrecy as well.

Ross knew I was attending today's game and asked me to wait for him afterward. Unfortunately, the Anchors lose again, and I watch Ross slap the hands of his players, defeat heavy on his shoulders, before I wander to the prearranged spot to meet him.

There, I wait and wait and wait, checking and then triple checking my phone until Kip Garcia exits the management building and sees me on the sidewalk.

"Verona?"

I smile weakly. "Call me Vee."

"Vee." He smiles wide, displaying white teeth, before his brows pinch. "Are you still waiting on Ross?"

"Yeah. He told me to meet him here, but it's been a bit." I glance toward the vacant grass parking lot, and the cars lining the road leading away from the stadium.

"Shit. There was another altercation in the locker room, and we had to handle it. He was chatting with Ford Sylver when I finally got the other player to leave the room."

Romero Valdez, perhaps? I don't ask, not wanting to give away I know a team secret or two.

"I could let you in." Kip hitches his thumb toward the management building.

"No. That's okay. I think I'll just send Ross a text and head home."

"Yeah. I'm certain he'll be there shortly."

I'm ready to argue that I don't know what Kip is talking about or that Ross isn't coming over, but remembering he knows our arrangement, I simply smile.

"Rough game," I tell him.

He shrugs. "Can't win 'em all. It's how you play the game that matters." He pats his chest. "Heart." And then taps his head. "And head. That's why Davis is a good coach. He's got both for the game. Eyes always on the prize."

Strange how he holds his gaze on me for a long minute, and I'm tempted to ask what the two men were discussing on the ballfield before the game started and they were looking at me.

However, I don't ask. Instead, I say, "Safe travels back to Chicago."

"We don't leave until next week."

"I know. But I leave tomorrow."

"Oh." His brows lift before some thought hits him and then his thick brows crease. "Oh." He adds softly, "Oh, fuck."

We stare at one another, while I wonder what he's thinking before he finally says, "Safe travels to you, then, Vee. Will we see you in Chicago?"

"Maybe." It's the million-dollar question.

Kip warmly smiles. "Want me to walk you to your car?"

"No," I shake my head. "I'm good." And I step opposite Kip, taking a final moment to admire the now empty stadium and the quiet slowly surrounding it.

The silent vacancy feels strangely prophetic.

+ + +

Ross sends a slew of messages.

I'm so sorry.

Leaving now.

On my way.

Almost there.

His panic would almost be comical if it wasn't endearing. I'd received similar, sporadic messages from Cameron when he was alive, and in hindsight learned they were platitudes. Fillers to stall my concerns when my suspicion ran deep that he was having an affair. My gut sensed the truth.

When I open my front door for Ross near seven o'clock, he's still dressed in his coaching attire. He instantly tugs his cap from his head and spins to face me while I'm closing the door behind him.

"I'm so sorry." The breathless apology has me chuckling.

"Relax, Ross." But the expression on his face has me instantly concerned and my gaze lowers to a small leather duffle in his other hand. "What happened?"

"Fucking Valdez." He shakes his head. "I don't want to be presumptuous, but would you mind if I took a quick shower here and then I can tell you."

"Of course. Go ahead."

There's no greeting kiss like we've had the past few nights, but I forgive him. Ross is clearly agitated by this young team member. He stalks off toward the primary bedroom and enters the bathroom while I tidy up the living room where I'd opened my laptop and my tablet, jotting down a few last-minute ideas for the next chapter in my book.

When I enter the bedroom, I set my laptop on the dresser without thinking about the fact the bathroom has no door to close off the space from the bed area.

I *know* this about the room. I've been staying here for four weeks, and yet it still throws me off sometimes, and I find myself reaching for a door to close the barrier behind me when I enter the space.

Still, I call out, "Hey, Ross. Do you want me to order some dinner for you?"

And then I turn toward the wide entrance to the bathroom and catch a glimpse of Ross beneath the shower. The glass enclosure does nothing to hide his body. One hand braced high on the tile. His head bowed, face toward the floor. The spray of the shower streams over the back of his head and along his spine. And his other hand is lower, fisting himself.

A series of events happen at once.

I gasp.

Ross turns.

I freeze.

He shuts off the water.

And with his eyes locked on me, he opens the shower door, reaches for a towel and wraps it around his waist.

Tongue-tied, I'm pinned in place. I don't know what I was thinking. *I wasn't thinking.* Although the layout of this room has become so familiar to me.

"I—"

"Don't. Move."

I don't. I can't. I'm mesmerized by this broad body. His slick skin. His wet hair.

In my head, I'm apologizing and pointing to the other room, like I intend to step away. Instead, I'm mortified, and close my eyes a second.

In that time, Ross exits the bathroom and tips up my chin. In front of me, he's dripping wet. His chest is flat planes with rivulets of water streaming down his pecs and over sharp nipples. The towel wraps snug and low on his hips. A trail of hair disappears beneath the covering where he is still long and hard. So long. So hard.

"Vee." His voice is soft as I open my eyes and swallow hard.

"I'm so sorry. That was such a gross negligence of your privacy. An invasion of it." I swallow again. Shame firmly plants in my chest and roots in my belly. I can't believe I did this to him.

"Invade my privacy, Vee." His gaze dances between my eyes. "Because you invade my thoughts."

When his mouth crashes on mine, I'm startled out of my initial shock and plunged into deeper surprise. His lips are warm and insistent. His tongue instantly sneaking forward, seeking mine. His hand cups my jaw while the other wraps around my back and tugs me against him.

Instantly, the heat and moisture from his shower dampens the jersey I'm still wearing with his name on the back.

His mouth lowers for my jaw and chin, moving down to my neck where he nips me where the column curls toward my shoulder, and *holy cow*, does that feel amazing. My knees give out as his hand travels up my back to cup my nape. His other hand smooths along my throat, blazing after his mouth until he reaches the top button of the jersey.

"Let me see you, Vee."

"I thought you didn't want that?" I whimper as he continues to suck my skin and maneuver a button on the jersey. How am I trying to be rational when my brain is short circuiting while my clit is begging for attention?

"I'm done denying myself," he murmurs against my flesh before moving back to my mouth and kissing me. "Done denying you."

In the meantime, my hands have found his waist and smooth over his warm skin. Along his sides and over his lower back then rounding to his stomach, tracing over those abs until I find that sexy trail of hair.

"But is this smart?"

"Smartest decision I've made in a long time."

Another button pops open on my jersey and another, and I'm lost to the way his hand suddenly palms my breast, inside the jersey. He squeezes tight and plucks my nipple, still covered by my bra.

I gasp and his tongue dives deeper inside my mouth. My fingers have found the edge of his towel and I curl them into the material, tugging at him, wanting him closer to me.

"Let me taste you, Vee."

"Oh God," I purr. It's been so long since someone's mouth has been on me there. Too long.

I don't exactly answer him before he lifts me, sets me on the edge of the bed, and works his way down the remainder of the jersey to open it. Then he leans forward and kisses my belly. With a hand on my upper chest, he presses me back until I'm flat on the bed and he kisses me again.

I'm dizzy and delirious and Ross Davis is so delicious.

Abruptly, he pulls back and stands upright, then reaches for the button on my jean shorts when another reality hits.

"Wait." With my heart racing, my head is galloping to catch up. "I'm not . . . I mean, I never thought . . . So I . . ." I blow out an exasperated breath and just spit out what I'm trying to say. "I'm not waxed or tidy or scaped down there."

I mean, who would have thought Ross Davis would be going down on me? Certainly *not* me.

"If you think a little hair is going to keep me away from you, think again, sweetheart." He arches a brow while his eyes give a final ask for permission to proceed.

I nod once, sighing in relief when the button on my shorts pop open. Ross makes quick work of the zipper, and with a sharp tug, my shorts are removed.

He eagerly spreads my knees and leans forward, running his nose over my covered center.

"You smell incredible, beautiful."

Or did he say you smell incredibly beautiful? I don't know. I can't think straight. My brain is scrambled with anticipation and a twinge of nerves.

With his fingers in the waistband of my underwear, he removes them slower than he lowered my shorts, taking his time like he's unveiling a masterpiece. Once he drops them to the floor, he leans forward again and slides his finger through my slit.

"Fucking soaked," he hums, like he didn't expect it, didn't know what he does to me, didn't know how he's been working me up for days. Or maybe he's being smug because I'm nearly dripping.

His thumb toys with me, spreading me open and circling the slick folds before he hits that sacred spot. I suck in air.

He hums again, a satisfied sound, before he applies teasing pressure, tiny circles of torture that cause my hips to buck upward. He claps a hand on my inner thigh, holding me still before his face is between my legs. The sudden flick of his tongue has my hips jolting again.

"Stay still, sweetheart." Only his palms are suddenly restraining my spread thighs, pinning me in place as he works his magic with that tongue. Long laps. Short swirls. He drinks me in before diving deeper.

All kinds of sounds are escaping me. Purrs. Hums. Moans. And I can't move my legs which is only amplifying the pleasure.

Ross removes one hand from my thighs to join his tongue, and my leg snaps upward, bracketing his head. One long finger glides inward as he works my clit with his mouth.

"Ross," I groan, the sensation too much. Earth, wind, and fire at the same time.

ELEVATOR PITCH

His finger slides in and out before he adds a second one. He blows over my clit, flirting with what has already been teased, then his mouth is on me again, warm and slippery.

"I'm—" My breath catches. "Ross, I'm . . ." I can't get the words out, all coherent thought leaves me and in its place is a release so sweet, so refreshing, so languid, I float through the rush of flutters and coast along the dips. My legs cage Ross's head as I ride out the gentle storm raining from within me.

Eventually, I reach for his head, needing him to stop while never wanting him to let me go.

With a final lap and then a soft kiss directly to sensitive folds, he pulls back and glances up at me. Those desert-bright eyes are full of pride and something deeper, something darker.

"Fucking delicious," he murmurs, climbing up over me and taking my mouth again, kissing me hard and fast, tongue thrusting inward, forcing me to taste what he's done to me. The moment is heady, thrilling, and dirty, while I'm lost to how carnal and raw it feels.

With my legs spread, Ross is cradled against me, the bulge covered by his towel not a mystery. I hitch my hips, seeking friction against him, wanting him to feel the way I do.

He pulls back and glances down at me. "I want to be inside you, Vee. Feel you collapse again around me."

"This will take our sleeping arrangement to a new level," I warn him. A level he explicitly said he didn't want to enter.

"Leveling up then."

He shifts so his knees are outside the cradle of my thighs, then he's climbing upward, over me, stretching for the nightstand on the opposite side of the bed. Only with his reach, his towel comes loose, exposing the long, hard length of him. As he's close to my face, I turn to lick up his length.

Ross freezes. "Vee." He hisses.

I repeat the motion, wiggling my arm free until I can fist him. I tug and stroke his thick, solid length before opening wide and sucking the tip.

"Don't play with me, sweetheart."

He barely finishes his command and I draw him into my mouth, unable to take the full length of him.

"Fuck." His curse is a soft plea, a strained prayer, and I honor him by hollowing my cheeks and dragging up and down his length, twirling my tongue and further teasing him.

Not much time passes, before his fingers curl into my hair, gently forcing me to release him.

"Enough, Vee, or I'll spend down your throat when I want to go off inside you."

We should probably discuss what that means, but then I understand why he was stretching over me. His wallet is on the nightstand, and he's prepared for this moment. Once a gold packet is retrieved, he clambers back over me, settling on his knees between my spread thighs. His towel is long forgotten.

I watch as he rolls on the protection, not certain I've ever witnessed a man do such a thing. As he handles himself, my channel clenches, greedy for him, anticipating him inside me. When he finishes covering himself, he glances at me.

"Gotta say, fuckin' you while you're wearing that jersey is a dream."

I gaze down at myself. Jersey spread open, bra on display. He reaches around me and unfastens the clasp at my back.

"Do that trick where you take it off without removing the jersey."

With a wiggle of my arms, and a tug and a pull, I'm braless while the jersey remains. Ross falls to his arm, braced above me, while he lowers his mouth to a breast and his other hand holds himself lined up at my entrance. His tongue twirls around my nipple while I cup his head, combing my fingers through his hair.

Then he bites my nipple and thrusts inward.

I lurch upward, taking him to the hilt and clutching at him. "Ross," I gasp, startled by the sting, the shove, and the sudden rush of my libido.

Filling me, Ross pauses and glances down at where he's entered me. "I've been fantasizing about this moment for weeks."

"For weeks?"

"Every day. Every night. Sleeping beside you has been heaven and hell." He pulls back then rushes forward again.

"But this. This right here is next level." He exhales and stills, using his arms to support him above me. Then he rolls his hips in a way that his pubic bone rubs against my clit, winding me up and up and up again. My legs are spread as wide as they can, my clit presses against him, loving the friction, the spiral, the build.

"Ross." My breath catches once more. I don't typically let go in this position, but the weight of him over me, the warmth, the pressure, and I'm suddenly on the verge of that floating sensation once again.

With my hands on his shoulder blades, pressing at him as if I want him to collapse on top of me, I clutch and claw until the flutters release, the relief sharp and quick, but no less intense than the first time.

I cry out his name.

"Sweetheart," he groans, going wild now that I've been reckless. He moves back and forth, rushing in, while teasing to pull out. Then he stills and every jolt, every flinch, I feel buried within me.

A vein on his neck strains. His heart hammers. My name is a sweet cry. "Verona."

Then he collapses over me, blanketing me.

Memories flash through my head. A warm jacket on a rainy day. An apology kiss against my neck. A camera flash and a captured moment.

Ross Davis will always be all these things to me and now this.

If only I could keep him.

Chapter 22

April
Regular Season

[Ross]

Vee left in the early hours of Saturday morning.

I told her I could take her to the airport, but she had a rental car to return.

But I was desperate for every last minute.

After such an incredible night, Vee was suddenly shy, almost avoiding eye contact while we stood in the dark parking lot.

I'd placed her suitcase in the trunk and finally caught her attention when I cupped her face, forcing her to look up at me. "Are we good?" I didn't want to say goodbye. I wasn't good at them.

A weak smile graced her face. "We're good, Ross Davis. Good luck this season."

The implied finality twisted my gut again. I didn't want to let her go. I also didn't know how to keep seeing her. Spring training was nothing compared to the hectic schedule of a regular season. Sure, we'd both be back in Chicago, but I couldn't figure out how to make us work when I was still the new guy for the Anchors.

Maybe after the season? I didn't like the excuse or the amount of time to wait. It could be almost nine months before the season ends.

So once again, Verona Huxley slipped through my fingers, although I held onto them until I had to shut the driver door and stood in a quiet parking lot, watching her drive away.

As our final spring series ended in a three-game win, the Ws were bittersweet. I'd wanted to call Vee with every success, but I didn't.

She'd already done so much for me. Bolstered my confidence with her pep talks. Given me her time and her tongue. And then our final night, which was special, sacred even. That night had nothing to do with my original proposal. All I'd denied us imploded into an incredible night I'll never forget.

"You alright?" Kip asked as we sat in the airport, waiting on our late-night flight back to Chicago.

"I will be," I lied. Because I'd fallen, hard and fast, and for the first time in my life, I was unsure of myself and whether I was worthy of a woman like Verona. A woman who hadn't asked for anything in return for all she'd ended up giving me.

"Why don't you call her?" he encouraged, concern in his voice.

"And say what?" *My superstition was all for naught.* Sleeping with Vee had turned into more of a personal mission than a new ritual.

Could I tell her my heart missed her? I'd wanted to feel something again, and I felt it.

Loss.

It wasn't fair to Vee. I'd been so back and forth, so hot and cold. I didn't have a plan for forward when all I wanted was to go backward and relish each of our nights together better.

"No, this is for the best," I whisper, ignoring the phone in my hand, fingers twitching to pull up her number. My screen saver was already the image of me kissing the side of her head and her surprised reaction. I was only torturing myself and I deserved the punishment.

"Man," Kip chuckled beside me. "Whoever said love is a battlefield hasn't been on a baseball diamond."

I had no idea what he meant, but my heart ached nonetheless, like I'd fought in a war, and lost.

If love was a baseball diamond, then my self-doubt just caused me to bench myself.

+ + +

It is said that March comes in like a lion and goes out like a lamb, but that didn't feel true when Mother Nature had other plans for the final days of the month. A snowstorm hit Chicago, delaying our return flight from Arizona to home. Once back, the team hustled to drop bags, kiss families, and hit the field. We only had two days before we are on the road again, heading to St. Louis for opening day.

Baseball season officially begins.

However, the real celebration happens when the calendar flips to April and opening day occurs in our home stadium.

There's no place like home, or in my opinion, the homelike feel of a place such as Anchor Field. The iconic stadium is one of the few landmark originals remaining among professional baseball teams. Set in a neighborhood north of downtown Chicago, the pride of this stadium is the ivy that lines the outfield wall, plus the bleachers above the twining vines, and a manually monitored score board that soars above the diamond.

And during this first home game, all I can think about is Vee.

Is she here? Has she brought a date? Does she miss me as much as I miss her?

Ten days have passed since our spectacular night together.

When the game begins, my enthusiasm for the season spikes as the Anchors start off strong until a pop fly arches toward centerfield.

Ford Sylver rushes forward from his position. Romero Valdez hightails it backward from his spot at short stop, then he spins to face Ford. Somehow the ball drops between them like something you'd see in a little league game.

Within seconds, Ford is in Romero's face, finger pointed at his teammate in a move that can only be described as aggressive.

My head is already shaking, recalling all the shit that has gone down so far this season between these two men over a woman.

Then, Romero reaches out, captures Ford's hand and twists. Ford's left arm is behind him in a move where I can imagine Romero demanding that Ford cry 'uncle'. Only his left arm is his *bad* arm. Ford drops to his knees.

"Aw, fuck," someone yells within the dugout.

"What the fuck?" another cries out, while a few of the guys empty the bench.

ELEVATOR PITCH

The animosity between Ford and Romero has placed a divide of loyalty among the men. Most favor Ford, as one of our captains and a veteran of the Anchors.

"Get back," I yell, clearing the dugout myself while Dalton Ryatt, my bench coach, tries to hold guys off, warning them to stay put.

As I cross the field behind the team trainer because my star centerfielder isn't standing up, my stomach flips. I only have a few seconds to make a decision here.

"What happened?" I snap before asking if Ford is okay. The pinch in his face and the way he's gingerly supporting his left arm, his throwing arm, already answers any question about his condition. He's in pain and has been since training started. I'm cognizant of Ford's medical history. He had extensive rehab over the last season on his left shoulder but he's creeping toward the need for corrective surgery. His age isn't helping either. He'll be turning thirty-eight this summer.

"I shouldn't have gotten in his face," Ford grits through the pain, accepting his responsibility in the wrong that happened. However, the altercation didn't stop with words.

We're men. We get heated, especially under the guise of competition. Typically, that competitive spirit is between teams, not *among your own teammates.*

I appreciate Ford admitting his fault but more happened on this field than a few harsh words and a pointed finger. Valdez responded.

And his physical reaction needs to be dealt with next. Valdez has been a thorn in my side since this season started. Taking liberties he doesn't have. Treating others with disrespect. Rude comments. Lewd motions. He doesn't represent someone I would consider a team player, nor is he someone I want on my team. However, I didn't make the initial choice to hire him. He was here when the team became mine. Now I'll have a potential investigation into intentional harm to determine if Romero purposely twisted Ford's *bad* arm.

"Thoughts?" I snap at the team trainer.

"He's out." A simple nod suggests we discuss the damage to Ford later.

With Ford closing his eyes, *he* knows the truth is as plain as the ivy on the wall behind him. He's finished for this game, and out for the foreseeable future, if not the entire season.

With the assistance of the medical staff, Ford stands and the crowd claps in relief when I'm certain most fans are still stunned.

How often does one see player against player *from the same fucking team*?

Trying to keep my head up, I follow behind Ford and the medical team who assist Ford to the dugout before he slips into the tunnel leading to the locker room.

For now, I have eight other guys to focus on and a substitution to make.

"Dane," I call out as I near the bench. "You're up." I hitch my thumb toward the field. We only have a few seconds to warm up the rookie we pulled up from the minors to shadow Ford for this type of incident.

Not necessarily one where his teammate takes him out, but Ford's arm not being at its best has been a concern, especially after a collision between the same two men caused an issue during the training season.

Stedman Dane is as green as they get. Small town kid in a big city. Almost as young as my sons.

"Think he's ready?" Dalton mutters beside me as I take my position in the corner of the dugout, up against the fence.

"He's gonna have to be, isn't he?" We don't have a choice because Ford is finished.

Dalton scoffs. The game recommences and while my heart goes out to Ford, because the older one gets, the harder it is to play this game, my thoughts rush to Vee, wishing I could talk to her about my concerns.

The Anchors are not off to a good start this season.

+ + +

With defeat in our hearts, the Anchors lose the game after the reckless display of poor sportsmanship between teammates.

While I refuse to let panic settle into my bones, panic is settling into my bones.

"Fuck," I mutter as I wait for the team to clear out of the dugout before following them through the tunnel to the locker room. I'd wanted one final glance around the stadium in hopes of locating Vee, but the scan was hopeless in a sea of retreating fans. I had no idea where her season tickets were placed anyway.

In the somber locker room, I address the team with what went well and what we need to work on with a final word of encouragement.

"Let's remember that we're a team." I glare at Valdez who has the grace to lower his head, but his mouth curves into a smirk. I narrow my gaze at him, knowing I'll have to deal with him privately when what I'd really like to do is kick him off the team in front of the other members, making an example out of him and his shitty behavior. His actions are inappropriate and intolerable. "And as such, that means we play together. Our opponent is the other team, not each other."

I don't need to remind them collectively, but as spirits are divided, I want the men to rein in their loyalties.

"Your dedication is to the Anchors." With a heavy exhale, I add, "However, any good thoughts or prayers for our teammate are welcome."

I won't speak out yet about Ford's ability to return or not.

First, I have a contractually obligated press conference to attend.

Then, an ass named Romero Valdez to chew out.

Then I'll be able to check on Ford.

And after all that, what I really want is to find Vee and snuggle in a bed beside her, where she might remind me this is what I wanted—to coach the Anchors—and then she'd give me one of her pep talks.

One that might end with more than just words, but with our bodies tangled together.

+ + +

In the medical room with Ford, a messenger who looks no more than sixteen-years-old knocks on the door. Anxiety is written in his expression and his voice quivers when he says, "Coach, I've got a message for you."

Fuck. I'm assuming the front office wants "a word" about the unsportsmanlike conduct that occurred on the field today. A reminder that they took a risk on me, or I've been given a second chance, *blah-blah-blah*. Although, I'm not so cavalier about the position I've been granted.

"Yeah," I mutter. "What is it?"

The poor kid swallows hard and lowers his eyes, fiddling with a slip of paper in his hands, before saying, "Tell him nightlight was here."

"What the fuck?" Kip chuckles, having found his way to the medical room as well.

"Women come up with all kinds of crazy shit." Max Bernard, the head trainer, huffs.

I arch a brow at the young messenger. "Was it a woman?"

He nods.

"Nightlight?" Max grunts. "Sounds like a stripper name."

Eyes wide, I glare at Max. He knows I'm not into that kind of thing. Respect to the women who do it, and whatever to the men getting off watching them, but that path isn't my pleasure.

Max clears his throat. "Or like the kind of thing you plug in at night so you can see in a dark room."

With gritted teeth, Ford adds, "My kid needs one of those to sleep at night."

Instantly, Kip and I meet eyes.

"Shit," Kip mutters, lowering his gaze while smiling.

And my heart rate soars when the messenger hands me the slip of paper.

Vee had been here.

Chapter 23

[Vee]

"What a game." Cassandra sighs while glancing at her phone, watching a replay of the aggressive arm twist that sent Ford Sylver to his knees.

My best friend cringes as she stares at the screen.

"Why do you keep watching that?" I admonish her while standing in my kitchen. Cassandra sits at the square high-top table that separates us in the small space.

"It's like a trainwreck I can't look away from."

My thoughts race to the man in charge of these men. So many decisions for Ross to make. How does a team come back from such aggression among members? Will Ford recover? Rumors have it his left shoulder has been a concern for a while. Will Romero get booted from the team? In my opinion, he's a terrible human being.

Reaching over the table, I cup my hand over her phone to cover the screen, and demand, "Well, look away. I feel terrible for Ford as both a captain and senior member of the team. Not to mention that Romero Valdez is a shit-stirrer."

Cassandra wrinkles her nose. "But he's so fine."

I scrunch my nose in return. "He's an ass."

"He has a nice one."

"Would you stop?" I chuckle while releasing her phone. "We don't foam at the mouth over adulterers."

Cassandra sighs. "True that. So, let's talk about Ross Davis and *his* fine ass instead."

"Let's not," I counter, because I don't want to think about Ross.

Ten days. *Ten freaking days* of nothing.

If I wanted more evidence that our arrangement ended, a stamped 'expired' on a contract would be less obvious than this silence.

Then again, I haven't reached out to him either. What does one say to a man who rocked your world, not once but twice in a night, and then didn't call the next day or the typical three days later? Is it still a standard three days after one has sex with someone? I'm so out of tune with dating, yet we aren't dating. We were only supposed to be sleeping together.

Obviously, Ross didn't want more from me. He didn't want to level up and start a relationship or call us anything other than what we were—a convenient tryst.

And as much as I want to hate myself for having sex with him, I don't. That night was special. Ross made me feel beautiful. While our first time was a rush of sensations and frantic energy, the second time was more an exploration of each other.

His fingertips traced over my body. My palms memorized him.

I shiver at the memory. While I'd told Cassandra I had sex with Ross, I tried to downgrade the experience, brushing past the confession, and skipping the finer details. Cassandra wanted more information but something in my face must have told her not to ask.

She'd been a pillar for me through everything with Cameron, and I didn't want to turn into that overly dependent friend again. This time, the choices had been mine. I'd willingly had sex with Ross Davis, and I hadn't done it for notoriety. I didn't want to share the night's happenings like he was just a notch on my bedpost.

Cassandra knew me better than that anyway. After Cameron's death, Ross makes only the third man in ten years. The statistic wasn't impressive, compared to my best friend, the perpetual bachelorette attracted to younger men.

"But you haven't talked about him at all," Cassandra pouts.

"What's there to say? He didn't call. He's done."

Cassandra sits taller on her stool. "Well, that's not how it works. No one ghosts my best friend and gets away with it, unless he is a ghost, and that'd be a good thing because it spares me the mess of killing him."

"You're ridiculous." I laugh.

"And he owes you an explanation."

I tilt my head. "But does he? He didn't ask for more. He didn't promise it either. It was just sex."

The declaration is easier said than my true feelings about Ross and that night. About the life-changing, body-reassuring, glorious sex we had.

I shrug and correct myself. "An arrangement."

"A fucking stupid one," Cassandra tacks on. "And lots of good it's done him to dump you. The Anchors lost their first three games. And look what happened today." She wiggles her phone in the air, once more referencing the altercation between teammates.

"*That* had nothing to do with me." I ignore the sting of her words about Ross. "The Anchors are just having a rough start. And he didn't dump me."

It was a mutual parting of the ways, right?

And today's display between Sylver and Valdez looked like more than a bad patch of grass, though. More like black ice on a slick road on the top of a mountain where the lack of shoulder is due to a steep cliff.

"Besides," I continue. "Are you suggesting I continue sleeping with Ross to save the team?" Even though she just called our arrangement stupid, she appears to be leaning in favor of continuing the practice.

"Look, sometimes you just have to take one for the team," Cassandra says. "Or in this case take the team's coach." Cassandra sticks her tongue in her cheek, making a lewd motion which only causes me to laugh.

"So, I'm to continue *having sex* with Ross Davis to save the Anchors?"

"A woman has to do what a woman has to do." Cassandra shakes her head, false sympathy in her expression. "And you know I'd volunteer as tribute, but something tells me you're the 'it' girl." With a hand at her chest, she sighs with mocking compassion. "Oh, the hardship of being you."

I scoff. "Clearly, I'm not *it*. And I don't want to be needed only for sex."

Cassandra and I glare at one another before bursting into laughter.

Why am I even complaining about sex with an incredibly built and sexually talented man?

Wait, I know the answer to this one. Because my feelings are in the way.

"So, if Ross Davis knocked on your front door, and said he wanted to have sex with you again, you'd turn him away?"

"He's not going to knock on my door and say, 'I want to sleep with you, Verona'." I drop my voice to imitate his rugged sandpapery tone.

"No. He might say, *I missed you, Vee. I can't live without you, Vee. I want you in my life, Vee.*"

My responding chuckle is bitter and raw while the sting of her teasing turns into a piercing pain. "That won't happen, so I don't need to think about it."

Because I have thought about those statements. *For ten days.* I've hoped for Ross to magically appear and wished for those sentiments to cross his lips. And nothing.

Silence.

The call button from the exterior of the building buzzes in my apartment and Cassandra and I both whip our heads in the direction of the front door. When our eyes meet, we break into laughter again, like schoolgirls high on adolescence.

"That was so freakin' freaky," she whispers, eyes still wide and focused on me.

"Probably mistaken delivery," I state then ignore the buzzer a second time as I'm not expecting anyone. The delivery person will eventually get the correct button.

My apartment building is in your typical Chicago six flat with two apartments on every floor opposite each other. I'm on the first floor which is raised above street level and faces the postage-stamp sized yard.

"Anyway—" I start but an insistent knock on my front door has me holding my tongue. "What the heck?"

I step away from Cassandra and walk down the narrow hallway to the door. Peering through the peephole, because I'm a single woman living alone and I'd never answer the door for a stranger, I flatten against the barrier as if *he* can see me.

Because once again, the last person I expect to see on my doorstep is the person standing on the other side of this door.

"Who is it?" Cassandra asks, her voice a mysterious hush, while standing at the opposite end of the narrow passage leading from my kitchen to the front entrance. "Vee-Vee?"

"Cee-Cee," I whisper, glancing down the stretch of the hall to her. "It's Ross."

"Well, it's about fucking time he showed up." With speed I hadn't anticipated, my friend rushes toward me, shoves me out of the way and opens my front door wide before glaring into the interior hallway. With her hands on her hips, she says, "You're late, mister." Like she's the one who's been waiting on him.

"I-I'm looking for Verona Huxley."

I step out from behind the door at the same time Ross leans back to check the numbers beside the door frame. As his gaze drifts back to the open doorway, his eyes catch on me, and he fights a smile. Standing before me, he wears snug jeans and a dress shirt, sleeves rolled to his elbows, exposing the colorful ink on his forearm, and looking sinfully hot, while holding a bottle of wine and a large bouquet of wildflowers.

"Vee." Whispered like a breath of fresh air on a warm day, I hate how the sound of my name in his rough voice clogs with relief.

"Ross." My responding call is more like someone has a chokehold on my throat.

He clears his. "I got your message."

"What message?" I hadn't called or texted him, not wanting to look desperate or dejected. After the three-day threshold on phone calls had passed, I didn't think there was any way of appearing one way or the other if I'd reached out to him. Needy or hurt versus flirty and wanton. I was struggling to find the medium ground labeled indifferent.

Ross doesn't take his eyes off me, but he smirks while tilting his head. "Nightlight."

I stare back at him, completely confused. "Nightlight?"

"Yeah, nightlight." His smile grows larger, not a hint of remorse or uncertainty or caution.

I turn toward Cassandra, my brows severely pinched, like *can you believe this guy?* Maybe he got hit in the head with a ball today.

"So," Cassandra drags out. "I'm the best friend." She extends her hand and Ross awkwardly shifts the wine bottle to the hand holding flowers to shake. "Cassandra Culpére." When their hands clasp, she holds a little longer than necessary and leans toward him. "Don't make me hurt you because you hurt her. Here's your second chance and only warning."

"Cassandra!" I croak.

She turns toward me. "Using my full name doesn't scare me, Vee-Vee." Then she wiggles her fingers in a wave and brushes past Ross.

"Cee-Cee?" My voice drops, confusion etched in the cry as I watch her descend the inner staircase.

"Keep the light on, Vee-Vee." She laughs to herself while Ross and I watch her disappear.

Like a lightbulb flickering on, the situation illuminates.

"Cassandra," I groan louder. *What did she do?*

"She's . . . fierce," Ross interjects, still focused on where Cassandra descended.

"You have no idea," I whisper, standing in my apartment while Ross remains in the hallway.

"So, your message . . ." He turns toward me.

"Was not from me." I glance toward the flowers in his hand which he holds upside down by the stems, wine bottle wedged between his fingers on the same hand. "I'm not sure what nightlight means, but it's evident Cassandra did something."

Ross softly chuckles before rubbing his knuckles underneath his chin, the move an anxious one. "So, you didn't send a message to tell me you were at the game or give me your address." He pulls a scrap of paper from his back pocket which I rip from between his fingers and scan.

My address is written in Cassandra's scribbled handwriting.

My mouth falls open. Speaking of killing people and turning them into ghosts, I'm going to unalive my best friend. What the hell was she thinking?

"No. I think this falls to my *former* best friend." I huff and lean against the open door while Ross and I stare at one another. The seconds tick by. I can smell his spicy cologne and freshly showered scent despite the distance between us.

"So, you weren't at the game?"

"No, I was at the game."

"And you saw what happened?"

"Who didn't see it?" I remind him.

Between the attendees at the game, plus the streaming service's live coverage, and all the sports news channels sharing the scene, not to mention it's making the clock app where Cassandra had been watching the replay in various meme forms, I'm not certain there is anyone left who hasn't seen what happened at Anchor Field today.

Ross hangs his head and swipes his hand over his short hair. "Vee, can I please come in?"

Cassandra's words come back to me.

"So if Ross Davis knocked on your door, and said he wanted to have sex with you again, you'd turn him away?"

I'm not turning him away because I can be the bigger person, but I don't trust myself to let him in. Like the big bad wolf standing on my doorstep, the only thing I want him huffing and puffing is an apology, and the blowing thing should happen on a part of me he won't get near again.

"I'm not having sex with you to save your team."

Ross's brows lift so high his forehead furrows. "I'm not here for sex, Verona."

I snort.

"That wasn't a snortle." His brows shift to a deep divot, like he's disappointed.

"No, Ross. It wasn't a snortle, and this isn't an open door to sex." I wave at the space between us.

"I know. I'm sorry. Can we just talk? I miss you, Vee."

The words instantly remind me of Cameron. His pleas. His regrets. But Ross isn't Cam. And I hate how my heart flutters. How he's repeating what Cassandra predicted. *"He might say I missed you, Vee."*

"Did Cassandra put you up to this?" I hate that I'm questioning him. That I distrust both his intentions and my best friend's generosity because I don't need a pity chat with Ross.

His eyes widen. "How could she put me up to anything? I just met her five seconds ago, and she threatened to cut off my balls if I hurt you."

"She threatened to kill you actually."

"Same thing," he corrects.

"You already hurt me. I'm sure your balls are still intact."

Ross's expression instantly falls despite my joke. Lowering his head again, the action one of shame, he pauses a second before looking up at me again. His eyes full of remorse. "I'm so fucking sorry, Vee. I shouldn't have let you walk away from me a second time."

My heart skips. I've heard apologies before from him. I want to be fierce like my best friend but I'm finding I'm weak when it comes to Ross giving me those sorrowful blue-eyes and slowly crooking up one side of his mouth, a weary smile taking over his face.

"Let me come in and apologize properly."

Properly would mean make up sex but we have nothing to make up. We didn't fight. We didn't even disagree. We came together as two consenting adults and then separated with an unspoken agreement. The sleeping arrangement contract was completed.

Still, there's something in the way Ross is looking at me. Hesitant while hopeful. Sheepish while sincere.

"Oh, fine." I press off the door and step aside, allowing Ross to enter my place, which strangely reminds me of all the other entrances he's made into my life.

Into my hotel room.

Into my Arizona rental.

Now, he's stepping into my home, and this is his last opportunity.

Strike three, and he'll be out on the curb.

Chapter 24

[Vee]

Ross steps into my medium-size living room and spins in a slow circle, taking in the large bay window overlooking the city side-street. My charcoal gray couch is littered with bright colored throw pillows. A large-ish television sits on top of a light-colored wood cabinet. Two high back chairs stand side by side with a dainty antique table between them like a cozy sitting space. My place is feminine as it is only me until Hannah comes home for a short summer visit between semesters.

Finally, he faces me and lifts the bouquet of flowers. "For you."

Flowers are always a sketchy gift, especially when it comes to apologies, as in, they aren't one, and Cameron gave them often as a cover for his conscience.

"I didn't take you for a flowers man," I state, accepting the bouquet and bringing the vibrant blooms to my nose. The array of spring flowers was not a cheap collection from a local grocery store.

Ross shrugs. "There are lots of things about me that might surprise you." His eyes don't leave mine and a shiver runs down my spine.

"Let me put these in water and get some glasses for that wine."

Ross glances down at the bottle in his other hand as if he's forgotten he brought something else with him. He nods, but then he follows me to my kitchen where his presence fills the small space.

While I fill a pitcher with water for the flowers and arrange them inside the container, Ross makes himself at home, opening a couple drawers until he finds a bottle opener, and does the honors to open the wine bottle and pour us each a glass.

Our motions feel rather domestic, like a couple comfortable with one another after years of living together.

Instantly, I scold myself for the thought, not wanting to get ahead of myself again with this man.

With my head, I motion for him to follow me back to the front room, but he helps himself to the seat Cassandra vacated in the kitchen.

"What can I do for you, Ross Davis?"

Ross digs his teeth into his lower lip and scans me from top to toe. "You can't lead with that kind of question, Vee."

"Then you lead. What do you want?" The question is harsher than it should be, but I can't find much grace for Ross. I'm sorry his team lost and I'm sorry his team members don't get along, but none of that is my concern. *He's* the manager.

"I should have called." He sighs, staring down at the wine glass on the table where his thick hands cup the stemless glass. "But I didn't and that's on me."

I don't respond.

"The thing is, Vee, I miss you in my bed." My mouth falls open and his expression turns stricken. "That didn't come out right."

"It certainly didn't, especially as I've never been in *your* bed. You've always been in mine." Like I'm some little secret. His superstition keeper.

Ross clears his throat. "Sweetheart, I didn't want to bring you to my hotel room. It wasn't . . . personal. Comfortable."

I tilt my head. "But that's how we met."

Ross wearily smiles again. "I know. And that night changed everything." He glances up at me. "But a hotel room wouldn't cut it again. The rooms can be so cold and nondescript. At least, at your place, at the rental, the sheets had your scent on them. They were softer, or maybe that was just my bedfellow." His smile grows stronger. "Plus, we weren't having some torrid affair. I wasn't keeping you a secret. I was just keeping you to myself."

He sighs and glances back at his wine glass. "You're the first woman who hasn't wanted something from me. Didn't have an agenda by being with me. And I just found more peace and contentment in *your* bed."

I'm fortunate I'm sitting because otherwise I might melt on the floor.

Then, Ross adds, "I meant what I said, Vee. I miss you. I miss talking to you and hanging out with you."

My shoulders lower, the tension tightening my back lessens a little more. Because I miss him, too.

Still. "So, you want back in my bed?"

He sheepishly glances away. "It's a little more complicated than that, isn't it?"

"Is it?" I arch a brow. "Because I won't have sex with you for superstitious reasons."

Ross's head lifts, his eyes wide. "Okay."

"Okay?" I huff. "That's it."

He sits taller, straightening his elbows while not removing his hands from the stemless wineglass. "I know the superstition seems silly. And Kip has his theories."

"What are his theories?"

"That my head needs to be focused on the field. That my heart should be on that diamond."

I nod, agreeing with his friend and coaching partner.

"But the thing is, I'm better with you around me. Superstition or not, it feels *right* having you in my corner to talk to each night."

He wasn't saying holding me or sharing a bed together feels right. But should I split modifiers?

There's something strangely comforting about Ross in my corner as well. He listened to me talk about writing and publishing. He showed interest in learning about my girls. He doesn't mind my quirks, often finding them endearing.

"I want you in my life, Vee. How ever you'll allow me."

Is this some weird voodoo? He's two for three from what Cassandra suggested he might say to me.

And who doesn't need another friend in their life? If we take sex out of the equation, I can keep Ross in a corner, right?

"So, we chat each evening then. No bed required." What do the kids call that? *Talking to someone*, in place of labeling their relationship status as dating. However, just like sleeping with Ross meant only sleeping, talking to one another is only going to mean we chat.

"If I'm the team manager's uncertified superstition keeper, do I get a special uniform?"

Ross chuckles and arches his brow. "Someone still has a coaching staff jacket."

Hmm. A souvenir I won't be giving back.

"And what do I get out of this new arrangement?" Because while I didn't ask for anything in return the first time, I want some reassurance this is a balanced proposal this round.

"What do you want?" His voice drops, a bit salacious, a lot sexy, but I'm not asking for sexual favors as *false* compensation.

"I want to pick your brain."

His eyes widen once more. "How so?"

"Since I've returned home, I'm stumped again in my writing." Could be that sometimes it's difficult to write romance when you feel like your romantic life is flailing. Or that I suddenly have my own experience in superstition. Without a certain spring training facility, or possibly the head coach for that team in my life, I'm experiencing a different type of losing streak. A loss of words.

"I want to ask you questions, without judgment, for research purposes."

"For your book?" His mouth quirks up on one side.

"Yes. You aren't my main character, but I still want to better understand a man's perspective."

"Okay." He draws out the word, as if hesitating to commit.

"On subjects like dating and sex. Not that the two are necessarily inclusive."

His brows severely crease. "Is this another two-men-sharing-one-woman thing?" He chuckles but the sound is more like he's being strangled and his bright eyes storm over. He almost looks angry.

"The semantics of that statement should be one woman pleasured by two men." I dismissively wave a hand. "I want to know *things*."

"Like?" Hesitation once again.

"How does it feel to kiss a woman? What emotion is involved? What's it like to touch her for the first time? To place your fingers there." I drop my gaze. "Or enter her."

Heavy silence fills my small kitchen. An empty sound as thick as Ross's fingers but as flavorful as our red wine. An electric energy crackles between us.

"Fuck, Vee." Ross exhales hard and scrubs his palm over his face before staring at me. "And this is what you want from me? I spill guy-secrets in exchange for you just talking to me."

I wrinkle my nose. "Sounds kind of detached, doesn't it?"

Ross stares at me long and hard for a moment, then he slowly stands. "In order for it not to be detached, I might need to give examples to express my answers."

With one step, he's before me, turning my stool so I face him.

"Like physical props?" I ask.

Ross hums, placing his hands on my knees and spreading them, then he moves between my legs. He cups my jaw.

"Question one. How does it feel to kiss a woman." He isn't asking.

Instead, he leans forward and presses his lips to mine. Featherlight at first. A whisper of a kiss that has me gaping in surprise before he dives in. His tongue invades my mouth. His lips crush mine. He kisses me like he kissed me the first time, when we were both startled by our response to one another. He kisses me like he did the last time before I left Arizona, when it felt like he was memorizing every swipe and swirl.

I try to school myself. Remind myself this is for research purposes, and I'm his willing guinea pig. But I'm getting as much as I'm giving in this kiss. Which is everything. All my hurt from Ross. All my happiness. He's been a constant contradiction, confounding yet surprisingly compassionate. He seems to appreciate who I am and accept what I do for him.

I'm a good friend.

With that thought, I pull back, cutting the kiss short, surprising Ross who chases my mouth, giving me one more nip before letting me go. His eyes are hooded. His lips swollen. His mouth slowly curls as I cover my own with shaky fingers.

"It's like sipping wine," he begins his instruction while rubbing his thumbs along my cheekbones. "A combination of tart and sweet. A balance on the tongue of tangy and tantalizing. A burst of flavor and then the slow swallow of warmth. The best is when the sensation lingers, like a phantom kiss, making my mouth water and want more."

His gaze drops to my mouth, the look ravenous, like he wants to strip me bare and enter me right here on this wobbling kitchen stool. I swallow hard, then I lick my lips like I can taste all the sensations he described.

"You aren't even a writer." I swallow hard, the warm comfort he mentioned clogs my throat. "And yet that was good." I clear my throat. "Good description. Good example." *A-plus-plus.*

"What can I say, I enjoy the finer things in life." He strokes my cheekbones once more and I remember him telling me something like that once before. "And you, sweetheart, are one of those fine things."

Oh, he's good. Very good. And I'm in trouble if I don't rein myself in. I should remind him we aren't talking about me. This is for informational purposes. For fictional characters.

Instead, I say nothing and lean back, but I can only pull away so far as the wall is directly behind my seat. My head taps it as I attempt to free myself from the constraints of his clasp and the invasion of his scent, not to mention the stirring buzz lingering from that kiss. Talk about wine analogies.

Ross's hands slowly retreat from my face, and he stands taller. "For insurance purposes, I think I'll hold off on answering the other questions for now."

"Yep," I choke out. If he provides any more examples, we're going to be naked on the floor and I can't allow Ross to expose me like that again.

"Then I'll call you tomorrow?"

ELEVATOR PITCH

I nod, preparing to walk him to the door but afraid to let go of the seat of the stool. I hadn't realized I'd been clutching it so tightly, holding myself back from touching him, from pulling him closer to me.

"I'll show myself out," he finally says, and I'm left sitting in my kitchen, wondering what just happened.

Did he kiss me to get what he wanted, or did he kiss me because he wants me?

Chapter 25

[Vee]

For the next week, Ross and I talk after his games which is late at night compared to spring training. The Arizona games were typically played during the afternoons, but the season games are more often in the evening, especially during the week.

By the end of the first home series, the Anchors had won two of three games and social media is breathing easier on the team's potential for success under their new leader.

Additionally, these are Anchor fans who will be loyal no matter who they hate or admire on a team, and it's become clear many people are not in favor of Romero Valdez and his antics. He's been suspended for his actions toward a teammate.

The announcement also came that Ford will be on the injury list for a few months, citing surgery and recovery time as the reason.

Of course, Ross told me most of this himself. He opened up to me about his concerns for his team's morale. His personal dislike of Romero's attitude. His heartbreak for Ford Sylver.

"He's a good guy. One I looked forward to coaching because of his leadership as well as his skill. Plus, I know what it's like to go out on a fizzle instead of in a blaze of glory."

Ross left pitching the year the Anchors won the pennant. He went out with a flaming inferno. Then again, his personal life had been smoldering embers while Ford's circumstances sound like a dumpster fire. I don't mention my concern that he's falsely compared the differing scenarios. Instead, I listen.

And every night Ross surprises me by asking, "How's the writing going?"

And I begrudgingly offer a variety of adjectives.

Slow.
Better.
Horrible.

ELEVATOR PITCH

Decent.

Until one night I admit, "I think I need a change of scenery." Like being in Arizona, specifically at the Anchor spring training stadium, where inspiration struck, I need a change of view.

For now, my characters are stuck. Literally.

I have him in her shower, and she thought she was being burglarized because she'd returned home to the water running. She's entered the bathroom with a baseball bat in hand, instead of calling 9-1-1, like any rational woman. Then he pulls back the shower curtain, finished with the shower and naked as the day he was born, skin steamy and slick, looking sexy as fuck.

He screams. She screams.

And somehow, I was interrupted while writing this scene and can't figure out what should happen next. The almighty, ominous question for two fictional characters attracted to each other—to have sex or not to have sex?

"Need a place to go?" Ross interjects, knowing I sometimes visit coffee shops or local libraries, just to get out of my apartment.

I shrug, although he can't see me. "Got a recommendation?" My old haunts don't seem to be sparking any new creativity.

"How about staying at my place?"

"What?" I choke on a sip of water. I'm sitting upright in my bed, comfortable in the same position I've been in each night when we chat. Like this is my therapist seat, although I was teasing about being his uncertified psychiatrist. Ross and I are friends. Friends who have carnal knowledge of one another, but friends, nonetheless.

"We play back-to-back out of state, so I'll be out of town for the next two series."

I hear sheets rustling. We don't discuss our *talking* positions. Where we sit, or what we're wearing, but I picture Ross laying in his bed, wearing only his boxer briefs. In my head, his room is dark, masculine, and moody.

"You could come here. Hang out. Use my place during the day or spend the night."

"Ross." I chuckle. "Aren't you worried I'd go through your things? Invade your privacy," I state, sounding eerie, as if I'd do such a thing when I wouldn't. "That I'd sleep in your bed like some superfan with a crush on you."

Oh, wait, I am that. And the idea of sleeping in Ross's bed without him should not appeal to me.

Ross laughs, lighthearted and easy. "First of all, I told you, you already invade my thoughts, so I'm not worried about my privacy."

My mouth falls open, surprised he remembered saying such a thing and wondering if he still feels the same way.

"And second, I want you in my bed, Vee. So permission granted to roll around in the sheets and do whatever you need to do to find inspiration."

"Anything?" I snortle.

"Ah, there's the sound I've missed. And yes . . ." He pauses. "Anything."

"What if I want to bring two men to your bed?"

Ross chokes so hard, it sets off a coughing fit, and despite me continually asking if he's okay, he can't catch his breath for several minutes before he groans in a strangled voice. "Never."

With a clearer tone, but still one that sounds rough, he adds, "I told you once I'd never share you, and I mean that, Vee. You'd be mine and mine alone."

A greater question might be, would *he* belong to me?

"I'll think about it," I state. "About staying at your place, that is." However, I already know I wouldn't be comfortable going to Ross's home without him present. The concept does feel like an invasion of his privacy.

"Consider it a vacation from your home, if you'd like."

"What I'd like is some freakin' inspiration," I mutter.

"You'll find it."

"Is that your idea of a pep talk?" I tease.

"It can be any kind of speech you want, sweetheart. Just as long as you're still talking to me."

I melt a little into the pillow at my back, slouching down further beneath the bedcovers.

"Good game today," I remind him, needing a change of subject.

"I didn't see you there." Ross now knows my seats are to the right of the dugout, off center from home plate, and roughly behind the WAGs—wives and girlfriends.

Laurel went to the second home opening game. I gave a set of tickets to Cassandra although I told her I wasn't speaking to her. She only laughed and told me I could make her my maid of honor at my *second* wedding. She's a funny one.

"Next one," I promise him. As he said, he'll be gone for a week with away games.

"And you'll be sleeping at my place while I'm gone," he reiterates, like it's a done deal.

"We'll see." I sound like I did when my girls were little, giving them the canned response when the real answer was *not going to happen*.

"I'll share my address with you. And send you the code to enter the place."

Something about the ease in which he shares both these things with me settles deep within my chest. Because Ross is showing he trusts me. He's telling me where he lives and offering me a key.

And his blind faith has me eventually accepting this generous invitation almost as easily as when I first agreed to sleep with him.

Chapter 26

[Ross]

If Vee won't sleep in my bed with me, maybe she'll sleep in my bed without me, which shouldn't sound as nefarious as it does. I don't have an ulterior motive. Having Vee in my life is the only win I need. There is just something about the idea of her in my bed that makes me rest easier. Like she'll be safer or more comfortable or whatever the word would be to account for this feeling of wanting her in my home.

With back-to-back road games, Vee and I will be separated for another seven days, and we're in a fragile place. She doesn't trust me or the feelings I've confessed to her. I'm strictly in the friend-zone.

So, I'm surprised when a text comes through first thing in the morning as I'm walking to the locker room pre-game to our match up with Milwaukee.

If the offer still stands, I'd like to take you up on a change of view.

Nothing makes me happier than envisioning her in my home, and I'm quick to respond.

Mi casa es tu casa. Or mi cama es tu cama. I chuckle to myself as I repeat what she once said to me. *My home is her home. My bed is her bed.*

When she only responds with a smiley emoji, I'm crestfallen.

Then minutes before the game begins, waiting on warmups to start, another text from Vee comes through.

Can't figure out the remote. Want to watch the game.

My chest swells again. Chandler never watched the games, and even when she attended them in person, she was more interested in being seen and who she would see than the game itself. Vee is actually invested in the games *for me.*

With quick instructions, I explain the remote.

Got it. Now, get your eyes on the ball, Coach. <moral support ass-slap>

With a chuckle, I click off the messenger app and slip my phone into my pocket. When I glance up, Kip is watching me.

"You called her, didn't you?"

"Maybe." I brace to defend myself. "Why?"

Kip and I have gone a few rounds about Vee. He felt I'd been unfair, bringing her into my superstitious nonsense, and then letting her leave so easily after Arizona. He didn't understand the scope of my conflict. Letting Vee go had been one of the hardest decisions. I wasn't good enough for someone like Vee, someone who didn't want anything from me. Someone who is more of a giver than a taker.

Now, the playing field between us felt a bit leveled. *For research.* Yeah, I'd answer any fucking question she had, and use all the props for examples until she learned this wasn't about baseball rituals. *We* are more.

"Because you've got that goofy grin again, like you get whenever she's texting you or you think of her. And it matters because your head needs to be here." He taps his head and points toward the ball field we can't see yet. "Not there." He aims his pointed finger in the vicinity of my phone.

Instantly, my mood shifts. Kip is a good guy and a great friend, but I don't need him questioning where my heart and head are at as the head coach. He knows as well as anyone that heart and head can be divided at times. Family comes first. Romantic matters come next. Vee is in that second category for me. But I'm present.

"I'm here," I tell him. My feet firmly planted in this locker room in Milwaukee. Rooted even more deeply knowing Vee is at my house, preparing to watch the game, because she believes in me.

+ + +

Hours later, I return to my hotel room and check Vee's status, hoping she took up my offer to spend her nights at my place, not just use my home during the day.

In my bed, nightlight?

Vee: **Is this my new nickname?** **It might work better as a code word.**

Me: **I'm calling you.**

Vee answers on the first ring and a sigh of relief escapes me. "Do we need a code word? And where did nightlight even come from?"

"Cee-Cee." Vee chuckles, the sound like a beacon in my dark hotel room. "My best friend has a strange sense of humor."

I smile. "Our word should be happenstance."

"Oh, do we need a word for something?" She laughs again. "And I thought you preferred *happy chance*."

I laugh quietly. "You remember that."

"I remember everything," she says in a poor imitation of me. Still, her voice is playful, and I smile wider, something warm and comforting washes over me.

"Happy chance is *my* phrase for you. To describe you giving me a second one."

The phone goes quiet a second. I've been trying to keep my feelings more to myself, not wanting to overwhelm Vee again and not able to make her promises yet. I just want to see where we go. She explained to me her characters lead her writing, tell their own story, and I want to see where my story takes me with Vee. Still, I worry that I've said too much, and I clear my throat. "Anyway—"

"I'm in your bed," Vee softly interjects, and I freeze. I'd been pacing back and forth before the hotel window like a caged animal.

"Yeah?" I swallow hard, picturing her in the dark blue sheets. The light on the nightstand dimly illuminating my room. Her soft curves in one of my T-shirts.

"Yeah." Her voice is quiet.

"What are you wearing?"

Vee laughs loud and hard. "Oh, are we doing that?"

I don't know what we're doing, but I want to know so I can picture her even better. "Tell me."

"I'm wearing an Anchors tee."

Yes. Mental fist pump. "With my number on it?" I choke, imaging the 33 on her back, or maybe on her chest, the top loop of each number curling around her breasts. It's been too long since I've seen those beauties.

"Nope. This is just a generic one."

"Still. A good visual."

"A good visual of what?"

I hear the smile in her voice.

"You, sweetheart. In my bed. Wearing an Anchors tee." I've put her on speaker phone, so I can tug off my shirt and shrug out of my pants. Then, I settle on the bed. "Vee, how would you feel about me answering question number two on your list? Might help you find some writing inspiration."

She's quiet a second, before she softly says, "I don't remember what question number two was."

"You wanted to know what it's like to touch a woman from a man's perspective."

Vee lightly coughs before her voice tightens, sounding professional while inquisitive. "Yes. How do you feel about the experience? Like does one vagina look like another, taste like another, or is one more memorable than others?"

I choke. "Holy shit, Vee. Just jump in with both feet."

She clears her throat again. Through the phone, I hear the rustle of sheets and wonder if she's settling beneath them or if she's sitting upright and grabbing a notebook. In Arizona, she kept a flower-covered spiral one on the nightstand beside the bed.

"Okay. So tell me—"

"I'd really like a visual aid for this one."

"No." Her tone is so adamant, I don't press.

But even if I'm not a writer, my imagination is good enough that I can picture her. Legs spread, pussy pretty, pink and swollen, wet and ready for me. I'd had a similar vision in my head when I stood in her shower back in Arizona. When I was fisting myself, preparing to release the pressure. Kissing Vee led to a buildup that ached, and to steady myself before I saw her each of those nights that we kissed like hungry teens, I took care of myself to ease the ache *before* I saw her. Still, she'd made me rock hard with only her mouth on mine and we'd often break apart breathless and greedy, needing a break before we could settle into her bed. *That night*, thanks to Valdez, I'd been late and needed that shower before my mouth hit Vee's, knowing I'd be hungry for more. I was surprised I'd heard her soft gasp over the roar of the shower.

Then again, I'm grateful I did because what a night we had.

With my hand flat on my belly, my dick twitches, eager for me to touch myself again. The reality of Vee is fresh in my head. But I'm not following through with any plan unless I get Vee on board.

"Okay. First, touching. For me, I like knowing that I'm giving you pleasure. That pressure point might be a trigger on you, but it makes me feel powerful as well. *My* fingers touching you there will be what gets you off. *My* tongue on your clit will tip you over."

"I . . ." More throat clearing. "We aren't talking about *me* directly. This is for research."

Ignoring her restriction, I continue. "Just touching that delicate skin. Edging around those folds, teasing you, flirting with entering you."

"Ross." Her voice strains around my name .

"Then, there's that tight nub, knowing it's the switch. But it's not just touching your clit. It's watching you light up. Your eyes brighten. Your lips part. The way your hips want to move, chasing my touch." I hum.

Vee moans.

"Your scent. Sexy. Musky." I inhale deeply, like I can catch a whiff of her from my memory.

"I like feeling how wet you get, almost greedy for me. Your slit slick. Your pussy eager."

"Ross." The struggle in her voice affects me. I want to feel her.

"My finger slipping through those slippery lips, dipping into you." Her breath hitches.

"Then there's the sounds you make. Like that one. Where your breath catches. Or you hum."

ELEVATOR PITCH

She recreates the sound for me and my dick jolts.

"You touchin' yourself, Vee?" My voice is tight, but low. I prepare for her to protest, to tell me no again, but I cut her off before she can answer. "I want you to touch yourself, sweetheart. Do it for me because I miss touching you."

"Oh, Ross." She purrs again in that sound she makes. Her voice is breathy when she says, "It only happened once."

"Twice." I recall our night together. The rush of finding her watching me from outside the shower. The thrill of kissing her. Then touching her. Tasting her. We came together two times that night. "And it wasn't enough."

I slide my hand lower. "Now tell me what you feel."

"I'm everything you said." She whimpers. "Wet. Greedy. Slick."

"Fuck, sweetheart. Tell me more."

"Are you touching yourself?" she whispers.

Hell, yes. "Do you want me to?"

"Yes." Another breathless plea. "Tell me what you feel."

"I'm hot and hard. Long and leaking from the tip. And greedy for you, too."

"Oh, God."

I picture her hand between her thighs, knees bent to the side. Her head tilted back. Her eyes lidded.

"Yeah? You like that? Like knowing you have power over me as well? You make me hard, Vee. You make me ache." I fist myself and stroke upward. "You're all I think about."

"I am?"

"Yes," I grunt, because Vee consumes me. "And how I feel when I touch you is incredible. Powerful. Invincible. You make me want to be better."

"Ross," she chokes.

"How ready are you for me, sweetheart? I want to taste you," I admit.

"What did I taste like?"

Mine. "Honey and musk."

She hums.

"And what did I feel like?"

Mine. "Like you fit me."

"Ross." Her sigh shifts, soft and sweet, but I want her as desperate for me as I am for her.

"Two fingers, sweetheart. Rub that spot. Feel how wet you are. You want my fingers to touch you."

"Yes."

I squeeze myself harder. "And my tongue to lick you up."

"Oh God, yes, please."

I yank faster at myself.

"And then you want me inside you, filling you up and—"

"*Yes!*" The sound of her breaking has me tipping over as well, spilling over my fist and dripping onto my belly.

"Fuck, Vee," I groan, continuing to fall apart from just the sound of her cries. I'm breathless and spent, and wishing she was here beside me.

Eventually, Vee quiets, her softening breaths whisper through the phone.

"You okay, sweetheart?"

"Yeah." Her voice is sweet once more, relaxed but distant. She's too far away when I want her here with me in *this* bed. The next best thing is her there in mine.

"I'm glad you're in my bed, sweetheart."

"Me, too." She chuckles softly. "Think the Anchors will win tomorrow."

My brows pinch. I don't like her doubt, and I know that I've done that to her.

"That's not what tonight was about." This was so much more. She trusted me to have this experience with her over the phone. I wanted to help her find inspiration, and I'm fucking thrilled she's in my home, beneath my sheets, taking her pleasure with me.

She doesn't respond to my comment, and I wish we'd video chatted. I need to see her face, but I don't press. Instead, we say goodnight after she wishes me good luck for tomorrow's game.

ELEVATOR PITCH

And when the Anchors win the next night, I try not to let guilt, or superstition, seize my chest.

Chapter 27

[Vee]

After waking up in Ross's bed for the third night in a row, and a final win against Milwaukee, making the series 2-1 in favor of the Anchors, I enter Ross's kitchen wearing one of his T-shirts.

Ross's home is incredible. He lives in a neighborhood where older homes have been restored to their original glory with modern amenities. His red-brick home is three stories tall and, like many classic homes in the city, it's narrow but long from front to back. He doesn't have much of a front yard or back but has professional landscaping with some seasonal flowers in the green mix.

His kitchen contains a huge island with four plush bar stools that face a large state-of-the-art set of industrial appliances and dark cabinets, and it's a favorite spot of mine in the house. From my position, seated at the end of the countertop, morning sunlight streams into the space from an Eastern window. In this location, I'm inspired to write.

After our night of sexy talk, I woke with a burst of energy and some new material for my stagnant manuscript. Last night after the final game, the Anchors traveled, so Ross and I only exchanged text messages while the team headed to another state.

With my tea prepared, I take a seat at the stool I've staked as mine and open my laptop.

Something causes me to look up. A flicker of movement in the corner of my eye before I glance up and squeak, jiggling my tea mug and drippling some of the hot liquid onto my hand. Quickly setting down the mug with a shaky *thunk*, I meet equally the startled gaze of a bare-chested college-aged boy standing at the opposite end of the island.

"Who are you?"

"Who are *you*?" I parrot, noticing the young man is only wearing a pair of boxer briefs. I don't need to clarify if this young man belongs to Ross. With dark blonde hair and bright blue eyes, he's exactly what I'd envision a younger Ross Davis to look like.

"I asked you first," he counters.

"Fair point," I reply, considering I should stand and offer my hand as way of introduction. Then think twice as *I'm* only wearing a T-shirt that belongs to this kid's father.

"I'm Verona Huxley," I state, using the open laptop as a shield. "A friend of your dad's."

The kid tilts his head. "You're older than his typical *friends*." Air quotes are implied in his exaggeration, and I should be offended on multiple counts. Implying I'm old; assuming I'm a certain *type*; labeling me as *that* kind of friend.

Clearing my throat, ignoring the lump in it, I state, "I'm not that kind of friend. And I prefer to consider myself as mature or seasoned." I tip my head and angle my gaze toward the ceiling. "Maybe delicately aged? Prime aged? In my prime?" I turn back to Ross's son and wave my hand. "Anyway, which son are you?"

"I'm Harley."

Silence falls between us a second before I say, "Your dad hadn't mentioned anyone would be here."

Harley tips up one bushy brow. His expression mirrors his father before he narrows his eyes. "Are you staying here?"

"I—" Suddenly, I felt excessively guilty that I've made myself at home in Ross's house for a few nights and used the setting of his kitchen as my writing space. I close my laptop, prepared to leave the residence once Harley leaves the kitchen, as I'm not going to walk around in only an extra-long T-shirt in front of Ross's son.

Harley watches as the laptop snaps shut. He steps closer to the large island, cell phone in his hand.

"I won't tell if you don't tell."

I chuckle at how quickly he wants to manipulate this situation. "Shouldn't you be concerned that a strange woman is in your dad's home?" Then again, does this happen often? Only last fall, Ross might have brought Chandler here.

Harley shakes his head. "Dad never brings his friends around. I only met Chandler Bressler once, and that was outside the house."

He might be trying to make me feel better, but I don't.

"I'm sorry," I reply not certain what else to say to him.

Harley shrugs. "Don't be. She's superficial. Now, if Dad were dating Aria Grendall, that would be a different situation." He pauses and wrinkles his nose. "Then again, that would just be wrong." He shivers. "He could be her father, which would make me her stepbrother." He pauses again, tilts his head. "Okay, that might not be bad. I could use all her connections."

As I have no idea who Aria Grendall is, or what she does, I let Harley have this argument with himself, although not liking the idea of Ross dating someone possibly as young as his own child.

"You attend DePaul, right?" I ask to defuse my thoughts.

Harley smiles slowly, his mouth wide and big like his dad's can be. "I do attend DePaul." He does that cute head tilt again. "Did Dad tell you about me?"

"Only that you're a freshman at DePaul and you're majoring in musical theatre. And he wanted to move back to Chicago to be closer to you."

Harley lowers his head, but I don't miss his dismissive scoff. "Yeah, well, two out of three isn't bad."

My brows crease, curious what he thinks isn't correct. "You don't attend DePaul as a freshman for musical theatre?"

He lifts his head and sighs. "No, those three things are correct."

Which means he doesn't believe his father wanted to move to Chicago for his son.

Watching Harley, he waves his hand, brushing off the conversation. "Anyway, I'm here to do laundry for free and raid his refrigerator."

I snortle. "Well, good luck on item number two. You might starve, buddy."

The kid laughs and wrinkles his nose again. "Yeah, I should know better when Dad isn't around. There probably isn't much in that fridge."

Slowly, I stand, using the island as best I can as a shield. "If you give me a minute to get dressed, I can see what he has and rustle us up something." I swing my arm before me like I'm an old-time cowboy on the range. I have no idea why I did that, and I slowly lower my fist to the countertop. "Or I could order you something?"

Harley watches me for a long minute, not taking in my appearance as much as trying to read me. Maybe wondering what my agenda is here, in his dad's house, making myself at home.

"You're different than the rest of them." His voice is soft, quieter as his gaze drops to the countertop where he flips his phone repetitively, like a nervous tick.

"Different how?" I don't think I need to ask different from who. He means all the other women that have passed through Ross's life. The repertoire of supermodels and influencers.

"Besides being *old*," I tease, trying to mask the gut punch to my belly from that comment. And any physical comparison to someone more Ross's type.

"You remind me of . . ." As his voice drifts, he stops the twirl of his phone and then lifts his head, not finishing his sentence. "Do you think you could make pancakes?"

I stare back at the boy, on the verge of being a man. Some kids are eighteen on the edge of twenty-eight while others easily slip back to being ten again. Harley is at that precipice.

"I'll certainly hunt around for the ingredients but if I don't find them how does The Syrup Tap sound?" A Chicago-area favorite, the waffle and pancake house is a place my girls love. "Or if you don't like that place, we could go somewhere else."

"No," Harley is quick to answer. "The Syrup Tap sounds great, Verona."

"My friends call me Vee," I tell him, and you'd have thought I'd shared my deepest secret with the kid by the way he smiles in response. Wide and big again.

"Vee it is. You can still call me Harley."

"Got it." I finger gun him, but he's already turning away from me.

"I'll get dressed."

As he disappears, I'm left standing in Ross's kitchen curious why Harley thinks his father wouldn't want to be closer to him. The moment also feels a bit surreal as I just had a discussion with Ross's son while wearing Ross's T-shirt, while his son was only in his underwear.

And now, I have a breakfast date with Harley Davis.

+ + +

Unfortunately, or fortunately, depending on how you look at the situation, I learn a great deal about Harley and his dad during our pancake meal.

"Aunt Rena essentially raised us after our mom died," Harley explains around a mouthful of silver-dollar chocolate chip pancakes. He asked for the full order, which amounts to a dozen of the chocolate pancakes smothered in whipped cream and covered in mini-chocolate chips.

"I'm sorry about your mom," I say, knowing the words are inadequate compared to the permanent hole in his heart. "I lost my husband, and my girls have been raised by a single mom."

Not certain why I tell him this information, Harley doesn't seem disturbed by it, but breaks into an inquisition about my girls. Their ages, occupations, and locations, plus something unique about each of them.

"Laurel is just social." I laugh as there isn't any other way to describe what she enjoys. "She's a good friend and I'd say going out on the town is her favorite activity. My Hannah loves baseball."

Harley scrunches his nose again.

"Not a fan?"

"If it wasn't forced down my throat, I might have been. I'm just not terribly athletic."

Now, I'm not about to admit I checked out a nineteen-year-old, but his lean body has definition, which could be good genetics, but also a sign of some physical training.

Still, I don't mention it.

"So, you don't like sports?"

"I'm more of a bleacher fan. As in, I'll go to a game if I must, and then I just want to have fun while I'm there."

I smile. "Makes sense. Hannah primarily got her love of the game from *my* dad. He had season tickets to the Anchors and often took my girls to the games as a Grandpa-and-Girls day out. He'd load them up on peanuts, popcorn, and *Cracker Jack*—"

"Like the song," Harley interjects before taking another bite of pancakes.

"Exactly. And then he'd bring them home all wired on junk food. But Hannah started picking up the game. The rules. The stats. The players and positions. She played softball as a kid."

"And she's the one in Milwaukee? Physical therapy major?" Harley confirms, showing he's paying attention to the details.

I nod.

In all our discussion, the one thing Harley doesn't ask me is how I met his father, and I'm grateful the topic doesn't come up.

As he finishes scarfing up his pancakes, his phone rings and he glances up at me as the Darth Vader ring-tone blares between us.

"I should answer this."

With my brows lifted, I respond. "Of course."

"Dad?" Harley says into the phone, gingerly lifting it like his fingers are sticky from syrup and melted chocolate. His gaze leaps to me after a brief second. "I called because there was a strange woman in the house this morning."

With his eyes still on me, he listens a second before speaking. "Yeah, that's what she said. You are friends, but not *friends*-friends, not like the kind with benefits."

My mouth falls open as my cheeks heat.

His brows crease deeply at something his father says, listening intently another minute before he defends, "I didn't kick her out. She took me out for pancakes."

He winks at me, like we share a secret.

"Actually, I'm with Vee right now," Harley clarifies. He listens another second before muttering. "Yeah, you too." Then he hangs up.

Glancing at me, he says, "Dad wants you to call him ASAP." Sarcasm drips from his voice.

Slowly, I smile, wondering what his father might have said, but then again, I'm not going to pepper a teenager with my curiosity.

"So, Darth Vader?" I nod toward the phone face down on the table.

Harley shrugs, falling back against the booth seat, his chocolate pancakes mostly decimated but now no longer of interest.

"Yeah, it feels appropriate."

With a soft laugh, I shake my head. "Well, I think Darth Vader can wait until we finish breakfast. I'm NIAH."

"NIAH?"

"Not in any hurry." I lift my tea mug for a slow sip and glance at Harley across the table, who has lowered his gaze but timidly smiles while his face lights up, seemingly pleased that I'm not in a rush to finish this meal with him.

Chapter 28

[Ross]

Not friends-*friends, not the type with benefits.*

Is that what she said? Why did she say that? I'd like to think we're something more. Special friends? That sounds lame. I don't know how to define our status. Strange? Weird? Strangely, weirdly serendipitous?

I mean, what are the odds that this woman keeps coming into my life and then the Anchors win. Although, being with her doesn't account for every win. And certainly, the way the team plays has more impact on the outcome of the game, but still, I'm more energized, clearly focused, and at ease knowing Vee is there for me.

She's *my* win.

And continual questions bombard me as I pace my hotel room in the few minutes I have between finishing my breakfast and heading to the field.

It sounded like Harley was enjoying himself whereas I can hardly get him to give me the time of day. I'm jealous my kid is having pancakes with my . . . friend who is a friend without benefits. But I'm also envious of Vee. She's spending time with my boy and making him happy. It should be me.

Am I being selfish with Vee? Do we need to clarify who we are to one another, or does friend encompass our situation? After the other night, plus our time back in Arizona, I'd like to think we are more than such a simple term.

I miss spending time with Vee. When we first reconnected, we talked and shared meals and wine, and spent a day together. I want more of that with her.

Dammit, why hasn't she called me?

My concern is doubled because I don't know what Harley is saying to Vee. He's a great kid. Smart, big-hearted, and talented, but he hasn't always been my easiest child. He wears his heart on his sleeve which means I am aware of how much he resents baseball and all he believes the sport has taken from him.

Most of all I hate when I tell him I love him, and he replies, *yeah, you, too*. Like he can't say the actual phrase back to me. It's a testament to how much I've failed as a father, especially since Patty passed away.

A knuckle rap on my door warns me Kip is ready. I hastily grab my bag off the bed and open the door with a little more gusto than necessary.

"Hey. Ready?" he asks, despite seeing my bag in my hand.

"Yep." I snap.

Kip staggers backward and blinks once. "Whoa. Easy, Coach." He raises his hand as if to hold me back.

As the hotel door closes behind me, I start down the hall.

Kip rushes to keep up with me. "Who pissed in your Wheaties this morning?"

"Do people even eat Wheaties anymore?" I ask, like it's actually an important question.

"Ross?" Kip questions, as if sensing my mood.

"It's nothing," I brush him off, pushing the down button between the bank of elevators. "I spoke to Harley this morning." And I *haven't* spoken to Vee yet.

"Kid still giving you trouble?" Kip chuckles, knowing Harley is a good kid, and by trouble standards, I could have it a million times worse than I do. Still, my son and I are disconnected in a way I can't seem to bridge. When Patty died, Rena filled the gap, but she wasn't his mother. She's his aunt. He missed his mom and maybe he even missed me as I was too wrapped up in my own grief and tossing balls to be present like my son needed.

However, Landon doesn't seem to hold the same resentments toward me as Harley.

Two kids. One household. Yet totally individual experiences and unique personalities.

When Harley decided he wanted to go to DePaul, I took it as a sign for myself. While I'm a native of Philadelphia, Chicago had been our home for eight great years. I wanted to come back to a city with fond memories, even if a few of them were also heartbreaking.

"He's . . . just Harley." I sigh.

Kip nods like he understands. He raised kids. He knows the trials and tribulations of being a dad on the road.

Kip claps my shoulder as the elevator doors open and we step inside. Lately, every elevator ride reminds me of Vee and how we met. How I was lost in my own head at the devastating championship game, and I hadn't noticed her in the corner at first. How she was awkward, doing a little bounce with her legs crossed. How she rushed off once our elevator ride resumed and we were released from the lift.

If that elevator hadn't stalled, I might have missed out on a chance with Vee. *Happenstance.*

"What?" Kip asks, and I glance over at him.

"What *what*?"

"You just chuckled to yourself."

"I—" I clamp my mouth shut, not wanting to share the finer details of how I met Vee. Kip simply knows I met her on the night the Flash lost, and we slept together, nothing more.

"You're thinking of her, aren't you?" Kip interjects.

"Got something to say to me about her?" I arch a brow, needlessly defensive when Kip's question was innocent enough. I think he's getting a kick out of watching me struggle with my own emotions and grapple with wanting a relationship with Vee that involves more than a sleeping commitment.

"No issue," he laughs. "Just enjoying the unflappable Ross Davis flapping. What I'd really like to know, though, is if the superstition factor is out of the equation?"

I sigh and tug my cap off my head, then lower it back down. "Yeah, the superstition is gone." Even if having Vee back in my life has brought on a few wins.

The elevator stops, and we exit the lift for the lobby while Kip continues.

"What a story. Superstition whisperer to—"

I stop quick and spin on my friend and former mentor. "She's more than that, okay?" My anger toward him is unwarranted but I'm feeling sensitive about Vee's status with me. "She's—" *A friend but not a friend-friend, like with benefits.*

"Fuck," I swipe my ball cap off my head again, scratch my scalp and replace the cap. "I'm not certain what she is but I care about her and I'm not going to let her sound *less-than* when I want her to be more."

"Okay." Kip's eyes widened, as if startled by my outburst. He lifts a hand to ward off my irritation and watches me, his green eyes nearly laughing when he says, "You're really falling for her, aren't you?"

Falling? The term is more like I fell. I didn't see this coming, but somewhere along the way, I tripped, and there was Vee. Sweet, kind, beautiful Vee.

My phone rings and with a quick glance at the caller ID, I'm stepping away from Kip without answering his question.

"Vee?" I exhale, as if I've been waiting for her call, which I have.

"Hey, Coach. You okay? You sound a little winded."

"Why didn't you call me?"

Silence fills the line a second and I take a deep breath, realizing my tone was too sharp.

"Well, I had this amazing breakfast date with a young man who told me all your secrets."

Fuck! "What did he say?" Again, my tone is sharp.

"What should he have *not* said?" Vee counters before she laughs. "Relax, all your secrets are safe with *you*. And the ones you shared with me are still safe with me."

I exhale and hang my head.

"But now I really am concerned. Is there something you should probably tell me, Ross?" Vee's voice is a bit more direct and serious.

"No. No, it's nothing. It's just . . ." I glance over my shoulder, noticing the team trickling out to our transport to the field. "Harley is a good kid. The best. But he doesn't think the best of me, and I don't want him to skew your impression of me."

"And what impression would that be?"

"That I'm an okay man, but a shitty dad."

"Ross." Vee sighs. "You aren't a shitty dad. You raised a polite young man who has the gift of gab but didn't spill anything dark. And can pack away some chocolate chip pancakes."

That's my Harley.

"Yeah, well, I didn't exactly do the raising. Patty did." The mention of my late wife feels like a dart hitting a board off center and silence drops through the phone between Vee and me. I really need to go but I don't want to end our call on this note. I've been wanting to talk to her all morning as we didn't get a chance to chat last night, and I was hoping for a recap of our *talk* the other night.

"Sweetheart, I hate to do this, but I've got to go." I glance back at Kip waiting on me just outside the hotel doors.

"Of course. Go, *go*."

I can almost imagine her pushing me out the door, maybe smacking my ass like she did back in Arizona. I want those moments again with her.

"Vee, when I get back in town, go out with me."

"What?" she chuckles, the sound a bit strained.

"I want another date."

"Okay." Her voice lowers, the word soft.

"Three nights. Then you're mine." The warning sounds salacious but the intent is the same.

I want Vee to myself.

+ + +

The days and nights don't pass quickly enough before I'm finally at Vee's front door, picking her up for our date. I'd wanted her to stay at my place. I would have loved to arrive home and find her there instead of the big, echoing house, that felt empty and a bit lifeless. However, I understood she didn't want to overstay her welcome. She'd gotten lots of words, which was writer speak for her progress in the story.

I'd also have loved to find Harley home. He went to school only fifteen minutes from the house, and yet I rarely saw him between his schedule and mine.

"You look beautiful," I tell Vee after she opens the door in that way she does, with a swift flourish like she can't wait to see me. The motion is how I feel about her and everything in me wants to rush forward, kiss her, and suggest we skip our plans.

However, I made a promise to be somewhere important tonight, and I need to show up.

Vee blushes sweetly while stepping back to allow me into her place. I hand over the smaller bouquet of flowers I brought her tonight. In the past, flowers had often been an apology.

I'm sorry I'm late. Sorry I missed dinner. Sorry I missed parent-teacher conferences.

But tonight, a certain joy fills me at gifting Vee flowers, no apology necessary.

"These are lovely. And you look smashing." She eyes up and down my slacks and jacket.

"Fuck, Vee, don't look at me like that." I chuckle, rubbing my forefinger and thumb around my mouth, stroking over my trimmed beard.

"How am I looking at you?"

"Like you could devour me."

Her eyes widen while her cheeks turn a deeper pink. We didn't have a repeat of sexy phone time; however, we did talk about it. How I wished I'd been here to see her in my bed, getting herself off. She let it slip that taking care of herself was the only way it's happened in a long, long time. I want to rectify that situation.

Vee steps forward and presses a kiss to my cheek. "Thank you for the flowers." Her voice is soft. Her lids lower as she pulls away from me, but I'm quick to catch her face, cupping her cheeks and giving her a more solid kiss. One that messes up her perfectly applied lipstick.

"Damn, I've missed you," I whisper to her mouth, knowing I might be admitting too much.

"I've missed you, too," she replies, blinking once I let her go, before we actually do miss our scheduled plans.

"Put those in water," I demand gently, swatting at her backside when she turns around, which causes her to yelp, then giggle, as she walks down the narrow hall to her small kitchen. Her apartment is tight, in typical old-world Chicago style. Galley kitchen. Tight hallway. Square bedrooms with minimal closet space.

Once Vee returns from the kitchen, vase in hand, she sets the arrangement on the television cabinet.

"Ready?" I hold out my hand and lead her out of her place.

Once I've helped her into my truck and settled into the driver's seat, she says, "I can't believe we're going to a play."

"Why not?" I laugh, starting the ignition.

"You don't seem like a theater kind of guy."

I ease onto the narrow street, pausing at a stop sign and giving Vee a glance. "I could be offended by that comment." I know the stereotype. Jocks don't like culture. Vee's already teased herself about once being a librarian and now a writer. Book nerd and star athlete, she called us.

Us. That's the one thing I want to talk more about with Vee—defining us. Because we should clarify some things, but not yet. First, our date.

"But you won't be offended," Vee interjects, giving me a soft smile. "I'm not stereotyping you, I'm just surprised. Surprised by all of this."

"Like what?" I once told Vee there were things she'd be surprised to learn about me, but maybe I meant it more about myself. Because I'm surprising myself lately with all I'm doing and saying, becoming a new version of myself. A version I'm enjoying.

"An actual date."

"We went on one before." Our trip to the Hole in the Rock.

Maybe now *is* the time for that *talk*. "Look, sweetheart. This arrangement isn't just a simple arrangement anymore. If you don't want to see me again, we can stop." I almost give myself a heart attack with the suggestion, but the truth is, if Vee wants out, she can exit. "But I'd like you to stick around. I'd like to see where this is going."

"This?" She hesitantly questions, and I catch a glimpse of her from the corner of my eye. Her wide eyes opening larger. Her teeth dig into her lower lip.

"Us." I point between us before reaching for her hand and giving it a squeeze.

As I brake for a stop sign, I sneak another peek at her, watching those teeth battle a smile from growing before she scoots closer and leans toward me, pressing a kiss to my cheek. "I'd like to stick around, too." Her voice is low, a bit sultry as she lowers back to her seat. Her smile grows, causing my own to spread wider.

Damn, she's so beautiful, and the way she's looking at me, devouring doesn't cover that craving. Or maybe that's me because I yearn for her in a way I've never felt before.

Vee suddenly giggles, the sound soft and sweet, almost shy but happy, and I want to park this truck on the side of the road and kiss her senseless.

However, a honk behind us reminds me we need to keep moving on this side street.

When we pull up before our destination, Vee's brows pinch and her head swings toward me. "We're at DePaul." A question fills her voice about the college location and the university theatre.

"Yeah, this is Harley's play."

Her eyes widen. "As in your son Harley? Is in a play?"

"*Rent*," I explain. "He plays Mark Cohen." I sigh. "I'm going to admit, I don't know much about this play. I think it's going to be a bit . . . morbid."

Vee pumps my hand in response. "Then we'll get through it together."

When we take our seats, she explains what she knows of the theatrical production which is about a group of friends, many HIV positive or with AIDS, in varying combinations of sexual relationships. I'm in over my head here and I'm thankful for Vee holding my hand most of the performance until the cast sings "Seasons of Love." Tears stream down Vee's face in reaction to the song about the minutes in a year, and how time should be measured by love.

Her response doesn't surprise me; Vee is sensitive. But what does shock me is my thoughts on the song. How have I measured my time? With wins and losses? By baseball seasons? By pitch counts when I was younger. By another year playing a game I love. But have I measured time correctly? Was Patty a season? My boys as children a season? Is a new season starting with them as men?

Watching Vee swipe at her cheeks, I wonder if she'll only be a season. I don't like the thought.

When the play finishes, we find Harley backstage with the passes he'd given me.

"You came." Harley rushes Vee instead of me, and they hug like old friends before he turns to me. "Dad." My name is said like he's surprised to see me. "Thank you for bringing Vee."

Vee turns toward me, her brows pinched, a question etched in her expression before she schools her face and offers Harley a warmer smile. "I wouldn't have missed it. You were amazing." She reaches for his forearm, affectionately emphasizing her compliment.

"Give your old man a hug," I gently demand, pulling Harley into me. "You did great, bud."

He claps my back before pulling away too soon. "Thanks, Dad." He looks me directly in the eyes. "Thank you for being here."

I didn't want to be anywhere else. I'm proud of my boy and it's on the tip of my tongue to remind him when someone calls his name and Harley turns his head.

He exaggeratedly waves his arm in the air before turning back to me. "I've got to go."

"Of course." Not going to lie, it stings that he is eager to rush off. I stare after him as he runs toward another young man, his arms pinwheeling at his sides before the two collide and embrace. Holding each other while tipping side to side.

Quickly, I glance back at Vee who is observing me, not watching Harley. I clear my throat. "My son has a boyfriend," I state, holding my head up high, prepared to go to battle, if necessary.

But Vee looks me directly in the eye, similar to the way Harley had, only she holds longer, more intently. "And you love him." Simple. Direct. Honest.

"Deeply." I exhale.

As an athlete, the stereotype of determination and grit comes with a perception of aggression and competition which includes diminishing those weaker or different from us. *A man is a man*, but that's an archaic attitude. What makes a man? Accepting all others? Being a good dad? Acting as a gentleman?

In sports, we take sexual orientation and mental health more seriously than ever before, especially with the number of former athletes coming forward about their past negative experiences.

When my son came out to me, my only response was that I love him. I had no other words. He is who he is. But I was upset because my son seemed hesitant to tell me, to open up to me, like he was afraid I wouldn't accept him, and that's the moment I knew I'd done a poor job of being his father.

"I know it's late, but do you want to grab something to eat?" I'm not ready for our night to end. With a glance back at Harley, I add, "He's busy." I make the excuse more for myself than him. I understand there are cast parties and time needed to unwind after a performance. The sensation is no different than playing a game, wanting to revel or commiserate with your friends after a win or loss. Teammates, cast members; there isn't any difference. People are people.

And as much as I want Harley to spend some after-the-performance time with me, so I can tell him how proud I am of him, maybe take him out for a celebratory dinner, I know he'd rather be with his friends.

Vee slips her hand around my bicep. "I know a great burger place nearby." Her tone expresses her understanding.

Being a parent is hard. You need to know when to hold tight and when to let go.

When we reach the burger joint, I express my gratitude. "I know you get it. Your girls are grown." I sigh, dangling a French fry from my fingertips. "Where does the time go?"

Dropping the fry onto my plate, I swipe my hands together. "I missed a lot when my boys were younger. Even more when Patty passed, and I moved on to coaching." I squint toward the window at my side as we sit in a booth across from each other. "Sometimes I worry I've missed too much."

Glancing back at Vee, she offers another compassionate smile. "It's never too late, Ross."

Patty comes to mind again. "Until it really is." Until you don't have another minute to make things right. To say what you should have said.

"My wife wanted me to quit." I lower my head, blindly staring at my nearly finished burger. "She hadn't been feeling well, maybe she knew internally something was happening. Women often have a sixth sense about things. She asked me to leave baseball for the boys." I shake my head, unable to look up, certain there will be judgement in Vee's eyes. "I didn't do it."

I was aging out of the sport but felt like I had one last year in me. *After this season.* Always my excuse.

Slowly, I lift my head and glance at Vee. "Instead of honoring Patty's request, I threw myself into the game, disappearing within it, and had one of my best pitching years. The Anchors won the pennant that year."

I swallow thickly, Vee allowing me a minute. "I'd suggested I quit after she passed. Been given leave to give myself a break. But my coach knew I was struggling." I wave a hand around my ear, signaling my head. "I was messed up and needed something to focus on. The game gave me the outlet I needed. My coach was right, but I'd done wrong by my boys. They needed me and I failed them."

After the season. I promised myself if the Anchors won, I'd leave the game, and I did. Took a year off and floundered. Baseball kept me grounded. When the offer from the Flash came in, I jumped at the chance to coach and moved my boys to Philadelphia, which was another change for them.

"My son needs the stage like I need a sandy diamond-shaped lot with a grassy outfield. And while some might argue baseball is just a game how would you feel if someone told you never to write again?"

Vee sucks in air. "Like I couldn't breathe."

"So, you understand me."

Vee does get me on a level no one else ever has. Her heart is huge. She listens and she cares. And she can make me laugh. She chases away dark thoughts. Her presence casts a warm glow in my life. I want to be able to do the same for her. I want her to know she's appreciated and adored, listened to and seen.

Vee and I are silent a second before she sighs and sits up straighter. "There's no way to measure grief or guilt. Is it a minute, an hour, or a season of our lives? Does it define us, or do we define it? Is grief only about death, or is it about time? Time lost. Time never used." Vee pauses. "I think, we allow ourselves the time we need, beat ourselves up if we have to, wallow if we must, but *that* needs a time limit. My grandmother once said she allowed herself two weeks at the loss of my grandfather. Then she forced herself out of bed, and it was one step at a time. One minute, one hour. A season."

Vee licks her lips. "We can't live with regrets, and yet the truth is, we all do. Regret over what we said or didn't say. Regret about what we did or didn't do. Remorse is part of life, and that's what's important to remember. We need to continue living, and be thankful time is in front of us right now, in this moment, and to make a change, if you wish."

I stare at Vee as she continues. "If you want a better relationship with Harley, tell him. Or better yet, show him. He's adult enough to understand that your job is demanding but maybe he doesn't understand why you love that job, or need it, or value it. Not value it more than him, but because it's something for you, like he has the theater for him." She tilts her head. "Which, by the way, why didn't you tell me he was in a play or that we were going to *his* play?"

"I just wanted to surprise you." While doing something nice for my son.

"Did you bring me to the play because Harley asked for me to be there?" Her eyes cast downward when she asks.

My forehead furrows. "Absolutely not. I didn't even know he'd want you there. I asked you to go *with me*, not necessarily for him, if that makes sense."

"For a minute there, I just thought you'd invited me to attend for him. And this wasn't a date."

I stare at her. "This is a date," I state, maybe a bit too adamantly. Maybe not the most romantic one as it involved my kid's play, and a discussion about my deceased wife, but still a date. "And I don't want to argue with you about my son."

Vee sits up straighter. "We aren't arguing about Harley."

"I don't ever want to fight." Guilt hits me once more at how often Patty and I fought near her end. Her struggles. My helplessness.

"Fights are going to happen, Ross. It's inevitable. You'll leave the toilet seat up or your socks on the floor, and I'm going to lose hair in the shower, clogging the drain, and drape my bra over a chair. Things happen."

Her scenarios lessen the tension and stir something inside me. The situations she describes imply we have a future to fight in.

I nod at her plate. "You finished?"

She's only eaten half of her mushroom-quinoa burger which she told me was life-altering, but I'm ready for our night to progress and move away from the sorrows of my past.

Vee nods, crumbling a paper napkin and tossing it onto her plate.

"Then let's get out of this place." I reach over the table for her hand as I scoot to the edge of the booth. After dropping a few bills on the table, we step into the brisk spring night, and I inhale.

This city and the woman holding my hand are the air I need right now.

This moment is a season I intend to enjoy.

Chapter 29

[Vee]

Once we arrive back at my apartment, I don't really want Ross to leave but I also don't trust myself to let him stay. He smells so good, and he looks so good, and he was rather stern about our date. But most of all he seemed so vulnerable talking about Harley and Patty. We didn't need to share all our sad stories, yet we seemed to understand one another on some deeper level.

Life is hard. Death is harder. Regret and guilt go hand in hand. Living with grief is the worst.

But we still have a life, and we owe it to those gone to live it as best we can.

Which circles me back to inviting Ross inside my place because I'm not ready to let him go.

And because I'm awkward, I jump ahead. "I won't have sex with you."

"Okay." Ross falters as he's lowering himself to my couch, pausing mid-bend with his ass back and hands reaching for the cushion.

"The Anchors are winning with or without that happening between us."

He finishes taking a seat, drapes an outstretched arm along the back of the couch and chuckles. "Okay." His eyes never leave me, where I stand in my living room which suddenly feels too small with him present.

I love my apartment. It's just the right size for one. A little cramped when Hannah is home, but I had to sell the house once Cameron was gone. The memories there were too much. Not to mention, a civil servant's compensation wasn't enough to pay that mortgage.

"And we don't even need to sleep in the same bed for them to win either." Wringing my hands together and swaying side to side a bit, displays my anxiety. If I get anywhere near a bed with Ross, I don't know that I can lie there pretending I don't want more with him. Because I want so much more than just a superstition proposition.

Us, he said in his truck. I want to stick around and see where we go, too. However, we should go slow.

"Okay," Ross states again, dragging out the word. "But how do you feel about sitting on my lap? Letting me kiss you? Consider it book research. Which by the way, you haven't mentioned. How is the writing going?"

Sit on his lap? My resolve is faltering, but I concentrate on the other part of what he said.

"You don't want to talk about my book right now." I instantly hate how I've diminished myself. Dismissed his interest in my work. I've been reading and re-working what I've already written, polishing up holes in hopes to solidify where the story should go next. Where the characters want to lead.

"I do want to discuss it, but I'd rather you sit on my lap while talking, and then let me help you find more inspiration."

My gaze falls to his muscular thighs covered in expensive suit pants. Is there anything this man doesn't wear well? Baseball pants. Athletic pants. Suit pants. No pants.

Nope. *Don't think about Ross naked.* Not yet.

We already discussed our one-night phone sex. How much he liked it. How it had helped motivate me. *Motivate my characters*, that is. Not me. I wasn't writing about myself. Or him. I was writing about fictional people.

Is it suddenly too hot in here? Because I can't take my eyes off Ross's lap.

Quickly, Ross stands, wraps his arm around my waist and tugs me to him. We tumble together to the couch, me landing on the lap I'm trying to ignore, narrowly missing our heads knocking. I release a strangled laugh, and my legs fall open when Ross cups the backs of my knees, forcing me to straddle him and settle on his lap.

"Better," he sighs playfully. "Now. Your book."

How the heck am I supposed to concentrate when I'm spread over his thick legs, conscious of my dress riding up and his soft suit pants against my thighs? *What's my name again?*

"I'm just at a standstill again, but it will work itself out." At some point, an *ah-ha* moment will strike, and I'll be back at the keyboard.

I toy with the collar of Ross's dress shirt, avoiding contact with his eyes which I feel watching me. He removed his suit jacket earlier, leaving it in his truck. Unable to help myself, I smooth my palms over his shoulders and then down his chest.

"Then let's talk about question two again." His sandpaper on wood sound rumbles up my middle.

My gaze snaps to his eyes. "We already discussed it." We had our moment on the phone together. A rather spicy moment that I had not anticipated happening. Ross's voice had dropped, and he was so descriptive. Like a damn good audiobook narrator, Ross made me feel the moment. My body reacted in a way I hadn't expected and the next thing I knew I was following his lead, touching myself, bringing myself pleasure with just the sound of his voice.

I shiver a little at the reminder, and the movement rubs my thighs over those soft pants of his. Ross notices my reaction. His hands cup my cheeks, and he gently pulls my face closer to his.

"This time, I want visual aids." Then his mouth captures mine in a kiss that's both seductive and sweet, drawn out by the slow lap of his tongue, sweeping against mine, before he pulls at my lower lip with his.

Suddenly, I'm hoisted into the air. Ross's uncanny strength on display. I squeal, wrapping my arms around his neck and latching my legs around his waist. He shifts only a foot or two, before settling me in one of the high back chairs. The lamp between the two seats is the only illumination in the room and suddenly too bright.

Ross lowers to one knee before me.

"What are you—"

"I've missed your skin." His palms smooth over my knees, forcing my dress to my lap and exposing most of my thighs. "You're so soft, sweetheart."

As the late April night is still cool, I wear knee-high boots. My legs quiver as he starts at the back of my kneecaps and massages up my inner thighs forcing them apart.

"Ross," I moan. Whether warning or wanting is yet to be determined.

"Let me see what I've been missing, Vee." He concentrates on my legs, his attention focused on massaging them, while keeping them spread.

"We don't have to have sex." His voice dips, like he'd very much like to have sex, but he'll respect my wishes. "And we don't have to sleep together." His voice drops, almost as if he's more disappointed in that loss. "But I want to touch you."

Permission is hardly out of my mouth before my thighs are pressed open as far as the chair will allow, and Ross tugs me closer to the edge of the seat. My dress is bunched at my hips. Then his head is between my legs, his nose nuzzling my center. He hums and inhales deeply before kissing me there.

I jolt. As if I hadn't been expecting the touch, anticipating it, wanting it. Because I *do* want Ross Davis. I want his hands on me and his mouth as well.

Quickly, he removes my underwear, leaving my boots on. I clamp my legs together, but Ross gently prods them apart again.

"Let's see what's mine."

My head falls back at the declaration. *I'm in so much trouble with this man.*

He hitches one of my legs over the armrest, then wedges his midsection against the other one, fully exposing me to him.

"So pretty." He stares unabashedly at me and my newly waxed area. His eyes are heated. His voice just as warm. "And so ready." With his finger, he swipes where I'm slick and anxious for more from him.

"Tell me you missed me, too, Vee." His finger teases me, taunting an area that *has* missed him. No one has ever touched me like Ross is. Reverent. Curious. Eager.

"I've missed you, too." My voice isn't more than a whisper.

Suddenly, he's cupping my backside, like a precious chalice, and lifting me just the slightest bit to better angle me to be licked and sipped, gloriously swiping his tongue across tender skin and teasing that precious nub. I clutch at the armrest with one hand while my other lands on Ross's head, holding him against me as my hips rock in short, sharp thrusts, begging his mouth for everything.

"Missed you," Ross mutters. Then swipes over my wet center. "Missed this." Then he's diving in again. Tongue on a mission. Mouth humming loud and proud as he devours me. His hearty noises make it known he's enjoying his feast and I feel myself dripping.

"Ross," I groan at the mess I'm certain to be making, and the stain he'll imprint on my heart. Because there is no doubt Ross Davis has marked me. A permanent scar. A lasting bruise.

Yet I don't want him to stop. I massage his scalp and Ross tightens his hold on my backside. With his fast-paced flicking tongue, I too quickly fall apart.

His name is again a strangled cry as he draws out the release, relentlessly licking me while I melt into the chair, dripping like candle wax, lazy and warm. Only he has made me feel this way. Bright, and hot, and seeking more.

When I've had enough, I give his head a gentle press and Ross pulls back, running his mouth against my inner thigh, his beard tickling me, while I slouch back into the chair.

"Oh my God," I mutter, blinking a few times. "I think I almost passed out."

Ross chuckles while his eyes flame. "So your question was how do I feel about that?" He trails a finger up my thigh and circles my sensitive area, taunting the skin that still tingles with aftershocks.

"As I told you on the phone, it's a powerful position to be in. Knowing I'm giving you pleasure. Knowing you want it from me." He pauses a second. "Because you want me, sweetheart."

While stating the obvious, there's a vulnerability beneath the confident voice. More a question of if he's correct in his assessment.

"I want you, Ross," I admit.

He smiles, wide and large, illuminating his face in a new way. "All the power." He teases over my center, tickling tender flesh. "And you make me so hard."

My gaze drops where the thick outline of him cannot be missed in the thin material of those suit pants.

"I like the taste of you, Vee. And the sounds you make when I taste you."

My face heats, a touch embarrassed that I make noise. "Am I too loud?"

Ross's expression sobers a little, disgruntled almost. Like he knows without asking that someone once complained. That finger of his, toying with me, thrusts inward and I gasp.

"Fuck loud," Ross counters. He works his finger in and out, producing a new sound between us. "I like how your body reacts to my touch. How you chase my finger like you don't want me to leave your body."

Oh God, this should be incredibly embarrassing, and yet I'm mesmerized by how open he is. How direct as he concentrates on where he's touching me, watching his finger disappear inside me.

"Tell me you don't want me to leave." Again, his voice is strong, but something deeper underlies his question.

"I don't want you to leave," I whisper, and I'm rewarded with a second finger, both rushing into me, filling me. My breath hitches again.

"You fit me, sweetheart." His gaze lifts to meet my eyes. "And I fit you."

There's something even deeper in that declaration, but my thoughts are scrambling as his fingers work within me. My back arches, thighs attempting to clench when one remains over the armrest and the other is trapped by Ross's broad body. He's building me up again. Winding me like a music box before released to sing.

"Ross," I whimper, shocked at the sudden rush up my center. My legs quiver once more.

"That's it, sweetheart. One more time."

I glance between us, catching briefly what he's doing to me before tipping back my head, closing my eyes, and falling into the moment.

Ross on his knees. His fingers inside me.

I hear him shift, feel his warm breath breezing over my slick skin. His thumb presses against that trigger spot and I unravel again. A piece of string, pulled and pulled and pulled, until the original material is nothing but a pile of loose thread.

I sag back on the chair, one leg dangling over the armrest, the other outstretched, while I stare at Ross who stares back at me. A smattering of heartbeats passes.

"I showed you mine, now show me yours," I flirt.

Ross chuckles, breaking our little bubble of breathy silence. Then, he's loosening his belt buckle and lowering his zipper, wrestling his pants and boxer briefs down enough to release what's long and hard, and *mine*. I don't want to share this man with anyone.

With his palm fisted around himself, he leans forward and swipes the tip through my essence.

I said no sex, yet Ross is so close, so tempting and hard. I did that to him. "We're a little old for just the tip," I tease, using humor to fight what I'm feeling. How I want to renege on my own injunction. I want to beg him to fill me up. To fit me.

Instead, I lower my leg and sit upright as best I can, forcing Ross back.

"Stand up." I demand, my tone is unfamiliar, commanding and powerful.

Ross and I meet eyes before he slowly rises to his full height. As he stands, I grip his pants and underwear and lower them to his thighs, then take over clutching his thick shaft.

"An amendment to question two." I stroke my fist down his length then upward to slide my thumb over the seeping slit. "How does this feel?"

"Like fucking heaven." His hips rock forward as I tug on him. His gaze aimed at where I'm stroking him.

I lean forward and swipe my tongue over the crown. Ross hisses.

"A queen, sweetheart." His voice strains. "You literally hold me in the palm of your hand. You own me."

I like the sound of that a little too much, and straightening the invisible crown on my head, I use the power he mentions to make him weak. I open my mouth and suck him inward, lapping at his length like I'm on a mission. He made me lose control when we were on the phone the other night. I want him to lose control as he stands before me.

"Feels so good," he hums. "Missed you so much."

Within seconds, one of his large hands is holding the back of my head and his hips gently surge forward. I slurp and lick like I can't get enough of him, allowing the sounds of my mouth around him to fill the room.

"Gonna come, sweetheart." It isn't so much a warning as a simple statement. He's nearing the end of his resolve. And with a final jolt that brings tears to my eyes, he spills down my throat.

When I pull back, releasing him with a lazy pop, Ross tips up my chin so I look at him. His thumb swipes across my lip, capturing a small droplet, and my tongue instinctively darts out for a final lick, not wanting a single drop of him wasted. Capturing his thumb, I suck it and he looks pleased, proud even. His eyes heat, his nostrils flare and his jaw tenses from our erotic position.

"Such a good girl." Ross winks.

For half a second, I understand the dominant-submissive lifestyle. Ross looks so content and sated. And I gobble up the praise kink.

Releasing his thumb, I smile up at him. "Hey, Ross Davis. Want to sleep with me?"

Asking is a risk, my playful tone a disguise for the overwhelming feelings I have for this man. How I want to please him. How I want to keep him. How I want him to truly be mine.

Ross chuckles, breaking through the intensity of the moment. "Verona Huxley, I thought you'd never ask." He bends, placing his hands on the armrests to cage me in and leans in, kissing me like we didn't just have our mouths on other body parts.

Like my invitation to spend the night was greater than the sum of everything else we just did.

Chapter 30

[Vee]

I wake from the sudden click of my front door closing. Swiftly, I shift my head on the pillow. Ross is still beside me, snuggled up close to my side. His arm drapes over my middle as I lie partially on my back, the other part of me resting against him.

Movement in my kitchen which is just outside my bedroom door snags my attention.

"Ross," I whisper-hush. "I think one of my girls is home."

Ross leans into me, pressing a kiss to my shoulder. We did not have sex last night. Not the conventional kind, but clearly the oral variety.

After our moment in my living room, we came to my bedroom where we shyly watched one another undress. Ross took care in removing his dress shirt and folding his slacks over a hanger I offered him. I had trouble with the zipper on the back of my dress and he helped me lower it, reminding me of our first encounter. This time, his knuckles slid down my spine after the zipper was separated.

"I love your back."

"I don't think anyone has ever said that to me."

Ross Davis has been a first in many ways.

"Ross," I whisper a little louder. "My daughter is here."

His eyes ping open, startling me with their brightness. "And?" He tips up his thick brows.

"You shouldn't be here."

"Why not?" His sleepy voice is gruff. His deeply pinched brows expressing his confusion.

I've never introduced my girls to a man in my life. Never had a man worthy of being introduced to them. And Ross walking out of my bedroom with me would make quite a statement. One I'm not certain we're ready to make, even if we discussed an *us* only last night.

What I say instead is, "Because you didn't want anyone to know about us."

"I never said that." His eyes widen.

Now doesn't feel like the time to argue with him, nor remind him that the first time we met, he said no one should know about our night together. We weren't public in Arizona. *Silly superstition.*

His pinched brows deepen. His eyes darken. "Lots of people know about us."

"Kip and Cassandra." *A whole two people.*

"You met Harley."

"That was different." Harley was an unexpected surprise in Ross's home. I realize that's not too dissimilar from whomever might be in my kitchen and just dropped something heavy on the floor.

"Well, I'm not climbing out the window." His tone is disgruntled, possibly hurt.

"Just . . . just stay in here until I can get rid of her." Another first. Something I never thought I'd say as a grown adult, before I scramble from my bed, rushing to slip on a pair of loose leggings. Not bothering to change the T-shirt I wore to bed, because whichever daughter is in my kitchen won't mind bra-less mom. I slip my fingers through my hair, conscious that Ross is watching me as I step around the bed.

He shifts quickly and efficiently, climbing up to his knees and snagging my wrist to catch my attention before I open the bedroom door.

"Hey," he whispers when I spin to face him. Proud chest on display. A thick wedge in his snug boxer briefs. "Good morning." He slips his hand to the back of my head and kisses me in a rough greeting that leaves me a little dizzy when he releases me.

"Stay," I warn, poking at his chest before I slip out my bedroom door, quickly closing it behind me.

Laurel tips back from behind the open freezer door. My brown-haired beauty's face lights up when she sees me.

"Hey," she greets me like it's perfectly normal for her to be standing in my kitchen, unscheduled or unannounced, rummaging through my freezer.

"Hey, baby. What are you doing here?"

"I was out of frozen waffles."

"Uhm. So you came to my house?" *Go to a freakin' grocery store.*

"You were closer than the store."

"Do I even have frozen waffles?" I stopped food shopping specifically for my girls a long time ago unless their visits are planned.

"No." She sighs and shuts the freezer door before facing me. "The Syrup Tap?"

"Is this your way of asking if *I'll* take *you* there?" I laugh. She isn't asking me out to breakfast, she's asking me to take *her* to breakfast.

"I live on a teacher's salary." Her hand comes to the hip she juts out to punctuate her financial status.

"And I live on a starving artist's one," I tease. "But give me a few minutes and we can go." The excuse is perfect, allowing me time to change and slip out of my own apartment before I'm caught with Ross Davis in my bedroom.

Only, said bedroom door opens and out walks the man himself. Suit pants and dress shirt on, but shirt untucked with only a few buttons near his waist fastened. His shoes are in his hand, socks tucked within them.

Laurel's mouth falls open. She lifts her hand, twisting it at the wrist to point behind me.

"Mom." Her voice is a strangled cry of shock, like she's frozen by the sight of a great big hairy spider on the wall.

"Mom," she repeats, not blinking.

"Mom." She sounds like she did as an insistent child, as if she doesn't have my full attention. "Ross Davis."

I shift, glancing over my shoulder while Ross crosses the very short distance in my narrow kitchen from my open bedroom door to me. He presses a kiss to my shoulder.

"Mom. Ross Davis just came out of your bedroom."

"I know." I sigh, a little embarrassed. Not by Ross but by the implication of what might have happened in my bedroom when nothing happened in there. It happened in the living room. In my bedroom, we talked more about Harley and then kids in general as they reach adulthood.

ELEVATOR PITCH

Which Laurel is clearly displaying she hasn't mastered, especially when she states in shock, "You're Ross Davis."

"I am."

"Coach of the Chicago Anchors."

"Yes," he says, slipping a hand around my back and squeezing my hip.

"Hot silver fox," she chokes.

"Uhm?" Ross chuckles.

"Laurel!"

"And you just came out of my mom's bedroom."

"Okay. I think Ross was just leaving and you and I can talk on the way to The Syrup Tap."

"Isn't that where you took Harley?" Ross asks, his voice close to my ear.

As I'm watching Laurel, her mouth gapes again before she says, "You went out with Harley Davis?"

For half a second, the announcement sounds like a reverse harem romance where the woman dates the dad *and* the son. Something I have no interest in doing, nor am I attracted to men young enough for me to be their mother!

"Laurel," I say a bit sharply.

"I think I'll let you explain that one." Ross chuckles behind me, then kisses my cheek. "I should probably go."

He steps away from me and addresses Laurel. "Nice to meet you." He doesn't offer a hand but tips up his chin. Laurel melts.

As Ross heads down the hallway leading to the front door, I hold up a finger to Laurel suggesting I want her to stay. Pinned to the hardwood floor, still in utter shock, I don't think she'd move if I asked.

"Wait," I call after Ross, quickly following him. He pauses near my front door and turns to face me. Lowering my voice, I ask, "What am I supposed to tell her?"

Ross stares at me a long minute. "Are you embarrassed by us?"

"No." I choke. "I just thought you wanted to . . . not be public."

"Why wouldn't I want to be public?" His eyes widen and then narrow, suspicious. "Unless you don't want to be public?"

The thought of Ross Davis being *my* dirty little secret is almost laughable. Who would I be hiding him from? He's the one with fans and paparazzi.

Still, I don't answer his question. I don't know how, so I snap. "This was *your* sleeping arrangement."

"Let's be clear." Ross stands to his full height. "The only sleeping arrangement is me in your bed. Or you in mine. Us. Together. We're more than some arrangement, Vee." He lets out a loud huff. "So let's have all the kids meet. Clear the air in one breath. We're public." His eyes narrow at me. "Exclusive. Monogamous."

I swallow down his meaning. "Okay," I whisper.

"Dinner. My place. Tomorrow night."

"What?" I snap again, surprised by how quickly he wants to make us public with our kids. I also remind him, "Hannah is in Milwaukee."

"That's only an hour away. Ask her to come home. And Landon will be home tomorrow anyway. He's going to the matinee performance of Harley's play."

"Don't you have a game tomorrow?" It's almost sad that I have his schedule memorized.

"Day game. I'll cook dinner." Then Ross leans forward, kissing me a little longer than a quick out-the-door kiss, and I'm left breathless and staring at the back of the shut door after his exit.

"Mom?" Laurel calls from the opposite end of the hallway, clearly confused by Ross's presence.

Maybe even more flabbergasted by the fact he kissed me.

And now we've been invited to dinner at his place. As a family. So my girls can meet Ross Davis and learn that we're together.

Is this even reality?

+ + +

Thankfully, Hannah isn't put out by my last-minute request to come home for a night. My blonde-haired girl is even wearing a summery dress, unlike her typical wardrobe of athletic wear.

"I have somewhere special I want to take you." Can I say I have someone special I want her to meet? Doesn't that imply he's my boyfriend or something? Can I have a boyfriend at forty-something? Calling him a man-friend sounds even stranger. And the truth is simply not an option.

I'm sleeping with Ross Davis.

I'd asked Laurel not to say anything to Hannah yet, but I'd been doubtful she could keep this secret to herself.

When Cassandra called me, I laughed, suspicions confirmed about my eldest daughter and her secret-keeping ability.

"Can't keep a secret from Aunt Sassy, can we?" I'd teased Laurel after the call where Cassandra squealed with delight before admonishing me for not keeping her up to date on the Ross situation.

What was our status? Sleeping partners? Research assistants? Even I was confused. We've called ourselves an *us*, but what does that mean?

When we pull up in front of Ross's house on the lush, tree-lined side street in a posh neighborhood, the girls gawk at the narrow, three-story brick home.

"Don't be weird," I warn them both.

"I don't think this situation could get any weirder," Laurel mutters. She's disgruntled that I didn't expand further about my relationship with Ross, other than mentioning that we'd met in Houston last year, reunited while I was in Arizona, and then bumped into one another again in Chicago.

"Is bumping some new term?" Laurel teased.

"Get your mind out of the gutter, kid."

"You're the one who taught me to have a dirty mind."

"I did no such thing."

But my girls read romance novels, following my love for them. Plus, I write them. Romance novels are full of life lessons, dirty minds appreciated.

"Where are we?" Hannah asks, interjecting into my memory of the conversation with Laurel.

"You won't believe this," Laurel mumbles, cryptic with her sister as we approach Ross's front door.

I ring the bell although I know the code. When the door opens on a rush, Harley eagerly greets me.

"Verona." He eyes the girls. "And her sisters."

I blush but the girls stare at him. Hannah's forehead furrows, concentrating, like she recognizes the nineteen-year-old in front of us but can't place him.

"Ladies, this is Harley. Harley, my daughters, Laurel and Hannah."

"Physical therapy." He points at Hannah. "Teacher." He looks at Laurel.

Laurel's head swivels. "He knows about us."

"You're being weird," I whisper. She's acting like Harley is some kind of teenage rock star heart throb, instead of an average college kid.

Harley steps back, allowing us to enter the house. "Dad's in the kitchen. I've never seen him so nervous. Then again, *we* should be nervous. He never cooks."

The three of us follow Harley into the large kitchen where Ross is rushing between a pan on the stove and items on the countertop.

"Can I help?"

Ross spins at my voice. His hands are cupped, chopped mushrooms spilling over the edge of them. "Hey." His smile is filled with both relief and concern.

"What's wrong?" I rush to his side.

The flame beneath a second pan sparks bright orange. Something sizzles. Ross turns toward it. "Shit."

He dumps the mushrooms into the first pan and reaches for a wooden spoon, stirring the mixture.

"Like I said, we might be in trouble," Harley mumbles somewhere behind us.

Placing my hand on Ross's back, I peer into the first pan. Whatever is inside is boiling at a high heat and giving off a slightly noxious fume.

"Whatcha making?" I don't want to be anxious, or critical, but it doesn't look . . . appetizing.

"It's supposed to be mushroom risotto."

I glance from the pan to Ross. "Do you know how to make mushroom risotto? Because I'm pretty certain it's not by boiling mushrooms, or with the goopy mess of rice inside the second pan.

"Not really." Ross lowers his eyes and rolls his lips. His broad shoulders fall. He's so disappointed in himself, it is endearing. He wanted to make us dinner. Me and my girls.

I reach for the stove and turn off the flames. "Maybe we should just order pizza." With my hand still stroking up his back, I try to sooth the blow to his ego while reassuring him pizza is a good idea.

"Are you . . . Ross Davis?" Hannah asks, echoing her sister's tone from yesterday morning, and reminding us of our audience.

I drop my hand, and Ross and I turn as one, watching Hannah's eyes widen. "You *are* Ross Davis."

"Brilliant. My family has strongly confirmed who you are," I mutter to him.

"And your mom is V. C. Hux," Harley states, sounding equally impressed by me when I haven't been the one to explain to him who I am.

I turn toward Ross. "You told him?"

"He asked questions."

"Kids have a nasty habit of doing that." I laugh.

Ross and I smile at one another until Hannah interjects again. "Are you two dating?" Her question is stated as if she can't believe it. Her mom. A famous baseball coach. *Like how incredulous would that be?*

"Who's dating?" The strong masculine voice comes from a dark-haired kid who is the image of his father in body stature. Height. Width. His face is round, but his eyes are molten chocolate.

"I think your dad is dating our mom," Laurel clarifies for the young man I assume is Landon.

"We aren't dating," I immediately state.

"We aren't?" Ross turns to me, eyes wide and hurt.

"Well . . ." How the hell do we explain ourselves to our kids? *I'm sleeping with your dad?* Only, it's not just sleeping anymore because he had his tongue, mouth, and fingers all over me last night, and yeah, that just does not need to be shared with the class.

Ross turns back toward his boys and runs his hand up my spine, squeezing the back of my neck. "Landon, this is Verona Huxley. Vee. And we are seeing each other."

"What does seeing each other mean?" Hannah asks.

"I think it's like *talking to*." Laurel crooks her fingers in air quotes. "You know, when someone isn't your boyfriend yet but you're exclusively talking to one another." Laurel turns toward us. "You are exclusive, right?" Her eyes narrow. Her question is direct and fired at Ross because my girls know their father cheated on me.

Thanks to the rather loud arguments Cameron and I once had, my girls heard things. Things I tried to delicately explain while not making excuses for their father. I refused to dismiss his adultery while attempting to forgive him.

What kind of example had I been for my girls, though? I wanted to portray fortitude in a marriage, but honestly, nothing would erase what he'd done. There hadn't been time for closure or forgiveness before he was taken from us. And, I should have shown my girls not to take shitty treatment, wedding band on your finger or not.

"We're exclusive," Ross states, squeezing my neck a little more firmly. Reminding me of what he said the other morning.

"And how long has this been going on?" Landon asks, his tone nearly as sharp as Laurel's.

"November," Ross says, when I say, "March." We look at one another.

He hasn't been with anyone since November? He explained the Chandler situation, but I still thought there had been others between our meeting in Houston and seeing each other in Arizona.

I glance back at four sets of eyes watching Ross and me. I've never been in this position before. My girls meeting a man. Or me meeting a man's children. The moment feels a bit surreal, especially if I add in that Ross Davis is who he is.

Hannah is still starstruck while Laurel is suddenly eyeing Ross with deeper concern.

Harley is smiling like he's been in on the secret for a while, while Landon crosses his thick arms over his chest and glares at his dad.

"How about pizza?" I choke out, wanting to derail the inquisition of Ross and me. And maybe wipe the scowl off Landon's face. Food can be a good distraction.

"Thank God," Harley dramatically states while Laurel pulls out her phone.

"What do you like?" she asks the room in general, taking over to scan for local pizza places. And suddenly four adult children are glancing at their phones, scrolling pizza options, and firing off ingredients they prefer, giving Ross and me a break.

"That went well," I mumble, turning in his direction.

"We aren't dating?" He scans my face, his eyes weary, concerned even.

"Ross," I warn softly. "Maybe we should discuss this later." We've narrowly gone unscathed just being in the same room as each other. I slip a quick glance at Ross's oldest son. "Landon doesn't look too happy."

Thankfully, the kids fall easily into conversation with each other, occasionally including the *older* adults in the room. Laurel goes into teacher mode, making certain everyone participates, keeping everyone engaged, while Harley has his theatre schooling on display. Hannah and Landon are a bit quieter but they each laugh at the antics of their siblings, and slowly any tension in the air dissipates until the girls and I prepare to leave.

"Don't you want to spend the night?" Harley teases. "You still owe me pancakes."

"I took you to The Syrup Tap," I remind him.

"What?" Hannah's head whips in my direction so quickly her neck must crack. Her offense is obvious in her tone. How dare I take someone to her favorite place without her.

"Tomorrow we can go there," I say to her.

"Why would you be spending the night?" Landon asks, his gaze going from me to his dad.

The conversation comes full circle.

"Because that's what Dad and Verona do," Harley continues. A smile graces his face, like what he's suggesting is no big deal. *Adult sleepovers anyone?*

"What do you mean, *that's what Dad and Verona do?*"

"Dad said Verona is his good luck charm. When she sleeps here, the Anchors win."

Uh-oh.

"What the fuck?" Landon blurts, turning toward his father. His folded arms slip to his sides, fists clenched.

"Hey." Ross glares back at his eldest son, agitated as well. "Watch it."

"Baseball players are so silly." Harley waves at my girls, as if the playful movement can unravel the blooming tension.

"On that note, I think it really is time to go. Thank you for the pizza. It was great to meet you, Landon." Although I'm not certain the sentiment is reciprocated.

"I'll walk you out," Ross states, stepping forward like he'll follow us.

I hold up my hand, then awkwardly twist it like I intend to shake his, making the moment even more ridiculous. "We've got it."

Ross stares at my outstretched hand, and for a second, I imagine him wanting to bat my hand away, cup my face, and kiss me senseless in front of all four of our children so I'll stop acting so strange. Then again, kissing me in front of our kids would be even stranger, and the image quickly vanishes.

"I'll call you later." Ross ignores my hand, which I eventually lower.

Harley saves the moment by reaching for Laurel and then Hannah, hugging each of them before coming toward me.

"I messed up, didn't I?" he whispers, but I shake my head when I pull out of his embrace.

Ross and I messed up as we don't know how to define what we're doing with each other.

Chapter 31

[Ross]

"Don't you think she's a little old for you?" Landon asks as soon as I close the door on that awkward as hell exit from Vee and her daughters. Sarcasm drips from my oldest son's tone.

"Excuse me?" I glare at Landon, who was an ass the entire evening. His tense body language. His sharp responses.

"I mean, your tastes typically run younger and flashier." His voice is full of accusation, one that expresses his displeasure.

My glare narrows even more, jaw clenching as I warn him, "Watch your step, son."

Not backing down, he continues. "She's almost . . . normal." The comment clarifies what I've known about my son for a while. He hasn't approved of me dating younger women, based on their age alone. A woman in her early thirties is closer in age to my twenty-two-year-old son. But I doubt it's always been their age that bothers him. It's their distance from him, as models, movie stars, and reality TV celebrities.

"She reminds me of Mom." Harley says.

The truth hits me hard.

Vee doesn't look anything like Patty, nor are they similar in personality. But I also understand what Harley means. Vee is sweet and considerate. Kind and gracious. She's fun to be around, funny in many instances, easy going in others. And she believes in me, like Patty once did. Vee is just . . . spectacularly Vee.

Glancing at Landon, I realize that's the crux. He's angry that I'm with someone resembling his mother because she *is* more my age. Vee has lived longer than his mother, too.

Jesus. How do I tiptoe around this?

"Got an issue with me dating her?" I question, not that his opinion would sway me, but I'd still like to understand what his problem is.

"You do you," he snarks and turns away from me.

"Hey," I bark, causing him to pause. "What's going on here?"

Harley is suddenly very still, head lowered, eyes aimed at the floor. "Do you have any idea what it's like being your son?" Landon rounds on me.

Of course, on a literal level, I have no idea what it's like, but figuratively, I imagine it's difficult at times. Kids can be cruel and when your dad coaches a beloved professional team that loses occasionally, kids have mouths that hurt. Then again, if your dad is a success, kids only want to be your friend because they think you have pull. Free shit, game tickets, special passes.

That bullshit I understand, and I've apologized over the years for other people's children.

However, I don't think Landon is specifically talking about how others react to him being my son. Rather, he's asking if I understand what it's like to be the child of Ross Davis.

"Lonely," I admit because I've been as present as I can but not present enough. Rena used to tell me I was doing the best I could. However, Patty had complaints before she passed.

Landon stares at me.

"Look." I brush my forefinger and thumb around my mouth. "I know I haven't always been the best dad. Maybe you think I'm the worst. But I am really hopeful moving here will be a positive change for all of us."

"I've heard that before," Landon mumbles referring to our original move to Philadelphia after Patty died. I had thought the change would be good for all of us. My sister was there to help. I could continue with baseball on a new level. My boys could have a fresh start. Chicago . . . hurt.

However, they did not need a new beginning back then. They'd needed me, and guilt eats at me that I hadn't been present often enough. With them both in the Midwest now, coaching for the Anchors was the fresh start *I* needed with them. The location keeps us relatively close to each other, at least geographically.

"Dad came to my play," Harley reminds Landon, his voice low, but defending me. "Vee brought him."

I sigh. "I brought Vee." It isn't that Vee wouldn't have willingly gone to see the play, if I'd told her beforehand where we were going. It's just . . . *I* asked her to attend. I wanted to see my son. That date was all me. "Because I wanted to be there for you."

"You haven't—" Landon starts but is quickly stopped when Harley raises a hand.

"But he is here now," Harley defends me again. My sweeter boy is becoming a stronger man.

I force my shoulders lower, but my back remains tight. One step doesn't give me a free pass to father of the year, but it's a start on the climb to building a better relationship with my boys. A start I need.

And Vee in my life is helping me do that.

I've never purposely brought a woman to my home. Never purposely introduced my boys to a woman I'm dating. Vee and I need to clarify that vocabulary.

Harley interrupts my thought when he says, "Mom is gone. And I miss her all the time."

My chest squeezes tight. Fuck, the ache for Patty runs deep sometimes.

"But we can't bring her back." Harley pointedly looks at his brother, sharing some secret conversation between them as siblings. Siblings who lost their mother too young and have had a relatively absent father. "And we can't live in the past either. We can't change if Dad had a game or not. If he was present or not."

Ouch. The truth hurts. It always hurts.

"But he's here now."

Jesus. Again. This kid will be my undoing as he sticks up for me with my other boy.

"And I like Vee." Harley turns his head, inspecting me. "She's good for you."

My face heats. My heart hammers. How does he know me so well?

"She is good for me. I like her," I openly admit. "She makes me laugh." I mean, what the hell was with that outstretched hand like she wanted to shake mine? I wanted to pin her to the wall and kiss her senseless right before our kids' eyes.

Fuck dating. Fuck defining us. Vee is mine and I am hers.

"She makes me smile." My face heats. "I like her quirks and her kindness. And she gets me."

I glance from Landon to Harley and back. "Maybe she is older than other women I've dated."

"In the past eight years," Landon mutters his correction, his gaze lowered.

"But." I exhale, setting my hands on my hips. "That makes her better." Wiser. Compassionate on a different level. A finer thing in my life. "She understands me."

That I need reader glasses and my knees creak when I stand upright, like after kneeling on the floor between her legs last night.

"She believes in me. That I can change. That I can be better. And I'm not giving her up." I stand taller, facing my boys. I want them to like Vee, but I don't *need* them to accept her. Vee is for me, not them.

"She's nicer than Chandler," Harley states.

Chandler wasn't cruel to my boys, she was worse, she'd been indifferent. She liked the idea of a single dad but not the reality of it. She didn't like kids, and although my boys are young, she didn't relate to them on the *one* occasion she'd been present around them.

Vee won Harley over with chocolate chip pancakes. Apparently, Landon is a tougher sell.

"It's your life, Dad. Date who you want," he dismissively states.

Still not liking his insolent attitude, I reply, "I will."

"But what's with this sleeping thing?" Landon wrinkles his nose in disgust while Harley laughs.

Yeah, I'm not finding it funny that Harley spilled the beans with the watered-down version of my relationship with Vee. The one where I told him I felt lucky Vee stayed in our home, and the Anchors had a winning streak on the road.

"Moment of truth?" I question which perks up both boys, their attention suddenly riveted to me. "I met Vee the night the Flash lost the championship. We got stuck in a hotel elevator together. Feeling sorry for myself, guilty that the loss was somehow my fault, I went to her hotel room, and we talked. *Only talked.*" I emphasize. "And the next day, I got the call from the Anchors, wanting me as their coach. I took the offer as a sign. Vee was good luck."

"That was one night," Landon reminds me, scowling and skeptical.

"But then I saw her again in Arizona, after Sylver and Valdez got into it on the field."

Landon groans. As much as he might have resentment toward my coaching position, he loves baseball. He played all through high school. He was a student athlete, and hoped for a college scholarship, but ultimately his choice had to come down to what he wanted to be in life. The scholarships came from universities that didn't interest him. He wants to be an engineer, and he recognized he needed to follow his heart more than money.

"And the Anchors won again." Maybe not as consistently as recently, but with Vee in my life, the Anchors had more ups than downs.

"Can't you just have a lucky pair of socks or something?" Landon asks. His concern shows despite the joke.

Tilting my head, I stare at my son. "Are you worried I'm using her?"

"Aren't you?"

Since when is my son such a defender? Then I recall my thoughts about people using him to get closer to me or a team. I fight a smile, pride swelling in my chest. My son isn't against Vee, he's actually more upset on her behalf. He wants to protect her.

With a smile on my face, I say, "I am not using her."

"She said you weren't dating," Harley reminds me. His brows creased with worry.

"And I plan to change that misconception."

Because as far as I'm concerned, Vee is my girl, not a good luck charm.

+++

"Hey," Vee sleepily whispers into the phone when I call her later that night. The hour isn't late, but I've clearly disturbed her.

"Are you in bed?" My ribcage tightens. I wish I was there with her, or she was here with me.

"Sudden headache."

"Is there anything I can do?" The boys are more than capable of taking care of themselves. I can go to the pharmacy for her or order a delivery. Or—

"It will pass. I just need to close my eyes and melt into this dark room."

My heart begins to hammer. I don't want her to brush off a simple headache. Patty did that too often.

"What can I do?" I ask, preparing to grab a jacket and leave the house. I'll stay with her all night.

"I'll be good by morning. Just need some sleep."

Did I keep her up too late the other night? The play, dinner, her living room, and talking.

"Did you write today?" We haven't discussed if our night together inspired her.

"The words can wait," she states drowsily.

"Okay, sweetheart. You rest. Call me in the morning?"

"You got it, Coach. I'm mentally smacking your ass."

Quirky. I chuckle, bidding her to sleep well, even if it is without me.

My bed is too empty without her. My heart full, though, whenever we talk. I love her ticks and teases. Her laughter and smiles. Even her awkwardness, like holding out her hand instead of hugging me goodbye earlier.

I love everything about Vee.

I think I *love* her.

The thought doesn't hit me as hard as I expect. Not like a fast ball coming at you at ninety-seven miles per hour. Falling for her was more like a perfect hit. One where your eyes are on the ball. The timing. The speed. You know you can't miss. And *bam!* It's still a surprise but you've been anticipating this hit. Waiting for the right pitch. Hopeful. Eager.

Longing for it. With the crack of the bat against the ball, you watch the ball soar and then you race. Run like hell for that first kiss, steal all the seconds for each touch. Marvel as you round third, praising all things heavenly for the opportunity, the chances, the freedom to be this close to her. Then you hit home plate, relief fills your chest, pride fills your heart. And love, so much love, and gratitude. I'll be thankful for every day I get to love Vee.

She's my homerun.

+ + +

The next day, I'm relieved to easily find Vee in the stands with Hannah beside her. The Anchors win, and when the game finishes I climb the dugout steps to the field, hoping to catch Vee's attention. With her back to the field, exiting her row, I call her phone and watch as she stalls, grabs her phone from her bag, and checks the screen. She stops walking, allowing people to go around her as she faces the field and answers.

"Good game, Coach." I hear the smile in her voice.

"Be a better game if you come to my place later."

"Wow, that's quite the invitation."

"So, you'll come."

A heavy pause falls between us, and I consider what I've said.

"You know, I'm a romance author and that means my mind goes dirty places sometimes."

I hum. "Definitely want to go dirty places with you, Vee."

"Is this a booty call?"

I watch as Hannah's head whips toward her mother and I chuckle. "Sweetheart."

Vee laughs as well, perhaps knowing she just embarrassed her daughter.

"If you want this to be a booty call, it can be. Or I can just check out your booty from here, watching you walk up those stadium stairs."

"Would you do that?" More laughter fills the question.

ELEVATOR PITCH

"Absolutely." My grin grows. I meant what I told my boys last night, I like Vee, but the word doesn't encompass my entire range of emotions. My feelings are so much more than just liking her, but I don't want to scare her with their strength. We still have a few things to iron out between us first. "So you'll come . . . over, that is."

"Let me send Hannah off. What about Landon and Harley? Are they both still around?"

"Landon left this morning. Harley went back to this apartment last night."

"Want to cook together?" she asks, not exactly mentioning my utter failure at making dinner yesterday, but it had been a disaster.

"I have a better idea. I'll order in."

"Sounds like a date, Ross Davis."

"See you soon, Verona Huxley."

I click off the phone and glance up to see Romero Valdez and Bolan Adler a few feet away from me. Each of them are chatting up women. Romero is unfortunately speaking with Ford Sylver's ex-wife. Bolan chats with his wife. He was married quickly before the season began and his wife Ruth seems sweet but standoffish.

"Gentlemen, locker room," I call out to them, knowing I've taken my own time to get to where I need to be.

Both men say their goodbyes and the echoing clomp of their cleats trails behind me in the tunnel leading to the locker room.

"Got a girlfriend, Coach?" Valdez calls out behind me.

If I did, I wouldn't trust him around her. Vee and I still haven't officially declared who we are to each other. Haven't confirmed the whole boyfriend-girlfriend terminology. And I wouldn't be sharing anything with anyone before talking to Vee. We're public but I don't need us sensationalized. I don't want that circus for Vee.

I don't respond to Valdez, not particularly liking to speak with him outside what's necessary for the team. It's a difficult position to be in. I want to like everyone. I want to treat them all equally, but Valdez is just one of those players I'm struggling to like as a human being.

"Ah, give Coach a break," Adler says. "We can't all be the Romeo you are," he teases our short stop.

"You were once a Romeo, too," Valdez reminds Adler of his former reputation. The one that sent him overseas for a while to play in Japan. His lawyer got him a new agent and brought Bolan back to the U.S., and the Anchors acquired the thirty-something catcher shortly before this season began.

"Now you've got that ring weighing down your finger," Valdez continues. "I don't know how you handle such a mouse in your bed."

The sudden scuffle of cleats and the definitive sound of a body slamming against a cement wall has me turning and rushing toward my players. Of whom, one is plastered to the tunnel wall by the forearm the other is holding against his throat.

"Don't speak about Ruthie like that. In fact, don't even look in her direction."

"Hey," I snap, slipping my arm between them. "Adler, step back." Not that Valdez's comments were warranted, but Bolan is the bigger of the two men, and he's the one holding the other against a wall.

"You're a shit stirrer," Adler states, not letting up on his teammate despite my attempts to whittle between them. "And no one likes you."

"*Ohh*, you hurt my feelings." Valdez's whimper is delivered in a taunting falsetto.

"Okay. That's enough." If Bolan hadn't pressed Romero to the wall, I might have done it myself. But even if I have a negative opinion of Romero, I can't let the team become divided again. With Ford's injury, and his absence because of it, the team has finally settled down a bit about the animosity between the two men.

And Valdez just came off his suspension for his role in that injury.

"Adler, back up," I warn, still trying to force them apart. Bolan is roughly my size but ten years younger than me, which gives him strength.

With a final shove against Valdez's throat, he presses off his teammate and takes a large step back. I'm left shielding Valdez, who is thinner and shorter, but no less scrappy than his larger teammate.

"Maybe what your little wife needs is a real man in her bed."

Goddammit.

Bolan rushes forward and I spin to face Valdez, attempting once again to body block Adler from getting to him.

"You're fucking toast," Adler hollers around me, his breath heated at the side of my head.

"Hey!" The call comes from my left before feet thunder down the tunnel and someone pulls Adler off my back. My hands have been against the wall, using the strength in my arms to cage in Valdez and keep Adler off his teammate, but I press off the cement and step back.

"You make another comment like that about someone's wife, girlfriend, daughter or female friend or otherwise, and I'll have you off this team."

Valdez's dark eyes narrow. His jaw clenches. He's only on this team because of a midseason trade last year, and I'll do the same to him this year.

"In fact, I'll go one further. I'll make certain you never play for anyone."

"You can't do that," he grits.

"Watch me." I've been in professional baseball for over twenty years. I know managers and front offices, and while my word might not be gold, it still would hold weight. There's a new alignment in sports with what's appropriate and not appropriate behavior, and trash talking someone's person is never acceptable. Not in my house. Not on my field.

"Get your ass in the locker room," Dalton Ryatt yells at Valdez. Dalton has good rapport with the guys, and at times, he's the only one who can handle a hothead. Sometimes I worry he might make a better head coach.

Valdez doesn't lower his head but holds it higher, as he steps away from the wall. But he can't let the situation rest and turns his head, spitting at the cement floor inches in front of Adler's feet.

"*Pendejo,*" Valdez mutters. *Asshole.*

Adler struggles beneath the hold of both Kip and another catcher, Cyrus Sawyer.

Dalton shakes his head as he follows behind Romero. As they leave, all the air seems to exit the tunnel.

"Coach, you need to do something about him," Adler addresses me.

"I'm handling him." *But am I?* One bad pitch doesn't ruin a game. But repeatedly bad throws? That player needs re-coaching or to be let go.

"Are you calm yet?" Kip asks Bolan, stepping back and holding up a hand near Bolan's chest, prepared to hold him back again if necessary.

"Yeah. I'm good." But the edge in his voice suggests he's anything but calm. We could use a few more minutes in this tunnel to settle him down, not to mention give time for Valdez to clear out of the locker room.

I don't want to be babysitter to a bunch of grown men, but I can prevent shenanigans from happening in that room. I'll need to be more vigilant and discuss this new infraction with my coaching staff.

I'd like to offer encouraging words to Bolan. Tell him that Valdez didn't mean what he said or that he won't go near Bolan's wife, but I can't make those kinds of promises.

Instead, I say, "Let me know what you need. For Ruth."

Bolan stares at me. "What do you mean?"

"If you're worried about her. Him getting anywhere near her, I'll file a restraining order myself, if you need me to."

Bolan bitterly huffs. "Yeah, I don't think that will be necessary. He's just talking shit. But that shit needs to stop." My catcher still looks rattled by Romero's words despite trying to dismiss them.

While I think his sudden marriage feels a bit too coincidental to the start of the season and a need to clean up his reputation, I don't question my men's personal lives unless it interferes with the team.

Romero has disrupted this team enough. He's crossed the line to foul territory and there might be no coming back.

Chapter 32

[Vee]

Ross greets me at his door in a pair of joggers and a white T-shirt, but we don't get much further than this entryway before his hands cup my face and he kisses me. His tongue rushes forward, slinking against mine as the kiss deepens.

"How are you feeling?" he mutters against my mouth.

"Good?" I giggle. Then, I realize he means my headache from last night. He already messaged me this morning to ask how I was feeling. "Better."

That answer satisfies him, and his mouth returns to mine, the kiss overwhelming. My tote slips from my arm, landing with a thud on the floor before I wrap my arms around his neck, leaning into the kiss more. Ross presses forward, pinning me against the front door, his large body flush with mine.

"This is quite the greeting," I tease, unprepared for such a welcome to his house and wondering what's gotten into him.

Ross stares into my eyes a second before leaning back and gently pulling me from the door by holding my hand. "Want a drink?" Still holding onto me, he leads me into his kitchen, and I stop near the large island, in the spot where I'd spent a few days finding inspiration to write within his home.

"This is where the magic happened." I whisper for some reason.

"What magic?"

"Words."

Ross stops abruptly as well and steps behind me. His arms wrap around my waist, and he presses his face into my neck, peppering me with kisses there. I tilt my head, the tender touch exciting.

"What do you mean?"

"I wrote. Right here." I point to the spot where I'd placed my laptop.

"Let's write another story." Ross hums against my neck. "I like you in my home." He tightens his hold, kissing me deeper along the column of my throat, sucking harder at my skin.

"You okay?" I ask, rubbing my hand over his strong, tattooed forearm around me.

"Rough day at the office," he mutters.

"How can I help?" I whisper, my senses overloaded by his kisses.

"Want inside you."

The request sends a sudden rush up my center. I've been the one to put the brakes on sex, yet my body is pedal to the floor prepared to speed ahead.

"Should we talk?" I murmur, as his kisses become more urgent against my skin. My head tips forward and he scoops up my hair, giving him access to my nape. He scrapes his teeth there and my knees buckle.

Holy shit, that feels good.

"Talk later?" he grunts, giving me an out when he doesn't want one. "Question three. For your research purposes. I can explain everything afterward."

"Okay," I moan, unable to speak my own name, unable to recall question three.

Ross hums at my ear. "Yeah?"

I sink my teeth into my lower lip and nod.

Ross lowers his hands and unbuttons my jeans, easily slipping a hand into them and beneath my underwear until he's cupping between my thighs. The first swipe of his finger, I jolt backwards, knocking my backside into the thick, hard, length bulging against his soft joggers.

I reach behind me, fumbling to feel him in my hands, noticing how thin the sweatpants are and easily disguising . . . "No underwear?"

"Let's get yours off."

"So bossy." But I'm quickly quieted as Ross removes his hands from my jeans and steps back, tugging my pants down, along with my underwear, in one fierce pull. I kick out of my flip flops and use my feet to pull my ankles free from my jean-underwear combination.

Bare from the waist down, Ross's mouth is on my neck again, as he presses my shirt upward and then over my head. He unclasps my bra, nudging the straps to slip free of my arms. Naked in his kitchen, with my hands on the countertop edge, Ross peppers open mouth kisses down my spine.

"God, I love your back."

Such a strange compliment. I can't see my back, so I don't suppose there is anything special about it, but with the attention he gives my spine, the sucking kisses along that ridge down the middle of my body, he makes me feel special. When he gets to my backside, he lowers to one knee behind me, spreads my legs apart and hitches one of my feet on the shelf of his leg. Open, and exposed to him, he leans forward and licks my center.

Mouth hungry. Hands roaming. Everything is happening so fast.

The first lap is quick and thorough before the tip of his tongue finds that tight nub, giving it all his attention. I lean forward, forehead resting on the countertop as Ross works his magic, melting me in the heat of his kitchen. My hands reach for the outer edge of the counter, needing something to brace myself as my hips rock with his eager attention to my core.

"Ross," I warn, surprised how quickly I'm rounding the bases, heading for a homerun. This isn't why I came here, isn't what I thought would happen. But who am I kidding? I want Ross as much as he says he wants me.

For research purposes.

Letting my thoughts drift and my body take over, I sink into the pleasure he's giving me. Licking. Lapping. Until his fingers are inside me.

I cry out at the sudden intrusion, relishing in the invasion, and dripping down his hand.

I'm a mess as I tip over the edge, a cresting wave crashing against a lakeside break wall. The thunderous roll of a rushing tide battering against the cement beach only blocks from this house. The release is quick, almost harsh, and over too soon.

When I finish riding the surf, Ross releases me, and I whimper at the loss of contact.

His knee cracks as he swiftly stands. I turn my head, watching as he shoves his joggers down his hips, freeing his hard length. Then, he's fisting himself and teasing my entrance with his tip.

I teased him about just the tip the other night, but Ross is on a mission. After a few swipes up and down the wetness coating sensitive folds, he awkwardly fumbles with the pocket of his joggers, down near his knees, before producing a foil packet.

"I like a man who's prepared," I kid, although I don't know why I'm making a joke. His preparedness should be a little disconcerting.

"I like you," he says, swiftly covering himself. The depth of his voice, the intensity of how he said what he said, has me standing upright.

I spin to face him, palming his jaw and drawing his attention to my face. "I like you, too, Ross." The words don't fully encompass how I feel. I like him more than I should. And when all is said and done, I'm certain I'm the one who will suffer a broken heart.

Ross's mouth comes to mine again, kissing me deeply, swiping his tongue inside my mouth as if lapping up my declaration.

I like you can sound so weak as a statement and yet still mean so much.

With his hands on my hips, he lifts me to his countertop and then lines himself up at my entrance again. I fall back, catching myself with my hands, bracing myself upright with my arms.

Ross concentrates, watching as he enters me. He pauses a second once deeply seated, allowing me to adjust. Except for the other night, it feels like it's been forever since we've been this close, this intimate.

With my mouth hanging open, his thumb and forefinger cup my jaw. "Fuck, do I like you a lot, sweetheart."

Me? Or this position? I don't ask. I can't think because he's sliding to the edge before surging inward again.

"When I'm with you, I feel . . . whole."

My breath catches as he's still cupping my jaw.

"Warm. Wanted. Home."

With him buried inside me, my heart races from both his words and the after-effects of my first orgasm.

Ross pulls back, then rushes forward, filling me again, stealing my breath a third time. In the weeks that have passed, I cannot believe I've forgotten how big he is. How deep he gets. How full he makes me feel.

Whole. Warm. Wanted. Home.

"Oh God," I whimper. "I like all of that." What he's saying. What he's doing.

"Yeah." He chuckles, repeating the motion, taking his time, finding a rhythm. The movement happens in such a way the ridge of his cock drags along that sensitive spot, tingling from my first release, yet quickly spiraling toward a second one.

I don't know how he's doing what he's doing, but I don't want him to stop.

"Want to feel you let go around me." He kisses me, hard and fast. "Want to feel everything with you."

He grips one of my ankles, placing my foot on the edge of the counter to open me up for him.

Clinging to his biceps, I use his body to support mine as he fills me over and over again. His hands press against my lower back to steady me. His arms around me pins my raised leg to my side.

"Ross." I gasp, shocked at my body's sudden response to him.

As I let go, shattering a second time, Ross moves faster, plunging deeper within me. His pace picks up until a final surge forces him still. Only deep inside my depths does he pulse and jolt.

"Ahh," he grunts, letting go within me while tightening his hold on my lower back, pinning me to him.

Eventually, he buries his face in my neck, and I wrap my arms around his, holding him to me, wishing I'd never have to let him go. He releases my leg and I collapse against him.

Never wanting us to end. Never wanting him to ever think I don't bring him good fortune.

+ + +

We clean up by showering together, where Ross takes his time to thoroughly wash my body before I scrub his. We don't make it sexual, but we tease one another in sacred places. I'm spent and Ross seems like he has something on his mind. The same something he tried to rid from his thoughts when I entered his place.

"Want to talk about it?"

"Talk about what?" He asks, twisting side to side in the shower for a final rinse of the body wash I spread over his tight skin.

"Whatever that was when I entered your house."

"Good sex?" His eyes sparkle.

"Well, there was that, too, but something else was on your mind first." And unfortunately, I don't think it was me. Do I feel used for sex? Used as a means of distraction? Not really, but I'm still a little unsettled by the rapidness of what happened. "But something else seems like it's bothering you."

Ross shuts off the water and I shiver, my body sensing what my head hasn't caught up to yet. Is he going to break up with me? After what just happened, I don't want to question him, but he's clearly upset by something.

He pops open the shower door and reaches for a towel before rubbing it over my hair and swiping down my body then wrapping the thick material around me. He grabs his own towel, and strokes down his chest before wrapping it around his waist, then runs his hand over his hair.

"Let's talk in my room."

"That sounds ominous." My stomach drops again, a nauseous slosh rumbling around within me.

Ross leads me to his bedroom attached to the ensuite bathroom and rifles through a drawer, presenting me with a T-shirt. The soft white material does nothing to comfort the unease tickling up my spine. Ross is suddenly pensive.

I climb up on the edge of his bed, desperate to pull the thick duvet over my legs and curl into the covers as a means to hide.

ELEVATOR PITCH

Ross tugs on the joggers he'd been wearing when I entered his house, and he faces me.

"I don't think I'm a very good coach."

"What?" The tension in my shoulders lessens. "Why would you say that?"

"Valdez and Adler got into after the game today. In the tunnel."

"Why?" I sit up straighter.

"Valdez made a crack about Adler's wife."

"Bolan Adler? The new catcher? I didn't know he was married." And I don't know why I'm speaking in questions.

"They were married before the season started. Rather spontaneously."

"Is she pregnant?"

Ross's brows lift. "I hadn't even thought of that, but I don't think so." He pauses like he's considering what I've asked. "Either way, Romero called Ruth a mouse, and Bolan reacted. Then Romero had to take it a step further suggesting he was more man than Bolan in bed."

"What the heck? Men are so ridiculous."

"Yeah, Adler did not appreciate either comment. Pinned Valdez to the wall like he was a swatted fly."

I chuckle softly at the image. "How does any of that make you a bad coach?"

Ross flings his arms out to the side before slipping his hands into his jogger pockets. "Because my players are always fighting with each other."

I watch Ross a second, taking in his sunken shoulders and lowered head. He isn't a bad coach. In fact, the Anchors are having one of the best seasons they've had since he played for the team nearly ten years ago. He's doing something right.

"Did your boys fight as kids?"

He chuckles bitterly. "All the time. They're so different from one another."

"It's no different on a team. You have all these diverse temperaments and backgrounds. Think about it. Your boys came from the same house, and they are vastly different from each other, right? Which makes them unique."

I take a deep breath. "These men are like your children. Same house, same rules. But they *aren't* your children. You're in charge of them, but not their emotions. Not their pasts. Not their personalities. You're top dog over the team."

"Top dog?" His head lifts as his eyes widen.

"You're the alpha male."

His lids lower, eyes narrowing. "Is this a romance novel thing?"

Ignoring the tease, I continue. "Leader of the pack."

He stares at me.

"And as such, you decide who stays or goes. Who plays or sits."

"You're saying I should bench Valdez."

"I'm saying, he needs a lesson in *teamship*."

"I don't think that's a word."

Forgiving his vocabulary correction, I carry on. "And as the coach, you need to mentor him. Teach an old dog new tricks."

"We're back to the dog allegory?" he teases, his mouth slowly crooking up on one side.

"Show him what it means to be a good team member."

"How?" Ross sighs. "Suggest *not* sleeping with your teammate's wife."

"He did that?" I sit taller, astonished by that news. Maybe I'd heard hints of such a thing happening, but who can believe what social media says, especially the clock app running rampant with rumors, thinking *they* created someone's fame and then undoubtedly ruining it.

Ross doesn't answer me, but his eyes confirm what I once thought was gossip.

"Well, in that case, off with his head." I chop the side of one hand against the palm of the other. "He's out of the pack. Left to starve on his own."

"Is this a pep talk?" Ross chuckles a little deeper this time. "Somehow, I don't think Valdez will starve. For attention or otherwise."

"Babe, you're in charge either way. If he doesn't align with your goals for the team, or the professional image you want to portray, cut him loose."

"Say that again." Slowly, the corner of his mouth curls higher and he takes a step closer to the bed where I sit.

"If he doesn't align—"

"Not that part."

"Oh, was cutting him loose too harsh?"

Ross leans forward, his face drawing closer to mine as he spreads his arms and braces a hand on either side of me on the bed. His voice drops. "Not that part either."

I swallow at his nearness, inhaling the scent of his body wash lingering on him. "You're in charge?"

"I liked hearing that, too, but I meant the first word." He smiles wide, like the Cheshire cat.

"Babe?"

His grin holds. His eyes dance. "Now say it like you mean it."

"You want me to call you babe?"

He shrugs, lowering his gaze, and suddenly retreating from me, like he's embarrassed he wants to be called an endearment. His vulnerability has me reaching out and clasping the back of his neck, so he can't get too far from me.

"I like when you call me sweetheart. And I'm happy to call you babe, babe."

"Now you're making fun of me." He scowls, leaning back against my hand like he wants to break free off my hold.

"Babe," I whisper. "Kiss me."

His smile slowly returns, twisting like he's fighting it. "Like a top dog?"

I laugh. "Like an alpha male."

Ross doesn't need a lesson in what that means because his mouth lands on mine in such a way, we're falling back on his bed, tangling together, and kissing like I'm his omega.

+ + +

After several minutes of heavy kissing and my relief that what was on Ross's mind was team related, and not personal, he suggests we crawl into his bed. He clicks on the television, orders us some dinner, and then asks, "Need any clarification on how it feels to have sex with you. For your writing purposes."

Right. For research purposes.

"I think I'm good on the basics."

"Basics?" Ross snorts. "There was nothing basic about the way you were perched on my counter, foot on the edge, open and wet for me, dripping to the granite."

"Ross," I moan.

"That pretty pussy on display and my hard cock slipping into you, getting deep."

"Jesus," I hiss, stirrings within me coming to life again. I swish my thighs together beneath the blankets over my lap.

Ross doesn't miss the movement and arches a brow. "Need more?"

There's no doubt I could go again but I don't want to be greedy.

For research purposes.

Saved by the doorbell, our food is delivered, and Ross asks me to stay in his bed. "We'll picnic." He disappears and returns quickly with the salad and pasta he ordered for us on a tray, plus a bottle of wine underneath his arm.

For the next hour we watch bad television and laugh, until Ross says, "Come to Philly next week."

The statement comes out of nowhere, and I snortle as a means to brush it off. "I can't just whisk off to Philadelphia."

With Ross perched up on his side, elbow supporting him, he gazes at me. "Yes, you can. I'll pay for your ticket."

"I don't need you to buy my ticket," I say a bit disgruntled. What I need is to understand where this invitation is coming from? Just like what happened earlier in his kitchen, this request feels sudden and a bit suspicious.

"What would I do in Philadelphia besides hang out in a hotel room?"

Ross frowns. "Why would you be in a hotel room?"

I huff. "Because we don't do this." Frustration builds. "We don't go out." While Ross said we can be public, I still don't know what that entails. Once again, we're hiding out in a bedroom. Mine. His. A hotel room. A rental. Does any of it make a difference? It's only us in seclusion. And it isn't that I don't want Ross all to myself, it's that I'm worried he's keeping me only for him. He doesn't want others to know I exist.

"We went to Harley's play."

He's right. His kid's play. And I'm not complaining. I actually think it was sweet he brought me to something so personal to him. I'm honored.

"We went to Hole in the Rock," he adds.

Now he's just being silly. So we've had two official dates.

"Aren't you worried the superstition whisperer will be revealed, though?" When people eventually ask who I am and how he met me, and then wonder what he's doing with someone like me compared to everyone else he's been with over the years.

A few years back a rather famous silver fox actor suddenly had a girlfriend who was closer to his age, and showed it with her gray hair, don't care, attitude. Jealousy prevailed in every negative comment about her while I cheered her on. Hail to the older gal snagging such a hot man. Or rather, praise to him, latching onto such a smart, accomplished, strong-minded woman.

I can't seem to apply the same principle to myself, for some reason.

"Our secret will be revealed."

"You aren't a secret." Ross scowls, his voice rising as well, and he lifts his body, using his arm to hold himself upright.

"Why would you ask me to go to Philadelphia?" The question is an honest one.

"Because I want my girlfriend to meet my sister."

"Your *girlfriend*? What? When did that happen?" When did I become his girlfriend? Not that I need some big declaration, but this is a large label to put on a sleeping partner, who only a few days ago became the other half of an *us*.

"Vee, I think we've established we're together." His tone is meant to soothe but it only prickles my skin.

We are together, but everything seems like it's happening too fast. I've gone from a sleeping arrangement with a stranger to a one-night stand of incredible sex to two dates and now I'm his girlfriend. He went out with Chandler more times than he's been out with me, and he refused to call her his girlfriend. The label seems like too much. Like it isn't reality when all I want is Ross and I to be real.

I should be honored but I'm off-kilter.

"What about Landon?" His son is only an excuse I'm using to stall. To process how we've arrived here so quickly.

"What about him?"

"He didn't seem too happy to meet me." We didn't have the chance to discuss his son's reaction to me because of my headache last night.

Ross lowers his gaze while a proud smile curls his mouth. "He was worried I'm using you."

I lift my head and blink at Ross.

He chuckles to himself and lifts his head as well. "He was upset with me, not *about* you." He quickly explains the disadvantage to being a child of someone famous.

"Oh." That's kind of sweet. "But we haven't discussed the whole dating, not-dating awkwardness from last night." I suddenly feel raw and exposed, unable to navigate the vulnerability swirling inside me.

For research purposes, echoes through my head again. The sex was for motivation.

"I think we can safely say we're dating." Ross looks at me, hesitation in his eyes as well. "Maybe we can't have a ton of typical dates during the season, but I'll try my best."

Typical. Non-typical. Traditional. Non-traditional. Wasn't I the one arguing I didn't know there were definitions to the types of dates.

ELEVATOR PITCH

"Did other women meet your sister?" I shouldn't care. I shouldn't ask. Why am I making a big deal about this invitation?

"No." He hesitates. "I haven't declared anyone else my girlfriend, either." His statement reminds me again that Chandler broke things off with Ross because he wouldn't call her his girlfriend.

"Do you not want to be my girlfriend?" The vulnerability in his tone should have me doubling back, reassuring him I absolutely want that honor.

Instead, I say, "I'm so different from anyone else you've dated."

Ross slowly smiles. "That's what I love about you."

My eyes widen.

"I love that you don't want something from me. That I can surprise you." He watches my face, seeing how truly surprised I am by everything he's saying. "I love how you listen to me and then offer advice. Your pep talks are one of my favorite things." His smile widens.

"How you laugh. Your wit. Your smarts." Ross reaches out and brushes my hair back over my shoulder. "I love that you're a writer. You see things differently, creatively."

For research purposes.

"It just seems like meeting your sister is . . . a step."

Ross tilts his head, trying to read me. Trying to understand my hesitancy. I don't know why I'm struggling. I'm being juvenile.

"You met my boys. That's an even bigger step. I want to take all the steps with you, sweetheart." Ross kisses my shoulder. "What am I missing?"

His sister is important to him. I should be thrilled by the invitation. I don't know what's wrong with me.

Or maybe I do.

I'm out of my depths here, overwhelmed by his raw honesty, afraid to believe in it. I haven't been in any kind of serious relationship since Cameron and look how that turned out. And I'd been in the same position when my relationship with Cameron began. I'd pined for him as a young, foolish girl. Crushed on him until he noticed me. Then I gave him my whole heart and he crushed me.

Gah. Even in death, I'm allowing Cameron to mess with my head and my heart.

"I'll think about it." I pluck at the blanket over my lap.

"That means no." Ross rolls from the bed and bends over it to collect our leftovers, still present on the tray he'd set on the mattress. As he hastily picks up a crumbled paper napkin and reaches for his empty wineglass on his nightstand, I shove the bedcoverings off my legs.

"I think I should go home."

He quickly lifts his head and freezes. "I don't want you to leave."

But I don't want to stay. Maybe I'm overreacting. Maybe I'm panicked. From the moment I've entered his home tonight, it's been a rush of emotions.

Sex in his kitchen. *For research purposes.*

A playful shower. A pep talk. A picnic on his bed. And now this . . . I'm his girlfriend?

The title doesn't hold the weight I thought it would. Or maybe it holds too much weight because I can't get it out of my head that everything started on a simple crush and a silly arrangement.

"I'm going to go." I need some space. Some air. I don't think clearly with Ross close to me. I make rash decisions, like wanting to sleep curled up next to him, or wanting to have mind-blowing sex with him.

Wanting to believe he desires me on some deeper level, like calling me his anything.

I wish I was a crier after sex, letting all the emotions rush out of me in a physical manner, releasing this tense overwhelm and sudden self-doubt.

"Will you be at my game tomorrow?" he sheepishly asks, displaying further vulnerability that only pisses me off.

The game. I don't want to believe all he cares about is baseball and winning. That all he cares about is his stupid idea that I'm some talisman, and now perhaps a novelty girlfriend for a little while.

I'm new and different from who he gravitates toward. The novelty will wear off, like Cameron's loyalty rubbed off. I'm a shiny coin, bringing good luck, but once worn, like stroking a talisman over and over again, the brilliance disappears, the newness gone, and a new lucky charm is sought.

Ridiculous, I know, but rational thought has flown out the window as I race to collect my clothing, that Ross neatly placed on a chair in his bedroom.

"We'll see," I respond, giving my mom-speak non-commitment answer.

I just don't know if I can stomach more baseball.

Chapter 33

[Vee]

"I think I made a mistake," I state to Cassandra the next morning when we brunch. She hates the busyness of Sundays, and we sometimes pick a weekday for the late breakfast meal.

We sit inside a swanky little café in the West Loop. With rain in the forecast, the interior is gloomy while typically sunny and bright. Tables fill the space, and a large bar runs along the back wall. Bloody Mary's are their specialty drink any day of the week. The place has a 1920s Art Deco-meets-modern-day vibe about it with arched mirrors and gilded bursts that look like flat palm trees.

"What happened?"

"Ross and I had a fight, of sorts." Or rather I had a full panic attack. Ross was getting real with his feelings, and I stepped back. I couldn't fully explain my reaction. However, I'd tossed and turned all night, arguing with myself, confused by my behavior.

"About what?" Cee-Cee casually asks, sipping a Bloody Mary while we wait for our orders.

"He wants me to go to Philadelphia to meet his sister." I drop my gaze from Cassandra to my utensils, still wrapped in a paper napkin.

My best friend chokes on her drink. "He what? Wow."

"I know, right? Like who takes their sleeping buddy to meet their siblings?"

Cee-Cee chuckles. "Girl, you're more than a sleeping buddy."

I sigh, flipping the rolled utensils. "He called me his girlfriend."

"He what?" She repeats louder, glancing around the room.

I reach across the table to grip her wrist because if I know Cassandra, and I do know her, she's about to blurt to this entire room that I'm Ross Davis's girlfriend.

"Would you keep your voice down?" My eyes warn her to also keep her thoughts to herself.

She lowers her head and her voice. "Vee, you're dating Ross Davis. Sexiest silver fox baseball coach, and most eligible bachelor."

"Since when is he the most eligible bachelor?" *What a title.*

"Since he ditched the streaming service queen."

"That's just it." I lower my head and retract my hand. "He told me he hasn't called anyone else his girlfriend. Ever. Since his wife passed."

I feel Cassandra's eyes on me.

"Anyway . . . don't you think meeting his sister is too soon. I mean, what do I say when I meet her? Hi, I met your brother in an elevator, and he decided I was a superstition whisperer, so we've been sleeping together, only now we're having sex, too. And now I'm his girlfriend after only a few months."

"Well, when you put it like that?" Cee-Cee chortles. "But let's back up. You're having sex with him again?"

I roll my lips, knowing I've opened the proverbial can of worms, and now I'm going to squirm.

"Yesterday, after his game."

Cassandra watches me for another long moment. "You slept with him before. Did the second time not measure up to the first?" She wrinkles her nose, lifts her pinky, and then bends it like it's wilting.

A strangled chuckle escapes me. "No, it was good."

"Sounds like it." Sarcasm drips from her voice as she reaches for her Bloody Mary again.

"No. It was . . . life-altering." The things he said. *Whole. Home.* The way he masters my body and moves his. The things he does to me, taking me over the edge not once but twice before he thinks of himself. What they say about women in their forties is true. Our libido comes back swinging and doesn't want to rest.

But Ross also makes me feel things. Things that frighten me, like I could love him. That I could trust him with my heart.

"Oh?" Cassandra lifts a brow before setting her elbow on the table and placing her chin in her hand. "Do tell."

"I'm not kissing and telling." I laugh a little harder.

"I'm asking you to fuck and share with a friend." She winks.

"Cee-Cee," I groan.

"Okay. Fine." She lowers her hand and waves dismissively. "So you had sex. He called you his girlfriend, and he wants you to meet his sister. Sounds pretty awesome to me."

"But don't you think it's unconventional. I mean, he's Ross Davis." I glance around me, hopeful that the couple seated at the nearest table, which is two tables away, doesn't hear us.

"First off, don't speak about him like that. Like he's some kind of god and not just a man. Maybe he's famous. Maybe he makes a lot of money. But at the end of the day, he's a guy with a job that involves playing a game."

I don't think Ross would appreciate his career being reduced to something so simplistic, but I understand what Cee-Cee means. He's a man. His talent or skill, fame or financial status, doesn't make him better than me.

"Plus, you're successful in your own right, Vee. You're V. C. Hux, author of numerous books about love and romance."

"Doesn't that simply make me a woman with a laptop and a wicked imagination?"

For research purposes whispers through my head.

"Do you think I used him?" I question. "Is he fulfilling some fantasy in my head?" I wave beside my head. "My real-life crush turned into a boyfriend."

Cassandra narrows her eyes at me, but I continue. "Have I made an original boyfriend into a book one?"

My best friend groans. "Vee, you've never used anyone in your life. You wouldn't know how. Plus, he called you his girlfriend first, right?" Her point is made.

"What's the real issue here?" she asks, tilting her head, further assessing me.

"I don't trust myself with him."

"You didn't trust Cameron." Her tone turns sharper. "That's what's tainted your faith." She sighs and lowers her voice, reaching for my hand across the table. "You had conventional, Vee. You married your high school sweetheart who turned out to be a dick."

"Cee-Cee," I moan, hating when she speaks ill of the dead, even if she's correct on some level.

"He cheated on you, Vee. He broke your marriage vows and your heart. And I tolerated him, because you're my friend, but he was kind of a dick in general. So, screw conventional. Or better yet, screw Ross, a hot silver fox who fills out baseball pants very nicely, and a man who called you his girlfriend, because he wants more than a *sleeping* arrangement with you."

I giggle weakly at her enthusiasm.

"Vee, you do trust yourself. You believe in Ross, right?"

"I do." I trust Ross, just not my feelings for him.

"Listen to your gut."

I don't think Ross would intentionally hurt me. He's too vulnerable himself at times. I lean forward, the ache in the pit of my stomach almost viable. "I messed up, didn't I?"

Cassandra smiles, squeezes my hand and releases it. "I think you just panicked because you don't trust that good men are out there. You had one not-so-great guy, and then a slew of poor dates."

"Sound familiar?" I tease. She's broken in many ways as well, and her perpetual bachelorette-hood is a front for that heartbreak. She's also stronger than me with her love-'em-and-let-them-be attitude.

"You aren't me," she continues, emphasizing how opposite our personalities are regarding relationships. "You crave stability. Something solid and secure. Trust is necessary for those attributes, but you're afraid to believe it exists in others. But believe in *yourself*. Hand over your heart."

"What if my heart breaks *again*." What if Ross wakes up and realizes the novelty has worn off, like I thought last night. What if he realizes I'm not good luck. I didn't change the trajectory of his team's wins and losses. I'm just an *average* woman, like he's a man.

"Hearts mend," Cassandra says, her voice turning more serious. "And you should allow yourself a little romantic reality from the fantasies you write."

"Most people want to escape reality and live through romantic fantasy."

"Live the reality." Cassandra leans across the table, placing her hand over my wrist. "You deserve your own happily-ever-after, Vee. And maybe that starts on a baseball field."

I glance toward the window. I haven't decided if I'll attend tonight's game or not. I'm a bit of a fair-weather fan, and a downpour and cold temperatures will definitely keep me away from the stadium. May can be so unpredictable in the Midwest.

"Isn't there some baseball saying about you don't score unless you swing at the ball?" Cassandra sips at her Bloody Mary and then signals for our waitress.

"You mean if you don't swing, you'll miss one-hundred percent of the balls?"

"I like my saying better. Go for the balls, Vee. You might score." She wiggles her brows. "Love and forty."

"Those are tennis scoring terms, not baseball ones. And that was all euphemisms, wasn't it?" I laugh.

"You know it." She lifts her empty Bloody Mary glass and taps against mine resting on the table. "I'm a sexual-innuendo-aficionado."

I shake my head, laugh at my friend. She's something alright, and unfortunately, she's right.

What I'm most afraid of is the heartbreak that could rest on the other end of Ross's season. However, if I don't go for whatever this is with Ross, I'll never know if my already damaged heart could eventually mend.

"Isn't that Romero Valdez?" Cassandra interrupts my musings.

Turning my head in the direction of the couple seated two tables away, who are standing to leave the restaurant, I answer her. "I think so." However, I'm not great at recognizing players outside the context of the ballfield.

Turning back toward Cassandra, I set down my glass. "Now enough about me. Tell me what's going on with you?"

"Funny you ask." However, her expression isn't filled with humor as she starts her tale.

+ + +

Good luck, Coach, I text. I leave off the ass-slap, which really should be an emoji, when I send Ross the message that I won't be at the game.

The Anchors game is rain-delayed by an hour. I predict the eightten start means the game won't end until sometime near eleven. As I make the decision not to attend, because rain and cold don't mix with my warm blood, I turn on the game on my television, and set the volume low as background noise while I work.

My writing has come in fits and spurts lately, and that's not an intentional innuendo about my fictional hero and heroine. Still, the story stalls and starts at odd times and tonight seems to be a moment where clarity reveals itself.

But as the game nears its end and my characters need a break, I make another decision for the night.

I don't let myself into Ross's home because that borders on stalkerish, not to mention, he trusted me with the code, but it didn't give me permission to come and go as I pleased. So, I anxiously stand outside his door near midnight, while the rain hammers the pavement behind me. I'm grateful for the small roof overhanging the raised landing before his front door.

With a shaky finger, which is trembling from a combination of the cold night and my rattling nerves, I ring the bell, waiting as I assume Ross checks his security camera before answering the door. When he doesn't answer within seconds, I ring the bell again. Waiting once more while second guessing my decision to be here, inventing scenarios why he couldn't come to the door.

He went out with his fellow coaches.

He had other obligations after the game.

He met someone else.

Angered by the imaginary woman I don't want taking my place, I ring the bell one more time.

As I wait what feels like long enough for a man to reach his front door or notice me through his security camera, I come to a final conclusion.

Three strikes. I'm out.

I turn for the stairs, watching the rain pelt the cars lining the dimly-lit city street. The heavy showers ripple up and down the street causing bursts of water to pop from impact with the pavement. Lifting my rain jacket hood, knowing a race to my car might be fruitless—I'm going to be drenched—I'm about to take the first step down Ross's front stairs when his door opens.

"Verona?"

I spin to face Ross, who clutches a towel that's wrapped loosely around his waist.

"Am I interrupting something?" *Clearly a shower.*

He glances beyond me. "I was taking a shower to warm up. I'm getting too old for rainy games."

"Well, I'll let you get back to—"

Ross steps out onto the covered landing, grips the front of my rain jacket, and tugs me forward, leading me into his house. The door slams behind me and he stares at me. We both drip on his entryway floor. He must have stepped out of the shower and walked directly to the door.

Not certain where to begin, I say, "I'm sorry about the loss tonight."

"You should be." His intention is clear. Without me in his bed last night, he faults me for the Anchor's loss this evening. His good luck charm failed him.

Still, I'm instantly hurt. That open heart Cassandra suggested is instantly pierced and raw. I came here to apologize for my behavior but maybe Ross is finished with my antics.

I hang my head.

But Ross's hand comes to my chin, his fist lifting my face so I look at him. His eyes search my face before his brows cinch.

"Vee." He groans. "I'm not thinking of you as a damn good luck charm." He begins as if he read my thoughts. "I'm not even mad that we lost the game. I'm pissed you ran off last night and didn't talk to me about what you were feeling. I'm upset that you weren't in my bed all night."

He tilts his head. "Do you realize you have yet to sleep in that bed with *me*?"

Instantly, I recall how I spent an entire week in his bed without him. And the things I did in that bed, with him, while on the phone.

"I didn't get to hold you, smell you, wake up to your beautiful face this morning."

His hand opens, cupping my jaw. "And I was preparing for another lonely night without you. And yet, here you are."

"Here I am," I whisper.

"Why are you here?" His voice lowers, sand grains in an hourglass. He steps closer to me, crowding me like he did yesterday, until I'm against the front door again.

"I . . ." I take a deep breath, feeling the warmth of his palm on my jaw. The heat of his shower radiates off him. His nearness is what I need. Whole. *Healing.* "I'm sorry."

His blue gaze is dull today, and darts around my face, searching for something.

"I might have overreacted last night." I lick my lips and lower my voice, the sound strained when I say, "I panicked."

Ross stays still. Close but rigid.

"I'm scared," I admit quietly and blink up at him. "I'm scared of how I feel about you. I'm scared that whatever this is will hurt when it ends."

"Vee." He exhales and lowers his head to mine. "I'm scared too, sweetheart. Frightened of all that I feel. I wasn't expecting this. Any of this." He pauses. "I wasn't expecting *you*."

"Me either." Ross Davis in reality is so much more than the fantasy that lived in my head.

"I haven't felt like this in a long, long time." His voice is fine gravel.

"I don't know that I've ever felt this way," I whisper, closing my eyes, afraid he'll see all the pain of my past and the fears for my future.

Ross pulls back and swipes his thumb along my cheekbone. His eyes are a bit brighter, wide and watching me. "Who says this feeling has to end, Vee?"

"You can't predict that it won't." I swallow around the thickness in my throat.

"I can't predict wins or losses, but I still play the game."

"I don't want to be a game to you." I blink as my eyes cloud.

"Sweetheart. Vee. You aren't a game." He tugs me to him, wrapping me in a hug with one arm. His other hand still clutching the towel at his waist. My face is against his warm, bare chest. My soaked rain jacket presses against his fresh skin.

Too soon, he pushes me back and holds my shoulder.

"Do you need a pep talk?" His mouth curls. The stiffness in him lessening. He pushes back my hood and then brushes back my hair, running his knuckles down the side of my neck.

I chuckle weakly. "Didn't know what you were getting yourself into by holding that elevator, did you?"

Ross stares at me a second. Maybe he's forgotten how he held the door when I raced to catch that lift back in November.

"Holding that elevator might have been the best thing to ever happen to me."

Ross and I stare at one another a long second before I slowly unsnap each closure on my rain jacket. *Snap. Snap. Snap.* The sharp sound mingles with our sudden ragged breaths. Ross watches as my coat slowly opens, revealing his jersey underneath. I let the rain-slicked material drop to the floor.

"Is this *your* idea of a pep talk?" His gaze doesn't leave me. Taking in his jersey on top. Jeans on the bottom. Feet in flip flops.

"Let's not talk," I whisper.

Then I tip up on my toes, palm his bristly face and tug his mouth to me. We shift until my back is against the hallway wall. Ross had been clutching his towel, even when he hugged me.

Within minutes, his towel is forgotten, dropped to the floor.

"Towels have a funny habit of slipping off you in my presence," I tease, taking the liberty to glance down at him, long and erect, and wrap my hand around his thickness.

"Funny. Only happens when you're around."

"Lucky me," I jest.

"No. Lucky me." His mouth is back on mine as I tug at his length, squeezing him harder, like he likes it. His fingers fumble with the jersey I wear.

"I thought you liked me in this," I remind him against his mouth.

"I'd like you better out of it."

I push him back until his back hits the opposite wall. Then, I remove the jersey myself, slowly revealing my body to him and letting the material fall to the floor with his towel and my rain jacket. I kick off my flip-flops and lower my jeans all while Ross watches me, biting the side of his fist. Eyes roam over me like I'm a precious jewel.

Standing before him in only my bra and underwear, we stare at one another for a second.

I shiver, both from his inspection and the coolness lingering in the hall from the rainy air outside.

Then Ross crosses the hall again, mouth crushing mine. The kiss says everything. He wants me as much as I want him. I'm his. He's mine. Us. Together.

Falling against the wall behind me once more, Ross kisses down my body, lowering to one knee. He props up my foot on his thigh, opening me up to him. Then his face is between my legs and my hands comb back his wet hair. His mouth is warm. His tongue thick, and quickly he finds that nub that triggers everything inside me to come undone.

He licks me with broad strokes and sharp flicks until I shatter, crying out his name in the dark entryway. Like fireworks exploding after a homerun. I revel in every starburst and explosion.

Ross lights up my life.

As I feel my knees giving up and the orgasm subsides, I cup the sides of his head, lifting his chin so he faces me. Then I lean down and kiss him again, swirling my tongue into his mouth, tasting me on him. Marking him.

"Fuck, that's hot," he mutters against me before standing, his knees cracking as he does. The hardwood must not have been comfortable.

I fist Ross again, stroking his thick length, teasing the head. I shift him and lift my leg, hooking it around his hip, guiding Ross where I want him go. He bends his knees a bit, lining us up and swipes through my slickness, but our heights won't allow us to finish the act against a wall.

"Condoms are in my room," he admits, still dragging through wet folds, teasing me, tempting us to go bare, right here in his hall.

I press at his shoulder, moving him back while I take his hand. Then I lead him up the staircase to his room.

When we reach his room, I climb up on the bed, scoot to the middle and wait as he opens the nightstand drawer for what we need. Once covered, Ross reaches for my ankles and tugs me back to the edge of the bed, my legs dangling off the sides as he stands in front of me. He leans down, one arm bracing him over me while his other hand guides his thick length to line up with my entrance once more. He strokes through my slickness, regaining hardness before he easily glides into me.

"Apology accepted," he grunts as he fills me to the hilt.

And I take a breath, as if I'd been holding mine since I walked into his house.

Keeping himself braced over me, he rolls his hips, the strength in his legs moving him in and out of me. He alternates between watching his entrance into me and looking at my face.

I only stare at him. His eyes are bright in the low light of his room. His smile is more of a smirk, but he looks happy.

Apology accepted.

Handing over my heart to him isn't going to be difficult.

Chapter 34

[Vee]

For a week, Ross and I continue in a pattern of showing up at one or the other's place and spending the night after heated moments. His dining room table. My living room couch. But afterward, we end up in bed together.

I don't know that I've ever been happier. Ross is an attentive lover but also a great listener, and he lets me hash out some plotline details with him, offering perspective. From a man's point of view, he says.

He surprised me one morning by arriving at a local coffee shop I frequent that has a calming tea I like, cutting into my writing time. The surprise visit was worth every minute we spent together.

Another time, Ross brought the tea to me at my place. He kissed me hard and too quick, and then left me to work my writing magic.

And one morning, he even had the calming tea delivered to his place, when I stayed to write in his kitchen, where inspiration always hits.

My book might soon reach its happy ending.

Being Ross Davis's girlfriend has benefits, and none of them are what people might expect. Simply put, Ross is good to me and good for me.

He tells me I'm beautiful. And he lets me show him how beautiful I think he is.

Our relationship isn't a secret, but it also isn't quite public either. Ross can't exactly go out to dinner at six o'clock, and he prefers the quiet of his place after a game. My schedule is more flexible than his and I mold my time around his.

Ross makes every second worth it.

We haven't returned to the Philadelphia invitation, and the home-games streak is shortly coming to a close, but not before a certain themed night game arrives. Most stadiums have themed nights, honoring cultures and professions, so Anchor Field is no different.

This topic is particularly difficult for me. A night honoring first responders in law enforcement, fire departments, and EMTs. A portion of the night's proceeds go to an organization for spouses of the fallen, which once benefited me.

I don't particularly like to draw attention to myself or to the circumstances of Cameron's death. I'm always torn between the obligation to miss him, because I didn't want him to die, and the facts, which is that his absence does not haunt me. My girls have missed out on having their father, and I'm sad for them. Girls need dads, and I had an amazing relationship with mine. I miss him all the time.

So, with the approach of the game, my thoughts drift to Cam the night before the honoring game. I'm in Ross's bed, and we've just had an incredible moment together, but Cam trickles into my dreams.

Him facing me, telling me once again he's sorry for what he did. How he hurt me. How he wrecked our marriage. How he wanted another chance. My stomach cramps with anxiety and heartbreak. The horrific moments he confessed what he'd done returned to me, like a powerful punch to the sternum. All my emotions are felt again in the dream. Suspicion and shock. Disbelief and disappointment. Anger. Grief for a love I felt slipping away long before Cam was taken from me. In the dream, he hugs me, and the embrace feels so real. Frighteningly real.

My heart races. I fear that I'm dead. I'm in heaven with Cam. And I'm about to ask him if I've died, when he releases me, steps away and turns his back on me.

An explosive crack shocks me awake but I'm caught for a moment in that thin line between dream state and wakefulness. Dreaming-me envisions Cam being shot. Something I didn't witness, and as I don't watch killer-shows or murder mysteries, I don't have many visions of Cam's demise. Waking-me realizes the crack was not gunfire, but the exhaust of a car or perhaps some kids letting off boomers late at night.

Cameron's name is on my lips. The residual effects of all my emotions pulsing within me as I lie on my back, hand on my chest, my heart hammering under my palm. My throat is dry. My eyes scan the room as if confirming I'm in Ross's house, his bed. I'm alive.

An arm tightens around me. "Hey, you okay?"

"Yeah." My breathing is ragged.

"You were making noises," Ross groggily states.

"I didn't mean to wake you." I don't look at him, eyes focusing on the ceiling, grounding myself in the present once more. I'm not dead. I'm in bed. In Ross's home.

"You called out your husband's name."

Forcing my head to roll, I turn in his direction. "I'm sorry." My voice is weak, soggy and raw. I should say more.

"Want to talk about it?"

I don't, and I tell him that. "Go back to sleep, babe." Then I roll opposite Ross and curl into myself, keeping my eyes open and aimed at the window, because I'm afraid to close them.

Seconds pass before Ross shifts, his arm looping over my waist. His strong arm pulling me back into his chest. His light snores tell me he's already asleep, but he's holding onto me.

And I'd like to imagine in his dreams, he's refusing to let me go.

+ + +

The Anchors game is rough. A moment of silence passes for the fallen men and women of our local community who race toward danger in our large, divided city. While Laurel shares the game tickets with me, in my dad's former seats, we are surrounded by policeman and their families, many of whom are too young to remember Cameron or what happened to him. I'm grateful the jumbotron does not play a running list of those who have passed. The reminder isn't necessary.

Inevitably, I excuse myself for the bathroom and run smack into someone from my past life—as the wife of a former police officer.

"Verona?"

"Hey. Paddy," I falter over the name of one of the last people I want to see tonight.

Padraig O'Brien was a police officer with Cam, and he easily embraces me although it's been a few years since I've seen him. He isn't a particularly attractive man, with a paunch belly and swollen jowls from too much alcohol. Additionally, he's known to often make inappropriate cracks to or about women. Following suit, his assessing gaze roams up and down my body when he pulls back from an uncomfortably long hug.

"Haven't seen you in a while."

"Yeah. I've been busy." He doesn't need to know what I do.

"Still writing those dirty books?"

Or perhaps he already knows. I'm surprised he'd remember. Cam must have mentioned my 'hobby' back when they were friends.

"Uhm, they aren't dirty." There's a fine line between writing what's a little naughty versus something considered truly filthy, as in unclean. Paddy doesn't need me to explain the distinction. "But yeah, I'm still writing." I expect the conversation to end there as most people don't know how to continue a discussion when they learn I'm an author.

"Must be hard without Cam. Or are you open to new adventures?" He wiggles his brows, and a cold chill runs down my spine.

"I'm good," I say, ready to step away from this unwanted reunion. "I'm headed to the ladies' room so enjoy the—"

"If you ever need some tips. Or *the* tip. I'm open to new experiences, as well."

There's no doubt he's just propositioned me and I'm about to throw up in my mouth. Caught between ridiculously thanking him for the offer and telling him to fuck off, because never in a million years would I consider Paddy, I fumble somewhere in between.

"Yeah, uhm. I have a boyfriend, but . . . Yeah, no thanks."

"You're dating?" He scowls, suddenly offended that I'm in a committed relationship versus open to a sexual free for all. "Cam would be so disappointed."

I bite my lip, before I blurt out the reminder that Cameron is dead, and even if he were alive, his disappointment wouldn't be an opinion I'd value. Especially as the man before me was in on the affair my husband was having and condoned it.

"Tell Melissa I said hi." After mentioning his wife, I step around him, disgusted by his embrace, and shaken by his words. He has no place in my head, but I'm still upset by the time I use the restroom and purchase a second margarita for Laurel and me.

"I just saw Padraig O'Brien." I take a hearty drink of my margarita after telling my daughter.

"What did he want?"

I'm not about to tell my daughter the married man offered me sexual favors for book research. Instead, I shake my head. "He's still a pig."

Laurel snorts. "He always gave me the creeps."

I turn my head toward her, worried he said something to her at a tender, young age. "Did he ever say anything inappropriate to you?" *I'll kill him.*

She shakes her head before sipping her margarita. "Just a bad vibe. I don't know how Dad could be friends with him."

I snort, knowing a few reasons they might have been friends, but not wanting to discuss them with my daughter. Cameron is gone and I made a conscious choice a long time ago not to linger on what happened between us. I can't change his decisions. I can't bring him back from the dead. He was simply a season of my life.

The thought hits me hard. Cam was a season I'd measured in love. With our youth. Our girls. My devotion to him. I can't help that he did not reciprocate the dedication or devotion I put into that time of our lives.

I'm in a new season, and my gaze seeks the dugout, although I can't see Ross from my seat.

"So, Ross asked me to go to Philadelphia next week when the Anchors play there."

Laurel's head whips up. "Why Philly?"

"He's originally from there and his sister lives there. She helped raise his boys."

Laurel nods. "That Landon was a little uptight, but Harley was fun."

Ross already explained how Landon's attitude had more to do with protecting my honor than disliking me. The thought is sweet.

But Padraig's words come back to me.

"You aren't disappointed that Ross is in my life, are you?" I don't know how comfortable I feel yet calling him my boyfriend, but Ross is everything to me and I wish there was a word to encompass that feeling.

"Disappointed?" Laurel snorts, the sound very similar to my snortle. "I'm thrilled for you, Mom. I mean, how many women get the chance to date Ross Davis."

"Um . . ." I'm hoping she doesn't want a real answer because I can name more than a handful who have dated Ross in the last decade.

"But seriously, he's hot and so are you. Plus, the way he looked at you at his house. It was really endearing."

"Endearing?" I chuckle. A rather antiquated word for my young twenty-three-year-old. "How did he look at me?"

"He sort of tracked you around the room, like he couldn't take his eyes off you."

My cheeks heat. *Did he really?* I hadn't noticed.

"As long as he's good to you, and faithful, that's all that matters."

Faithful. So far Ross has been very committed to our arrangement-turned-something-more. Between practices, games, and our nightly routine, I don't know how he'd fit another woman into his life, and I hate the doubts that creep into my head. Because he isn't doing that to me. He isn't sneaking someone else between the cracks in our lives. There aren't any cracks.

I make a decision on the spot.

"He's a good man. And I'm going to go to Philadelphia for him."

Chapter 35

[Ross]

I didn't like that Vee was dreaming about her late husband last night. Whatever was running through her thoughts, she was deeply disturbed and mumbling his name before waking with a start. I also didn't like how she rolled away from me, wanting space between us when we don't do that. We sleep close, parts always touching if I'm not draped over her like she's my personal body pillow.

This morning, she was quiet.

I don't want to be jealous of a dead man. He'd lost his life through a tragic circumstance, and that's nothing to be envious of. Still, he hadn't been a good husband from the bits and pieces Vee has shared about him. I hadn't been a perfect husband either, but I hadn't cheated on my wife. I'd loved Patty, but that love changed over time. It ebbed and flowed as I suspect marriages do. Given that I'd married Patty in my late twenties, and then we weren't together more than a dozen years, I don't know how our marriage would have fared, but I'd been dedicated to her and the boys. Devoted. Loving as best I could.

Last night's events with Vee are shaken up again, when the game tonight opened. The field honored the men and women in blue serving this city, along with those who have fallen. Maybe that's what triggered her dream. Losing someone so suddenly, so unexpectedly, has a way of haunting you. Hitting you out of the blue before crawling back into the box where you lock away those forbidden thoughts of someone you love who was instantly gone.

Morbid thoughts have me sneaking a peek in the direction of Vee's seats. She'd been absent the last time I looked but now she's back. She and her daughter look like they are deep in discussion instead of watching the game. Not that I expect her to watch every second. Hell, I'm not even a player, so it isn't like she can watch me. Still, it'd be nice to learn her eyes are on me.

A firm hand on my shoulder rouses me. "You still in there?" Kip asks from beside me.

"Yeah. Sorry. Did you say something?"

"I'd like to put in Royal." Flynn Royal was sent down to the triple-A after spring training, but we recently brought him back up to us. We're winning tonight's game 8-1 and one of our best pitchers has had a good run.

"Sure." I don't typically weigh in on pitching changes unless things are going downhill fast. Kip is the coach for my former playing position, but that doesn't mean I don't have thoughts about pitchers.

You can take me off the mound, but you can't take the mound out of my heart.

I wait out Kip's call to the bullpen, fighting the pull to glance in Vee's direction while the pitching change is made. I step out of the dugout to fist bump Harlan after he exits the hill.

"Good game."

He grunts. No pitcher likes to be called off, but to save his arm, it's the right move, especially when we're doing so well in tonight's game.

With Royal on the mound, he goes two more innings before our closer is called out and the Anchors finish with a W.

And I finally allow myself a glance into the stands, seeking Vee in my excitement at the win. She gives me a wave as the crowd stands and sings our winning anthem. Unable to help myself, I give her a single wave as well.

"Coach?" Adler startles me, turning my head in his direction, where he's facing the stands as well. "You got a girlfriend?"

He isn't teasing me, just smiling like a fool, searching for his wife as well.

I called Vee my girlfriend and it upset her, but I don't know how else to define her because the long litany of saying—she's someone I've fallen for and want to further explore—seems a little too detailed.

Isn't that what a girlfriend is, anyway? Maybe I am an old guy. *Yeah, fuck that.*

"Yeah. Her name is Vee." I nod in the direction just past the WAGs section. "She has season tickets," I state as if explaining why she isn't sitting in the section for significant others.

"Lucky lady," Adler claps my shoulder.

I snort. "Actually, I'm the lucky one." He has no idea how I started out with the belief Vee was my good luck charm, but I've come to realize that just knowing Vee is the real blessing.

Having her in my life is a gift.

+ + +

When Vee tells me she'll go to Philadelphia, I nearly drop the glass of wine she offered me. I'm thrilled. "What made you decide to go?"

Standing in her small kitchen, she simply shrugs. Her place is quaint and cute, very classic Chicago, but tight, and I prefer we hang out at my house. In fact, I have visions of Vee permanently staying there.

"I'd like to meet your sister, if the offer still stands."

"Of course, it still stands." I set down my wine glass and step toward her, bringing her in for a hug. Holding onto her, she settles into my chest, and I like how we fit together. How right we feel. I press a kiss to her head, and she tips back, lifting her face to me.

"So how does this work? I assume I fly separately, and I can't stay in your hotel room, without it seeming like something clandestine."

"Most guys share a room, and sometimes Kip and I do. Other times, we don't, but in general, we don't want the men having random women in their rooms, and we don't let wives and children stay with the players either."

I smile. "But I could purchase your hotel room, and then spend the nights with you which does sound clandestine." I chuckle. "Did I ever tell you Kip reads romance novels? I've never thought to ask if he's read your books, though. I don't want my best friend envisioning my girlfriend in the situations you describe."

Vee snortles in my arms and I grin. "It's not *me* in the books."

"It better not be," I joke.

Vee sobers a little in my embrace and lowers her eyes, placing a hand on my chest. "I saw one of Cam's old partners tonight." She twists her lips side-to-side, as if debating to tell me something. "He offered to help me with *experiences*, for writing purposes."

"What the fuck?" I tighten my hold on her. The comment is a reminder that Vee could be with anyone she wants to be. Someone else could help her with her writing. Someone else could warm her bed. Someone else could hold her, and I don't like that thought.

"He's a dick. He's actually married."

I tighten my hold on her. *What the fuckity fuck?*

"I'd still never consider him. And he's a dick," she repeats.

I don't want her to consider anyone but me for her. "If you need inspiration, you come to me." I squeeze her again.

Vee chuckles, toying with the front of my shirt. "I already do."

My mouth ticks up. "Are you writing about us?"

She shakes her head. "Not exactly, but I'll admit you have inspired a few scenes."

"Really?" Pride hits me. Not that I want our sexual exploits exploited but I'm glad she finds our relations worthy of her fiction. "On that note, maybe we should do some research."

Her brow tips. "For inspirational purposes?"

"I'm inspired," I tease.

"I could get inspired."

I love her playful side. "*Could get* inspired?" I chuckle. "And how could that happen?"

She flattens her hand on my chest. "I'm thinking it involves your tongue and then that massive—"

I don't need the details spelled out for me before my mouth is on hers and I'm leading her to her bedroom.

Fully inspired.

Chapter 36

[Ross]

I want everything to be perfect for Vee meeting Rena. Instead, it's one clusterfuck after another.

As the team has a contracted airline, Vee flies separately, and her flight is delayed due to thunderstorms. Then, the team's hotel was changed at the last minute, because of some scheduling mix up, which means Vee will be at a different hotel than mine. And finally, Landon and Harley decide to surprise visit Philadelphia as their colleges are on summer break.

This summer, Landon will remain near Purdue, living in a house with friends, and Harley plans to stay in his apartment as it's a twelve-month rental, but they'll have the freedom to visit me more often. However, this surprise visit means Vee and I need to re-arrange our sleeping arrangement.

And this introduction with my sister.

Rena is cool as far as little sisters go, and being the youngest of three, and the only girl, she's rolled with having unruly older brothers. She jokes she's a spinster, a term I never understand, as she's still young in my opinion. She looks exactly like our mom did with strawberry blond hair, cut just above her shoulder in springy curls. Her eyes are bright blue like mine. Once upon a time, she claimed to have found the One, and then he broke her heart. And she's given almost ten years of her life to help me raise my boys, so I owe her the world.

But with Landon and Harley suddenly present, meeting Vee won't be the quiet, easy affair I wanted it to be between two special women in my life. The boys have safely arrived at Rena's home, and they'll stay here for a week. They've also quickly ditched the house in favor of meeting up with old friends from when we lived here.

"Landon tells me she's not like the other women in your life," Rena states, sitting across from me in her muggy backyard. The heat of the day kicks in after the rainstorm. With my night free before the three-game series, I sip a beer while waiting for Vee's delayed arrival.

"I don't have other women."

Rena lifts a brow. Her eyes are warm, curious. "What makes her special? Special enough you invited her to Philly to meet me?"

I shrug at first, then lean forward and brace my arms on the outdoor table. "She's just different. Harley says Vee reminds him of Patty. In some ways she is like her, but in most ways, she isn't." I pause trying to describe Vee. "She's sweet and funny. Kind. Pretty. Quirky. And she's nothing like any other women I've dated."

Rena gives me a knowing look. She's seen the tabloids and knows the truth. I'm a serial dater who was monogamous with each woman but never called any of them my girlfriend.

My sister once said to me, *you could do so much better*.

"Vee is that better," I state and smile at how great it is to have someone like Vee in my life.

"How?" Rena lifts her beer after asking, watching over the bottle as she sips.

"What is this, twenty questions?" I chuckle.

"It's grill-my-older-brother to protect his heart."

I huff. "Shouldn't this older brother be protecting yours?"

Rena softly smiles. "Tell me more about her. How did you meet again?"

Oh boy. But, I spend the next hour explaining how Vee and I met, where and when, and then how we saw one another again.

"Happenstance," I explain, then lower my head, a bit bashful when I say. "I think Vee might be a second chance for me."

"She's your *happy* chance." Rena's mouth curls on one side, pleased by her own assessment, while unknowingly stealing my line.

"Yeah." I agree.

"Then I can't wait to meet her."

Only introductions are on hold as Vee doesn't arrive until almost ten at night, nearly a twelve-hour delay for a two-hour flight.

"I could have driven here faster," she gripes, once she's inside her hotel room, and I'm on my way to meet her despite team curfews before games. A blizzard at two a.m. couldn't keep me away from her.

"I'll make it up to you." My Uber stops outside her hotel, and I cross the lobby for the elevators. My feet move almost faster than I can keep up. I'm that eager to get to her. I feel like I haven't seen her in weeks when it's only been thirty-something hours.

I'm also unsettled being back in Philadelphia. Restless. And I want to be near Vee. She keeps me grounded. She calms me. She's my home plate.

"I don't know that I'd be great company tonight." She sighs, exhaustion in her voice. "Even though I'm wired, I think I'm just going to go to bed."

"Hold that thought," I state, stepping into the elevator and worrying that I'll lose the connection to her. The call does disconnect, and I phone her again as soon as I'm on her floor. "Sorry about that."

"Don't worry about it." She sounds disheartened. "I'll just see you tomorrow."

"Or you could see me right now?"

"Ross," she groans.

"Open your door, sweetheart."

"What?"

I pause outside her hotel room, waiting on her to cross the room, and open the barrier in that way I adore. Where she yanks it open wide, like she's been expecting me, like she can't wait to see me.

Because that's exactly how I feel about her. I can't wait to see her.

The door opens with a flourish, and I speak into my phone when our eyes meet. "Hey."

"Hi," she answers through hers before clicking off the device.

I step forward, into her room, and she steps toward me, into my arms. She didn't spend the night at my place last night and my bed was cold without her.

Now, my mouth is warm against hers. Her body is pinned to mine as I lift her straight up, her feet dangling a few inches off the ground while I carry her deeper into the room before setting her back on her feet.

"What are you doing here?" Her voice is filled with renewed energy. "Don't you have a curfew or something?"

"Or something. And that something is you, sweetheart." My mouth is on hers again, sipping and sucking.

"Let me erase your bad day," I murmur against her mouth.

"You don't need to do that."

"I want to." I want her. Good days, bad days. Bad dreams, good ones.

"I'm just wound up," she mumbles against my lips.

"I'm here to unwind you, then." Releasing her mouth, I press her away from me and reach for her shirt, lifting it over her head. Spinning her around, I kiss across her shoulders, digging my teeth gently into the tight muscles while my hands massage her lower back.

"Holy shit. That feels incredible."

I hum against her skin, while I unclasp her bra. Still sucking her shoulders, I tug the bra off her and knead her breasts, cupping each swell, pressing them together before plucking her nipples which are instantly erect.

"I love how you respond to my touch." Speaking into her skin, I reach for the button on her jeans, popping the closure at her waist before slipping my hand into her pants, diving directly between her legs.

Sliding my finger over the dampness of her panties, I hum. "So ready for me, sweetheart."

Vee tips back her head, leaning against my shoulder. "The things you do to me, babe. My body can't help but respond."

"I like the sound of that." Her calling me babe. Her admitting I do things to her.

With a quick tug, her jeans are lowered, underwear removed as well. Vee remains facing the bed, while I pull my shirt forward, over my head, then press my warm chest against her back.

Vee hisses. "Your skin is on fire."

"I'm on fire. For you." I nip her neck hard and her knees buckle, but with one arm around her waist, and my hand between her thighs again, I support her body. Quickly, I find the spot that spirals Vee out of control. Her hips rock back, her ass seeks friction against my hard length.

"You want me, sweetheart?"

"Always."

Damn, I like the sound of that, too.

Working at her clit, I pause to dip into her warmth, soaking my finger with her essence. Sliding back out of her, I circle that trigger point again and again, before breaking rhythm, and diving two fingers into her.

"So full," Vee cries out, arching her back and pressing her ass against me again. She leans forward, hands catching on the edge of the bed.

"Want you like this," I tell her, sliding my hand up her spine, staring at that back I adore.

"Yes."

I release her to kick off my shoes and step out of my pants. With her lush ass aimed at me, and her head turned to watch me, her hair drapes over her opposite shoulder. I'm struck by how pretty she is. Sunshine on a cloudy day. A refreshing sip of water on a hot afternoon. Comfort.

And waiting on me to fill her up.

"All the power," I remind her. While I feel strong being with her, elevated, electric, she's the one with the strength to break me.

Fisting myself, I bring my firm tip to her entrance, sliding through that wetness. Teasing both her and me with where I want to be.

"I'm on the pill," she quickly states. "For feminine reasons."

I don't know what that means but we can discuss it later. For now, I have her permission to slip inside, and my breath catches at first contact. When just my tip breaches her heat.

"Fuck, Vee." I grunt, gliding easily into her, sliding home.

I still and reach around her, flicking her clit. Vee's hips buck.

"I should have fucked you that first night." I kiss her shoulder while rubbing that nub and hanging out inside her. "I wasn't in the right headspace, but I didn't know what I was missing."

I draw back, teasing us both by nearly exiting her body before rushing forward again. My fingertips circle that trigger point on her.

"Want to feel you come around me, Vee." I want her to fucking milk me dry.

"You feel so good," she whimpers, arching back, matching my thrusts. She lifts one leg, bracing her knee on the bed, opening herself up to me.

"Damn, Vee. That just—" I can't speak. Curled over her, working her clit and sliding in and out of her channel, I'm a mess of sensation. Her heat around me. Her sweetness coating me. The sound of us coming together.

"Vee," I warn. "I'm so close." But I won't go over the edge without her. I can't think about baseball, but I'll find something else to hold off my release.

"Yes." Her legs stiffen. Her hips stop rocking but roll like a slow drizzle. She sucks me into her, clenching around me, as she crests and cries out again and again. "Babe. Ross. Yes."

I'm quick to follow, pulling back once before slamming into her, holding still, and letting loose like a fountain.

"Fuck." I grip her hips, bury deep within her, and hold her tight against me. Silver stars dance before my eyes, and I blink several times.

Vee pulls off me, flips for the bed, and lays back. "One more time," she begs, holding out her hands.

I can't. My dick won't last, but her legs are spread, pussy weeping, so I climb over her, wedging myself between her thighs, and using my fingers again, working her with two thick digits while my thumb presses at her clit.

Simultaneously, I rock my hips, simulating what I wish I could do, but I'm forty-seven, not seventeen.

Tipping her head up to kiss me before arching her back and tilting back her head, Vee goes off rather quickly. She lets out a long, low groan as she releases a second time.

"Fuck, that's hot, Vee."

When she slowly subsides, coming back to earth and this bed, I lazily stroke between her thighs before holding my hand over her center.

"What was that?" I tease.

Vee blinks a few times before draping her arm over her eyes. Her lower lip quivers.

"Vee? Sweetheart." I tug at her arm, but she refuses to look at me. A tear escapes her eye. "Talk to me."

"Sometimes I'm just overwhelmed by . . . us. By what you do to me. How you make me feel. The way my body reacts to yours." She sucks in a breath. "And I guess . . . it's just that . . . I'm in my forties, so that means I'm horny."

I chuckle, but not in jest. "Sweetheart, you can be horny all you want with me."

She drops her arm, smacking the bed beside her. "What are you doing with me, Ross?" Her question is asked so seriously, and on the tip of my tongue is an answer.

I'm loving you.

Instead, I say, "I'm horny for you, too."

She huffs. Then chuckles. Then snortles, and we both break into the easy laughter that happens between us.

She overwhelms me too, in all the best ways.

Chapter 37

[Ross]

In the early morning, I leave Vee because of batting practice and warmups. And when I finally catch up to her in the restaurant of her hotel, she's not alone.

"Look who I met." When I lean into Vee and kiss her cheek, seated at the table is my sister and sons.

"Dad, you didn't mention Vee would be here," Harley states, displeasure in his voice, thinking I purposely held back this information. He stands to hug me.

Vee gives me a puzzled look. I hadn't purposely omitted her visit, I guess I just forgot to tell the boys as I hadn't seen them yesterday at my sister's house.

Landon is watching me, and I take a seat at the table set for lunch, between Landon and Vee, squeezing his shoulder as he doesn't stand to hug me. "I think the surprise is you guys being here. What happened to letting me know where you'll be?"

The rule is to tell me if they leave their respective campuses.

"We wanted to surprise you," Landon states, not a bit of menace in his voice.

"Well, I am surprised. In the best way. I have all my favorite people at one table." I turn to Vee. "So, you've met Rena." I nod toward my sister. "How did this happen?"

Harley answers. "Vee told me you were meeting her for lunch, so I asked if we could join you."

I glance at Vee, my head spinning a little bit. "I gave my number to Harley when we first met. Being that you're busy, and away a lot, I told him he could call me if he needed anything local."

Harley is newly moved to Chicago, like me, but unlike me, he doesn't remember as much about living in the city. I should be grateful for the adult contact. For Vee's offering. However, I'm out of sorts that I didn't know.

ELEVATOR PITCH

The restlessness of being in Philadelphia is back. Almost like an itch beneath my skin. I'm off.

Still, I say, "That was generous of you."

I side-eye Rena, feeling her watching me, and catch her pinched expression. She doesn't like my tone, and I clear my throat.

"So, what have y'all been talking about?"

"Vee's career," Rena excitedly states glancing at Vee before looking at me again. "You didn't tell me she is V. C. Hux."

I look from Vee to my sister, a bit surprised that my sister sounds like she knows Vee. I'm reminded that Vee's husband wasn't overly interested in Vee's career, and I'm upset with myself that I haven't bragged more about *her* success with my sister.

"Are you familiar with her books?"

"Aren't you?" Rena asks, her puzzled expression back. "She's amazing. I've read her Huntley brothers series, and now I'm working my way through her former rock stars collection."

While Vee and I discuss her writing, I still haven't actually read any of her books. We've fallen into more of me asking her if she's written during the day, but not always the details of what she's written. Like someone might ask me if I practiced pitching, back when I pitched, but not asking for an explanation of how I pitched. Only I'm not a pitcher anymore, I'm a coach. And I should have more information about what exactly my girlfriend is writing.

My annoyance with myself grows, feeling selfish and frustrated. How many games has she attended for me? How many times has she let me talk about my issues with players in the locker room? How many times has she swatted my ass to wish me luck?

And what have I done for her? Bought her a couple cups of her favorite calming tea?

I haven't read a single book. Not even asked to see a chapter. I've been so wrapped up in baseball. Again.

The restlessness of being in Philadelphia turns to unease about Vee. Am I doing enough for her? Am *I* enough for her?

"She's very impressive," I state, but I sound a bit tightlipped, almost offended, when I'm actually mad at myself. And I feel Vee watching me. I can't look at her, ashamed of myself for not coming across like her biggest fan.

Rena is clearly a fan.

Fortunately, Vee and Rena are both good at making conversation and draw the boys into discussions. I'm not much of a conversationalist today. My mind is all over the place, and too soon, it's time for me to head out.

Dismissing myself, I address the table as I stand. "I'll see you guys at the ballpark." It's not really a question. I bought tickets for Rena and Vee to attend together. Rena purchased tickets for the boys in the same vicinity.

And I pause half a second waiting for Vee to stand and walk me out.

Instead, she offers me a wink. Playful. Flirty. Girlfriendy, but it's not enough. My irritation is back and it's not really at Vee. I'm mad at myself. Upset that I didn't introduce her to my sister like I had planned. Harley did. Upset that I don't have time to hang out with my kids, and my girl, and my sister and linger at this lunch. Upset at this uncomfortable prickle, gnawing at me as I'm back in Philly.

I step to Vee and cup her face, looking her directly in the eyes. "Wish me luck, sweetheart."

"Luck," she whispers, her eyes heated before she licks her lips. I want to kiss her senseless. Instead, I settle for a quick kiss, hoping to swallow her wish.

By the time the game starts, I'm a wreck, and the Anchors look more like a bunch of fumbling tee-ballers than professionals making millions of dollars. As I'm not a screamer, keeping that shit in my head, I have a headache by the sixth inning that rivals the crack of a metal bat against a ball on repeat. The constant *ting-ting-ting* makes my stomach queasy.

Plus, the Anchors are losing.

Rena and Vee are in the stands with my boys, and I'm an anxious mess, feeling the pressure of everyone watching. Me as a coach to a new team. Me as the former coach of our opponents. Philly fans are a tough crowd, and I anticipated the boos. The catcalls of being a traitor. The insults for lost loyalty. From the same fans who demanded my release. Philly is a rough city. Fans love hard; hate harder.

And the tension builds.

When the game ends, the Anchors lose, 0-10, and we hang our heads entering the locker room.

"Guess his lucky charm didn't work this time," someone in the locker room says.

I still as I'm the last to enter the common space.

"Who said that?" I glance around the room of men in various states of undress. Some sit. Some stand. A collective breath is suddenly held. My eyes shift from man to man before landing on a smirking Romero Valdez.

"Want to repeat what you just said?" I sound like a teacher, asking a kid in a classroom to share his thoughts with everyone.

Valdez stands tall. Or at least as tall as his five-eight will allow him compared to my six-three. "*I said*," he emphasizes. "Looks like your lucky charm didn't work this time."

"What lucky charm?" I cross my arms, defensive, while also certain what, or rather who, he means.

"The one you're fucking."

"What the fuck?" I take a few steps toward him before Kip and Dalton are in front of me. Not holding me back but blocking any further approach. "What the fuck did you say?"

"I said that piece you're fucking didn't bring you luck after all."

"That's it." I call out, jabbing a finger at my short stop. "You're suspended." He's already endured a suspension for his actions toward Ford earlier this season, but his current comments are insolence against a superior. His fucking coach.

"For what?" Valdez questions, facing off with me, meeting my glare between the shoulders of Dalton and Kip.

"For being a dick." It's the most unprofessional thing I've said as a coach, but I can't help myself. I know who he's insulting, and I don't like what he's saying.

I am not fucking Vee for some superstitious reason.

"You've crossed the line this time," someone states, and Valdez turns his head in the direction of Bolan Adler.

"Fuck you, and your fake wife."

A shift occurs again. Men rustling to catch Adler before he gets to Valdez. Valdez getting pinned back by others.

And just as this happens, photos are snapped, capturing the chaos in the Anchor locker room.

And within hours, headlines read:

Chicago Anchors. A sinking ship.
Rumors of inappropriate behavior and nefarious superstitions.

+ + +

After a lengthy call with the front office, and a detailed discussion with the general manager of the Anchors, Romero Valdez is put on a second suspension for his insubordination. He's also put on the books for a trade when the mid-season gap opens. He doesn't represent the ideals we hold for this Chicago team, and his previous behavior toward Ford, documented complaints from Bolan, and now this verbal altercation with me witnessed by the team are grounds for termination of his contract.

I'm relieved but saddened. I failed him as a coach and failed my team as their leader.

Their top dog. Their alpha male.

When I finally call Vee, it's after midnight. "I think you should go home."

With the headline what it is, I don't want Vee's name to suddenly be linked with the suspicion of "a superstition whisperer" as the news reports have coined her. Ironic, as she called herself the same thing a time or two. I don't believe for a second Vee sold her own story to some tabloid. Even if she loves a good story, she's into the fictional kind, not the sensational ones. And I want to protect her.

"You don't want me here for you?" Her voice is quiet and small when she questions me. I hear her hurt and know that it's because she feels I'm pushing her away when I'm trying to protect her.

Her life will implode if the media gets ahold of her. Glorify her or rip her apart, the media is a double-edged sword, and I don't want that kind of press for Vee. Plus, I'm reminded from our lunch, she is a success in her own right. She has a following and fans, and what would this kind of press do to her? Her career? Her success? Her personally.

Selfishly, I want her here, but I don't want her dragged through even more muck, spouted by Valdez, because he's a vengeful dick. As I'm convinced Vee would never use me, or us, to elevate herself, I'm still curious how Valdez knew about Vee as only a select few know our truth.

Whipping off my ball cap, I scratch my head. I've been wearing the cap almost all day. I'm still partially in my uniform. I need a shower. I'm exhausted, and I just want to hold Vee. But I can't.

"I just think it's best if you go home. Lay low."

"I didn't know I was lying high." Her snarky reply stings as I pace in my hotel room like a caged animal.

I pause, glancing toward the window and walking toward it. The drapes are still open. The city lights glow in the distance. I press my head against the cool glass as if I can see Vee across the vast space.

"Our secret is about to be revealed, Vee." My voice is low and rough. "I don't want the shit that can come with a media surge flung at you."

The phone is quiet a second, and I close my eyes, trying to envision Vee. Maybe she's sitting on the edge of her hotel bed, in the same spot I took her last night. Vee and I have had sex in a lot of locations and positions, but it hits me that we haven't actually made love. Slow and controlled. Taking our time.

I need more time.

And everything feels like it's spinning out of control. This feeling I had entering Philly. Almost like a premonition that returning here, something bad would happen.

"I see." Vee says eventually, but her tone suggests otherwise. She sounds subdued, almost resigned. Not understanding I don't have a choice but to send her home.

"Look, it's been a rough day. Let me help you book a ticket."

"I can book my own ticket, Ross. Thanks." Her tone shifts, sharp and tight.

A heavy pause fills the phone again before she says, "Good luck to the Anchors, Coach."

She hangs up as I'm trying to say, "Please, don't be like that."

I hate that Vee's reaction is eerily similar to Patty before she passed. Bitter. Angry. Hurt.

A wave of nausea churns through my stomach as I glance down at the now quiet phone in my hand. Vee is gone. I'd pushed her away. Perhaps I've pushed her too far.

Fear and guilt collide. Panic settles in next. What if I don't ever see Vee again?

That night, I toss and turn. I don't hear from Vee despite calling again and again, leaving messages, then sending texts. I don't know if she got a plane ticket and went home immediately or if she leaves tomorrow. I don't know where she is or how she's doing with all this.

She sounded so sad, and it kills me that I'm responsible for the pain in her voice. She doesn't understand how much she means to me.

I love her.

Of course, I want her here with me, but it's best for her.

I hardly sleep, worried I might never get to hold Vee again. The restlessness of being in Philadelphia is back in triple force. I wake groggy, feeling like I'm hungover even though I didn't touch a drop of alcohol. Dread is like a thick slug inside me.

In the morning, I finally answer a call from my sister.

"Are you okay? How is Vee?" I imagine my sister and my girl are instant best friends, and it warms my insides that Rena is concerned for Vee. Unfortunately, I don't have more descriptors for Vee.

"She's angry." I sigh, drained and the day has hardly begun. I'm angry, too, underneath my exhaustion. Angry at Valdez. Angry at who ever talked. Angry that I might have lost the only woman I've loved in ten years.

"With the press?" Concern fills Rena's voice.

"With me." I hang my head, cupping my nape as I sit on a corner of the mattress, toes digging into the lush carpeting. God, I wish Vee was here. I wish she would answer her phone.

Rena gasps. "Ross, what did you do?"

"I sent her home. To protect her."

Rena is quiet a minute. The silence is almost deafening. "Ross. I love you, but I don't think Vee needs protection. She needs a man who will stand beside her. Stand up for her."

"How the hell do you think I got into this mess?" I snap, my head lifting as well as I glare at myself in the mirror across the room. I look like I feel. Wrecked. "Fucking Valdez was spewing shit, and I went after him, defending Vee."

The headline and photograph come back to me. The one where I'm being held back by my assistant coaches and Bolan is being held back by others. Valdez has a shit-eating grin on his face while another player has a hand on his chest.

"Did you tell her that?" Rena asks.

"I—" I didn't. I should have started with that. Instead, I started by suggesting she leave.

"Fuck, Rena." I sigh and hang my head again.

"Don't dump your happy chance in the river, Ross."

I know that, I want to snap. Instead, my irritation shows when I say, "Which river?" Certain she means the Delaware River.

"Any of them. Rivers only flow in one direction. Away."

Fuck. I pick up my cap on the bed beside me and chuck it across the room. My sister is right, and I messed up. I want to hop on the next plane and chase Vee. Tell her how I screwed up, apologize properly, and finally tell her I love her.

Of course, I want her with me. Always.

But for now, my stomach curls again. My gut is sick because I don't have a choice here. I have to choose baseball over Vee because I have games to coach. Hell, I even have another away series after we leave Philadelphia. I can't just leave and go after the one thing more important to me than anything else.

Baseball always wins out, but how many more times will I lose my heart?

Chapter 38

[Ross]

The next few days are more than rough, as we move from Philly to Phoenix, and the rumors continue. Speculation about Valdez's future on the team. Gossip about me and my superstition whisperer, who has been upgraded to *slumber-party princess or lady luck*.

"How you holding up?" Kip asks me as we stand side by side watching Royal take warm-up pitches. With summer almost here, Phoenix is a furnace outside this enclosed stadium. Even inside, it's warm. The team is in various stages of stretching and final batting practices are being completed.

Staring at the field, I blindly watch my young pitcher and simply shake my head in answer to Kip.

We've already discussed how it wasn't him who told anyone about the arrangement Vee and I had. He also checks in with me almost hourly, knowing my head and heart are some eighteen-hundred miles away.

"If you're worried about where my mind is—"

"I'm not." He's been a good friend, knowing I'm hardly holding it together. He also knows Vee is all I can fucking think about right now. I'm focused on the field when game time arrives, but every other minute is pre-occupied with her.

"How's Vee?" he asks cautiously.

"Still not answering any of my phone calls or texts." Defeat is in my voice as I scrub my forefinger and thumb around my mouth, arms crossed over my chest. The position is casual but internally, it's like I'm trying to hold myself together. My chest aches. I miss Vee more and more every day that passes without contact.

Her snortle. Her smile. Her sexy sounds and pep talks.

Being back in Phoenix is torture. This is where I hatched my plan and Vee, sweet, generous Vee, agreed to my nonsense. My *happy chance* was propositioning her and her accepting the challenge. I never expected to fall in love.

I certainly never expected anyone to find out how we started, and frankly, I don't give a damn about our beginning. All that matters is how we end. What we have, which is rare and beautiful, special and life changing. Vee in my life has changed everything, and I refuse to believe this is the end of us.

I swipe my cap off my head and run both hands over my scalp before slapping the cap back in place. Then I rub the heels of my hands against my eyes, as if I can focus on this field better, and clear my mind only momentarily of the woman I need to chase.

"You look exhausted," Kip teases.

"I'm a mess," I grunt, not even hiding how tired I am. Worn down by the distance. Worn out by her absence.

I'm still stuck on the road for three more games.

I feel like I've dropped the ball on the most important game of my life. Only Vee isn't a game. She's everything to me.

Kip claps me on the back. "Let me know if you need anything."

What I need is Vee.

"You'll get her back," Kip adds, as if reading my thoughts.

I want to have the same faith he has, but each day that passes I become more and more certain.

"What you need is a grand gesture?"

I tip back my head and stare at the ceiling of the enclosed stadium, blinking several times. "Kip, what the fuck, man?"

"Don't you read her books?"

My head snaps back, my neck cracking at the move. As a matter of fact, I have been reading one of her books.

"I don't want to give anything away but near the end, the hero always needs to grovel. And it's best done with a grand gesture."

"Like what?" I turn to him, forgetting we're standing on a ballfield. I'm ready to beg him for his knowledge.

Kip chuckles. "I should torture you and make you finish the book, then you'll understand."

"Kip, I swear." The desperation in my voice, along with something in my face has my friend chuckling again. "Just tell me."

ELEVATOR PITCH

"Okay, here's what I suggest."

Chapter 39

[Vee]

"Hello?"

"Cassandra," I groan as I cross my living room when she took the liberty to answer my phone. I didn't block Ross's phone number because that felt childish, but I also haven't answered his calls. I got the message. *Again.*

When he told me to go home. When he wanted to keep me a secret.

Lay low? What did that even mean? This wasn't some mafia romance where henchmen were out to get me. Ross and I had an arrangement, and clearly someone found out about it. As only Cassandra knows from my side, I assume the information leaked on Ross's end. Maybe it was locker room talk. Men sharing their superstitions and how they acted on them. Maybe it had all been a joke to him, although I doubt that. He couldn't have faked the orgasms he had with me. He just doesn't want anyone to know we're beyond the sleeping pact. Way beyond.

So much for being his *girlfriend.*

I'd held myself together, though only barely, as I headed to the airport the following morning, feeling despondent and rejected. Once I hit my apartment, the crying began. I'm heartbroken and pissed. I knew it would hurt when we ended, I just didn't think it would end like this. How Ross took it upon himself to *protect me*, by pushing me away. Like he's embarrassed by our situation.

Shouldn't all that matter be the happily ever after no matter how the tale began?

Then again, I'm the writer, not him.

"Cee-Cee." I hold out my hand, wiggling my fingers. We've been arguing once again about how I should hear Ross's side of the story. I don't have to make a decision, just hear him out.

But I'm tired of excuses from men. And I'm sad that once again I haven't been a partner's first choice.

ELEVATOR PITCH

When my phone rang on the coffee table, and Cassandra was closest to the device, she took the liberty to snatch it up and answer.

"Actually, this is Cassandra. Hang on a minute. She's right here." My best friend holds out the device, waving it at me with a strong jab of her arm while mouthing: *Talk to him.*

I shake my head, glaring at her before taking the phone from her.

Fine, I mouth back.

"Hello."

"Vee?" Relief washes through his voice. The sound is both strained while exhilarated.

"Ross." We've established who we each are. I don't know what else there is to say. Silence falls between us a second before he clears his throat.

"God, I wish I could just get on a plane and talk this out face-to-face." He exhales. "Kiss you. Hold you. But I can't."

I sigh. "I know you can't. I would never ask you to or expect you to. You have obligations and responsibilities. I'm not mad that you couldn't drop everything and run home to me, Ross." I pause, willing myself not to cry again. "Baseball is important to you, like writing is important to me. I'm mad because you pushed me out, practically put me on a flight, like I didn't matter. Like I don't have a voice in any of this."

"I don't know how things got so out of hand."

Between us? I bite my lip, not willing to ask, not wanting to argue.

"I should have led with what happened in the locker room. You saw that picture. Valdez was spewing bullshit about you. And he somehow knew about the superstition pact."

My mouth falls open.

"I was coming to your defense. Suspending him, actually, when that photo was taken."

I don't need to ask which photo. It's made quite the rounds on social media. His assistant coaches standing in front of him. Someone with a hand on Valdez. Two guys restraining Bolan Adler.

Ross sighs. "Things got out of control. I lost my temper, which I never do, but I won't let someone talk about you, Vee. Belittle what we

307

have." He pauses. "Because there is something between us, sweetheart. Superstition went out of the ballpark long ago. It's you. You're good for *me*."

I roll my lips, holding back any comments, and taking a deep breath to keep myself in check.

"And I want to be good for you. Thought I was pushing you away when all I was trying to do was protect you. I hurt you, but I was only worried that if you'd have come to the next game, someone would see you, and hound you, not me. I don't want that kind of limelight for you."

"Because I'm not a supermodel." I clamp my lips shut, mad at myself for interjecting.

"Because you're so much more. Vee, you don't need supermodel as a status. You're beautiful, inside and out, and you're right for me. And I miss you."

My heart hammers. I want to believe him, but even if I miss him, too, I've learned my lesson about men who grovel.

"What did Valdez say about me?"

"Sweetheart." Ross sighs. "It doesn't matter but he knew about our arrangement. Not who we are now, but how we started."

"How did he know?"

"He said he overheard two women talking. Called you a superstition whisperer. He took the conversation and ran with it."

Oh my God. I glance at Cassandra who is watching me as my eyes bug out.

"Ross." I choke. "I'm so sorry. I think it was me. Cassandra and I were talking about our situation at brunch one morning, and Valdez was at a table a few feet away from us." And Cassandra can be loud, although I love her for it sometimes.

Silence fills the phone again before Ross says, "It doesn't matter. Our secret is out." He bitterly chuckles.

"I'm sorry to embarrass you."

"I'm not embarrassed." His tone turns defensive.

ELEVATOR PITCH

"Then I don't understand why you're apologizing. The secret is out. The superstition has been over for a while. Wins. Losses. Our sleeping arrangement hasn't made a difference."

"It's made a difference to me," Ross says, his voice softening.

I don't know what to say. He's made an impact on me as well. All the sorrow I've had for the last week unleashed a torrent of words, and my writing is nearing the end.

"I downloaded one of your books," he finally says.

My gaze leaps to Cassandra again, who is still watching me, but making a heart symbol with her hands.

"Why?" I ask, fighting the thrill that rushes through me that he purchased one of my books.

"I want to know more about you, Vee. I want to experience your talent and read all the words that come from that creative brain and those beautiful fingertips."

I glance down at my hands, recalling all the times Ross massaged my fingers.

"Actually, I've bought all your books. They'll be waiting for me at the house when I get home." He chuckles softly. "Might take me a few years to read them all, but I'm willing to put in the time. I want the time, Vee. To know everything there is about you. All the fiction, and all the facts. I only want you as Verona Huxley. No one or nothing else."

"Ross." I whisper, touched by his purchase and sudden dedication to read all my work.

But words are just words.

"Good luck in Phoenix," I say, my voice thick. My heart breaks that he's where the magic happened. If only I could turn back the clock. But would I?

Happenstance. The chance to see him again after that elevator stuck.

Happy chance. The unlikely event that we'd meet again, and a whirlwind of events would get us to where we are now.

Suddenly, I'm choking up after promising myself I would not cry anymore. "I need to go," I whisper, the soft tone strained.

"Can I see you when I get back to Chicago?"
"I'll think about it." But he knows what that means. It's mom-speak for probably not.

+ + +

I can't avoid the Anchor games. I mean, I could sell all my tickets and make a nice profit, but the thing is, I enjoy the games, and reliving the memories made with my dad and my girls.

So, on a Thursday evening, a day after the Anchors return to Chicago, Cassandra and I go to the game where I purchase two extra tickets for Laurel and Hannah to attend.

Girls' Night Out at the ballfield. I can't think of anything better.

To my surprise, Landon and Harley are sitting with their aunt, Rena, in the same section.

"Hey, guys," I question when I notice them noticing me.

Landon gives me a long look. "What a strange coincidence, right?"

"Us here at the game in the same section as you," Harley adds.

I tilt my head. Strange indeed, but even stranger is how they are both acting . . . weird.

Rena taps the back of Landon's head, eyeing him in a silent conversation before turning toward me. "It's so great to see you again." Her hug is a comfort. We had a good time meeting each other in Philadelphia. Under different circumstances, we might have become good friends.

"Well, enjoy the game." I smile, attempting to avoid looking toward the dugout as I return to my seats.

Puzzled by their presence, I'm thrilled for Ross that he has family here to support him. With the boys here, I'm hopeful this means the father-son relationship is on the mend for all of them. Healing hurts. Promising a better future.

From our seats, I continue to try to ignore the dugout, sipping my margarita and staring at the field, while hardly concentrating on the game. With the antics of Aunt Sassy around my girls, the night passes with laughter despite the anxiety humming through my body. *My* family is a good distraction for me.

In the middle of the fifth inning, the jumbotron board lights up with birthdays, congratulations, and marriage proposals, and it's a highlight of the game as we try to find the proposals in the crowd.

But tonight, as the board nears its broadcasting end, one name flashes across the screen.

VEE.

My gaze leaps to the dugout where Ross suddenly appears, climbing up on top of the roof, holding a poster in his hand. Bubble letters printed in Anchor red and blue on the sign reads:

Hey, hey, Laurel and Hannah.
I'd like to date your mom.

"Oh my God," Cassandra gasps, clutching at my wrist.

"Mom?" Laurel whispers, her head snapping toward me.

Hannah stares at Ross, eyes wide.

Around us the crowd noise slowly lowers to hushed whispers and turning heads, people searching for the *mom* on the sign.

My gaze falls to Landon and Harley a second, both of whom have turned in their seats and face me.

Voices closest to us catch on.

"Didn't someone hold up a sign years ago asking if Ross would date their mom?

"Whatever happened to that woman?"

"Oh my God. Does he mean her?"

Someone claps, setting off an echoing wave, before more hands are coming together and people are chanting. A combination of *Ross-Ross-Ross* and *Mom-Mom-Mom*.

I glance around me, until I see myself highlighted on the video screen. Then more heads are turning, and cameras are flashing.

Someone cries out, "There she is."

Tears blur my vision. Ross still stands on the dugout rooftop aiming the sign toward my section. Glancing left then right, I see security at the end of the row, waiting for me.

"Vee-Vee," Cassandra whispers, implying what I need to do.

"I know," I choke.

"It's like that movie *Never Been Kissed*," Laurel squeals.

Only I've been kissed, a number of times and in a number of places, by the man holding up a sign waiting on me.

Flustered, I'm already moving down the row. "Excuse me. Pardon me." I don't have far to go before security surrounds me and I'm hopping down the stairs toward the dugout entrance from the stadium seats.

As I near the dugout, I see Kip Garcia standing on the dugout stairs, arms crossed, shaking his head with a big grin on his face.

Comments fire toward me from the players watching their coach.

"*Damn, who knew coach was such a romantic?*"

"*Do you think she'll date him?*"

"*There she is.*"

I reach the entrance to the dugout from the stands, where I'm assisted under the netting and over the fence. Then I'm helped up to the dugout roof by a number of players' hands, but it's Ross I'm concentrating on, who has dropped the poster and holds out his hand for me.

"Hi," I whisper after he tugs me close.

"Hey, happenstance," he says, bringing me closer to him. "So, what do you say?"

"Will I date you?" I glance at the posterboard face up near our feet. With tears in my eyes, I laugh. "I'll do one better, Ross Davis. I'll sleep with you as well."

Ross chuckles, the grin spreading his round face. Then, he's cupping my cheeks and bringing me in for a kiss before forty thousand fans.

Suddenly, "hit it' blasts over the loudspeakers and I pull back, laughing at Ross's former walkup song. Happy tears stream down my face.

ELEVATOR PITCH

"Think I should share my rap dance moves with everyone?" I ask him, unable to contain my glee.

He chuckles as well, noticing the past video of me waving my arms and swinging my hips which is suddenly projected on the screen.

Nothing is sacred on the internet.

"Let's keep all your moves just for me, sweetheart," Ross says.

"Whatever you say, Coach."

"I say kiss me, Vee, because I love you."

"I love you, too."

And I do kiss him, to the cheer of baseball fans and the background sound of Rob Base and DJ EZ.

Epilogue

August
Mid-season

[Vee]

"The End." The bold type-print is dead center on the page.

"And they lived happily ever after?" Ross jokes, turning his head toward me as we both sit upright on his bed.

"Happily for now," I explain.

Ross scowls over the reading glasses at the edge of his nose. His broad, naked chest is on display. "I don't like that ending."

"Why not?" I scoff. "They ride off into the sunset."

"There was no sunset in that ending." He narrows his eyes at me, having listened to me read the ending of my next book. This is his new demand. I read him what I write, but when I get to the sexy bits, he shuts me up, telling me he doesn't need any instruction in that area.

My voice rises. "It's figurative."

"And it's weak. The ending needs something brighter than a sunset."

I chuckle. "You read one romance novel and now you're an expert?"

"I've read three," he reminds me, keeping his gaze on me before removing his reader glasses.

My heart does a little skip. We're reading my books together, which makes me nervous, but it also thrills me. His interest in what I do for a living. His care for my career. The way he loves me.

I dig my teeth into my lower lip, suddenly a little anxious he might be right. Maybe the ending needs a little more. "What would be brighter than a sunset?"

Ross shoves the covers off his legs and scoots from the bed to kneel beside it. "I really wanted to do this on the mound at Anchors Field, but can you believe I had to make an appointment for such a thing, and they are booked for months out?"

"You don't say."

"So, I'm doing it here. Where I want you to live with me. Where I want you to share my bed and my home because you own my heart and occupy all my thoughts."

He tugs open his nightstand drawer and pulls out a little black box, flipping it open to present something shinier than a sunset. Something brilliant and solid and I can wear on my finger.

"Ross." I swallow hard, tears blurring my vision.

"Marry me, Vee. Because I'm superstitious, and I want you in my life always. To chase away concerns and bring me peace. And love me."

"I do love you," I whisper, my throat too thick to speak any louder. "And yes. Yes, I'll be your secret keeper, superstition whisperer, and your wife. Oh my God, Ross Davis, you're asking me to marry you."

"I sure am, sweetheart. So, is that a yes?"

"That's a holy cow yes, and play ball, and swing for the bleachers."

Ross laughs. "Okay, I don't need the rest of those things."

"Yes, yes, yes. Now get on this bed," I demand, setting my laptop on the nightstand that became mine a few months ago.

Ross scrambles up from his knees, while I hold out my hand. Then he slips the beautiful square-cut diamond on my finger.

"Now, that's a homerun," he chuckles, staring down at his gift.

"You're my homerun, Ross."

I'm tackled to the bed and peppered with kisses before he travels all the bases and we both score.

Because the biggest win is Ross and me together. Always.

Thank you for taking the time to read Elevator Pitch.
Please consider writing a review on major sales channels where ebooks and paperbacks are sold and discussed.

Want an extra inning of Vee and Ross?

Elevator Pitch Bonus

Want to read who is next at bat?
Check out CATCH THE KISS.

Catch the Kiss

More by L.B. Dunbar

Sterling Falls
Seven siblings muddling their way through love over 40.
Sterling Heat
Sterling Brick
Sterling Streak
Sterling Clay
Sterling Fight

Chicago Anchors
When your eyes are on the silver fox coach more than the game.
Elevator Pitch
Catch the Kiss

Parentmoon
When the mother of the groom goes head-to-head with the single father of the bride.

Holiday Hotties (Christmas novellas)
Holiday novellas certain to heat the season.
Scrooge-ish
Naughty-ish
Grouch-ish

Road Trips & Romance
Three sisters. Three destinations. All second chances at love over 40.
Hauling Ashe
Merging Wright
Rhode Trip

Lakeside Cottage
Four friends. Four summers. Shenanigans and love happen at the lake.
Living at 40
Loving at 40
Learning at 40
Letting Go at 40

The Silver Foxes of Blue Ridge
Small mountain town, silver foxes. Brothers seeking love over 40.

L.B. DUNBAR

Silver Brewer
Silver Player
Silver Mayor
Silver Biker

Sexy Silver Foxes
When sexy silver foxes meet the feisty vixens of their dreams.
After Care
Midlife Crisis
Restored Dreams
Second Chance
Wine&Dine

Collision novellas
A spin-off from After Care – the younger set/rock stars
Collide
Caught

The Sex Education of M.E.
The original sexy silver fox.
When a widowed professor decides she'd like to date again, and a local fireman volunteers to give her lessons.

The Heart Collection
Small town, big hearts - stories of family and love.
Speak from the Heart
Read with your Heart
Look with your Heart
Fight from the Heart
View with your Heart

A Heart Collection Spin-off
The Heart Remembers

ELEVATOR PITCH

BOOKS IN OTHER AUTHOR WORLDS
Smartypants Romance (an imprint of Penny Reid)
Tales of the Winters sisters set in Green Valley.

The World of True North (an imprint of Sarina Bowen)
Welcome to Vermont! And the Busy Bean Café.

About the Author
www.lbdunbar.com

L.B. Dunbar loves sexy silver foxes, second chances, and small towns. If you enjoy older characters in your romance reads, including a hero with a little silver in his scruff and a heroine rediscovering her worth, then welcome to romance for those over 40. L.B. Dunbar's signature works include women and men in their prime taking another turn at love and happily ever after. She's a *USA TODAY* Bestseller as well as #1 Bestseller on Amazon in Later in Life Romance with her Sterling Falls, Lakeside Cottage, and Road Trips & Romance series. L.B. lives in Chicago with her own sexy silver fox.

To get all the scoop about the self-proclaimed queen of silver fox romance, join her on Facebook at Loving L.B. or receive her monthly newsletter, Love Notes.

+ + +

Connect with L.B. Dunbar

Printed in the USA
CPSIA information can be obtained
at www.ICGtesting.com
LVHW021615291024
795102LV00012B/387